WITH SEDUCTION IN MIND

Serena glowed with enjoyment as she watched the fireworks. "Lord Beaumont, how wonderful. I have never seen anything as interesting as the flames going around like a wheel in the sky."

She glanced up at him at the same moment Robert smiled at her. His gaze held hers and he let her see his desire. A slight shiver ran through her and confusion appeared in her lovely eyes. His chest swelled. She'd reacted to him without his even touching her.

It was time.

"Walk with me." Robert twined her arm in his, drawing her nearer than he should. He led her down the dimly lit paths, his thigh brushed against hers, as he told her about the gardens, pointing out one feature or another. Each time they touched, her breath caught, and he felt more confident of his plan.

When they reached the Grecian temple, he led her up the stairs. It was dark, but not so dark he couldn't see her face as she gazed around the folly.

"How very beautiful this is," Serena exclaimed.

He lowered his voice, making it soothing and caressing. "Not as beautiful as the one viewing it."

Robert was attuned to her scent, her smile, her every movement. He'd wager his fortune she'd never been kissed, never touched intimately. He intended to be the first—the only—man to kiss her and learn her body . . .

Books by Ella Quinn

The Marriage Game
THE SEDUCTION OF LADY PHOEBE
THE SECRET LIFE OF MISS ANNA MARSH
THE TEMPTATION OF LADY SERENA
DESIRING LADY CARO
ENTICING MISS EUGENIE VILLARET
A KISS FOR LADY MARY
LADY BERESFORD'S LOVER
MISS FEATHERTON'S CHRISTMAS PRINCE
THE MARQUIS SHE'S BEEN WAITING FOR

The Worthingtons
THREE WEEKS TO WED
WHEN A MARQUIS CHOOSES A BRIDE
IT STARTED WITH A KISS
THE MARQUIS AND I
YOU NEVER FORGET YOUR FIRST EARL
BELIEVE IN ME

The Lords of London
THE MOST ELIGIBLE LORD IN LONDON
THE MOST ELIGIBLE VISCOUNT IN LONDON

Novellas
MADELEINE'S CHRISTMAS WISH
THE SECOND TIME AROUND
I'LL ALWAYS LOVE YOU

Published by Kensington Publishing Corp.

ELLA QUINN

The TEMPTATION of LADY SERENA

ZEBRA BOOKS
KENSINGTON PUBLISHING CORP.
www.kensingtonbooks.com

ZEBRA BOOKS are published by

Kensington Publishing Corp.
119 West 40th Street
New York, NY 10018

All Kensington titles, imprints, and distributed lines are available at special quantity discounts for bulk purchases for sales promotion, premiums, fund-raising, educational, or institutional use.

Special book excerpts or customized printings can also be created to fit specific needs. For details, write or phone the office of the Kensington Sales Manager: Attn.: Sales Department. Kensington Publishing Corp., 119 West 40th Street, New York, NY 10018. Phone: 1-800-221-2647.

Zebra and the Z logo Reg. U.S. Pat. & TM Off.

First Kensington Books Electronic Edition: January 2014
First Zebra Books Mass-Market Paperback Printing: December 2021
ISBN-13: 978-1-4201-5322-4
ISBN-13: 978-1-4201-5323-1 (eBook)

10 9 8 7 6 5 4 3 2 1

Printed in the United States of America

Chapter One

1816, Scottish Borders region

The Earl of Vere scowled. "Damn it, Serena, you can't back out now. Not after the plans have been made. If you don't go to London who will you marry? What do you have left here?"

Lady Serena Weir stared out the solar's window, studying the bleak late February landscape. Snow covered the ground, more gray than white; the trees lifeless and black against the gloom. She glanced over her shoulder at her brother, James. "I could marry Cameron."

"Do you even care for him more than moderately?"

"No, but he needs to marry, and he likes me." She turned back to the window. Snow still covered the hills. In another month they'd be the feeding ground for the castle's sheep and cattle. But if Mattie, her new sister-in-law, had her way, Serena would not be there to see it.

James snorted with derision. "Cameron likes your dowry.

Mattie has made all the plans. She assures me you'll have a wonderful time."

Serena pressed her lips tightly together. *The plans,* he'd said, as if they had taken on a life. *The plans* for her to go to London for her first Season at six and twenty years of age. A little old to be making a come out. *The plans* meant she would leave her home. The place she had been born and raised and never before left. Tears pricked her eyelids. She would not cry. Not in front of James. If a London Season was such a good idea, why hadn't he sold out of the army after their father died, when she was still young? Instead, he'd left her here to manage the estate while he remained on Wellington's staff.

James had returned shortly before Christmas, with his bride, Madeleine—Mattie, as she liked to be called—and Serena's ordered life was thrown into turmoil. She no longer knew what her future held.

Despite her warm cashmere dress and woolen shawl, Serena shivered. No matter how many fires were lit, Vere was always cold and damp, even in the solar, the warmest room in the castle. London would probably be warmer. That might be a good reason to go.

James teased her in the local dialect. "Serena, lass . . ."

She bit her lip. "James Weir, I *know* you did not speak Scots with Wellington."

"Please, Sissy?" her brother said, reverting to his childhood name for her. "Stop looking out the window and talk to me."

Serena sighed, but turned. Her brother was tall with dark brown hair, like their mother's, whereas she had her father's auburn curls. She'd known he would marry, but it never occurred to her that he would bring a wife home with him. Or that she would be forced to leave.

Serena fought her sudden panic, but there truly was nothing here for her anymore. "Fine. I'll go."

"Good girl!" He smiled. "I'll tell Mattie it's settled."

James gave Serena a peck on the cheek and strode out the door.

"Do. Go tell Mattie," Serena muttered in frustration. *What didn't he tell Mattie?*

London was Mattie's idea to rid herself of her unwanted sister-in-law. Serena had been presented with the plans *au fait accompli*. Somehow, she would have to make the best of it.

Early the next day, Serena and James left on the week-long journey from the Cheviot Hills to the home of their Aunt Catherine, the Dowager Marchioness of Ware. James spent the night, but left early the next morning.

Mary, Serena's lady's maid, was still unpacking her trunk, when her aunt entered the bedchamber.

"Let me see what you've brought with you," Aunt Catherine said.

Serena tried to smile, but tears filled her eyes. Aunt Catherine was her mother's twin and Serena wished her mother was here to reassure her. In answer to her aunt's question, she replied, "I'm afraid none of it is fashionable."

"You've had no reason to think about being stylish, have you?"

Serena shook her head.

"Will it hurt your feelings if I told you I'd suspected that?"

She was still too numb to feel much of anything. "No."

Mary stood aside as Aunt Catherine sorted through the clothes, discarding most of them. She held up Serena's riding habit. "Well, this, at least, seems to be in good condition and not too out of date."

Serena grimaced. "It's probably the newest piece of clothing I own."

"No matter at all, my child. I knew you would need a new wardrobe. It will be much easier to toss everything and begin anew. A visit to a good modiste in York will start you. When we arrive in London, we shall visit Madame Lisette on Bruton Street." Aunt Catherine paused. "Have you danced at all?"

"I had a dancing master when Papa was well."

"When was that? No, don't tell me. It was too long ago to have mattered. We'll hire one in London." Aunt Catherine made a face at the pile of clothes on the floor. "Other than your riding habit, is there anything you wish to keep?"

Serena glanced at the now-empty trunks and shook her head. "No, only something to wear until I have new gowns to replace the old."

Her aunt's kind, patient gaze stayed on Serena for a few moments. "Good. I am glad to hear it. There is nothing more unfortunate than being attached to a gown that is quite out of style and in no way useful." Aunt Catherine turned to go. "We'll visit York to-morrow."

After she left, Serena said, "Mary, please leave me for a while."

"Yes, my lady. Is there anything I can get you?"

"No, I'm fine." Serena sat on the window seat. Her throat hurt from holding back the tears she would not allow to fall. How anyone thought she was going to find a husband at her age, she didn't know. It was as if she'd been set adrift. How was she going to learn everything required when she'd only been in small villages? She'd never attended a proper ball or been to a modiste. Serena bit her lip to keep the tears at bay.

Darkness seemed to surround her. She pressed her head against the cold glass. Eventually the weak winter sun faded and the room dimmed. By the time a knock sounded on the door, Serena had stopped feeling sorry for herself and vowed to carry on. She was the daughter of an earl and the granddaughter of an English marquis. Rising, she went to the basin and splashed water on her face. "Come."

"Her ladyship wants to know if you'll join her for dinner." Mary lit the candles. "If you're not up to it, she'll send a tray."

"No, I'll be down shortly, unless she expects me to change."

"No, my lady, she said to come as you are."

The next few days were spent in such a whirl of shopping Serena felt she'd been turned upside down. Never in her life had another person made her a priority.

She gazed at her aunt, then at the large pile of new gowns and packages, and laughed. "I'm sure I cannot wear half so many."

"Well, I'm happy to hear you laugh, my dear, which you haven't done since you arrived." Aunt Catherine's humorous gray eyes sparkled. "You will need many more when we arrive in Town. You will have routs, balls, dinners, afternoon teas, and morning visits to occupy you, as well as other entertainments."

Serena trembled. A Season would be worse than she'd thought. "I had no idea."

"No, I daresay you did not, but there is no need to take fright." Her aunt smiled warmly. "I am extremely pleased with you. Your manners are very pretty and self-assured, and your mind is well informed. You will do splendidly."

"But *my age*. I'm no longer in my salad days."

"Serena, my dear," Aunt Catherine said in a no-nonsense tone, "even your age may be put to advantage. Not every gentleman wants a young miss. You know how to manage a great house and an estate, and you do not want for sense. I can think of any number of gentlemen who will not look upon you amiss."

Unconvinced, Serena merely agreed and allowed the matter to drop.

Early the next morning, Serena ordered a stableboy to saddle Shamir.

After he'd done as she bid, he glanced toward the stable. "I'll just get your groom, Will, to go with ye, my lady."

Serena's nerves were strung too tightly for company. She needed a good gallop this morning, and Will would slow her down. "No, I'll be fine without him."

The boy helped her mount without arguing. After she'd cleared the stable yard, Serena cantered south up a rise and gazed out over the still barren fields. The frost was not as heavy this morning, nor the air quite as cold. It was late, but spring was coming. The land tugged at her. She'd rather be planting than dancing.

A man on a large black horse appeared in the valley and stared up at her. He looked tall, but it was hard to tell at this distance. A breeze ruffled his fair hair as he rode toward her. After a few moments, Serena realized he was riding not simply in her direction, but to her. Her aunt had warned her not to ride alone. Was this man the reason for the warning? Whirling Shamir around, she gave the horse his head and rode back to her aunt's house as if someone was chasing her.

Robert Beaumont rode toward the woman on the crest of the hill. She sat atop a raking roan, much too large for a lady. Her riding habit, a dull rust color, reminded him of autumn leaves. Her long auburn hair curled down her back, and she wore a small hat with some sort of feather—pheasant, by the way it stuck out. He wondered how the devil she kept the hat on her head with her hair down. His interest piqued, he urged his horse to a trot. As he neared, she took off at a fast gallop.

She was gone when he reached the top of the hill. Beaumont looked out over the valley. A horse and rider were in the north. How had she gotten that far so quickly? Disgruntled, he turned and rode home. After throwing his reins to a groom, he strode through the doors into the main hall and called to his housekeeper, "Norry!"

She came out from a parlor. "I'm here, my lord. There's no reason to shout."

"Who lives to the north?"

"Well, my lord," she muttered, "if you were here more often, you'd know. It's a widow lady. I can't remember her name right off the top of my head. Why?"

Ignoring Norry's all too familiar complaint, he pressed for more information. "Does she have any children?"

The housekeeper narrowed her eyes. "I heard all her children are grown. She moved here after her son married. Now, if you'll excuse me, my lord, I have work to do."

"Norry, let me know if you remember. Especially if it concerns an auburn-haired female."

"Master Robert," she began in a censorious tone, "we'll have none of your carrying on up here. You leave it in London." She nodded her head curtly and left.

Beaumont clenched his jaw and stormed off to his study, cursing the fact that so many of his servants had been with him since childhood, and never let him forget it.

Shamir's hooves clattered on the brick of the stable yard. Serena slid down from her horse and, hoping to avoid her aunt, hurried to a door on the side of the house. Serena had not yet found a way to explain to her aunt how riding calmed her fears so that she would understand.

"Serena," Aunt Catherine called from the breakfast room.

Serena jumped. *Damn,* caught again. "Yes, Aunt Catherine?"

"Come here, my dear."

She was certain her aunt planned, once again, to kindly explain why Serena could not ride alone. Though, after seeing the man on horseback this morning, she acknowledged her aunt might be right.

Well, there was no avoiding it. Serena straightened her shoulders and entered the breakfast room braced for a reprimand.

Her jaw dropped.

Two very fashionable couples were with her aunt—one older, about her aunt's age, the other couple near her age. The men wore close-fitting dark coats and beautifully arranged cravats. They and the younger woman, shorter than Serena by a few inches, rose. Her gown was of a light brown cashmere, trimmed with dark brown ribbon, and tied under her bosom with a darker brown and gold twisted cord.

Serena shut her mouth and stood, rooted in place. The younger woman approached, smiling and holding out her hands. Serena, in her dull russet riding habit, felt like a duck to this lady's swan.

"I am so happy to finally meet you," the woman said. "I'm your cousin Phoebe. May I call you Serena? It is such a lovely name. We are here to help you make your debut."

When Phoebe embraced Serena warmly, she awkwardly returned the gesture. Serena blinked back tears and her tension seeped out as Phoebe then led the way to the table.

"You're surprised, I'm sure," Phoebe said, in a warm voice. "I've just been told your aunt did not inform you we were coming."

Serena glanced toward her aunt, who immediately introduced the others present. "Serena, do you remember your uncle Henry and his wife, Ester? Phoebe is their niece. Her husband is Marcus, Earl of Evesham."

The tall dark-haired man inclined his head.

"Your uncle Henry has been very interested to hear of you over the years and has invited us to stay at St. Eth House for the Season." Aunt Catherine smiled. "There is no one more able to help you through your Season."

Serena's throat ached. She did remember her uncle Henry, the Marquis of St. Eth, her mama's brother. He'd come to her mother's funeral. But her father hadn't liked her mother's family, and there had been very little contact after her mother's passing. When her father died, Uncle Henry wrote her with an offer of help. She wished she'd taken it and desperately wished she'd made her come out when she was younger. "I—I don't know what to say. Your generosity is almost too good to be true."

Phoebe took her hand. "Please, don't let us frighten you. We truly only wish to help. When Uncle Henry told Marcus and me about you, and asked that we accompany him here, we couldn't allow the opportunity to pass us by."

"I am just stunned. I had no idea Aunt Catherine would . . ."

Phoebe glanced at her husband and grinned. "Yes, isn't that the nice thing about family? They are always there to help one, whether they tell you or not."

Serena smiled. She'd moped long enough. She would make the best of her new life and she had help now, when she needed it. Running an estate was nothing compared to entering the *ton*. "I—I am a fish out of water. I never thought to have a London Season. I've never really been in a town, except for Edinburgh as a child and recently in York to shop. My whole life has changed."

Phoebe nodded. "Your aunt said you have never been in Polite Society."

Serena gave a short, mirthless laugh. "I've never been in

any society. We have no towns near the castle and no close neighbors. Except for my dependants, I've spent the last eight years alone."

Phoebe smiled reassuringly. "You're not alone anymore. We'll make your come out as easy for you as we are able to. And you may surprise yourself by having fun."

The next morning, Serena rode out with Phoebe and Marcus. Unlike Will, Serena's groom, her cousin and husband didn't complain when Serena wanted to gallop ahead. She waited for them at the rise she'd visited the day before. "I like having you two as company. I usually ride alone, although Aunt Catherine is not at all happy about it."

Phoebe bit her lip. "Serena, in London you may not ride alone. It's considered fast for an unmarried lady to ride or indeed to walk unaccompanied. It will harm your reputation, and you'll not be able to obtain vouchers for Almack's."

Marcus smiled at Phoebe. "Phoebe didn't like to ride with a groom, either. It enabled me to escort her."

She met his gaze. "Yes, that did greatly advance your cause, my love."

The small signs of affection between Marcus and Phoebe, and between her Aunt Ester and Uncle Henry, intrigued Serena. "I have no wish to seem impertinent, but yours is a love match, is it not?"

Phoebe glanced warmly at Marcus. "Yes, indeed. I was out for over six years before I married."

"And Aunt Ester and Uncle Henry are a love match as well?"

Phoebe nodded. "It is the tradition in my family."

"And a very good tradition it is," Marcus said. "Else she'd have been snapped up long before I returned to England."

A love match seemed to be a very nice thing to have. "Do either of you know the area here? I was riding alone one morning and stopped here, on the crest. A man upon a great black horse was in the valley." She frowned. "I left when he rode toward me."

Phoebe shook her head. "No, I don't know the area well. Marcus, do you know anyone up here?"

Marcus cast a gaze around again. "A large black horse?"

Serena nodded.

"Was the man fair and tall?"

"Yes."

"Most likely Robert Beaumont."

"Hmm," Phoebe said. "Very proper for you to have ridden off. There is no knowing what a gentleman encountering a lady alone would do."

One week later, Serena arrived at St. Eth House.

Phoebe met her on the pavement. "We'll visit Madame Lisette in the morning. I've already written her, and she'll be happy to design a wardrobe for you."

Serena admired all of Phoebe's clothes. "If she's the one who designs your gowns, I very much look forward to visiting her."

"I shall leave you to settle in and see you in the morning." Phoebe bussed Serena's cheek and left.

The comfort and opulence of St. Eth House amazed Serena. Built in the last century, it was one of the larger residences gracing Grosvenor Square and one of the few free-standing houses. The nicely laid-out gardens in the back and the smaller ones on each side of the house softened the imposing aspect. Serena's room had a view of the fountain in the back. She stood gazing out a window when her maid entered.

"Have you ever seen anything like this?" Serena smiled happily. "Feel how warm it is. What I'd have given for this comfort at Vere Castle."

"Aye, verra warm it tis." Mary ducked into the dressing room.

"I am beginning to feel as though this adventure was meant to be. Everyone has been so very kind." Serena sat on the window seat and called to Mary, "How have you fared?"

Her maid had been with her for many years. Serena had been grateful, and surprised, when Mary agreed to leave Scotland and accompany her south. With matters as they were at Vere Castle, Serena did not think she would ever return home. Her goal now was to find a husband, and she decided it must be a love match.

"I'm getting on well, my lady. Rose, Lady Evesham's maid, has been so good as to show me the newest ways to dress hair and care for your new clothes. And Lady St. Eth's grand dresser, Perkins, is nice as well."

"Are you comfortable here?"

"Aye, my lady, and happy, now that I havena got Lady Vere's French maid telling me I'm doing it all wrong."

Serena was concerned about the answer to her next question. Her groom, an older man, not used to traveling, had insisted on remaining with her. "Has Will said anything to you about how he's doing?"

"He'll miss Vere, but he's happy to stay with you. Says the other grooms know what they're about."

London was indeed warmer and friendlier than Vere Castle, for everyone.

Chapter Two

Serena entered Madame Lisette's shop on Bruton Street with Phoebe and their two aunts.

Madame, a small lady, her dark hair streaked with silver, greeted them "Ah, the new *mademoiselle. Bien.*"

"My dear Lisette," Aunt Ester said. "Lady Serena Weir, my niece, desperately needs your help. She requires everything!"

"Bon." Madame walked around Serena. "I have made some designs that are *comme il faut.* Just the thing."

Aunt Ester tapped her chin. "She'll need several walking, carriage, day, evening, and two or three ball gowns within the week. That should be enough to start."

Serena's eyes rounded at the list her aunt rattled off. She'd never even heard of some of them. How could she hope to wear as many as her aunt was ordering? She'd have to change several times a day to make use of them all.

Madame measured her. "I have a few things ready from

the information sent me, my lady." Madame clapped her hands and what seemed like a parade of garments was carried out for their inspection. "They are *très* *élégante* for Lady Serena."

Madame called to an assistant then left them.

Looking at the number of gowns the modiste expected Serena to have fitted, she whispered, "Phoebe. Is shopping always like this?"

"Only at first. Madame will soon learn your taste and then it's not so chaotic. Give it some time. Once we have some carriage and walking gowns, we'll look for hats, and shoes. Oh, and we can't forget fans, reticules, gloves, and muffs."

Serena plopped into a chair. "I'm exhausted just thinking about it. This is as busy as harvest time. How *do* you keep up?"

Phoebe chuckled. "When you already have your basic wardrobe, it is easy. *Your* difficulty is that, other than the few things you bought in York, you do not have a wardrobe to begin with. Once you are married you'll need more new clothes."

"But won't the new ones do?" How many could one wear?

"Well, some of them will, because of your age, but as a married lady, one may dress differently, and there are *other items* a married lady needs."

Serena looked at Phoebe in confusion. "What items?"

A wicked glimmer entered Phoebe's eyes. "Oh, you'll find out in time."

Serena's fear of her eligibility returned. "But, Phoebe, *do* you think some gentleman will want to marry me?"

"Serena, you have all the attributes needed to make a good, if not brilliant, marriage. What's more important is that you find a gentleman you wish to marry. I am a great proponent of being selective."

The ladies completed the first of their shopping and returned to St. Eth House. Phoebe followed Serena up to her parlor, sat down at the small writing table, took a sheet of paper, and dipped the nib of the quill into the standish.

"Now then," Phoebe said, in an efficient tone, "tell me what you want in a husband. What must you have to make you happy in a marriage?"

"You make it sound like shopping." Serena grinned. "Are you really going to make a list?"

Phoebe's lips tilted up. "Of course. There is a reason it's called the Marriage *Mart,* you know. It's very much like shopping, although choosing a husband is more frustrating—and enjoyable—at the same time."

Serena sat on the small chaise. "I've never seriously considered the question of what I would like." She paused. "The attributes with which he must be endowed." Thoughts jumbled, then fell into place. "Very well. Sufficient fortune to support a family. A country estate. Kindness. He shouldn't want to rule me. I realize that, under the law, he is allowed to do so, but I could not bear it."

She glanced at her cousin. "It would be nice if he were handsome. Though, if he met my other requirements, I could overlook that. Superior understanding. I could not abide being married to a stupid man. A sense of humor is important. As long as he is a gentleman, I don't care about his rank. And I want a love match."

Phoebe put her pen down. "I should warn you, the heart is an independent organ. It is very difficult to tell it whom to love and whom not to. We must hope yours chooses wisely."

Robert, Viscount Beaumont rose when Phoebe entered the library, and watched as his besotted friend, Marcus, strode quickly to greet her. Their unbridled joy at seeing one another caused Robert to shudder.

Marcus took her hand. "Ah, there you are, my love."

His friend turned her hand over to kiss the pulse at her wrist. They'd been married for over a year and their son was eight months old, but he always greeted her as if they were still courting. Marcus smiled when she blushed.

Beaumont tried to clear his head. That kind of marriage wasn't for him. He could never cede control to a woman as Marcus had to Phoebe. Experience was a harsh teacher, and Beaumont would not love again.

Robert bowed. "Phoebe, how well you look. I've always said that Marcus stole you from me."

"Robert, what a bouncer. You had no notion of marriage, and I would never have accepted anything less."

He flushed. "With you, my dear, anything would have been possible."

She shook her head. "You are a desperate flirt."

Marcus narrowed his eyes. "*You* are very lucky I don't take offense, Beaumont."

"Pistols at dawn!" Robert cried, but couldn't keep the humor from his tone.

Phoebe laughed. "I remember the first time I heard you and Marcus insulting each other. I told him he had been very cruel to you. I was quite wrong. What a pair you are."

Beaumont smiled wickedly. "Ah, but, my lady, if only you would have walked with me."

"Enough, Beaumont, else I will throw you out on your ear." Marcus scowled, but his lips twitched. "I'll not stand here and watch you make love to my wife."

"You could leave . . ."

"Oh, no, you must stop." Phoebe gasped, chuckling. "I will shortly be in tears."

Robert opened his mouth again, but Phoebe said, "Really, Robert, enough."

She collapsed on the sofa next to where her husband stood. Once she'd taken her place, the gentlemen returned to their seats.

"I swear," she said with a gurgle of laughter, "I am never so diverted as when I listen to the two of you."

Marcus snaked an arm around her. "How was your day, my love?"

"It went well, very well indeed. We have much more to do, but we made a start. Robert, would you like to join us for dinner to-morrow? It will be just family."

"I shall be delighted to join you." He enjoyed taking his potluck with Phoebe and Marcus. One never knew what their cook would serve.

"Good. We'll see you at seven. What are your plans afterward?"

"I've arranged to join a party at Lady Re . . ." Robert broke off, realizing Phoebe would not approve. "Nothing at all."

"Would you like to accompany us to Lady Sale's ball? It will be quite unexceptional."

Robert regarded Phoebe suspiciously. "Why?"

She gave him an innocent look. "Why for the pleasure of your company, to be sure."

Marcus pulled her a little closer, and Robert wondered fleetingly what his life would have been like if things had been different.

"My love, don't you remember?" Marcus said. "To-morrow we're attending the theater. That new comedy. Robert, what is it called?"

Beaumont not only knew what it was called, but intimately knew Collette, the starring actress. *"Love in a Village."*

"Yes, that's it. Will you join us?"

Some small part of Robert warned it was a trap, but he ignored it. "Yes, I'd be very happy to attend with you. Nothing I'd like better."

The door opened and a nursemaid brought in eight-month-old Lord Arthur, Marcus and Phoebe's son. Arthur bounced with excitement, threatening to fall out of the nursemaid's arms into his father's. Once safely in Marcus's grip, Arthur looked around and spied his best friend.

"Uf, uf." The baby held his hands out to Robert.

"Apparently Arthur has a preference for you. I don't understand his taste." Marcus grimaced. "Still, the baby is young yet and has time to come to his senses."

Robert took Arthur and jiggled him on his lap. The baby smiled, showing new teeth. "You are growing to be quite a handsome young man. Mind, you don't decide to look like your father. Your mother is much better looking." Robert cuddled the baby, breathing in the child's sweet scent.

Marcus gazed thoughtfully at Robert. "Isn't it about time you think of setting up your own nursery? You're past thirty, you know."

Robert frowned. "Have you been talking to my grandmother?"

An hour later, Phoebe walked swiftly into the morning room at St. Eth House.

"Phoebe!" her aunt greeted her. "What brings you here? I was sure you would be playing with Arthur."

"He decided he liked male company more than mine. Although, I imagine it won't be long before he wants me again." She was one of the few *tonnish* women who chose to nurse her son.

"I have come to ask Serena to join us for dinner and the theater to-morrow evening." Phoebe smiled at Serena. "Would you like that?"

Serena's eyes sparkled with joy. "Oh yes, of all things! I have never seen a play."

"Perfect," Phoebe said. "We will expect you around seven o'clock to dine with us."

"Who else will form your party?" Ester asked.

"I don't know yet." Phoebe glanced at her aunt. "This has been very last minute. Perhaps Lord and Lady Rutherford. Rutherford always enjoys a good comedy. Serena, you'll want to meet Anna. She is great fun and a good friend."

Phoebe stayed for a while longer before returning home. She found Marcus still in the library with a very fussy Arthur.

Sitting, she unhooked her gown as Marcus handed her the baby. "I think he wants you more than me."

She took her son.

"It was a good idea having your gowns specially made," Marcus said. "Patience is not our son's strong suit."

"It was very fortunate that Madame knew how to make them," Phoebe replied. "Serena agreed to join us. It will be her first play. Please send round to Rutherford's and ask if they can accompany us. I do not wish to be too obvious. Oh, and invite them to dinner as well."

Marcus grinned. "My love, are you playing matchmaker?"

"Now, why would you think that?" Phoebe caressed her son's cheek and smiled.

Entering his home in Berkeley Square, Robert's gaze lit on a letter which lay on the ormolu hall table, the seal already broken. When he picked it up, his nostrils were assailed by the strong, sickly sweet scent of ambergris. Holding the letter at arm's length, he gently shook it open and perused the contents.

Collette complaining he neglected her and insisting on his attention that evening. Robert sighed. The lovely, lush, and accommodating actress had just become too demanding. It was time to give the fair Collette her *congé* and move on to other fields.

He strode into his secretary's office. "Charles, please go round to Rundell and Bridge's and pick up some bauble for Collette. Send it to her with a note telling her that I shall no longer be availing myself of her pleasures. Word it however you like, so long as she understands."

Charles shook his head slightly.

"Ah, my poor Charles, you do not approve of my methods."

"My lord, at the risk of offending you, I do not understand how you can so coldly cast off your—your . . ."

"Liaisons?"

His secretary nodded.

"Perhaps someday I shall tell you. For now, do as I ask."

Serena had been informed she could gallop if she rode very early in the morning and took her groom. She availed herself of the first opportunity to do so. As the sun was rising the next day, a man on a large black horse trotting along Rotten Row caught her attention.

She stopped under a tree and watched him, admiring his seat. Perhaps she should add riding to her list of requirements for a husband. He reminded her very much of the man she'd seen in Yorkshire. If he was the same man, he was larger than she'd thought. Chastising herself for staring at him, she headed to the exit.

Robert turned and stared in disbelief at the woman riding

out of the park. Could it really be the lady from Yorkshire? She had the same habit and auburn hair. Excellent seat. He gauged the distance between them. Damn, there was no way to catch up with her. Cursing his luck and the stupid fool who'd decided one could only gallop on the tan, he turned Démon to race back down the track.

Did she ride every morning? Why hadn't he seen her before? How could he meet her? That he would, he'd no doubt. Robert's blood raced at the thought of spearing his hands through her long curls. He smiled slowly, yes, he would definitely find a way.

Later that morning, Serena visited Hookham's. Having never before lived in close proximity to a bookstore, she was in heaven. Upon her return to St. Eth House, she found her aunts discussing to whom Serena should make her first morning calls and which teas she should attend. Between the plans being made for her and the dancing lessons due to begin to-day, butterflies fluttered in her stomach.

Serena wished she was not so nervous. "Are you sure I'm ready to make morning calls and attend teas?"

Aunt Ester smiled warmly. "Serena, you will be fine."

But Serena knew she was as good as on the shelf. "I'm so old now."

Aunt Catherine patted her hand. "I'll not argue your come out should have been long ago. Still there is no reason to be concerned. You're much more self-assured than you could possibly have been at eighteen."

Serena took a breath. She didn't feel self-assured. "At eighteen, I would not have known enough to be afraid."

Ferguson, her uncle's butler, entered to announce that Monsieur Dupont, the dancing master, had arrived.

"Well, my dear," Ester said, "shall we go?"

Uncle Henry was already in the ballroom when Serena entered with her aunts. Her stomach churned. Monsieur Dupont put her at ease with some country dances she remembered. Soon she forgot her nervousness and began to enjoy herself. Although, when they progressed to the waltz, Serena faltered.

She'd never stood so close to a man to whom she was not related. She blushed hotly, and when Monsieur Dupont placed his hand on her waist, she jumped and looked to her aunts for support.

Aunt Ester was stern. "If you do not learn to waltz, you'll be branded a provincial."

Serena swallowed and tried, but in Monsieur Dupont's arms, her movements were wooden.

"Mademoiselle, perhaps next week you will feel better," he said. "It is, perhaps, too much for one day."

"Nonsense." Aunt Ester tapped her foot. "Henry, take Monsieur's place."

Monsieur Dupont bowed and stepped aside.

Uncle Henry took Serena's hand and whispered, "You'll be fine. Follow my lead."

Feeling safer with her uncle, Serena soon forgot her embarrassment.

"You're doing very well," he said, grinning.

Aunt Ester nodded. "There now, you see, it is not at all difficult."

Serena breathed a sigh of relief. "It's really not as hard as I thought it would be. Monsieur Dupont, may I try it with you now?"

"Dance with Marcus first, then Monsieur Dupont," Phoebe suggested from the doorway.

Serena agreed. "Very well."

Marcus danced with her, then Monsieur Dupont; he declared that with a little more practice she would be perfect.

He bowed. "Mademoiselle, you are a quick learner. I shall see you next week."

Aunt Ester smiled at Phoebe. "Who are you here to see, my dear, and did you bring Arthur?"

"Yes, your housekeeper is entertaining him, or rather he is entertaining your housekeeper. I'm not sure which it is. I came to help Serena choose a gown for this evening."

"Very well, I shall leave you to it."

Phoebe and Serena went off to her dressing room, and searched through her new gowns.

"Here. This one, I think." Phoebe held out a pale yellow silk evening gown with a twisted cord of green and gold. "Now you tell me what you'd like to wear with it."

Serena studied the gown and selected a spangled shawl and a reticule with seed pearls. "I think these will go well. What do you think?"

Giving Serena an enigmatic smile, Phoebe said, "Perfect. Serena, you'll look lovely. We'll see you this evening."

Shortly before seven o'clock, Serena entered the drawing room.

Uncle Henry rose to greet her. "Serena, that yellow suits you. You look charming, like a fresh daffodil."

She curtseyed. "Thank you, Uncle Henry."

Aunt Ester smiled. "My dear, how do you like your gown?"

"I like it very well indeed. I had no idea my wardrobe would arrive so quickly."

"Yes, Lisette is very good at delivering what one needs just when one wants them."

Aunt Catherine took Serena's hand. "I've never seen you in better looks."

Uncle Henry glanced at her. "Dunwood House is only a

few houses down the street. Would you prefer to walk or would you like the carriage?"

"I think I shall walk."

"I'll send a footman to accompany you."

Aunt Catherine kissed her cheek. "A whole new life is about to start. Have a wonderful time."

Robert took his hat and cane from Finster, his butler. "I am dining at Dunwood House and shall attend the theater afterward. Send the town coach to meet me there."

As he turned the corner from Carlos Place onto Grosvenor, an elegantly dressed lady glided down the street on the other side of the square, followed by a footman. There was something familiar about her. As she walked between two houses, the setting sun, hanging low in the sky, set off the dark red curls dancing around her face. It was the lady with the auburn hair. Robert strode rapidly to the opposite side of the square, but when he reached it, she was gone. Why was she always disappearing? Cursing his luck, he continued on to Dunwood House.

Chapter Three

Phoebe greeted Lord and Lady Rutherford as they were announced.

Anna kissed her cheek. "You look as if you have some plan afoot. What's this about?"

Phoebe told her about Serena and her debut. "I've invited Serena to accompany us to the theater. Robert Beaumont will also be coming."

Rutherford raised a brow. "How did you manage to convince Beaumont to be introduced to her? Hardly his type of lady."

"Well," Phoebe said, a little guiltily, "Robert doesn't exactly know he'll be meeting her, and she doesn't know she will be meeting him."

Rutherford's expression became severe. "You're playing a deep game using Beaumont."

"The very reason I have not told Serena. I would not for

the world see her hurt. They will either be attracted to each other or they will not. We shall see."

Anna perched on a chair. "Phoebe, I like Robert very well as a friend, but his reputation, my dear. He reminds one of a butterfly taking a taste of each flower before moving on."

Rutherford held a decanter of brandy suspended over a glass. "And how would you know?"

Waving her hand, Anna replied. "Gentlemen are not the only ones to know about certain reputations. I also know he is a favorite with many of the *ton's* matrons."

Her husband scowled. "Matrons whose husbands don't know enough to keep them busy at home."

Marcus handed Anna a glass of sherry. "Anna, if Serena were a widow, I'd join in your concern. But Robert's conquests don't run to gently bred, *unmarried* females."

Anna looked unconvinced. "I hope you're correct."

Serena was announced and Phoebe moved to greet her and introduced Anna and Rutherford.

Marcus asked, "Serena, would you like a glass of sherry? It's quite good. Or would you prefer a glass of wine?"

"A sherry, please."

The ladies drew Serena into conversation about the upcoming Season. Marcus and Rutherford spoke in low voices several feet away.

"Phoebe is to be congratulated on her protégée," Rutherford said. "She's a beautiful girl. What's her portion?"

"Substantial."

Rutherford glanced at Serena. "Yes, I'm quite impressed. You'll not have any problems marrying her off. If Beaumont doesn't take the bait, someone else will."

When the butler announced Robert, he stepped into the room and languidly surveyed the company. He smiled at the Rutherfords, but his attention was arrested by the lady he'd seen walking and on horseback. He had trouble catching his breath and even greater difficulty maintaining his countenance. He cast an experienced eye over her.

The lady wasn't a young miss. Perhaps she was a widow. She was far lovelier than he'd thought she'd be. Her hair was dressed high, curls dropped and bounced around her shoulders from the loose top knot. One curl caressed her breast. He itched to twist that curl around his finger. Her rosy lips tilted up at the corners. What would it be like to kiss those lips? He intended to find out.

Phoebe took his arm and led him to the woman. "Lady Serena, may I present Robert, Viscount Beaumont."

Lady Serena? Perhaps she'd been married to an untitled gentleman. He brought his attention back to Phoebe.

"Robert, Lady Serena is my cousin. Her brother is the Earl of Vere. This is Lady Serena's first time in the metropolis. We're introducing her to our particular friends as well as all the entertainments London has to offer."

Brother? Not married or a widow *and* Phoebe's cousin. Of all the bad luck, this was the worst. She was unavailable, and his senses refused to believe it.

Beaumont bowed over Serena's hand and held it. "I am enchanted, Lady Serena. I believe I saw you riding in the Park this morning. On a large roan?"

Serena curtseyed. The movement so graceful it was like a dance. "It is my pleasure to meet you, my lord. You are referring to Shamir. Did I not see you riding in Yorkshire? You have a large black gelding, I believe."

"Yes. His name is Démon." Robert could scarcely tear his eyes away from her. If he'd had a dream, she was the embodiment of it. Her eyes were an unusual shade of amber fringed by lashes a little darker than her hair.

He frowned slightly, it finally dawned on him what she'd said. "How did you know he was a gelding?"

Robert fought to keep his gaze from dropping to her lips.

He wondered how she'd taste and shook himself. He was unlikely to ever find out.

Serena smiled. "I know a great deal about horses, my lord. A gelding is hard to miss."

Robert's frown lightened to a humorous smile. "No, not if you know what you're looking at." Belatedly, he remembered he'd taken her hand, and brought it to his lips, grazing them across her knuckles.

She blinked slowly. "No, not then."

Serena had focused on Lord Beaumont the moment he'd entered. He was tall. She only came to the middle of his broad chest. On horseback, he'd reminded her of Ares, the Greek god of war. But that was an illusion. His manner was too refined and his dress too fashionable to hide the soul of a warrior. He bowed so elegantly. A provocative smile played on his well-molded lips, and his voice was deep and silky when he greeted her. Her chest tightened as his eyes, the color of bright moss, caressed her. Her heart skipped as she fought to regain control of her traitorous senses.

She'd been inured in the country for much too long. Even through their gloves, his fingers heated hers, and when his lips touched them, she'd had to remember to breathe. Was this how she would react to every gentleman she met? Or only him?

They dined informally and arrived at the theater in time to partake of champagne prior to the first act. Serena took in the plush velvet hangings and chair coverings, there was gilt everywhere. "Phoebe, I've never seen anything so grand!"

Phoebe grinned and squeezed Serena's shoulder.

The ladies sat in the front of the Dunwood box, leaving the gentlemen to sit behind them. The second-row chairs were just off-center to the seats in the front so that one could easily converse between them.

Phoebe glanced at the pit and spoke quietly to Serena. "Do not look down. There are a number of gentlemen trying to catch your attention. It would not do for you to acknowledge them."

Suddenly nervous, Serena averted her gaze. "What are they doing?"

Phoebe's lips tightened. "Some have their quizzing glasses out and others are waving."

Lord Beaumont took Serena's arm. "Don't worry about them."

Serena felt a little panic, afraid she might do something gauche. "I don't know where to look, if I cannot look down."

"Look at me," Lord Beaumont whispered.

She did and her heart jumped at the warmth in his eyes. "At you?"

"Of course." After a few moments, he broke his gaze and glanced around, looking slightly disconcerted. "Or at any of our party. Just not to the pit."

He handed her a glass of champagne. Serena loved how the bubbles tickled as they made their way down her throat.

Everyone seemed to settle down and the curtain on the stage was drawn back.

Once the play began, Serena's attention fixed on the performance, but Robert couldn't focus on anything but her.

She seemed so different, so enchantingly naïve for a woman of her age. Her skin was like sweet, warm cream. Small wispy curls gathered on the back of her slender neck. He was so near he could almost feel their softness. He leaned closer to take in her scent. Light, almost lavender, but different. How would she taste?

He pulled back his hand, surprised, he'd almost touched

the curls. What the devil was he thinking? He was far too interested and she was an innocent—and Phoebe's cousin. He had no intention of allowing his affections to be engaged. Not again.

The intermission brought not only their refreshments, but a number of gentleman friends seeking an introduction to Lady Serena. Robert stood off to the side, scowling. They may be some of London's most eligible marital prizes, but they were making cakes of themselves, flattering her.

She held back now, somewhat shy, but later . . .

A cold sensation washed over him. She'd be spoilt within a week. She'd become the same as all the other females on the catch for a husband.

Finally, the visitors left and the third act began. Despite trying to distract himself by watching the voluptuous Collette, Robert returned his gaze to Serena, to her lovely profile and unfeigned delight. She was captivating.

At the end of the performance, Serena, with innocent joy, said to Phoebe and Marcus. "I don't know when I've laughed so much, or enjoyed anything so well. If I see nothing else of London, the trip will have been worth it just for this. I don't know how to thank you."

"I am delighted you enjoyed it. That, indeed, is enough for us." Phoebe glanced at Beaumont. "You're quiet, Robert. Did you not enjoy the play?"

"Yes, delightful." His attention was once again drawn to Serena. "More than that, I took pleasure in watching Lady Serena's delight in it."

Serena's eyes widened and she colored prettily, but said nothing.

He took her hand and placed it on his arm to escort her from the box and, though her hand trembled slightly, she moved gracefully beside him. He wanted to put his arm around her waist and draw her close, or bury his face in her hair. But that would cause a scandal. Then again, it might be worth it.

Serena gazed up at him with delight. "I'm glad you joined us this evening. I had such a wonderful time."

His mouth dried. Her lack of artifice stunned him. "It was my honor."

At the theater door, he raised her hand to his lips. "Until we meet again." He softly brushed his lips across her knuckles. "Good-night, my lady."

Robert bowed and bid the others a good evening. *The devil,* why had he announced he'd liked watching her? It was the truth, but it wouldn't do to give Lady Serena any thought of trapping him into marriage. He'd need to be more careful around her. Better yet, he'd leave and stay away from her. His estate in Newmarket should do.

Robert arrived home and startled his senior staff by telling them he planned to leave in the morning.

When Finster ventured to inquire how long his lordship expected to be away, Robert snapped, "As long as it bloody well takes." Then he stomped off to his room.

After escorting Serena home, Phoebe and Marcus were enjoying a brandy with the Rutherfords at Dunwood House.

Phoebe caught Marcus's eye. "What do you think? Is Robert interested?"

"Sweetheart, it will not be as easy as you think to bring them together. He has spent far too long running away from marriage."

"But did you see how he looked at her?"

"I did. Much like a wolf discovering a nice soft lamb."

Phoebe frowned.

"Don't worry," Marcus said. "He won't try to seduce her unless he means to marry her."

"I don't want him *seducing* her at all."

Marcus chuckled. "I think he's taken with her. More than that, I can't say."

Anna regarded Phoebe. "Do you think Serena likes him?"

"I wish I knew. I don't want to encourage any thoughts she may have until I know how Robert feels."

Rutherford, who had, until then, been silent, said, "I'll tell you, if what we saw tonight is any indication of the reception she'll receive from the *ton,* Beaumont better move quickly, or someone else will snap her up."

Phoebe smiled proudly. "Serena *was* very well received. Perhaps rivals for her affection will spur Robert on."

Serena stared unseeing into the mirror while Mary combed her hair out. She'd been so unsure of herself at dinner and the theater, but Lord Beaumont's presence had comforted her. He'd been so kind and attentive, with his quiet manner. She liked the way he kissed her hands, his gaze warm on her. Not at all like the other gentlemen who made flowery compliments and jostled one another, making her feel as if she were on display. Serena would have gladly stood next to Lord Beaumont all evening. If only she could control her breathing and her heart. He was the only one who'd affected her that way. How strange?

Serena climbed into bed and thought of watching him ride. He had such a good seat. He'd turned her way and his wonderful moss-green eyes rested upon her. What did it mean? The effect he had on her breath, and the way her body flushed. Serena threw off the duvet. It really was warmer in London.

* * *

A few days later, Serena and Phoebe drove around the Park in her high perched phaeton. It was so far off the ground that at first Serena was concerned it would tip. But Phoebe was such a good driver that Serena was soon at ease and able to take a view of the Park and the many people walking and riding. They'd driven about half-way around when two ladies in a landau hailed them.

"Phoebe, who are they?"

"Lady Jersey and Lady Sefton."

"Oh." Aunt Catherine had told Serena about them. They were leaders of the *ton* and gatekeepers of that bastion of the Marriage Mart, Almack's. Lady Jersey was known as "Silence" because she talked constantly.

Lady Jersey greeted them enthusiastically. "My dear Lady Evesham, please introduce us to your . . . cousin—is it not?"

Phoebe performed the introductions. "Lady Serena is St. Eth's niece. Lady St. Eth and Lady Ware are sponsoring her."

Lady Jersey regarded Serena for a few moments. "You are Maria's daughter."

"Yes, my lady."

"I was so sad to hear of her death. Be assured we will do what we can do to make your Season successful." Lady Jersey turned to Phoebe. "Have you procured vouchers for Lady Serena yet?"

"No, ma'am, not yet."

"I shall send them along to St. Eth House."

Serena and Phoebe thanked her. They bid the other women a good day, and Phoebe moved her phaeton back into the carriage way.

"Serena, you're garnering a great deal of notice."

"Phoebe, you wouldn't *believe* the number of gentlemen paying morning calls during the last couple of days!" Serena had trouble believing all the attention she'd received. "And they're leaving all sorts of gifts. I wanted to return them, but Aunt Ester and Aunt Catherine tell me they are quite unexceptionable, and it would be wrong of me to do so."

Phoebe laughed. "You'll become used to it. I predict when it comes to a husband, you, my dear, may be as picky as you choose. Is there anyone whom you like better than the others?"

Clutching her gloved hands together nervously, Serena responded. "I did think Lord Beaumont very nice, though I've not seen him since the play."

Phoebe's tone was ambiguous. "Yes, he is handsome."

"Yes, very." Serena sighed. It appeared as if every other gentleman had called on her, why hadn't he? He was not in the Park that morning either, she'd looked.

Soon they were stopped again, this time by Mr. Ned Carver, a long-time friend of Phoebe's, who asked for an introduction.

He bowed. "Lady Serena, I would be most honored if you would walk with me."

Phoebe fixed him with a jaundiced look. "Ned, *do* look around. Do you see a groom hidden anywhere on this phaeton? Lady Serena cannot walk with you alone. It wouldn't be proper, and I can't leave my horses. If you wish to stroll with her, you will have to arrange to do so when she is not driving with me."

"Lady Evesham," Mr. Carver exclaimed in frustration, "what has Evesham been doing to make you act like an archwife?"

Phoebe gasped. "Oh! I am not a virago, and I am very happy with Marcus. You know the proprieties as well as I. Go to St. Eth House and do the pretty. You may console yourself with the knowledge that no one else will be able to walk with her to-day either."

Mr. Carver lost his place to Lord Huntley, who also demanded an introduction. The ladies were stopped so often that it took an hour to travel the short distance between the Park and St. Eth House.

Serena fought her laughter as Phoebe made more pithy comments to the gentlemen wishing to stroll with her.

When Serena and Phoebe drew up in front of St. Eth House, Phoebe heaved a sigh of relief. "Serena, do you drive?"

"I have only ever driven a gig and a wagon. Though I'm told I drive well."

"Have you thought about buying a curricle or a phaeton while you are in Town?"

Pursing her lips, Serena gave the suggestion some thought. "The idea had not occurred to me, yet I can see it might be very useful. Though I'd miss hearing your masterful set-downs."

Her cousin chuckled. "Let's talk to Uncle Henry."

Phoebe knocked on the door to his study and walked in. "Uncle Henry, Serena needs her own carriage."

He did not appear at all surprised. "Serena, do you know what type you would like?"

"Well, I would like to—to cut a dash. But I am not sure my driving skills are up to Phoebe's. Is there something between a gig and a high perched phaeton?"

Henry gave a shout of laughter. "Yes indeed, my green girl. We shall plan to visit Longacre and find something suitable. To-morrow if you'd like. Soon you'll be the envy of the *ton*."

The next morning they visited one of the coach-makers. Serena couldn't believe all the different carriages on display and had a great deal of fun perusing them. "Oh, look, Phoebe, Cinderella's carriage."

The carriage resembled a double-perched chariot slung between large wheels. It was painted a bright yellow with gold scrollwork. The cushions were in a light blue velvet.

"Yes, it certainly does look like Cinderella's carriage." Phoebe grinned wryly. "But wouldn't one look a quiz in it!"

In the end, Serena settled on a very smart-looking curricle, painted a dark brown with gold-on-tan piping. "What shall I do about horses?"

"Ladies are not allowed at Tattersall's." Henry asked, "Will you trust me to select a pair for you?"

"Of course." Serena glanced at Uncle Henry. "I trust you. What do I need to know to drive the curricle?" She could scarcely contain her excitement. This was much more fun than buying clothes. "I do think I should practice before I drive during the fashionable hour. Don't you? Do you have time to teach me?"

"For that," he said, "you want Phoebe. She is the best whip in the family."

"I'd be happy to take you out to practice," Phoebe replied.

Phoebe and Serena met two days later to begin her lessons. She learned the correct way to hold her ribbons and the whip, and how to feather a corner and tickle the wheeler's ear.

They were in the Park after breakfast and Serena was thankful there was no one around to see her. "I had no idea driving a curricle was so much more involved than driving the gig."

"If it were only the driving, we would not have much to do. You have a nice light touch. In London, you must learn to drive with style, or open yourself up to being branded a mere whipster. I wouldn't worry. You're learning quickly and will soon be able to drive during the Grand Strut without embarrassment."

In a few short days, the fashionable in Hyde Park were greeted by the sight of Lady Serena tooling an elegant curricle drawn by a matched pair of bays. She saw Phoebe and hailed her.

"You look very smart, cousin," Phoebe said.

Serena grinned. "Well, I certainly feel it. This was a wonderful idea!"

They chatted for a few minutes before Serena's attention was demanded by a gentleman waving at her.

"Now remember," Phoebe said primly, "you may only take up gentlemen to whom you've been introduced."

"I'm not so green as that." Serena shook her head. "Phoebe, this is a great deal of fun."

Taking Lord Wively up beside her, Serena bid her cousin farewell.

"By gad, Lady Serena, you do drive well." Lord Wively sat back.

"Thank you, my lord. I am pleased you think so." Pretending to pay attention to her horses, Serena looked in vain for a tall man with blond curls. The only man who'd captured her attention.

Midway through the following day, Serena giggled as her uncle peeked into the morning room before opening the door.

"Is the knocker never still?" he asked with an air of frustrated amusement. "We've not had so many young men in this house since Phoebe's come out."

His wife laughed with delight. "Yes, my love, isn't it wonderful? We are enjoying it immensely. We have had gentlemen here on the slimmest of pretexts, and more than one mama has been induced to meet Serena."

Catherine's voice quivered with enjoyment. "And the

poetry, my dear brother, from odes to her eyes down to her feet, not to mention budding couplets."

He shuddered. "What a paltry set of fellows. Odes. Ester, did I ever write poetry to you?"

She grinned. "No, my love, and I thank you for it. I wonder if any young man has married on the strength of his poetry. Well, other than Byron, of course."

Serena sat on the sofa set between two tall windows. "Uncle Henry, I've received so many gifts, I don't know what I shall do with them. All this attention is making me feel giddy."

He smiled warmly. "Serena, I think it is safe to say you have taken the *ton* by storm. Ester, did Phoebe procure the vouchers to Almack's?"

"Yes, Sally Jersey dropped them off last week. She is very impressed with you, Serena." Ester turned back to her husband. "I don't know if you remember, Henry, but Maria showed such kindness to Sally when she made her come out, that Sally wants to help launch Serena."

Serena's expression grew wistful. She glanced at her Aunt Catherine. "I wish I had more memories of Mama when she was—oh, how can I put it—still herself. For most of my life she was . . ."

Catherine smiled a little sadly. "Your mother would have loved to see your success. Do you drive out this afternoon?"

Serena knew her aunt was right. Her mother would have enjoyed this immensely. "Yes, with Lord Huntley. It seems as if I am never at home." Serena sighed. "Aunt Catherine, you were correct when you told me I would need all the clothes we bought and more. I've already had to call upon Madame again, and Phoebe took me to Pantheon's bazaar where I could find all manner of things for a pittance."

"Ester," Henry asked, "when do we hold our ball for Serena?"

"At the start of the Season in two weeks."

"Won't London still be a little thin of company?" Catherine asked.

Ester shook her head. "No, you should see the invitations we have already received. The wet weather in the shires seems to be driving people back to Town. The Season will begin at St. Eth House. Phoebe's ball will be a couple of weeks later. You have no idea the work she has had to do to put that ballroom back in repair. It's not been used since Marcus's sister, Amabel, married." Ester glanced at Serena. "It wouldn't surprise me at all if we have a marriage to celebrate this Season."

Serena looked at her aunt and sighed. Yes, she must marry, but whom?

Chapter Four

Robert arrived at his estate on the outskirts of Newmarket the day after the disastrous theater visit. He'd pushed his horses so hard, he'd had to change them. But no matter how fast he drove, he was unable to outrun his growing attraction to Lady Serena.

The minute his hand touched hers, he'd felt the connection and, what was worse, his customary aloofness began to slip. He'd loved once and chosen badly. Robert bore no desire to travel to those depths of misery with any lady again. Just the thought strengthened his resolve. His marriage would be one of convenience, where he could control the outcome.

He needed an heir, not another broken heart. All he had to do was to stay out of London for a week or two and regain his wits. By the time he returned, Lady Serena would have chosen the highest title that offered for her, or the one with the most money. She might even be betrothed.

For some reason, that thought didn't comfort him.

Robert stalked out to the stable determined to erase her from his mind, but he couldn't stop thinking about her. Lady Serena haunted his dreams, coming to him and offering her lips, then fading away when he tried to touch her. Last night, he'd awoken trying to stroke his pillow.

If that wasn't bad enough, no one appreciated his help. His trainer said to Robert if he came to the track once more, he would quit. And his housekeeper had the gall to tell him to stop giving everyone orders without consulting with her first.

Robert stood surrounded by stalls. "Pitchley," Robert said to his groom, "I want the brick in this floor taken up and replaced."

Pitchley regarded him with a jaundiced eye. "My lord, give over do. The floor was done last year. It don't do you a bit o' good driving us all mad."

Robert's temper flared and he snapped. "I'm the master here, Pitchley, and I'd thank you to remember it. If I want to make changes, I shall."

"Master Robert," Pitchley continued undaunted, "I've been with you many a year, and I ain't never seen you so testy. I dunno what bee you got up you, but you're 'bout to drive 'em all to Bedlam."

Robert faced his long time henchman and growled, "Why is it whenever I do anything you don't like I become Master Robert again?"

"Iffen you don't like it, then don't act like you was six years old ag'in," Pitchley said, unrepentantly.

Robert ran his hands over his face. "I need to return to London. Be ready to leave in the morning."

"Aye, my lord. They'll be reet glad to see the backside o' you this time, I reckon."

Robert glared, his tone frigid. "Remind me, please, why I haven't let you go?"

Pitchley met his eyes. "Ain't no use a-telling me you's going to let me go. Wouldn't go iffen you did. Promised your da I'd stay with you." The groom sniffed. "Serve you right if I did leave."

Robert turned sharply on his heel and walked out of the stable.

"You'd better figure out what's wrong with you, Master Robert," Pitchley called to him, "afore somebody decides you need to be locked up."

Robert stopped. Responding would only encourage Pitchley's impertinence. Better to ignore him. "Pitchley, did I ask for your opinion?" A mistake—Robert knew it as soon as the words left his mouth.

"At least you ain't a-kick'n and a-scream'n like you did when his old lordship wouldn't let you sit his hunter."

Resisting an urge to give as good as he was getting, Robert strode firmly to the manor-house door, his shoulders hunched against the advice Pitchley was throwing at him.

He could not understand why that *damned woman* insisted on staying in his head—he adjusted his buckskin breeches—and was affecting every other part of his blasted body.

The following evening, Robert arrived at his London townhouse in time to change and have dinner at Brooks, his club. What he found when he entered the hallowed, male-only sanctuary, was talk of Lady Serena. Her assured manners and informed conversation, sense of humor, skill with the whip, and, most irritating of all, how well she dressed and her beauty. Her creamy breast adorned with a curl floated in his mind.

After being asked several times if he had either made her acquaintance, or could he use his influence with Evesham for an introduction, Robert stormed back to his house.

Later that evening, he sat in his study staring into the fire-place—an untasted glass of brandy in hand. Damn the woman. Damn all women. He drained the glass and went to bed, only to be haunted, once again, by visions of her.

The next day did not begin any better for Robert than the previous one had ended. He was dressing when his butler brought in a note from his grandmother. His presence was requested to drive with her in the Park that afternoon, prob-ably to discuss his need for an heir. Fate was laughing at him.

Robert took himself off to Manton's Shooting Salon, then to Jackson's Boxing Parlor, where he found Marcus and Rutherford emerging.

Rutherford looked at him closely and, although his friend clamped his lips shut, he could not keep them from twitch-ing.

Beaumont fumed knowing he had the look of a man being driven to madness by his own devil.

"You here?" Rutherford asked. "What happened to New-market?"

"I decided to come back to Town. Have I missed any-thing?" Robert asked with feigned indifference.

Marcus's eyes sparkled with wicked glee. "Not much. The Season is just starting. You should've received a card for St. Eth's ball as well as our own."

Absently rubbing his jaw, Robert replied. "I only returned last evening. Mariville, my secretary, will have them."

As hard as Rutherford tried, he couldn't stop his lips from

curving up. "Robert, no wish to intrude, but I've seen you in better looks. Is everything well?"

Beaumont ran his hand through his usually carefully styled curls. "No, damn it, it's not at all well. I got to Brooks last night and was besieged by people wanting an introduction to *Lady Serena*. Then I received a note from my grandmother this morning. How she knows where to find me is so frightening I don't want to think about it. I must attend her this afternoon. The prospect is enough to drive a man over the edge."

Rutherford grinned. "Lady Serena has become very popular. Anyone who has the slightest acquaintance with Evesham is being asked for an introduction."

Marcus said innocently, "St. Eth told me the knocker is never still. Got them writing odes to her face."

Robert's mouth dropped open. "Odes to her face?"

Marcus rubbed his chin. "Yes, and Phoebe said Serena already had an offer. Of course, Serena won't say who it was, but the betting in the clubs is that it was Hampton. He was puffing off that he'd offer for her. Didn't think she'd turn down a duke."

"She turned down Hampton?" Robert attacked his hair again.

"It's really not so difficult to understand," Marcus replied provocatively. "I would imagine Serena wants a love match."

"A love match." The devil. Beaumont turned and flung himself back out the door.

Rutherford played idly with his pocket watch. "Marcus, I believe Beaumont is becoming truly disordered."

Swinging his quizzing glass, Marcus replied, "Indeed, as his friends, we should assist him in his time of need."

"I would say the game is on. Can I interest you in a private wager?"

* * *

Robert walked back to Berkeley Square trying to regain his customary cool. He would go to Lady Harkness's house tonight. Her parties always provided a distraction.

First he had to see his grandmother.

Robert presented himself at her home on Upper Brook Street just before five o'clock. His grandmother was an irascible old lady who always seemed to get what she wanted, which was humorous when her edicts were directed toward other members of the family. She dressed only in black bombazine and favored the style of the previous century, both in fashion and in speech.

For most of his life, she had been his favorite relative. But two years ago she'd begun to harp on him to wed. Now he avoided her whenever he could, though if summoned, he would go.

Robert assisted his grandmother and his aunt Frederica, the Dowager Lady Stanstead, known as Freddy, into their landau. He was seated with his back to the coachman, who was as deaf as a doornail, allowing his grandmother to say whatever she wished. Not that anything *could* stop her from saying what she wished.

"Robert, I am an old woman. I want—and I shall see— the succession secured before I die. You must marry. One disappointment in youth is not an excuse to fail in your duty. I daresay you could have any chit you wanted. You're the head of our house. Get on with it."

Robert opened his mouth to protest.

"Don't tell me about your reputation. I know what it is. But I'll tell you what I've never heard, and wouldn't believe it if I did, is that you've ever toyed with the affections of a well-bred virgin. Decide what you want in a wife, my boy, find her and marry her."

Robert was silent. Thoughts ran amok in his head. He'd thought he'd known what he wanted. A wife who would stay in Yorkshire, bear his children, and enable him to continue with his life. Then he'd met Lady Serena. What was so different about her he didn't know and couldn't guess. So far, she'd not lived down to his expectations. But Marcus said she was waiting for a damned love match.

Love was not for Robert. Could he have her without it?

He kept himself from running his hand over his face and glanced up at his grandmother, who stared at him with a sharp, almost knowing, look in her eyes. Good God! She couldn't possibly perceive what he was thinking. He glanced around, in what he hoped would appear to be calm unconcern.

Lady Serena was tooling down the carriage way in a fashionable curricle with *Covington* seated beside her. *Blast him.*

Beaumont's muscles clenched as he stared at Serena, unable to tear his eyes away.

Lady Beaumont grinned. Robert was so preoccupied by the lady in the carriage, he wasn't paying attention to anything else. She exchanged a humorous look with her daughter.

"That is all I have to say, my boy. You may make your escape." Lady Beaumont waited. It had been a long time since he was this taken with a lady. *"Robert."*

His head swung around as if on a swivel.

"I said you may leave."

"Thank you, Grandmama. I mean. Oh, damn it." He leaned forward, kissed her cheek, and bolted from the carriage.

She chuckled merrily. "He's just like his grandfather. I haven't been so diverted in years, Freddy."

Her daughter's gaze followed Robert making his way

after the carriage. "He certainly appears to be a case. Does he really think he'll catch her on foot?"

"Freddy, poke Joe Coachman. I need to go home before I make a spectacle of myself and find out about that girl so we know with whom we are dealing."

Late that evening, Robert arrived at a house on the edge of Mayfair. Lady Harkness, the widow of a rich Irish peer, who, having never been admitted to the drawing rooms of the Polite Society, decided to amuse herself by attracting gentlemen and ladies of the *ton* seeking distractions in a discreet house.

Her rooms were opulently furnished in creams and gold of the popular Egyptian style. Lit by soft lamps and wall sconces, they contained dark alcoves designed to encourage the pursuit of passion. Her refreshments were always of the highest quality. A string quartet played softly in the background. Couples gathered, speaking in low, well-modulated voices. Lady Harkness's house served both those ladies who had not found happiness in marriage and the high-born rakes who were pleased to service them.

She came forward to greet Robert. "Lord Beaumont. I've not seen you in a while. Where have you been hiding yourself?"

He bussed the powdered and perfumed cheek she offered, but he couldn't keep the tension from his voice. "I've been in the wilds of Yorkshire and in Newmarket."

"You sound as if you need a distraction. Would you like me to introduce you to one or two of the ladies present?"

He smiled thinly. "Not just yet."

Robert, a glass of champagne in his hand, prowled the room. He took in the glances and sidelong looks he received from several ladies, some of whom he'd already enjoyed.

They all seemed so vulgar, and he wondered what he was doing here.

Frustrated, he flirted with a ripe brunette, before finally turning away, disgusted. The woman's charms couldn't compete with his vision of auburn hair and innocent amber eyes. Unable to find his escape in another woman, he went home.

He poured himself a brandy and stared into the fire's flames. Since avoiding Serena obviously hadn't helped, he'd decided to spend time with her. He'd discover her true character and would, surely, be bored in a week or two.

After tossing off the drink, he threw the glass at the fireplace.

Serena galloped down the tan on Rotten Row, while another horse strived to close in behind her. She urged Shamir faster. Upon reaching the end of the track, she glanced over to see Lord Beaumont cantering up on Démon. He reined in and trotted toward her and her breath quickened.

He smiled, and Serena's heart beat so hard, she was sure he could hear it.

"Lady Serena, I wish you a good morn."

Willing herself to be calm, Serena turned up her lips slightly. "A good morning to you as well, my lord."

Beaumont's brows lowered. "Are you alone?"

She pointed to Will, on the side of the track. "I have my groom."

"Would you like to ride with me?"

Her chest constricted, and she drew a shaky breath. She'd thought and dreamed about just this—riding with him, his gaze upon her—perhaps, he'd even kiss her hand again.

Serena smiled. "Yes, I'd like that. Usually, I ride with

Phoebe and Marcus, but poor little Arthur is cutting teeth and had a bad night."

Lord Beaumont grinned, his eyes enigmatic, almost as if he had a secret. No other man had looked at her that way.

"What a shame they can't be here. I hope the baby recovers quickly."

Robert and Serena set off at a trot through the Park, riding silently for a time. Serena cast a sidelong glance at him. Her heart jumped. He was looking at her as well. Lord Beaumont was held to have wonderful address, but surprisingly, he seemed nervous. She wished he'd say something. Surely he wasn't waiting for her?

Finally he spoke. "You ride well."

She realized what high praise that was. Lord Beaumont was a member of the Four-Horse Club. "Thank you. So do you."

"I've never known a lady to have such a large horse. What is he, seventeen hands?"

"Close. Sixteen three. But he has wonderful manners."

"Have you ridden him long?" he asked, with curiosity.

"Since my father died." Serena started to feel at ease with him, like she had on the evening of the play. No other gentleman had ever asked about her with the same amount of interest Lord Beaumont did. She patted the horse's neck. "In a way, we found each other. Papa bought Shamir but never rode him. I was in the stables one day when he was kicking his stall. The grooms were unable to calm him. Yet he settled immediately for me."

Serena turned to face Lord Beaumont. He looked at her with those beautiful green eyes. Her hands trembled on the reins.

He seemed thoughtful for a few moments. "I've heard of horses that choose their masters. You must be very special."

Her mouth dried. She'd driven with other gentlemen and spent time talking to them, but she'd never had trouble breathing. If she didn't leave soon, she was going to make a fool of herself. "I must go now. Thank you for your company, my lord."

He bowed to her gracefully, a difficult maneuver on horseback. "Until we meet again, my lady."

She broke his gaze. "Yes, until we meet again."

Serena trotted toward the gate, but her heart yearned to remain. It was all she could do to keep herself from looking back over her shoulder to see if he still watched her.

Beaumont stared at Serena as she rode away. Where was his vaunted charm when he needed it? Robert sucked in a breath, picturing Lady Serena's long auburn hair curling over her creamy shoulders, her head thrown back for him as he nibbled and placed feather-soft kisses on her jaw and neck. His body clenched in desire and need.

By God, she was the most beautiful woman he'd ever seen. She'd employed no arts to attract him, yet he craved her. He didn't even know if Lady Serena was happy to see him. Until the end of their ride, when he held her gaze, she'd barely lifted her eyes to his. Was she interested in him at all?

He should have been able to draw her into conversation. Lord, he was losing his touch. It was then that it dawned on him that spending time with Lady Serena wasn't going to end his torment. Every time he saw her, he wanted her more.

Damn. He whirled Démon around and thundered back down the track.

Upon returning home, he wreaked havoc on his desk, searching for the invitations to St. Eth and Evesham's balls.

"Charles!" He strode down the corridor to his secretary's office. "Have you seen an invitation to St. Eth's ball?"

"Yes, my lord." His secretary glanced up warily. "I was about to deny you."

"No, accept it." Beaumont ignored Charles's incredulous expression and paced. "When is it?"

Charles picked up the gilt-edged card. "In three days."

"I should have a card to Evesham's ball as well. Do I have any other invitations?"

"Nothing out of the usual, my lord. Lady Remington is having a soiree—"

No others? Of course not. He hadn't been to a *ton* event in years, but those are the parties Lady Serena would attend. How could he start receiving the right sort of cards again? "Send my excuses to Lady R. and accept St. Eth."

His secretary tapped the papers on his desk, before asking hesitantly, "My lord, I have no wish to seem impertinent, but are you feeling quite the thing?"

"Charles," Beaumont glowered. "If you care at all for me—or for your position—you will not again mention my health."

Charles smiled. If he didn't know better he'd suspect Lord Beaumont had a tendre for some lady. Interesting. Charles had been in Beaumont's employ for seven years. His lordship had never been so testy, and Beaumont hated *ton* events.

Hearing voices, Charles entered the hall to find Henley, Lord Beaumont's valet, and Finster in conversation.

"Mr. Mariville," Henley asked, "has his lordship seemed a bit surly of late?"

Apparently, Charles wasn't the only one who'd noticed a change. "Why, what's happened?"

"Well, normally I would never mention it, however, this morning he bit off my nose simply for asking if he would dine at his club." Henley sniffed. "I've been his lordship's valet since he came upon Town, and he has never been churlish before."

Finster cut in. "I have been in service with the Beaumont family since before his lordship's birth," the butler said, in his supremely lofty manner. "Never has the master flung himself in and out of the house as he's been doing lately, not even when he was a young man."

Charles glanced at them. "He has seemed a little out of sorts lately, but I don't doubt it will work itself out."

Lighthearted, Charles returned to his office to refuse the invitations he normally accepted—and accept the invitations he normally refused.

Things were becoming very interesting.

Lady Beaumont glanced up as her daughter entered the morning room in Upper Brook Street, where she was sitting with Robert, who'd arrived unannounced.

"Robert, what are you doing here?" Freddy asked. "I don't remember Mama summoning you."

He glared. "A pretty state of affairs it's become when a man can't visit his grandmother when he wishes."

"Freddy, leave the boy alone," Lady Beaumont said, then paused, asking her daughter, "Did you discover what we want to know?"

Freddy's eyes sparkled with mischief. "Yes, Mama, I did, and very intriguing I found it. Unless you need me here, I'll attend to our mail."

"Go on. Return when you're finished." Lady Beaumont turned her attention to Robert. "To what do I owe the pleasure of your visit?"

He paced, picking up objects and setting them down. His

grandmother watched with amusement until he scowled at an old, expensive piece of Chinese porcelain. "Robert, sit."

Robert took a seat in the chair next to the sofa upon which she sat. "Now, you may tell me what you want."

He stared into the fire for a moment. "Grandmama, I have—there is—well, I think I would like to make a . . . push."

She studied him, taking in the desperate, haunted look in his face. "Robert, are you trying to tell me you've found an eligible lady for whom you are thinking of offering?"

"Yes, that's it." He looked relieved by his grandmother's prescience.

"That's wonderful, but there must be something amiss for you to be here. What's the problem, my boy?"

He let out an anguished groan. "There is no getting near her. The only time she is not surrounded by a crowd of others is when she's riding in the morning. I've refused invitations to the types of parties she attends for so long, I don't receive them anymore."

"We shall speak with your aunt to see what she can arrange."

At that moment, Freddy reentered the room. "What do you want me to arrange?"

"Robert wants to attend *ton* parties again. He'll need vouchers for Almack's."

At the mention of Almack's, Robert rolled his eyes.

Freddy pressed her lips together. "Robert, if you want to do the pretty, you'll need to attend all the entertainments. I'll ask Mrs. Drummond-Burrell for a voucher for you. Clementina has always had a soft spot for a rake." Freddy pursed her lips. "Have you received any invitations at all?"

"For St. Eth and Evesham's balls. Other than that, nothing."

She tapped her chin. "I'll visit Lady Bellamny again tomorrow. Once I tell her, word will go round quickly. If you're still close to Evesham, you'd be well advised to ask Lady Evesham for help. She's very discreet and well connected."

Robert's countenance lightened. "Yes, that's a good idea. Phoebe will be able to do the trick."

Lady Beaumont nodded. "Good, now take your fidgety self off. You'll give me a spasm if I have to watch you anymore."

Robert smiled with amusement. "Grandmama, what a faradiddle. You've never had a spasm in your life."

"No, but there's no saying I won't start having them," she retorted.

"Would you like me to bring you some vinaigrette or feathers to burn when I next visit?" he asked with credible solicitude.

His grandmother threw a pillow at him.

He ducked and blew her a kiss as he left the room.

"His grandfather, to the life," Lady Beaumont reminisced with a misty smile. "Now Freddy, what have you found out about our mystery lady?"

"Her name is Lady Serena Weir . . ."

Chapter Five

As Robert walked toward Grosvenor Square, he felt better than he had in weeks. Wilson, the Dunwood butler, showed him to the library, where Marcus, working on some papers, glanced up as Robert was announced.

"Robert, what brings you here?"

He took in the stack of documents on the large mahogany partner's desk. "I don't wish to disturb you. Do you have time?"

Marcus waved his hand at the papers. "Don't let this bother you. I don't have to do it all myself. That's one of the joys of having a wife who knows as much about estate management as do I. Please, come in."

He motioned Robert to a chair.

Robert sat and tried unsuccessfully to sort his thoughts. This was not going to be as easy as he'd supposed. "Marcus, when you were courting Phoebe, did you feel, well, crazed?"

"Crazed, exasperated, murderous, as well as a number of other things," Marcus said. "What has my courtship with Phoebe to do with you?"

Robert swallowed. "Well I—I, I'm not quite sure how to put this . . ."

Marcus's face darkened. "Put what? Is it something to do with Phoebe?"

"No, no. I need advice because . . . I am not feeling at all the thing lately, and I came to ask for Phoebe's help."

Marcus's lips twitched. "Robert, are you trying to tell me you think you might be in love?"

Beaumont recoiled as if his friend had thrown a punch. "*Love?* No. It's not possible."

He slumped in the chair and sunk into his own thoughts. The problem was they weren't telling him anything useful.

Marcus waited.

After a few moments, Robert gave up trying to sort out his muddled mind. Lifting his head, he fixed Marcus with a stare. "How would I recognize if I'm in love? *Not that I am,* but, with Phoebe, how did you know?"

"I was in a pretty fair way to being in love, but when my beloved wife knocked me down, I was sure of it. Though I don't recommend it as an experience."

"Phoebe hit you? Why?"

"I was stupid."

Robert stared out the window as Marcus went to the side-board.

"Would you like anything to drink?" Marcus asked.

"A wine, thank you."

Marcus tugged the bell pull and a footman popped his head in the room. "Yes, my lord?"

"Please ask her ladyship to attend me."

The door closed. Marcus gave a glass of wine to Robert and took one for himself.

A few minutes later Phoebe entered. She glanced at Robert.

Marcus shrugged. "The only thing I've been able to determine is Robert's not in love. Perhaps you can discern what the problem is. I have great faith in your powers of perception, my dear."

Phoebe sat on the small sofa next to the chair Lord Beaumont occupied. "Robert, what is it and how can we help?"

If he knew what the deuce was wrong, he wouldn't be here. Frustrated, he said, "I'm having these feelings, and—and I don't know what they are. Marcus says I'm in love, but I can't be . . ."

Phoebe bit her lip. "You have an attraction for someone?"

Attraction? Damned obsession might be more accurate. "Yes, that's it, and I can't seem to think of anything else. I feel as if I am walking in circles, and—"

Marcus interrupted. "Just to be clear, Beaumont, you are talking about a gently-bred female, not a . . ."

"Marcus, do be quiet. Of course he's talking about a lady." Phoebe turned back to Beaumont. "Go on Robert. Tell me about her. Is she someone I know?"

"It's Lady Serena." He groaned.

Marcus handed Phoebe a glass of wine. "You may need this."

She smiled at him. "Come Robert, it cannot be that bad. If you think you like Lady Serena you should come to know her better, and then, if you find you suit, you may try to fix her attention."

Suddenly Robert felt a glimmer of hope. "My aunt Freddy is going to arrange for me to receive cards again and to be admitted to Almack's, but that will take weeks. So many gentlemen are interested in her. What can I do until then?"

Marcus's brows rose. *"Almack's?"*

"Marcus, shush. Of course Almack's." She once more addressed Beaumont. "Robert, there is nothing easier. You shall attend entertainments with us until you begin receiving cards. I am sure Rutherford will help as well. My dear friend, you will, no doubt, be amazed at how eagerly hostesses will send you invitations. You're very eligible you know."

Robert stood up. "I shall go see Rutherford now."

Marcus pushed Beaumont back down. "I'll send for him. There is no reason for you to go through this all over again. I daresay Phoebe will be happy to explain."

Marcus muttered to himself as he once again walked to the bell pull. "You'd drive Rutherford mad."

Within a short period of time, Anna and Rutherford were shown into the library. Anna glanced at Phoebe, who imperceptibly nodded her head as she motioned for Anna to sit next to her.

Anna grinned at her husband. A look of unholy amusement lit his face as he took a chair next to Marcus. Phoebe briefly explained Robert's problem.

Anna forestalled Rutherford as he opened his mouth. "We shall, naturally, be happy to help you, Robert. Phoebe, do you attend Worthington's party this evening?"

"Yes, we are chaperoning Serena."

Robert's head popped up like a jack-in-the-box, and he stared at her intently.

Phoebe's lips quivered. "Yes, Robert, you may accompany us. However," she said and narrowed her eyes at him, "I forbid you to try to fix her attention whilst you are unsure of yourself. If she were to develop a tendre for you, and you did not return her regard, she would be badly hurt. That, I will not allow."

Rutherford took a sip of wine. "I wouldn't be surprised if her card has been filled for a week."

"True." Phoebe was quiet for a minute. "I don't suppose either of you have requested a dance?"

"I am to stand up with her for the quadrille," Marcus replied.

"You've never danced the quadrille with me," she protested.

Marcus smiled wolfishly. "No, of course not. Waltzing with you is much more interesting, my love, and eminently more satisfying. Serena wanted to practice her steps with someone she knew."

"I am to dance a waltz with her." At Beaumont's glare, Rutherford quickly added, "Also because she wanted to practice her steps."

"Robert," Phoebe asked, "how long has it been since you have danced a quadrille?"

"Even in the underbelly of the *ton,* we dance."

Phoebe pursed her lips. "I think both of you should give your dances to Robert."

"As long as Serena agrees," Anna said, "I think it would be unexceptional."

"Good, it's settled then. Marcus and Rutherford shall ask that Robert be allowed to take their places." Phoebe smiled at Robert. "There, that was easily solved."

Serena waited to be handed up to the Dunwood coach. To her surprise, Lord Beaumont alighted, elegantly attired in a black coat, a nicely patterned waistcoat, and black breeches. His cravat was fashionably and neatly tied. He must be the best looking man in the *ton.*

He bowed and Serena hid her surprise when he dismissed the footman and insisted upon helping her into the coach himself.

Her hand tingled when he touched it as it had before, and

in her dreams. Serena peeked up at him through her lashes. He gazed down at her. His green eyes smoldered with a heat her body reacted to, but that she didn't understand. She had trouble swallowing and her breathing was shallow. Did she affect him in the same way he affected her? What did it mean?

Once there, Robert escorted her into the ballroom. Serena thanked him and joined a group of ladies.

Miss Featherton, a young woman of two Seasons, greeted Serena. "Lady Serena, who is the gentleman that accompanied you?"

"Were you not listening when he was announced?" Miss Emerson, a plump lady in her early twenties who'd joined them, asked.

Miss Featherton glanced at the ceiling and huffed. "No, I was *looking* at him."

Serena gave a polite smile. "He is Viscount Beaumont."

"He reminds me of a Greek god." Miss Featherton sighed. "I've never seen him before. He must not spend much time in London."

"Oh no, I believe he spends most of his time in London." Miss Emerson lowered her voice. "I heard Dowager Lady Worthington say to Mama he'd not attended a ball like this for years, and he must be thinking of marrying." She frowned slightly. "Then Mrs. Carter said she'd heard of a lady in despair over him, and Mama said she knew the lady and that the lady should have known better than to behave as she did."

Serena's grip on her fan tightened. This gossip about Lord Beaumont didn't sound at all good.

Miss Featherton's eyes grew wide. "Did they say the woman's name?"

"No, they saw me and Lady Worthington just remarked that the ball would now be a success because he'd attended.

Mama said I could stand up with Lord Beaumont if he asked me, but I mustn't go anywhere alone with him."

Miss Featherton's eyes grew even wider and her voice dropped to a whisper. "Do you think he is a rake?"

"Well . . ." Miss Emerson glanced around and said in a conspiratorial tone, "I think he must be. Otherwise why would Mama stop talking about him when she saw me? If he's looking for a wife, perhaps he's reforming."

Serena pressed her lips together. How dare these girls blacken his name so carelessly? "I wouldn't repeat idle gossip. He is a friend of my cousin, Lady Evesham, and he's been very kind to me."

Miss Emerson's face fell. "But wouldn't it be romantic to have a reformed rake fall in love with one?" She sighed. "I'd be happy just to dance with him."

For the first time since Serena had arrived in London, she felt the differences in the ages of the other ladies making their come out. She wasn't at all sure rakes did reform, which boded ill for her if the talk was true. When Lord Beaumont was near, she had trouble remembering any other gentlemen existed.

Robert bowed and lifted Serena's hand to his lips before placing it on his arm. He'd wanted to talk to her and keep her by his side. Unfortunately, the quadrille was not conducive to holding a lengthy conversation.

He smiled, confident in his ability to charm her as easily as he did any other female. "Lady Serena, you dance delightfully."

She glanced up shyly. "Thank you, my lord. I have not danced the quadrille long. I'm a little concerned I might miss my steps."

Robert blinked, caught off guard by her guilelessness. "I

would never have guessed you'd not been dancing it for years."

Serena smiled delightedly up at him, and he stopped breathing.

"I am having such a good time in London. I feel almost like a princess," she confided.

And he was lost, struggling not to respond to her innocent joy. Collecting himself, Robert replied with practiced grace. "You look like a princess."

The paces of the dance parted them and brought them together again. Serena glanced at him, gratefully. "Thank you, my lord. You are too kind."

Robert searched her face when she spoke the words he'd heard too often while engaging in a flirtation. Yet unlike other females, she meant what she'd said and he didn't want her gratitude. He wanted . . . He didn't know what he wanted, except for her to smile again. "I am only telling you the truth."

She did look like a princess and was easily the most elegant and beautiful woman in the room. Her gown of Pomona green set off the red in her hair and was cleverly fashioned to make her shoulders appear almost naked. What would the rest of her look like? She wore only a long strand of pearls looped low over her luscious breasts. Breasts he desperately wanted to touch and taste. Matching pearl drops highlighted her shell-like ears, and there was that curl over her left breast, tempting him to touch her.

A light pink infused her cheeks and Serena lowered her gaze.

Drat. Could she have read his thoughts? Now what was he supposed to say? "So tell me, Lady Serena, what is it you enjoy most about being in Town?"

When she glanced up, he became lost in her eyes.

"People have been so kind to me."

He didn't expect that. Anger rose at the thought she might have been hurt. "Did the people you knew before not treat you as they should?"

"Oh, it wasn't that. All of them were my dependants." Serena's answer reassured him. "I—I didn't have much inter-action with anyone else. I never truly thought to find the people in London so welcoming."

Robert held her gaze for a few moments. Once again, her candor was unexpected and for the first time in his life, he had no witty response.

He returned Serena to her circle and retreated to a pillar he could stand against to watch her. His plan to grow tired of her had failed. Each time Robert saw her, he wanted her more. Touching her made his body yearn for what it couldn't have and awakened a desire he'd never experienced before. His battered heart stirred. Lady Serena was far more danger-ous than he'd thought.

Serena's thoughts drifted to Lord Beaumont while she chatted with the other ladies between the dance sets. He'd seemed concerned, as if he wanted to protect her.

Lord Waverly claimed her for the next set, a country dance she knew well. Serena glanced over at Lord Beau-mont. He was hopelessly handsome and appeared so alone. The thought that he could have a bad reputation disturbed her more than she wanted to admit. He'd gone to great lengths to stand up with her this evening, and she didn't know what to make of it.

Serena looked up at Lord Waverly. This was so different than her dance with Lord Beaumont. Serena's experience with gentlemen, other than in her family, could fit in a thim-ble. Even her brother and father hadn't been around very much. She'd not been out of the schoolroom when her mother passed away. After her father died and her brother remained on Wellington's staff, she'd been alone. Serena was out of her depth when it came to men, but now Phoebe and Anna could advise her.

Lord Waverly returned Serena to her friends and Lord Beaumont claimed her for his second dance, a waltz. She hid a grin when Miss Emerson sighed.

Serena steeled herself to feel Lord Beaumont's hand on her waist. It didn't help. She drew in a sharp breath as her heart pounded in her chest and her knees almost gave way. This was far, far worse than with the dancing master.

"Is anything wrong?" Lord Beaumont asked.

"No, no. I'm just not sure I know the steps of the dance well enough," she lied.

He twirled her down the floor and into the turn. "But you waltz delightfully. Why were you worried?"

"It is my first time waltzing in public. You dance very well, my lord. Though I have only Uncle Henry, Marcus, and the dancing master to compare you to."

He had only a polite smile on his face. "A leveler. Thank you for your praise, particularly considering my competition."

Her anxious gaze flew to his. This was not going well at all. "Did I say something wrong?"

His eyes softened. "No, not in the least." His murmur was deep and his green eyes heated as they had before. "Would I could dance every set with you and keep you in conversation all evening."

Serena blushed again but did not answer. He was certain to think her some sort of dunce. She needed to think of something to say.

They came to the turn and he drew her a bit closer. Lady Serena was so quiet and had not responded. Had he offended her? Was she even more innocent than he'd thought? His body's near constant desire faded a bit with his concern that she was unhappy.

For some reason, it was very important that he draw her out and make her smile again. "Oh, no, you must converse, Lady Serena. People will think I've said something I shouldn't have if you blush so delightfully and don't speak."

"I am unused to these types of conversations. I thought with you, as you are a friend of my family, I could be more myself."

Her hand trembled in his, but she gave him a small smile. There, that was better.

Enjoying her artlessness, Robert grinned. "Then I'm honored you feel you do not have to speak with me."

He tightened his hand on her waist through the turn, making sure not to hold her as tightly as he wished.

"You are funning with me," she said in consternation. "I wish you would not do so while I am dancing. I might miss a step."

Taken aback, he searched for another subject. "You don't live in Yorkshire. Where do you live?"

She tensed during the last turn. Maybe that was the problem. She was unused to dancing so close to a man.

"I live—I used to live in an old and drafty castle, Vere Castle." Her smile did not reach her eyes. "It's in Scotland, almost on the border. You must live very close to my Aunt Ware."

"Yes, my principal estate is in Yorkshire. Your aunt's land and mine march together. Of recent years, I've remained mostly in London. But I must, of course, visit Yorkshire several times during the year on estate business. We are coming to the next turn, and I shall need to hold you closer."

She nodded, but still stiffened as his arm drew her in and only eased when he loosened his grip.

"You visit only on estate business? How sad. I found the country to be very beautiful in its own right."

Well, that was better. He forced himself to relax his hands. "If I had a family, I'd spend more time there. When I was a child, we had parties during Christmas. All the men, even my father, who was a very high stickler, went out to the forest to bring in a Yule log. I remember it burned for months."

"Oh, yes," Serena said animatedly. "At the castle, we have a Christmas party for all our dependants, and they help bring in the Yule log. It is my favorite time of year."

The music ended and he brought them to a stop. Robert leaned in as close as propriety would allow and tried to breathe in her scent. "How did you happen to come to London?"

"My brother returned recently with his new wife, and it was decided I should finally have a London Season."

He could tell Serena was making an effort to keep her tone light, but pain lingered in her voice, so he changed topics. "Have you been to any of the museums? They have some very interesting exhibits."

"No, I would love to see them. There's been no time."

Robert met her gaze. Those amber eyes haunted his sleep. "Perhaps I may escort you."

Serena innocently returned his look. "Yes, thank you. I would be delighted."

"Do you know if you are free to-morrow at two o'clock?" He held his breath—

"Yes, I think I am."

—and released it. "May I come for you then?"

Serena smiled, her pleasure unfeigned. "How wonderful. I'll look forward to it."

Robert was unable to believe she was looking at him with

such simple joy. Had a woman ever gazed at him in that manner?

He reluctantly released her hand and bowed, first to her, then to Phoebe and Anna, who'd appeared from nowhere. Not allowed to stand up with her again that night, yet unwilling to either leave the ball or dance with anyone else, he leaned back against a wall with his arms folded and scowled at Serena's next dance partner, oblivious to the other ladies in their brightly colored plumage.

"Robert, you are making a spectacle of yourself." Phoebe's lips were tight. "You cannot dance only with Lady Serena, then stand there staring at her. You will cause just the sort of talk you should be trying to avoid. Find some other lady with whom to partner."

That was not what he'd planned. "I suppose you're right. Phoebe, will you dance with me?"

"No, she will not." Marcus frowned. "You asked for this, now you must play propriety."

As Robert walked away from them, he glanced around hoping for an escape. He had no desire to dance with anyone other than Lady Serena, but the Dowager Lady Worthington found him and introduced him to a young lady in need of a partner. Hiding his chagrin, Robert prepared to endure the unmitigated torture of young females in their first Season.

At the end of the evening, Robert walked home, annoyed. Other than his two dances with Lady Serena, he'd spent the rest of his evening dancing with several chits, in whom he had no interest. To make it worse, he didn't understand the depth of his reaction when Lady Serena danced with other gentlemen.

Robert had never minded seeing a woman with whom he was intimate dance with others. Why it should matter with Lady Serena, he could not fathom. He scowled. Nor had his hands burned when he had held another woman, but they did when he'd danced with her. Why had he felt the need to draw her body against his during the waltz? Or drag her away from her dance partners?

If this was love, it was a damned uncomfortable feeling. He lengthened his stride in irritation.

Was it love, or did he just want her? What could he do to end his agony?

Chapter Six

Early the next morning, Serena, mounted on her horse outside of St. Eth House, was surprised to see Phoebe ride up on Lilly without Marcus.

"Marcus is with Arthur," she explained. "The baby had another bad night. I cannot tell you how happy I shall be when he has all his teeth."

They galloped down Rotten Row. The Park always reminded Serena of the country, but to-day, even the trees leafing and the new flowers pushing up in the beds couldn't distract her from thoughts of Lord Beaumont.

Dropping Shamir to a walk, Serena considered how best to approach Phoebe with her questions. Questions that had kept Serena awake most of the night. In the end, she decided candor was the only way forward. "Phoebe, is there some reason Lord Beaumont was with you last evening and that Marcus and Rutherford gave their dances to him?"

"Robert asked us to help him with you." Phoebe pulled a

face. "Beaumont is in difficult straits. He's spent years running away from love and marriage only to find he now wants both, and it terrifies him." Phoebe sighed. "We agreed that he could attend entertainments with us, but only on the proviso that he would not fix his attentions on you until he knew his own mind."

Serena's heart somersaulted and her horse tried to pick up his pace in response. Could he really have the same feelings for her that she had for him? Rather breathlessly, she asked, "Do you mean he thinks he might be in love with me?"

Phoebe shrugged in exasperation and reined in Lilly. "I wish I could tell you. Robert only knows that thinking of you makes him walk in circles."

But what did that mean? Serena wished she knew more about men.

"Serena, how do you feel about him?" Phoebe asked, concerned. "Could you love him? If you cannot, we should end this now."

Part of her felt buoyant. But her practical Scots common sense made her pause. Serena thought for a few moments, her innate sense of caution guiding her. "I don't have much experience with gentlemen, but I won't deny that I'm very interested in him. I have been since the first time we met. He's charming and good looking."

Serena slowed Shamir to a walk. "Is Lord Beaumont really a rake?"

"A rake?" Phoebe rode silently for a minute before responding. "Robert is a good friend. I like him very well," she said. "If he loves his wife, he'll make an excellent husband and father."

Phoebe paused for a moment. "I can say with a certainty, he'd never seduce you and leave you. His intent would be marriage. Yet, I am not sure he would see the need to *love* his wife. I am most concerned for you, my dear. I do not wish to see you hurt."

Phoebe brushed a hand against her forehead. "This is so difficult because I care for you both dearly. Still, I must tell you, I do not think you would be wise to allow him to engage your heart until he is sure of his. Though, how you are to do that, I have no idea."

Serena felt more vulnerable than she had since she left Vere Castle. If she fell in love with Lord Beaumont, and he didn't love her as well, she'd be forced to live with the result for the rest of her life. Serena worried her bottom lip. "He's taking me to a museum this afternoon at two o'clock."

"Indeed?" Phoebe said, astonished. "I am quite sure I've never heard of Beaumont stepping foot into a museum but, lately, he's doing many things I never thought he'd do."

Hope bloomed in Serena's heart again. If he was making these changes, surely he must have feelings for her. "Phoebe, I don't know what to do. It's all so confusing. I have heard he has great address, yet he always seems a little at a loss in conversation with me. People say he is a rake, yet he has not been at all rakish with me. I do not know what to think, and I'm afraid I *will* lose my heart."

"Considering the moonstruck way he's behaved lately, I can't say I am surprised. I'm sorry I cannot advise you more," Phoebe said uneasily.

Serena glanced up. "Oh, no, here comes Lord Bromley. Can we hide?"

Phoebe laughed. "Bromley is quite harmless."

"But such a dead bore." Lord Beaumont's deep voice came from behind them.

Serena jumped.

Phoebe merely said, "Very true. Good morning, Robert. To what do we owe the pleasure?"

"I have developed a taste for early morning rides." He breathed deeply. "The air is so fresh."

Phoebe seemed to consider him. "Robert, if you can rid us of Lord Bromley, you are welcome to remain, else we must leave."

A sparkle entered his eyes. "Nothing easier. Bromley has the worst seat in the country. Come, let's gallop."

They headed in the other direction, quickly outpacing Lord Bromley before he could hail them.

Robert glanced at Serena. "Show me how fast Shamir is." With his dare hanging in the air, he took off down the track.

Unable to refuse the challenge, she dashed after him and soon drew ahead, beating him to the turn.

When he finally caught up with her, she asked, "Does that answer your question, my lord?"

She laughed as Shamir pranced around.

Robert frowned, but his eyes were amused. "Devil a bit. Where did you learn to ride like that?"

"My brother and I used to race each other."

"I didn't think you'd beat me."

Serena assumed a haughty mien. "Then, my lord, you should not have issued the challenge."

His eyes warmed again, and he brought his horse closer. "Vixen, next time I'll know better."

Phoebe, who had ridden up behind them, asked, "Serena, would you like to breakfast with us?"

"Yes, thank you. Will François make the croissants I have heard so much about?"

"We shall ask him." She turned to ride home. "You may come along as well, Robert."

After breakfast, Robert left Dunwood House more confused than ever. He was sure Serena liked him, at least a little, but he couldn't understand why she threw out no lures to encourage him.

At two o'clock, he waited in the hall at St. Eth House and glanced up to find Lady Serena gracefully descending the stairs in a light brown walking gown, made high on her neck, worn beneath a spencer in a military style.

He raised her hand to his lips and lightly kissed it. "You look beautiful."

"Thank you, my lord."

When he caught her gaze, she smiled, and her face turned a pretty shade of pink. A warm feeling infused him as they continued to stare at each other.

Ferguson coughed pointedly.

Serena blinked. "We should go."

Robert hadn't been to the museum since he was a child. Still, he did a credible job of guiding her, and he enjoyed the exhibits almost as much as she did.

They were both attending a ball that evening and as they left the museum, he ventured to ask, "Is your dance card full for the ball?"

"Yes, though two of the places are held by Rutherford and Marcus." She smiled shyly. "They are both waltzes."

His chest tightened and his heart raced. "Would you allow them to give up their dances to me?"

Her cheeks flushed. "If you wish it, I would be delighted to dance with you."

Robert searched her eyes. All he saw was innocent joy and grinned. "Have you had an opportunity to sample Gunter's ices?"

"No." She looked entranced. "What a treat that would be."

"It is entirely my pleasure," he said, amazed that it was perfectly true. Doing things to make her happy pleased him more each time he was with her. This was trouble, but he couldn't stop.

* * *

Lord Huntley and Mr. Featherton watched Beaumont enter Gunter's with Lady Serena.

Mr. Featherton raised his brows. "Have you ever seen Beaumont escort a lady to Gunter's?"

"Wouldn't have believed it if I hadn't seen it."

Featherton rubbed his cheek. "Heard he has started attending balls and other entertainments."

"Beaumont?"

"Got it from m'sister. Said he's finally given in to his grandmother's pressure to marry."

"I'd like to see the day Beaumont agrees to be leg-shackled," retorted Huntley skeptically. "And I wouldn't wish it to be with my sister. He's deemed a cold fish by any lady he's involved with, from what I've seen."

Mr. Featherton raised his quizzing glass. "Yet, he's very popular with the ladies. Heard several of them say so."

"But Beaumont usually only goes for married ladies or widows. Charms them, gives them a couple of weeks, then moves on. If he's thinking of marriage, it won't be for love. I doubt he knows the meaning of the word."

Robert presented himself at St. Eth House the evening of the ball. He was greeted by Lord and Lady St. Eth and Lady Ware before finally reaching Serena.

She smiled. "Lord Beaumont, I'm pleased you could come."

Robert bowed. "My lady, I would not have missed it."

She was elegantly dressed in a ball gown of dull gold, over an underskirt of cream embroidered with small gold and green bees, and she seemed even more beautiful than before. He focused on the long thick curl that lay on her bosom and his blood boiled.

When Serena looked at him, he'd wanted to drag her away. Away from all the other guests in the overly crowded ballroom. Away from the lascivious men who imagined, as he did, her naked in their arms. He glanced at her low-cut bodice and almost reached out to tug it up, just a little, to hide the view from the other men. Robert now understood the reason Mohammedans covered their women. But Serena wasn't his, yet.

Robert restrained himself and claimed his first waltz.

"How are you enjoying your ball?" He held her a little closer than necessary in the turn, not caring who noticed.

"It is wonderful, and the room so beautiful. We were all very busy to-day directing where the decorations would go. I thought we'd never finish in time."

Robert looked around the room. Mirrors, spaced between the wall panels, enhanced the light from candles set in wall sconces. The room was decorated in a watery blue with greens and yellows. "Yes, you've done well."

Serena colored. "Thank you, but it was Aunt Ester's idea. Other than trim at Christmas with greenery, I'd never done anything like it before. This was much more exciting. We didn't entertain at Vere Castle."

"Never?" Robert didn't understand why. Most ladies he knew lived for balls.

"No, my parents were very ill before they died, and my brother was gone for so many years. Of course, we always had the normal fetes for the workers and the small village, but nothing like a ball."

"You must make up for your isolation now and indulge in all the *ton* has to offer."

Serena's eyes sparkled. "Yes, particularly this evening. My aunts have gone to so much trouble for me."

When the waltz ended, he led Serena back to Lady St. Eth, where her hand was immediately claimed by her next dance partner. Robert tried not to scowl as she went off on another man's arm.

Once again chastised for standing against the wall glaring—this time by Freddy—he allowed himself to be presented to more young ladies in need of dance partners. Robert bowed and smiled, but their simpering adoration left him disgusted. He'd been out of the Marriage Mart for over ten years, nothing had changed.

Thankfully, he'd had the forethought to arrange to take Serena for a drive the next afternoon. He left after their second set, before he savaged the next gentleman who danced with her or kissed her fingers. What he wanted to do was spirit her out of the room and into his arms. Better yet, throw her over his shoulder and take her home. Maybe then, she and everyone else would understand that Lady Serena Weir was his.

Later that evening, as Mary prepared Serena for bed, she relived her waltzes with Lord Beaumont. When his hand had circled her waist, she'd been tempted to close her eyes and lean against him. The pressure of his fingers sent shivers through her and her knees weakened.

After their first dance, he'd once again lounged against a wall staring at her. Serena had tried not to look, but she had felt his heated gaze, compelling her to glance at him. She'd missed most of what her dance partner had said and just smiled, hoping to cover her distraction.

When the movement of the dance brought her around, Lord Beaumont had gone and her heart plunged to her slippers. During the next set, Serena had seen him dancing with a young lady and, for the first time in Serena's life, jealousy took over. She'd wanted to stop the woman from touching him. It was silly and uncharitable, but Serena couldn't stop herself. She'd tried to focus on the dance, but her gaze strayed whenever Lord Beaumont came into view.

Finally, it was time for his second waltz with her, and her body hummed, waiting for his touch. Then it was there, his hand strong and firm on her waist. Serena's heart had pounded and, although she calmed herself before glancing up at him, she was almost undone by the look in his eyes.

Even with her limited experience, his desire was evident. He'd held her even closer than before. But Serena hadn't been sure if it was because the floor was so crowded or he'd wanted to. All she'd known was she hadn't wanted the waltz to end.

She remembered the way his hand gripped hers and his fingers moved on her back, creating tiny fires and sending delightful shivers through her body. When she'd glanced up, he'd gazed at her as if he wanted to devour her.

Serena wondered what it would be like if Lord Beaumont held her close and kissed her. What it would be like to touch his strong face and run her fingers through his blond curls.

Her maid's voice intruded on her thoughts. Serena tried to focus, very glad Mary couldn't read minds. "I'm sorry, Mary. What did you say?"

"Just that you must have had a very good time. You've been woolgathering since you got back."

"Yes." Serena stood. "I had a very pleasant evening."

Two days later, Robert attended the gala opening of Almack's. Having been carefully coached by his Aunt Freddy, he presented himself, correctly attired in a black coat and knee-breeches, to his grandmother's house.

Upon entering the assembly rooms at Almack's, he stifled a groan at the thought he'd once more have to stand up with other ladies. The only bright spot in this evening would be dancing with Serena.

He assisted his grandmother to the seats set up for dowagers and spent a few minutes conversing with her and Freddy. Robert searched the room for Serena, intending to ask her to waltz, but remembered she could not until approved by one of Almack's patronesses. He glanced at his aunt, silently pleading for her help before another gentleman could waltz with Serena.

"Very well, come, I will take you to Mrs. Drummond-Burrell." Freddy placed her hand on his arm and maneuvered him through the crowded room to a haughty-looking matron.

"Clementina, my nephew, Viscount Beaumont, would like to be recommended to Lady Serena Weir as an acceptable dance partner."

A slow smile graced Mrs. Drummond-Burrell's countenance. "Indeed, I would be happy to propose him."

Robert offered Mrs. Drummond-Burrell his arm and escorted her to where Serena stood with her aunts.

Mrs. Drummond-Burrell did not even bother to introduce herself, before saying, "Lady Serena, you do not dance. May I present Lord Beaumont to you as a desirable partner?"

Serena curtsied and thanked the patroness.

Triumphant, Robert led Serena out to waltz.

"How did you do that so quickly?" she asked with amazement. "I was quite certain I would be made to wait forever before being allowed to waltz."

"I used my influence." He smiled smugly. "My Aunt Freddy is an old friend of Mrs. Drummond-Burrell."

"That was well done of you, my lord."

"I am glad you think so. Once I take you back to your

aunts, you'll be surrounded by your court. Will you grant me another waltz before they're all taken?"

Serena grinned. "Yes, of course. After all, you must be rewarded for making it possible for me to waltz so soon."

Robert studied, sure he'd find an arch look or a flirtatious smile. There was nothing but happiness in her eyes and on her face. Something tugged inside him. Elation and a warmth of a different sort rose as he twirled her around the dance floor. It was as if he'd won some sort of contest.

When he returned her to her aunts, the gentlemen, now clamoring to dance with her, abused him for stealing the march on them. Robert's chest puffed out; he was proud that he'd accomplished what none of the others had.

He considered remaining next to her, but the platitudes and flattery from the other men irritated Robert. He made his way back to his grandmother hoping to hide from the patronesses. But, with what he could only describe as a gleefully evil expression on her face, Lady Jersey insisted on introducing him to another young woman.

Ignoring the envious looks from the other gentlemen, Beaumont claimed his second waltz with Serena. Once he had his hand on her back, he snapped (he'd tried to soften his tone, but hadn't succeeded), "You're surrounded by admirers."

She tilted her head. "Yes, I suppose you could call them admirers. Is something wrong?"

"No." Only that he wanted to claim her for himself and this was not the proper venue. He resisted tightening his hold on her. "You must be gratified to have so many gentlemen dancing attendance on you."

"I would rather have one man that I cared for, and who cared for me, dance attendance, as you put it, than be surrounded by a court of admirers."

Her sincerity stunned Robert, and his stomach clenched like he'd been punched. When she said care, she meant love. Did that mean she was starting to care about him, and how would she feel if she knew he was incapable of the emotion?

He changed the conversation to Arthur's teething and Serena regaled him with a story. At the end of the dance, he led her back to her aunts.

Sir Gregory Moreham regarded Robert with a sapient eye. "What is your game, Beaumont? Never known you to attend Almack's before."

Robert responded with a bored drawl, "It pleases my grandmother, of course. Must do the pretty you know." Beaumont strolled away to do his duty by leading a young miss out for a country dance, but could not stop thinking about what Lady Serena said, or her serious expression when she'd said it. He wanted badly to possess her.

Serena tried to keep her mind on Sir Gregory. Used to waltzing now, she made the startling discovery that only when Lord Beaumont held her did she feel breathless and aware of every move her partner made. No other gentleman made her legs feel weak or her breathing quicken.

She caught him glancing at her and heat rose to her cheeks. She quickly turned her attention back to her partner. Had she been clear enough in her response to Lord Beaumont? Did he now understand that all the attention she received from other gentlemen was not equal to one man who loved her? He'd changed the conversation so quickly, Serena couldn't be sure and she must be. Perhaps she should retreat a bit and give them both time to think.

* * *

At a soirée three weeks later, Serena, surrounded by her court, watched Beaumont join Marcus, Phoebe, Anna, and Rutherford. Phoebe glanced at Serena, and she returned Phoebe's inquiry with a silent plea for rescue. The gentlemen were all very nice, but none of them affected her heart. Sick of the pretense, she'd been trying, without success, to escape.

As Phoebe linked arms with Anna and walked toward Serena, she hid her sigh of relief.

"Lady Serena," Phoebe said, "Lady Bellamny is asking for you. Come, I'll take you to her."

Worried now, Serena excused herself and, though her group of admirers frowned, none of them attempted to accompany her.

"Phoebe, what does Lady Bellamny want with me?"

"I don't even know if she is here." Phoebe grinned wickedly. "But, I do know none of the gentlemen will follow us if they believe she's seeking you."

Serena laughed. "Phoebe, what will you think to do next?"

"Yes, unscrupulous of me, was it not?" Phoebe's eyes sparkled wickedly. "But most effective."

They strolled around the garden lit with lanterns bobbing in the trees and set on the sides of the paths.

"Now, what is wrong?" Phoebe asked. "You look to be in a brown study instead of enjoying yourself. You should be taking pleasure in your success."

Serena sighed. "I find my life a little empty. When I first arrived in London, there was such a lot to learn, and so much to do, it took all my time. In the past, I've been devoted to helping people. Now, all I do is attend parties and indulge myself. I no longer have a purpose. It's as if my life is stalled."

"I understand." Phoebe sympathized. "Yet for the present, you must concentrate on finding a husband, which means attending entertainments. How goes it with Beaumont?"

Thinking of him deepened Serena's frustration. Ever since that evening at Almack's when she'd blurted out her desires, she'd held back, waiting for him to show her how he felt. "I see him many mornings while riding, and he ensures that he waltzes with me twice at each ball. Frequently, I've caught him staring at me. If he is interested in me, I don't understand why he'll say nothing to the point!"

She shrugged. "We never have a conversation that is deeper than inane civilities. He looks as if he expects me to do something, but I've no idea what. Am I meant to read his mind?"

Anna shook her head in disgust. "It sounds very like what Rutherford did. He took a long time to recognize his feelings and then to figure out what to do about them. I had time to spare; what will happen to you if you return to Scotland unmarried?"

Serena frowned. "I cannot. My brother as much as told me there was nothing there for me anymore. I don't want to live with Aunt Catherine. She is all that is kind, but it simply would not do. I am too much used to managing my own life."

Lines creased Phoebe's forehead. "Have your feelings grown any deeper for Robert?"

"Yes, if only he did not keep me at arm's length. Every time we begin to discuss anything of importance, he changes the subject. I like him very much. More than that actually, yet I am all out of patience with him."

"We need a plan," Phoebe said. "Let me think on it a bit. We shall come up with something."

Anna patted Serena's arm. "If anyone can make up some sort of scheme, we will."

* * *

Irritated, Robert turned to Marcus and Rutherford. "I don't know what to do about her. I've been to every drum, ball, and rout party Lady Serena's attended for the past month. I've ensured that I've danced with her twice at each ball. I ride with her frequently, and I've even taken her driving during the Promenade, but I'm not making any progress. What *has* happened," Robert scowled, "is I've become the target for every matchmaking mama in Town."

Rutherford's expression was thoughtful. "What do you discuss when you're with Serena?"

Robert shrugged. "I speak with her on very unexceptional subjects, of course."

"Which unexceptional subjects?" Rutherford asked.

"You know, the usual topics of conversation one has with a female. The latest *on-dits*, the weather. How Arthur's teething is progressing. It's amazing how ladies love the infantry."

He could have easily finished with the epitaph: That one is not trying solely to bed.

Rutherford snorted with disgust. "Has it occurred to you to ask what her life was before she came to London?"

Marcus narrowed his eyes. "Or what her views are on estate management?"

"Are you mad? How should she have any ideas on that?"

Marcus shook his head. "Because, you profligate chucklehead, that's what she did while her father was an invalid and continued after he died. Her brother was away on Wellington's staff." Marcus sighed. "I don't understand how you could have spent so much time in Serena's company and know nothing about her. What the devil ails you?"

"I know exactly what ails him," Rutherford said with disgust. "He's never before been interested in knowing more about a female than it takes to get one into his bed. All of his interactions have been strictly of the physical nature. Robert, you must decide if you care enough about her to change your ways."

"I *have* changed my ways." His jaw firmed. "Why the deuce do you think I'm here, or at Almack's, or anywhere else I've been in the past month? It isn't because I'm enjoying it."

Marcus rubbed his hand over his face. "Robert, do you have feelings for Serena?"

Beaumont waited several moments before replying. His voice was a low growl. "Yes, damn it. I can't touch her hand without craving more. I can't see her dance with another man without wanting to thrash him and drag her away. I've never felt like this before. But will these feelings last? What if they don't? Phoebe made me promise I wouldn't try to fix my attentions until I am sure of myself."

"Well, you'd best become sure." Marcus warned. "Serena will—"

Rutherford coughed. "—be arriving any second with our wives."

"Damn it to hell."

Marcus kicked Robert and he turned.

The tension Serena's mere presence created rolled off him. She feigned calm, but her quickened breathing was evident in the movement of her breasts.

Dear God, had she heard him?

In the midst of the unspoken drama, a titter was heard. The group turned as one toward the noise. Miss Tice and Miss Martindale were approaching.

Robert groaned.

The young ladies curtsied and greeted them all, then Miss Tice looked meltingly up at Robert. "Lord Beaumont, we wanted to know if you would like to escort us around the gardens. They are so beautiful tonight." She giggled.

Robert struggled to hide his dismay. He glanced at Serena, noting the sudden amusement in her eyes.

She smiled gently at the young woman. "I am terribly sorry to disappoint you, but Lord Beaumont just offered to escort me around the gardens."

Robert threw Serena a grateful look.

Holding out his arm, he replied. "Indeed I did. Shall we go?" When they were out of hearing, he said in a low voice, "I cannot thank you enough."

Her lips curved up. "I daresay it must be an interesting experience for you to be the hunted, rather than the hunter."

"Do you know, I have never thought of it in quite that way?" Some of his tension eased.

They spent the next half hour wandering by gaily lit gardens. Night-blooming jasmine and nicotiana wafted through the air. Robert made a concerted effort to encourage Serena to talk about herself. In turn, he told her a little about himself, until the talk turned to his home, and he deflected the conversation back to her. "When you spoke of your life in Scotland, I assumed you had a steward managing your estate. Marcus just told me you did it yourself."

"Why would you think otherwise?"

"I hadn't given it much thought, since you're a woman."

Serena's lips tightened, and he knew he'd made a mistake. Now would be a good time for someone to kick him. "How did you manage?"

Serena stared at him as if surprised he'd continued the topic. "I'd had years of practice before my father died, and running an estate interests me. Do you not manage yours, my lord?"

"No." His tension returned. "I have an excellent steward." Robert didn't want to talk about home. It engendered few happy memories, and he spent as little time there as possible. He immediately changed the topic. "If you are interested, I could get up a party to Vauxhall. Everyone should attend at least once."

Serena's smile returned to her face. "I have wanted to go to Vauxhall since I was told of it. You always seem to offer to take me to places I've not visited before. Thank you."

"I'll arrange the outing and let you know when it will be."

They'd stopped near a lantern. Serena gazed trustingly up at him. He captured her look, and a longing he'd never felt before coursed through him. What was this woman doing to him?

He raised her hand and brushed the knuckles with his lips.

She blushed and her breath hitched.

Robert might not know if he loved her, but he was almost certain she loved him, and God knew he wanted her, for a very long time. Possibly for the rest of his life—and the only way to have her was to wed. Smiling to himself, he placed her hand on his arm, and strolled with her to the terrace.

Chapter Seven

The next morning, Robert entered his secretary's office at shortly after nine.

"Good morning, my lord." Charles glanced at the clock. "I didn't expect to see you at . . ."

Robert smiled. "At this time of morning? Such a frippery fellow you must think me. I've been riding early every day, you know." Now that he'd made his decision, nothing could spoil his good mood. "Charles, I wish to make up a party to attend Vauxhall. The Eveshams, Rutherfords, and Lord Huntley. Ask if there is a lady he would like me to invite. Also add Lady Serena Weir."

Charles stared at Beaumont as if he'd lost his mind.

Patiently, Robert waited for Mariville to regain his countenance.

"I see." Charles shook his head as if clearing it. "My lord, would you like to attend the Gala night? It's a mask."

Robert paced. "A mask is perfect. When is it?"

"I believe it's in a couple of days."

"Yes," Robert smiled, satisfied. Women were always less inhibited when wearing dominos. "Arrange it."

In the end, the party included Lady Serena, the Eveshams, and the Rutherfords, as well as Lord Huntley and a Miss Marlow.

Robert arranged a private boat to transport them across the water, as well as a box and supper, which included the wafer-thin slices of ham for which Vauxhall was famous while champagne, wine, and rack punch completed their menu.

Once they'd finished eating, Robert suggested a stroll before the dancing began. Serena exclaimed over the clever way the lanterns seemed to dance in the trees. Because of the anonymity of a mask, Robert was able to dance every dance with her, holding her much closer than was proper, and no one would notice. Before midnight, he led his party to find the best position to view the fireworks, which included a Catherine wheel.

Serena glowed with enjoyment as she watched the spectacle. "Lord Beaumont, how wonderful. I have never seen anything as interesting as the flames going around like a wheel in the sky."

She glanced up at him at the same moment Robert smiled at her. His gaze held hers and he let her see his desire. A slight shiver ran through her and confusion appeared in her lovely eyes. His chest swelled. She'd reacted to him without his even touching her.

It was time.

"Walk with me." Robert twined her arm in his, drawing her nearer than he should. He led her down the dimly lit paths, his thigh brushed against hers, as he told her about the gardens, pointing out one feature or another. Each time they touched, her breath caught, and he felt more confident of his plan.

When they reached the Grecian temple, he led her up the stairs. It was dark, but not so dark he couldn't see her face as she gazed around the folly.

"How very beautiful this is," Serena exclaimed.

He lowered his voice, making it soothing and caressing. "Not as beautiful as the one viewing it."

Robert was attuned to her scent, her smile, her every movement. He'd wager his fortune she'd never been kissed, never touched intimately. He intended to be the first—the only—man to kiss her and learn her body. The primitive beast inside him clamored to take her now.

He turned Serena to face him. Her wondering eyes met his, searching. She was so lovely, so innocent, and, though she might not realize it yet, she belonged to him. Robert touched her lips softly with his, teasing hers to respond. Finally, after hesitating for what seemed like an eternity, Serena's gentle lips moved beneath his.

Excitement raced through him.

He *was* the first to kiss her and he wanted everything she could give him.

"Robert." Her whispered word, more of a tender sigh.

He'd never known how sweet his name could sound, how hearing it on her lips could stun him. A previously unknown sense of protectiveness and possession came over him. No other would ever have her.

He slowly dropped his hands from her shoulders to wrap her in his arms and draw her close. Her head didn't even reach his collarbone.

Serena expected the kiss, but not the tremor it caused. Strange warmth simmered within her, and her knees wobbled. Robert held her more tightly. Her breasts, touching his hard chest, tingled and ached. His lips were firm, but soft, moving against hers gently.

When she responded, his kisses grew more insistent. He moved his tongue over the seam of her lips. Curious, Serena opened her mouth. Robert entered, his tongue caressed hers and her burning boiled over. She moaned; her heart beat so quickly she thought she'd swoon. Instead, she returned his caress. Soon their tongues were tangling. His body hardened and the evidence of his desire rode against her stomach.

Serena desperately wished someone had talked to her about kissing, and how his hands stroking her back would make her feel so different, so willing to be with him. Bereft when he lifted his head, she wondered if she'd done something wrong. He pulled her closer and kissed her again. She opened her mouth, eagerly responding to him. How had she lived so long without knowing this wonderful, ravening feeling?

In the past, Robert's passion had been solely physical, his only goal to slake his and his lover's lust. Serena's innocent fervor spurred him to want more for her.

He'd planned to use all his considerable experience to bind her to him, tonight. To make her crave what he could give her. No one could light the flames of desire in a woman better than he. Yet, with each heartbreakingly guileless kiss she gave, his vaunted control slipped.

Robert's breathing became ragged, his blood heated and he grew hard. His unexpected passion for her was so strong he struggled to harness his more primitive desires. His body urged him to press her up against the wall and take her. *Mine.* With real effort, he reined in his demons and brought himself under control. God, and this was just a kiss—or was supposed to have been.

Robert slowly lifted his head. Serena's rosy lips were swollen, and her face flushed. He wondered if her breasts were tinged with passion. Her nipples hardened and brushed his chest. Robert groaned. He'd attend to them later. Holding her tightly, he stroked the length of her back and recaptured her lips, plundering and laying claim to them. He drew back to gaze at Serena. Her wide eyes returned his stare.

"Did I do something wrong?"

The vulnerability in her voice humbled him.

"No, you did everything right." *Too right.* He was well and truly caught. How was he to keep Serena and remain in control? "We need to return before they begin to search for us."

Robert kissed her lightly before leading her out of the folly. His plans for her leapt forward. He must marry her, and soon.

Phoebe and Marcus were waiting for them when they returned to the box. Phoebe's sharp eyes looked from Serena to Robert and back. A slow pink rose in Serena's face.

Robert assumed a bland and uninformative mien. "Where are the others?"

Marcus scowled. "They've left. Miss Marlow had to go home. Anna and Rutherford are playing gooseberry."

Robert looked down at Serena, willing her to feel his gaze. She glanced up. "Would you like to ride to-morrow morning?"

"Yes."

He held Serena's hand and her attention, while Marcus helped Phoebe into the carriage.

Serena was taking one last look around, when Robert heard Phoebe mutter to her husband.

"He'd better be intending to tell her he loves her and wants to marry her."

Robert stiffened.

"I've no doubt he intends to marry her," Marcus responded quietly. "Just don't expect him to tell her he loves her. He'll not want to give her that much power over him."

"Then she won't accept him."

Robert's gaze flashed to Serena, who approached the coach with a contented sigh. He would not lose her, no matter what he had to do.

Serena lay in bed and touched her lips.

It seemed if they'd crossed some sort of invisible barrier tonight that had held them back before. His heat and his need were tangible. As for her, flames of desire flickered just below her surface, ready to rise again at the thought of him. Yet, somehow she knew, despite their passionate kisses, that he still held her at a distance. Something held him back from declaring his love for her.

It was too late to guard her heart. She'd lost it when he'd pleaded with her to rescue him from the young ladies at the soirée. She wanted her marriage to be a sharing of power and love—most definitely love—and he remained silent. There could be few worse things than to be hopelessly in love with your husband and have him not feel the same.

Robert had tossed and turned the night before, wanting Serena with him. He wondered how quickly they could marry, after he asked her. What Phoebe had said gave him pause, but he couldn't believe Serena would refuse, not after she'd kissed him.

Robert wanted a large wedding at Haythrope Hall, his ancestral home. He supposed he'd have to discuss the settlements with St. Eth, after which, Serena would be his. Beaumont would never have to watch another man dance with her—or touch her—again.

Robert arrived in the Park the next day for his morning

ride to find Serena with Marcus and Phoebe, trotting toward the tan. The weather was perfect. The leaves rustled in the trees, and the first flowers, finally bursting forth into bloom, decorated the landscape.

Phoebe's eyes narrowed when Robert rode up. It took a while, but he managed to smooth her ruffled feathers and give her the impression he'd done nothing with Serena of which Phoebe would not approve. It wasn't precisely true, but, well, he did mean marriage after all. He rode ahead with Serena, racing her up Rotten Row, before heading back to Grosvenor Square.

Robert helped Serena down from her horse and said nonchalantly, "Lady Talgath's garden party at her villa in Merton is to-day. Her bluebell wood is famous. I'd be honored if you'd join me."

Serena smiled. "This is supposed to be the perfect time to see it. I'd love to accompany you."

"We'll take my curricle. I'll come for you at eleven o'clock." Bringing her hand to his lips, he turned it and placed a kiss on the inside of her wrist just above her glove. Finally, she'd be alone with him without all her sharp-eyed—and even sharper-tongued—chaperones.

"I shall look forward to it," she said breathlessly.

As I am looking forward to making you mine. "Until then, my lady."

When Robert arrived to collect Serena, she was a vision in a modest-looking, long-sleeved, teal carriage gown trimmed with Brussels lace. He sucked in a breath. Lady Serena was more ravishing each time he saw her.

They filled the hour-long drive to Merton with pleasant conversation. Serena exclaimed over the countryside and pointed out the various plants and birds. She was so happy. Later to-day, he'd make her even happier by asking her to marry him.

Lady Talgath's villa was set in a park with views of a meadow and an ornamental lake. On the opposite side of the property from the water, the bluebell wood could be reached through a gate. In the dining room, refreshments were laid out.

After everyone had consumed a substantial repast, the older guests relaxed in the rare spring sunshine, while groups of younger people walked to the lake.

Robert led Serena out through the terrace doors. "We can follow those heading to the water, or visit the bluebell wood. I recommend the wood first, then, if time allows, we can walk to the lake."

Not waiting for her response, Robert twined her arm in his and started toward the wood.

She tugged him to a halt. "Lord Beaumont, you didn't let me answer. What if I'd wanted to go to the lake first?"

Robert sounded concerned. "You didn't, did you?"

She gestured to the gate. "Not particularly, we may walk this way first, if you like, though I *do* wish to see the lake before we leave. Yet, if you ask me a question, please deign to hear my answer."

"I stand corrected," Robert said, chagrined. "Please, lead on, my lady."

Several minutes later, they arrived. Serena was enchanted by the thousands of bluebells dotting the wood and field beyond. "Oh, how lovely it is. We *are* here at just the right time. They are all in bloom! What a wonderful idea this was."

Robert stopped breathing when she looked up at him, her face filled with wonder. His heart warmed when Serena smiled. He took a breath. They walked on a little farther before he was certain they were alone.

Leading her a little off the path, he paused under an osier, the willow's long weeping limbs just beginning to leaf. "You like this place then? You're glad we came this way first?"

Serena glanced at him, her eyes soft. "I thought you a little dictatorial in your insistence, but the prospect is lovely. Yes, I'll admit I am glad we came here first."

Robert leaned back against a tree, drawing her to him. There was a good reason he had brought her here now, when the others were at the lake.

He bent his head and kissed her, running the tip of his tongue tantalizingly across her lips. He captured her mouth as she opened to him. Tilting his head to deepen the kiss, he slowly stroked her from her nape to her waist, urging her closer still until her breasts touched his chest. He reveled in the light scent of her hair, of her.

She shivered as his tongue played with hers, and her hands slid from his chest up to his shoulders. Even through his coat, he felt her heavy breasts and hard nipples. His desire for her grew. He held her more tightly. Women had always responded to him, but never like Serena did.

Shivers of delight ran through Serena as his tongue played with hers. She slid her hands from his hard chest up to his shoulders and wondered why the ache in her breasts was relieved a little when he pulled her hard against him. Fire burned within her, and her thoughts fled. Only feelings remained. His hands set tiny flames in her skin. A desire she'd never known and didn't understand grew. Robert's lips and tongue made her want more of him. More of the heat. Serena's heart thudded.

She clung to him, breathing through him. Her knees

weakened and she slipped. His strong arms tightened to hold her more firmly. She stopped trying to understand how he could make her feel so alive and accepted it as a truth. She had no resistance against him when he held her and kissed her; she couldn't have stopped if she'd wanted to.

Robert didn't understand why she affected him so deeply. How a kiss could move him to madness. A possessiveness he'd never felt toward any female took hold of him and urged him to claim her, to make her his. She couldn't refuse him. He'd not allow her to decline.

High-pitched voices floated on the light breeze. Robert could have stepped away from Serena so they'd not be seen. Instead, he ravished her mouth, stealing her thoughts, he stroked her more intimately, cupping her breast. She shuddered and pressed into him. He knew she was enthralled and wouldn't hear the others coming toward them on the path.

There was a gasp and a titter.

Robert lifted his head slightly and raised a haughty brow. Slowly he released her breast, ensuring everyone saw him lay claim to her.

Serena opened her heavy lids and turned toward the direction of his gaze. Miss Tice's mouth hung open.

Serena turned her head away. Her heart beat so quickly she was sick, mortified to have been caught like this with Robert. The shame she would bring on her family. She'd ruined herself and she knew better. *Oh Lord! Please let this be a bad dream!* Serena was barely aware of him still holding her tightly against him and wholly unprepared for what happened next.

Robert addressed the group with a languid drawl. "You must excuse us. We are celebrating our betrothal. You may wish Lady Serena and me happy."

Miss Tice abruptly closed her mouth.

Mr. Camp and the others stuttered. "Yes, yes, my lord, of

course, very pleased to wish you happy. If you will pardon us, we didn't know."

Mr. Camp quickly led his party farther down the path.

In a voice loud enough to be heard by the retreating group, Beaumont said, "My love, did you not express an interest in viewing the lake? I believe we may now do so."

He bent his head to kiss her again and unable to resist the temptation he offered, she returned his kiss. Slowly he took her hand and put it on his arm. As her body tingled, her mind numbed. The very thing she'd not wanted to happen had. Now what was she to do? She couldn't marry him. Not now! Not like this. Serena glanced up at him, expecting to see the same concern and consternation. A smug smile graced his countenance.

Like a blinding light, comprehension struck her. She stumbled, and he caught her. Robert did it on purpose! He purposely placed them—her—in a compromising position. One he knew would lead to an immediate declaration of marriage. He had arranged this! Serena's breath came more rapidly, and anger and chagrin rose within her. How stupid she'd been.

Beaumont looked down at her now, but, his smile was gone, the disquiet she'd wanted to see earlier showed in his eyes.

"Serena, are you all right? It'll be fine. I'd already planned to ask you to marry me to-day."

Her breasts heaved and she allowed her anger to show. "But I, sir, would not have accepted."

"What do you mean? You'd not planned to agree! You can't kiss me like that—and the way you did last night—and not marry me." His face hardened. "I may not have been around gently bred virgins for some time, but *that* I know has not changed. It's not, of course, as if I'd organized their arrival, but what does it matter?"

"You may not have arranged it, but you surely took advantage of the circumstances. And it matters a great deal to me, *my lord*. You have taken any choice I might have had for my future out of my hands. You have ruined me." Her tone was harsh, but her voice trembled.

"As we are to marry, I, in no way, ruined you. People will merely think I'm hot for you, which I am."

"Oh! How dare you say that to me? You—you unprincipled . . . unprincipled . . ."

"Rake?"

"Yes, *unprincipled rake!*"

"Not as unprincipled as you will be considered, my lady, if you don't marry me."

She stopped abruptly. "I shall not be entrapped."

Robert's eyes hardened to flat stones, and he dragged her forward. "Not another word until we are beyond the gates. No one must think that you are not in complete agreement with our marriage."

She clenched her teeth. "There is not going to be a marriage."

"Smile."

Serena entered the lawn of the villa and forced a pleasant smile to her face. She had been in the *ton* long enough that nothing of her seething tumult showed except in the rigidity of her arm entwined in his. If she could have broken his hold and run away, she would have.

Beaumont greeted the other guests milling on the lawn. He smiled charmingly at Lady Talgath with all his customary address. "My lady, we do not wish it to be widely known, as we have not yet informed our families, but you will soon hear the news. I was so overjoyed, I was unable to restrain myself. You may wish us happy. Lady Serena has agreed to be my wife."

Lady Talgath fluttered with delight. "Lord Beaumont, how pleased I am that you chose my home to make your offer! I do indeed wish you both very happy. Was it in the bluebell wood? *Very* romantic, is it not?"

Serena pinched Robert hard as she gracefully accepted Lady Talgath's good wishes. He stiffened.

Serena deepened her smile.

Robert bowed. "Lady Talgath, thank you for such a pleasant afternoon. We must hurry back to Town before the news precedes us."

Serena inclined her head and bid her hostess adieu.

By the time they walked outside, Robert's curricle was ready. He handed her into it and silence reigned until they were clear of the gate.

Serena turned on him. "I cannot believe you told her we were marrying. What were you thinking?"

"Serena."

She glanced at him coldly. "I have not made you free of my name, sir."

"Oh, have you not? The minute you made free of your lips, my girl, you made me free of your name. Get used to it."

She had whirled in her seat to face him, but at that last jab, she shifted and faced stonily ahead.

Beaumont bent closer. "If I'd not told Lady Talgath the news, she would have heard we'd been seen from Miss Tice and the others." His tone was soothing. "Do you really wish your name bandied about the *ton?*"

Serena blinked back tears, despair enveloping her.

"The announcement will appear in the *Morning Post* no later than the day after to-morrow."

She held her head high. "Lord Beaumont, I told you, I will not marry you."

Robert replied cheerfully, "Oh, you'll marry me, my lady. If I have to carry you to the altar, you'll marry me. By God, I didn't know I was taking a shrew to wife."

"I happily release you," she snapped.

He struggled to tamp down his anger. "I have no desire to be released, and I have no desire to see you ruined. You are mine, and I will have you."

She loved him. What the devil was the matter with her?

"But, you don't love me," she insisted. "You don't really want to marry me."

"You're out there. I do want to marry you."

She faced him, her eyes brimming with tears. "Lord Beaumont . . ."

"Robert."

"*Lord Beaumont,* why? You do not *love* me."

"But you, my dear, love me, and I want you. Extremely badly, as it happens. Enough to take you to wife."

Serena cried out as if struck, "I do not love you! How could I, when you act like this and—and trap me as a hunter traps an unsuspecting rabbit?"

Robert's stomach tightened. Dread ran through him. He looked quickly at her and forced himself to relax.

"You may not want to be, but you are in love with me." His words were clipped. "Do not lie to me again."

The rest of the journey was made in silence. Serena glanced once more at him. His face had hardened into stark planes. His jaw was clenched, as if he were made of stone. Why had she allowed him to kiss her? How could she have been so wantonly stupid as to confuse his desire with love? She'd gone willingly into his arms, like a lamb to slaughter. And now what was to become of her? She refused to marry him.

When she would have allowed the footman to hand her down from the curricle, Lord Beaumont stopped him. Reluctantly, she gave her hand to Robert. It trembled as he took it gently in his much larger one. She refused to look at him as Ferguson held the door open. Her first impulse was to flee to her chamber, but Robert held her fast.

"Ferguson, isn't it?"

That worthy inclined his head. "Yes, my lord."

"Please be good enough to inform Lord St. Eth I am in need of private conversation with him."

"My pleasure, my lord."

Robert waited until Ferguson left before bending his head and saying in a low, fierce tone, "You may go, *after* you politely bid me adieu. I'll not have the servants talking."

She struggled to draw a breath and smile. "My lord, I bid you *good-bye*."

Withdrawing her hand, she walked to the stairs, head high. Once she reached the corridor, she fled to her chamber.

"Mary." Serena tried to still her panicked breathing. "Please find a footman to go round to Dunwood House and ask Lady Evesham to come to me."

"My lady, what's wrong?"

"Please, just do it, Mary. It's urgent."

"Yes, my lady, at once." Mary ran from the room.

Alone, Serena sank onto the sofa set between the long windows. Her thoughts jumbled and whirled, and she dropped her head into her hands. Why couldn't she think? Serena didn't know how long she sat there, but finally, she heard a light knock on the door and it opened.

"Serena?" Phoebe whispered.

Serena jumped up and pulled her cousin into the room. "Phoebe, oh, Phoebe! I have been such a fool, and I think I am well and truly caught. I don't know what to do. I cannot marry him, and I'm ruined." A tear slipped down Serena's cheek.

Phoebe opened the door and asked Mary to have tea and sherry brought, then placed an arm around Serena, and led her back to the sofa.

"Now, tell me what happened. Nothing is ever as bad as it might appear. Whatever it is, we shall find a way to help you."

"It is Lord Beaumont." Serena sobbed. "He—he has destroyed me." Serena tried to hold back the bitter tears as Phoebe comforted her.

"How?"

"We were at Merton, and he took me into the bluebell wood. We were discovered kissing and he told them we were betrothed. Yet he looked so smug, I know he purposely created the opportunity. *Phoebe, I trusted him.*"

Phoebe gasped. "I never thought Robert would do something like this."

Serena's voice broke. "I cannot marry him if he doesn't love me and Robert as much as confirmed he doesn't."

Phoebe was still for several moments. "We need reinforcements." She rose to tug the bell pull. Mary answered.

"Please ask Lady Ware and Lady St. Eth to attend to us here."

Mary nodded and left.

"Serena, we *will* think of something. Robert shall not get away with this."

"So," Phoebe said with disdain, when their aunt's arrived, "that is what we are dealing with. It appears Robert Beaumont has reverted to type."

Serena looked at them. "I'm so sorry."

Aunt Ester's gaze was level. "Serena, I am afraid you must marry him."

Tears started in her eyes again. "No, no, please!"

Ester took her hands. "But, you do not have to marry him soon. We can easily put off the ceremony until he admits he loves you."

"Do you think he *does* love me?" Serena asked, desperately wanting to believe it was true.

Phoebe nodded. "Without a doubt. He is madly in love, or he wouldn't have acted like such a fool, but, for whatever reason, he doesn't want to—or cannot—admit it. You *are* right. Robert needs to acknowledge his feelings for you. It would give him far too much power over you if he does not."

"Absolutely," Ester said. "Look at everything he's done to try to come close to you. It's been most unusual. Robert Beaumont has not attended a *ton* party since a year or two after he came on the Town, and I am not sure I ever saw him at Almack's."

Phoebe and Catherine agreed.

"But," Ester continued, "you chose a very autocratic rake, my love. It will take him time to change his ways. *Not* when it comes to other women, of course, but definitely when it comes to admitting to his feelings for you. He must be threatened by them. You said he asked to speak to Henry?"

Serena nodded.

"Yes, for Beaumont, it's a good choice. Henry is a very high stickler. He will insist you marry." Ester pursed her lips. "We must think of a good reason to put off the wedding until Beaumont comes around."

Aunt Catherine frowned. "I suppose escaping to your family's home in Scotland is out of the question."

Serena snorted with frustration. "My brother and sister-in-law would have me in the chapel bound, gagged, and waiting."

Ester regarded Phoebe thoughtfully. "Phoebe, did you not tell me you and Marcus bought a house in France?"

Phoebe's brow cleared. "Yes, in Paris. The agent just finished the renovations." She smiled broadly. "Aunt Ester, you're brilliant. We could take the *Lady Phoebe* over and travel up from Dieppe. Didn't you tell me you were not able to visit France when Mama did?"

"I had the chicken pox. Phoebe, what a nacky idea. Do you think Marcus would mind?"

"Not if he's allowed to accompany us. He'll be very disappointed in Robert. I remember when he ripped up at Rutherford for not admitting he loved Anna."

"Catherine," Ester asked, "what think you?"

"I think," Catherine said, with great emphasis, "that I have never been to France and would love to go."

There was a burst of laughter. Serena's heart lightened, and the knot in her stomach finally loosened.

Phoebe nodded with decision. "It's settled then; when shall we meet to discuss our travel plans?"

Ester mused. "Do you mind if we meet at Dunwood House to-morrow for breakfast?"

"No, that is perfect. I shall ask François to make croissants." Phoebe grinned at Serena. "Don't worry, cousin, you will come out of this. Robert Beaumont will be made to admit he loves you, or you'll have the longest engagement in history."

Chapter Eight

St. Eth waved Lord Beaumont to a chair in front of St. Eth's large mahogany desk, and offered refreshment. Beaumont accepted a glass of wine.

"Lord St. Eth, I have come to inform you that Lady Serena and I shall marry."

Henry waited for an explanation. When Beaumont said nothing, he raised a brow. "This is sudden. What happened to bring it about?"

Robert didn't meet Henry's gaze, but brushed an imperceptible piece of lint off his sleeve, stalling. "We were at Merton in the bluebell wood and were seen in a compromising position. As I had already planned to propose to Serena while we were there, I informed the young people who came upon us we were merely celebrating our betrothal. I also told Lady Talgath, as she would hear it when the others returned to the villa." Beaumont faced Henry. "I'll send a notice to the *Morning Post* immediately. I expect the marriage to take place as soon as the banns can be read. Just over two weeks should be sufficient time."

In a deceptively dulcet tone, Henry asked, "Have you discussed the date with Lady Serena?"

"No. I saw no reason to do so. We must marry. I will allow no hint of scandal to attach to my wife."

Henry stiffened and stifled a curse. Beaumont should have thought about that before. "Send the notice," Henry said, firmly. "*Do not* give a marriage date. I will discuss with the ladies what date best suits them."

Lord Beaumont clenched his jaw and put his wine glass down with a snap. He rose. "Very well, my lord, it shall be as you wish. I do not plan to wait long."

Henry walked Beaumont to the front hall. Once the door had closed behind him, Henry said, "Ferguson, find Lady St. Eth."

"My lord, all the ladies are in Lady Serena's chamber."

"Ask her to attend to me, please."

"Yes, my lord, of course."

"Immediately."

"There you have it, my love, that is the story and our solution in a nutshell." As Ester studied her husband's face, myriad emotions passed quickly through it.

"Damn . . . forgive me, my love. Are you certain your plan will work?"

"I think so."

"How dare Beaumont purposely compromise her? It's a trick I would have expected from a fortune hunter. Not a landed peer with great wealth."

"Yes, well, we must work with what we have."

A knock sounded on the door. Phoebe entered smiling, followed by Marcus carrying Arthur. Marcus and Phoebe were dressed in evening clothes.

Phoebe took Arthur and handed him to Henry. "Marcus believes we have too much planning to do to wait until morning to discuss the trip."

Henry chuckled as he took the baby. "Marcus, what are you thinking?"

Evesham went to the sideboard and poured sherry. "That we should leave as soon as possible." He lifted the glass in a toast. "Counter-attacks should be made with stealth and by surprise. Turnabout is only fair."

Not long after leaving St. Eth House, Robert was ushered into his grandmother's parlor. Lady Beaumont gave him a long look. "Something is wrong. What is it?"

Robert smiled, but his tone was hard. "Grandmama, the notice of my betrothal will be in the *Morning Post*—if not to-morrow, then the next day."

Lady Beaumont regarded him suspiciously. "Lady Serena?"

"Naturally," he said affronted.

"Robert, I want no fustian from you. What did you do to bring about your betrothal?"

"I made it impossible for her to refuse."

"You did what?" Lady Beaumont demanded angrily.

"Really m'dear, it's no matter. She's in love with me. I merely placed us in a position that demanded an immediate announcement of marriage."

"Why was it necessary for you to compromise her?"

Robert ignored the question. "I told St. Eth I expect to marry in a little over two weeks. To-morrow, I'll post to Haythrope Hall." Beaumont took one of her hands and kissed it. "Adieu, Grandmama."

He returned home and informed his staff of the pending change of his marital status. Charles was tasked to write the notice to the *Morning Post* and begin an invitation list. Robert changed and walked round to Brooks for dinner. To his satisfaction, word of his betrothal had already begun to circulate.

"That was fast, Beaumont." Mr. Fotheringale took a pinch of snuff. "You were only given long odds in the betting. The real money was on Fairchild."

Robert, who had frequently participated in the Marriage Mart wagers, observed his friend coldly. "Fotheringale, I would appreciate it if you would not mention my affianced wife in relation to betting."

The man's head snapped up. "Yes, yes, of course, m'boy. Not another word. When is the marriage to take place?"

"We've not yet set a date. Lady Serena must discuss it with her aunts. I've told them I wish to be married immediately."

"You seem very determined," Fotheringale commented.

"Yes," Beaumont agreed. "I am indeed."

Marcus sipped his sherry. "I'll have the *Lady Phoebe* ready to sail in two days time."

"Is your ship large enough for everyone?" Henry asked.

"Yes, sir. I sailed over from the West Indies on her. We'll stay in Dieppe until the carriages and horses arrive, and then travel by easy stages to Paris. Phoebe has already written to our agent in France. He'll arrange the lodging and insure the Paris house is ready."

Phoebe glanced up from her lists. "If there is no objection, I'd like to invite the Rutherfords to join us. Rutherford, especially, has an insight into how Robert might behave, and Anna's not had an opportunity to travel to France."

Ester chuckled. "With all of us, the children, their maids

and nurses, not to mention the valets and dressers, we shall need to hire an entire *hôtel* to hold us."

"That's something I'd not considered," Marcus said. "Phoebe, did you . . . ?"

She tilted her head at him. "Of course, my love, for every stop we make we shall have the entire building."

Marcus puffed his chest out with pride. "You could have been Quartermaster General, my darling. I don't understand how Robert thought he'd be allowed to get away with this."

Phoebe narrowed her eyes. "Overweening conceit and a dictatorial nature."

The following morning, long before the fashionable made their visits, Ester was surprised to greet the Dowager Lady Beaumont and Freddy in her morning room. Ester welcomed them warmly and with a great deal of curiosity.

"Lady Beaumont, Freddy, to what do I owe this pleasure? I have not seen either of you for an age."

"Ester, you owe our visit to my scapegrace nephew," Freddy replied. "*We* had the dubious pleasure of receiving him yesterday afternoon, when he informed us he was to wed your niece, Lady Serena." Freddy frowned. "It was not the news, which was welcome, but the fashion in which it was delivered that raised our suspicions that all may not be right."

The look on Freddy's face told Ester they hoped to be wrong about Beaumont's actions.

Ester was sorry to disappoint them. "The betrothal is not as we would have wished it."

"Drat the boy!" Lady Beaumont's face turned red and she pounded her cane on the floor. "Why can't he behave like a normal man, fall in love, admit it, and marry? I don't know what ails him to act like a rascal. Don't *you* tell me you are going to let him get away with this . . . this infamy?"

Ester laughed. "No, we will not. We are, the whole family and then some, leaving for France to-morrow. In our haste, we may have overlooked informing a certain person."

Lady Beaumont chuckled. "I always knew you for a smart chit."

"I have to give credit to my niece, Evesham."

"Well, that doesn't surprise me either. Gets her brains from her mother's side, I'm sure. So tell me the worst. What did Robert do?"

Lady Beaumont's frown deepened as Ester told her Serena's story.

"What an idiot. He's mad in love with the girl! Why, he practically flew out of my carriage when he saw her with another man driving in the Park. That I should live to see a grandchild of mine act without the least delicacy of mind!"

Freddy's face took on an appearance of unholy delight. "Mama, would you like to visit France?"

Lady Beaumont scowled. "At my age? What a ridiculous . . ." Then her eyes twinkled with mischief. "Freddy, I've always said you had my brains. It's just the thing to stop any gossip. All of us ladies traveling to Paris to buy Lady Serena's bridal clothes. It's perfect. Robert will be furious. I'll see that young jackanapes admit he loves Lady Serena *and* be happy about it, if it is the last thing I do. Freddy, make the plans."

Ester said, "I must ask Evesham, of course, but you might be able to travel with our party if you can be ready to-morrow."

"If you have room for us, we can be ready. Freddy, let's go. We've packing to do."

Ester helped Lady Beaumont from the sofa. "I shall send you word as soon as possible."

"We'll wait to hear from you." Freddy kissed Ester's cheek. "What fun this will be. I've not been anywhere in years."

Each lady told only one or two friends, in the strictest confidence, that they were traveling to Paris with Lady Serena to buy bridal clothes. To make sure word spread, Freddy made another visit to Lady Bellamny.

The betrothal announcement appeared in the next day's *Morning Post*. Two days later, the *Morning Post*'s notices included the news that Lord and Lady St. Eth, Lady Serena Weir, and Lady Ware would visit France for an unspecified period of time. Farther down the page was a statement that Lord and Lady Evesham would be in residence in Paris for the immediate future. The notices also included Lord and Lady Rutherford's visit to France.

Everyone in the party wondered how long it would take for the news to reach Robert.

Captain Jonathan Benedict, the *Lady Phoebe*'s captain, welcomed everyone aboard in the small hours of the morning, just in time to catch the morning tide. The stiff wind had them in Dieppe by noon.

The landlord of the Coq d'Or, an inn the Eveshams had used before, greeted the party warmly. Once they were all settled and dinner ordered to everyone's satisfaction, the ladies found a nearby café to sample the local pastries.

While they were enjoying their repast, Lady Beaumont assumed a patently innocent expression. "Robert decided to post immediately to Yorkshire to ready the estate for Lady Serena's arrival. For some reason—most likely because he left so quickly—I think I may have forgotten to tell him we were traveling to France when he came to see me, and I seemed to have neglected to send a notice to the *Post*, as well." The matriarch grinned. "What a shame. The dear boy will not know where we are."

Marcus gave a shout of laughter and leaned over to Phoebe. "You know, I've heard Beaumont describe his grandmother as irascible, but I didn't fully appreciate what he meant until now. She really is a grand old lady."

"Oh, Marcus, I will strive to be like her when I am old." Phoebe succumbed to giggles.

Serena paled. "But Phoebe, Robert will be so angry with all of us for disappearing, especially me."

"Serena, we are all here to protect you."

The ladies drew her into a comfortable coze, and the gentlemen gathered together to converse.

Marcus glanced at Rutherford and St. Eth. "Serena is right. Beaumont is going to be in a towering passion to find no one in Town when he returns."

Rutherford lowered his brows. "He has no one to blame but himself. By God! If I had to tell Anna I loved her before she'd marry me, he should be put through the same torture!"

St. Eth commiserated, "It's never easy. I almost didn't win Ester. Fortunately, a little bird told me what I needed to do."

"We tried," Rutherford said. "Our little bird would need the subtlety of a peacock in full feather to be understood."

Marcus took a sip of wine. "How shall we handle it when Beaumont shows up, as he is bound to, since we have spirited his bride away?"

"We cannot allow him to be alone with her," Henry said.

"No indeed," Rutherford agreed. "The ladies will help with that as well. Just how susceptible is Serena?"

Marcus raised a brow. "Considering what happened at Merton, we must assume she's *too* susceptible to take any risk at all."

*   *   *

The next day, Serena gazed from the window of the inn's first-floor parlor and wondered when Robert would arrive. She knew he'd follow and that he would be very angry. She told herself, with her family and his surrounding her, she had no reason to fear him, but her stomach twisted itself into knots. How could she have been so lost to propriety, so *wanton,* to have allowed him to kiss her like that? She covered her face with her hands.

A noise from below made her jump. The low rumble of masculine voices echoed up. She listened for a moment and sighed in relief, it was not Robert. Deep in reverie, she'd not been aware Lady Beaumont had entered the room until the dowager's cane struck the wooden floor.

Serena hurried to the older woman. "Oh, Lady Beaumont, please allow me to help you."

Serena assisted Robert's grandmother to the small sofa.

"Well, my girl, I've heard from everyone but you regarding this affair. Tell me, do you love my mutton-headed grandson?"

Serena contemplated Lady Beaumont's tight-lipped countenance and sensed the older lady's concern for her. Even though Robert's grandmother had accompanied them to France, Serena had not expected such kindness and understanding from Lady Beaumont. Surprisingly, Serena felt she could speak more freely with this woman, than she could with her aunts or Phoebe.

"Yes, I do love him, desperately. Most of the time, he is incredibly gentle and charming. I've watched him play with Arthur and Ben, Lady Rutherford's little boy. Robert is almost never high in the instep. He has gone out of his way to entertain me."

Serena hesitated. "He's doing all sorts of things he would

not normally do, but he will not allow me to know him more deeply. He has told me about his estates and his horses and all manner of *things,* but never shares his *thoughts* and *feelings.* I'd never seen him act—never knew he could act—the way he did at Merton and on the drive back. He was so *hard* and . . . dictatorial. The way he spoke to me and the things he said . . ." Serena looked down at her hands.

"And you've been jumping every time you hear a loud noise outside, afraid it will be him," Lady Beaumont said.

"Yes, I have the greatest dislike of contretemps. That was the reason I agreed to leave my home and come to London, to avoid . . . the situation there."

"I've heard your brother married. His wife didn't want you around, I take it."

Serena nodded.

"Well, that was a mighty pretty way to thank you for keeping the estate in good repair for him until he was ready to finish playing soldier. He should have sold out when your father died."

Serena blinked back tears. After all the years she'd struggled to do her duty, all the years she'd spent alone, this woman was the only one who'd ever acknowledged what she'd done, given voice to what she'd sacrificed. "I tried not to think of it, but I wished he'd come home. I'm so much older now." Her voice was suspended by tears.

"Come here, my girl."

Serena sank to the floor beside the sofa.

Lady Beaumont patted Serena's head. "You just have a nice cry. You've been used ill by some of those who ought to have had your best interest at heart, and I'll include Robert in that. We will not allow it to happen again."

Lady Beaumont sat with Serena until she'd cried herself out.

Serena finally lifted her head. "Phoebe and Marcus think

Robert loves me. You're his grandmother. What do you think?"

"Oh, he loves you well enough. He would not have done what he did if he wasn't afraid he'd lose you. Until now, Robert has been very clever avoiding the parson's mouse-trap. Too clever. They'll tell me I ought not to talk to an innocent like this, but I'm from a different generation. We were not so mealy-mouthed. And you, my dear, have been kept in ignorance. If you'd had a better understanding of what happens between a man and a woman, you probably wouldn't have made the mistakes you did."

Serena blushed. "I was so foolish."

"Well, you're not alone. Robert had his heart badly broken when he was young. I don't know what happened. He would never talk to me about it. Since then, he's become used to taking his pleasure from a particular sort of woman and discarding them the minute he is done."

"Do you mean a . . . high-flyer, ma'am?"

Lady Beaumont chuckled. "Not usually, although, I am sure there were some of them as well. No, I am referring to well-bred ladies with the hearts of courtesans. Kept him safe from any entanglements."

"Do you think he might discard me after we wed?"

"No, my dear, where Robert loves he'll be very different. But, if he doesn't admit his love, he'll use your love for him to get what he wants. You will not have the influence over him you should have. Like his father and grandfather, he'll remain in control. If you mean to marry him, you must make him admit his feelings before you're leg-shackled. If you don't want to marry him, tell me now and we will arrange it so you need not."

"But I don't understand." Heat rose in Serena's face. "We were seen . . . together."

"Arrangements can be made. I don't say you can remain

in the *ton,* but you would be free of the betrothal. Do you wish to marry my grandson?"

"If he loves me and allows me to be close to him, yes. If he holds me at arm's length, then no, I could not live like that. I would die a slow death, without any freedom. I'd rather live quietly, as a spinster."

"Then you must trust us to help you bring him around. Mind you are not to be alone with him in a dark corner of a terrace, or anywhere else for that matter. He'll take full advantage of you, and he has the charm and experience to do it. Not to purposely hurt you—never that—but to show you and the world that you are his."

Serena stiffened her spine and anger surged within her. "He said something very much like that on the drive back from Merton."

Lady Beaumont grinned. "Keep that day in mind, and don't allow him to run roughshod over you. You'll be much better for it. Come along now. The other ladies have some entertainment planned for us."

"Yes, ma'am." Serena rose, vowing that when Robert came, she'd be ready for him.

Robert returned to London two weeks later to find the knocker off the door at St. Eth House, meaning the family was gone for a significant period of time. He walked to Dunwood House and found the same state of affairs.

Scowling, he drove to his grandmother's, where he was greeted with the news that his grandmother and aunt were away from Town and had given no date for their return.

Robert stormed into Beaumont House in a black rage. "Charles!"

Mariville popped his head out from his office. "Yes, my lord?"

"Do you happen to know where my grandmother, the St. Eths, the Eveshams, and Lady Serena might be? The devil take them, they've all disappeared."

"I believe I saw an announcement in the *Morning Post* that the St. Eths, Lady Serena, and the Eveshams were all traveling to France. I know nothing about Lady Beaumont."

"Did it not occur to you, Charles," Robert asked in a sweetly dangerous tone, "that I might like to know that information?"

"It did not occur to me, my lord," Mariville responded pointedly, "that you were in ignorance of it."

No, why should it? Robert glared at Charles. The *Post* was delivered by express mail when Robert was in York-shire. It was his own damn fault he didn't read it. "When did they leave?"

"I'm not sure. I'll have to find the notice again."

"Do so!"

Frustrated, Robert entered his study and poured a brandy. France? Why France, of all places? He'd told St. Eth he wanted to marry as soon as possible. What the devil were they thinking?

They'd left without a word. *Serena was his affianced wife.* He'd made sure of it. He should have been told.

Then again, Serena had been exceedingly angry at him when they returned from Merton. Maybe he shouldn't have taken leave of her so quickly. He'd thought that his time in Yorkshire would give her an opportunity to become used to the idea of being his wife. Actually, he'd hoped she'd miss him, at least a little.

He'd missed her damnably. Now that she'd be his, he couldn't stand to be away from her.

He sat twirling the glass until Charles knocked on the door. "Well?"

Robert's heart raced when his secretary hesitated.

Charles spoke carefully. "It appears, my lord, they all left the day after you did."

Robert surged to his feet. "They've been gone for *two weeks?*"

"So it appears, my lord."

Beaumont paced the room, unable for a minute to think. "Do you have any idea where in France they've gone?"

"One of the announcements mentioned Paris."

Robert stilled. "Make arrangements for me to travel there immediately. I'll leave from whichever port has the first passage."

Robert waited in Dover for three days, until the wind was, once again, in the right quarter. When he arrived in Calais, his mood was blacker than when he'd left London. Fear of losing Serena made his breath quicken. He had to find her and bring her home.

Chapter Nine

In the parlor of the Coq d'Or, Serena glanced at her cousin. "Phoebe, when shall we continue on to Paris?"

"To-morrow. The horses and carriages have arrived. I wanted to give them a day to recover." Phoebe grinned. "It really is time to leave. We've seen everything there is to see here."

"Yes, we've had a very good time," Serena said. "I've never seen a beach made of pebbles before, and the excursion to the château that Aunt Ester arranged was wonderful."

"I think we've had something to eat or drink in every café and restaurant in Dieppe." Phoebe took a sip of tea.

"Are the cafés in Paris similar?"

"Most of them are more elegant. All the French towns seem to have any number of good eating establishments," Phoebe said. "There are some wonderful ones in Rouen, where we shall stay for a couple of days."

The next morning Serena stood with Phoebe, checking off items on the lists they'd made.

"I think that is it." Serena studied the carriages, six for traveling and three for baggage. "The coachmen have the directions for to-day in the event we are separated, though I do not know how that could happen with this cortege."

Rutherford strolled up to them. "All we need are brightly colored ensigns to make us more noticeable."

Phoebe laughed. "True, there is no disguising us."

"I'd say not." He lifted his quizzing glass. "Where are we changing horses?"

"I've decided not to change them," Phoebe replied. "The countryside can still be uncertain. I don't know what we'd find in the way of new horses, and I do not want to leave ours behind."

Serena enjoyed the trip. They made a very merry party as they traveled by slow stages to the ancient city of Rouen, where they rested for a few days, visiting the cathedral and the Abbey of St. Ouen, the oldest parts of which dated back to the early fourteenth century. They also saw the astronomical clock, the site where Joan of Arc was said to have been burned, as well as the Church of Saint-Maclou.

Their twelfth day in France found them entering Paris through the Porte de Villiers in the northwest section of the city. By midafternoon, they drove through large wrought-iron gates which gave way to a circular drive leading to the front steps of the Hôtel Charteries, Phoebe and Marcus's Paris residence. Wilson opened the door as their carriages came to a stop.

The house, built in white stone, was situated near the Jardin de Tuileries and not far from the British embassy. It had a main building and two wings. Walled gardens bordered three sides of the building.

Serena alighted from the carriage and stared up at the window-filled façade. "It is beautiful!"

Phoebe looked pleased. "Thank you. We've put a great deal of work into it. But come, tea will be ready soon."

They all gathered in a drawing room overlooking the front drive and drank tea while the baggage was being settled. Soon footmen showed them to their respective chambers. Serena's suite had lovely painted panels in both her bedchamber and the small parlor. Long windows, overlooking the side garden, adorned both rooms and allowed the afternoon light to shine through. The fireplaces were already lit.

Serena was the first one down to the morning room on the ground floor in the back of the house. She walked out the wide double doors onto the terrace to view the garden and the fruit trees beyond. Espaliered tree branches bearing small fruits ran horizontally on the old stone wall surrounding the garden.

Phoebe joined her.

"Phoebe, I could stay here forever. I've always wanted to have a wall upon which I could train trees and vines."

"I am so pleased you like it. We had a lot of work putting the house back together. The previous owners were caught up in the Revolution and the next occupants, no better than squatters, took possession of the house. Fortunately for us, the property was never taken over by the government. I am well satisfied with the results."

Serena creased her forehead. "What happened to the original owners?"

"Murdered. We bought the house from an heir who did not wish to ever return to France."

Phoebe took Serena's arm to walk back inside. "The gentlemen have gone to the embassy to register our arrival. They will no doubt return with at least one invitation. Sir

Charles Stewart, the ambassador, and his wife, Lady Elizabeth, entertain extensively. We shall begin morning visits to friends of ours who are here and take a trip to the shops tomorrow." Phoebe reached for the bell pull. "Have you decided how you wish to handle Beaumont?"

"Yes, I have given it a great deal of thought. I'll deal with him honestly. There is no point in prevarication. If he cannot admit he loves me, I will not marry him." Serena paused. "Phoebe, I cannot be alone with Robert. I—whenever he touches me, even my hand . . ."

Phoebe leaned forward. "I understand. We'll make a point of providing you with a chaperone at all times. Even if you stroll in the garden with him, one of us will always be in sight. Will that do?"

"Yes, perfect!"

Phoebe's eyes lit. "And if he does try anything, one of us will dash out to protect you."

Serena worried her lip. "He'll be so angry. I'm dreading our first meeting."

The door to the terrace opened and Anna joined them smiling. "Phoebe, what a perfect house. I shall have to convince Rutherford we need a Paris residence as well."

Tea was served as they made plans for the next day.

Anna took a sip of tea and nibbled a small biscuit. "I cannot wait to see the Paris shops. Serena, you should have seen the clothing Phoebe brought back from her wedding trip."

Serena turned to Phoebe. "I want to stop at a café and taste the hot chocolate I've heard about."

"You will eat your way through France," Freddy said. "I don't understand how you can eat so much and never seem to gain any weight at all. It must be your youth."

Serena looked at Freddy's slim form and hid a grin.

The ladies all turned when the gentlemen entered.

"We've an invitation to an embassy ball to-morrow,"

Marcus informed them. "And a rout party the next day." He rattled off the names of their countrymen and women currently populating Paris.

Phoebe frowned. "Marcus, do you know if word of the betrothal has gotten around?"

"I don't know how it could not have, with the announcement in the *Post,*" Henry said. "But yes. I was congratulated on my skill at marrying my niece off so well."

Serena, who had been talking with her aunts, said, "Uncle Henry, what did you say?"

"My dear, your engagement is common knowledge at the embassy."

She frowned slightly. "But what does that mean?"

"Only that you must behave with propriety, my dear, which I'm sure you will do anyway. And if Beaumont attends any of the events, you will accord him his place by your side."

"I don't agree with you, St. Eth," Lady Beaumont said, as she entered the room. "There's no reason I can see why Robert should be rewarded for his bad behavior. When he shows up—and if he decides to attend any of the entertainments at which Serena is present—she may treat him as she wishes."

Henry looked as if he'd argue, then his face lightened. "Of course, if we were to put it around that there was a little tiff . . ."

Marcus snorted. "And this *is* France. Tiffs occur on a much more frequent basis here."

Phoebe's eyes sparkled. "If one of the French noblemen begins to pay a little too much attention, as they are wont to do . . ."

"Perhaps my nephew will finally smarten up," Freddy finished.

* * *

Traveling with his valet and groom, Robert hired a chaise
and horses. They arrived in the quiet *hôtel* in Rue St. Hon-
oré, not far from the British embassy, in the afternoon on the
third day after he departed Calais. Leaving Henley to take
care of the rooms, Robert strode quickly to the embassy. He
was searching for the registry when he heard a familiar
voice.

"Beaumont! What are you doing here?"

Robert turned to see an old friend from Oxford, Sir Walter Thrashridge. "I could ask the same about you. The last I
heard you were in Portugal. Are you posted here now?"

"No, unfortunately, merely passing through to my new
posting in Brussels. I've seen Evesham."

Robert fought to keep his irritation at Marcus hidden. "I
have come to join them. I was in Yorkshire when they made
the decision to travel here. I understand it's a rather large
party. Who else came with them?"

Beaumont waited while Thrashridge thought.

"I remember now. Lord and Lady St. Eth, then a Lord and
Lady Rutherford, St. Eth's sister and other niece, Lady Serena. What a beautiful girl she is, made quite an impression at
Lady Elizabeth's ball t'other evening. In fact, Lady Evesham, Lady Rutherford, and Lady Serena were the principal
attractions. Evesham and Rutherford took care to stay by
their ladies. With all the expatriates and the Frenchies hovering around Lady Serena, there wasn't any getting near her."

Robert stopped himself from grinding his teeth. "Don't
happen to know Evesham's direction, do you? I only know it
is some house he bought."

"I don't, but the registry will have it. Are you going there
now?"

"That is my intent."

"Well, I'll show you the way. There was something else I

thought I should say to you." Thrashridge rubbed his chin. After a moment he smiled. "I've got it now. I'm to wish you happy. Who is the young lady?"

"Lady Serena," Robert said gruffly. *And when I find her, I'm going to drag her to Yorkshire where she belongs.*

Robert went directly from the embassy to the Hôtel Charteries on the other side of the Jardin des Tuileries. The walk did nothing to clear his mind. He couldn't even think of what he would say when he saw Serena, not to mention his best friends who'd spirited her away. Wilson ushered him in, then kept him waiting in a small parlor. Unable to sit, Robert paced.

Serena had been looking through a first-floor window when she saw Lord Beaumont approach. She fled down the corridor and back stairs to the morning room, where the other ladies were sitting, bursting into the room in a very unladylike fashion. "He's here! Oh, what shall I do?"

Lady Beaumont took her hands. "Now, now, calm yourself. You don't have to see him if you choose not to."

"No, indeed, but, Serena, he is in Paris," Aunt Ester said. "You will have to meet him at some point."

Anna worried her lower lip. "Serena, what say we remove to the long drawing room? That way you may have some privacy, and we will still be there for you."

"Thank you, Anna."

Robert's fury grew as he was made to wait in a small parlor off the foyer. Wilson finally came and escorted him to Marcus, Rutherford, and St. Eth. Marcus motioned Beaumont to a chair and let the silence stretch.

"Well, aren't you going to say anything?" Robert flushed

angrily. "Are you not going to explain why you took Serena out of the country without a word to me?"

Marcus raised a brow. "Didn't you promise Phoebe that you would not attempt to engage Lady Serena's heart before you knew your own mind?"

"I do know my own mind. I am going to marry her. You—all of you—know that! She loves me!"

Rutherford raised his quizzing glass. "If you were so sure of her feelings, why did you find it necessary to place her in a position where she couldn't refuse you?"

Robert flinched, but did not answer.

Marcus continued. "It was because you knew that, unless you loved her in return, she wouldn't marry you."

Pressing his lips together, Robert harnessed his rapidly rising temper and made his demand. "I will see my affianced wife now, if you please."

St. Eth, who had been standing next to a window, met Robert's eyes. "But *I* do not please."

Beaumont clenched his jaw.

St. Eth, under his breath, added, "This young man needs to be taught a lesson."

He met Robert's gaze. "Lady Serena is here under my protection. You will have speech with her *only* if she wishes it. There is, however, one person here who does wish to have a word with you."

Robert, now in the devil's own temper, growled, "And who might that be?"

St. Eth smiled humorlessly. "Your grandmother."

"My *grandmother*. Here?"

The door opened, and Phoebe walked in. "Robert, I will take you to Lady Beaumont. She wishes to talk with you before you see Serena."

Phoebe rounded on him, hands clenched at her sides.

"Despite your peccadilloes, I never thought I should be ashamed to call you my friend. You have gone far beyond the line of what is pleasing."

She strode out of the room.

Robert followed her up the stairs to a parlor.

"My lady, here he is." Phoebe turned and shut the door behind her with a snap, leaving him to face his family's matriarch.

He bowed and regarded his grandmother with a haughty stare. She may be a gorgon, but he would not give an inch. She had no right to go against him.

"You, my boy, may sit and tell me what you think you're about, acting in this reprehensible fashion."

"Grandmama, I am trying to do what you told me to do. I am trying to marry."

"Good God, boy! Don't you think you can get a girl to marry you without compromising her? What's addled your brain?"

He was the head of the family. Who was she to question him? He did what was necessary. "Grandmama, despite how Serena and I got there, we are betrothed and she must marry me."

Lady Beaumont narrowed her shrewd eyes at him. "Oh, she *must,* must she?"

"Her reputation will be ruined if she does not. You know that."

"I know nothing of the sort," Lady Beaumont said. "If Lady Serena doesn't wish to marry you, I shall do everything in my power to help her out of this betrothal."

"You cannot." Robert's voice was like steel. "I will not allow it."

"Robert, you may be the head of this family, but you do not rule me. I shall act as I think right. And it will not be helping you to browbeat that poor girl into marrying you. If you want to marry Lady Serena, find a way to make your suit acceptable to her."

"I want to see her. Now!"

"And what will you say?"

He scowled.

"Just as I thought. You shall not see her in the mood you're in. You're like a surly bear. When you can curb that nasty temper of yours and act civil, you may speak with her. Until then, go away."

"Grandmama. Please, no."

"Robert, you did very wrong by Lady Serena. You hurt her, not only possibly her reputation, but her heart. She is a charming, capable young lady who would make you an excellent wife *if* you can convince *her* of it. I told you before, you cannot allow a disappointment in your youth to guide your life."

Robert's bluster faded. "Grandmama, I don't know what to do."

"You have friends here who will help you, if you'll let them. Now give me a kiss and go. You may call to-morrow."

Robert allowed himself to be guided back to the front door and thanked Wilson as he left. As his fury withered, his mood became more thoughtful. He walked back to his lodging. He knew he'd angered Serena, but it had not occurred to him he'd hurt her. The thought that his grandmother would help Serena jilt him didn't bear thinking of. Maybe he shouldn't have done what he did. Clearly, it had caused everyone to turn against him. But how could he fix it?

He absently agreed with his valet as to the dinner menu, and decided to remain in that evening. Unable to sleep, Robert sat in front of the fire, one long booted leg crossed over the other. To-morrow, he'd ask Serena what she wanted; he prayed it included him.

* * *

The ladies, joined by the gentlemen, were waiting in the long drawing room to hear the result of Lady Beaumont's discussion with her grandson. Serena, unable to stay still, paced the length of the room several times before Anna drew her into conversation.

The door finally opened for Lady Beaumont. Robert was not with her. Serena's gaze flew to the older woman's face.

Lady Beaumont smiled. "He has gone to his lodgings to mend his temper. I told him he could not speak with you until he had. I believe we shall see him to-morrow."

"Ma'am, what did you say to him? He looked so angry when he arrived. He wasn't much happier when he left."

"I told him he'd hurt you. I had the impression he hadn't thought of it before. Come, you may escort me to the morning room. It must be time for tea."

Phoebe laughed. "It is more than time for tea. I quite frankly think I could use a sherry. Marcus?"

"Indeed." Marcus crossed to the sideboard. "Serena?"

She sank down onto the sofa. "I'd like a tumbler of my father's twenty-year-old scotch whisky at this point, though I'll thank you for the sherry."

When Robert was ushered into the drawing room the next afternoon, his mood was subdued. He'd spent the morning walking Paris, trying to think of what to say to Serena. Something he could promise her. Was there something more important to her than love?

Serena met with him at one end of the long drawing room. His grandmother and aunt sat at the other end, not watching, but ready to step in.

When Serena met his gaze, Robert was abashed to see how pale and tense she was. She blinked back tears. The beautiful amber eyes that used to smile up at him held sorrow and pain. She allowed him to take her trembling hands, and they sat in silence.

What had he done? He'd never intended to injure her. Until his grandmother mentioned it, it never occurred to him that he'd harmed her. Robert had expected anger at his admittedly ruthless methods, but this level of anguish? His heart wrenched to see her like this. If he could only take her in his arms and show her how much she meant to him.

She was waiting for him to say something, but what could he say to make up for his treachery?

After a longer silence, he spoke. "I'm sorry for my actions. To have caused you so much suffering was never my intent. I hope you can find it in your heart to forgive me."

Standing, he bowed and took his leave.

Serena swallowed and dashed a tear from her eyes. She'd anticipated a rebuke, perhaps an eruption of anger, but never the misery in his green eyes as he watched her. Robert was her downfall. If Lady Beaumont and Freddy hadn't been there she would have wrapped her arms around him and given in at once.

She loved him so much, but it would kill her to live with him if he didn't feel the same. What would happen when he left her bed for another's? If she was ever to get from Robert what she needed, she'd have to be strong now. Much stronger than she was being. She rose and went to Lady Beaumont.

"Well, what was that about?" Freddy asked. "For all his insistence on seeing you, he certainly didn't stay long."

Lady Beaumont chuckled lightly. "If I know our Robert, as Nurse used to say, he's at the end of his rope. Freddy, tug the pull and summon the others."

The rest of them piled into the room.

Phoebe's eyes were burning with curiosity. "What happened?"

Serena shrugged. "I'm not sure. Robert sat and held my hands for such a long time, then told me he was sorry and left."

"He left?" Phoebe and Anna glanced at their husbands.

"What do you make of it?" Anna asked.

Rutherford rubbed his pocket watch. "I wish I knew. *If* he attends the embassy ball this evening, we may learn more."

Serena gripped her hands tightly together. If Robert was at the ball, how could she stand it? Waltzing with him, having him touch her. How would she resist him? But worse, what if he didn't come at all?

Chapter Ten

Robert stared when Serena descended the stairs to the ball-room. She was easily the most beautiful woman he'd ever seen. The bodice of her pale yellow evening gown was cut low in a deep square of gauzy georgette, pleated and tucked, barely covering the perfect, creamy mounds of her breasts. Breasts he wanted to touch as he had in the bluebell wood. His fists clenched, then he scowled at a Frenchman who ogled her.

Robert cursed under his breath. He must find a way to make her his wife.

He went to her and bowed, saying softly, "Lady Serena, I would be honored if you'd accept my escort this evening."

Serena glanced at him warily. "Why do you wish to accompany me?"

He met her gaze. "Which answer do you want, Serena, the conventional or the truth?"

"Both."

"The conventional answer is that almost everyone here has seen the betrothal notice. It would appear odd if we were not together and would cause unwanted gossip." He stepped closer and lowered his voice. "The truth is that I need to be with you. I know this is all I'll have until we are able to . . ." He broke off, unable to finish.

"Let us stroll, my lord." Serena placed her hand on his arm and raised her chin. "And, Robert, if we are to keep up appearances, you must at least smile."

"Yes, my lady." For the first time in a long time, he did just that.

Two weeks passed. Robert visited every day, sat with Serena, and left. In the evenings, he appeared at the balls, parties, or dinners and almost silently escorted her. At the beginning of the third week, they sat alone in a large parlor with the door opened slightly to a smaller room, where their chaperones waited.

Serena made her demand. "Robert, we have been going round and round with this *'betrothal'* for weeks now. You know what I must have from you in order to marry. Yet, I have no idea what you desire. What it is *you* want. Why are you holding back from me?" At his hesitation, she insisted, "I shall have it in plain speaking, even if you think it is something a lady should not hear."

Beaumont narrowed his eyes. "You, my love, have been spending far too much time around my grandmother. You are starting to sound like her."

"There is a great deal to be said for your grandmother's directness. Are you going to tell me or not?" Serena couldn't stand this purgatory he'd consigned them to anymore. "Because, I warn you, my lord, if you do not, I shall end this farce here and now!"

Robert stared at her for a long time. "It is not a pretty story, nor one that a lady should hear. Particularly not an innocent lady." He rubbed a hand over his face. "Yet, if that's your price, I'll pay it."

She bit her lip. "That is my price."

He walked to the sideboard and poured a glass of brandy for himself and a sherry for her, then held it out. "You might need this."

Serena took the glass from him, then Robert sat on the chair closest to her.

"Shortly after I'd attained my majority, I was in London for the Season. Not looking seriously for a wife, but testing the waters, as it were. I developed a violent passion for a lady. She was in her second Season, tall with dark hair. Beautiful, or so I thought at the time." Robert took a sip of brandy, then another.

When he did not continue, Serena said, "I am aware that young men frequently form violent passions. Go on."

"Her mama was very encouraging and gave me the direction of her daughter's guardian. Her father had died some years previously. I was on the point of asking for permission to address her." He grinned ruefully. "I was a very high stickler in those days."

"Would that you still were," Serena said dryly.

He gave a bark of humorless laughter. "It would have made it easier for you, would it not?"

"And you as well, Robert."

"You may be right. Nevertheless, I had been very particular in my attentions to her, but I'd not yet approached her with my desires. The betting in the clubs was narrowing and it was clear to most of the *ton* I was infatuated with her."

"What *gentlemen* find appropriate to wager on never fails to amaze me."

"Remind me to tell you of the betting on who would finally win your hand. It wasn't me."

"It may still not be you, if you don't get on with it."

Robert gazed at her innocently. "But, my dear, you were the one who took us off on this track."

Serena folded her hands in her lap. "Very well, I shall not utter another word until you have finished."

"As I was saying, I wanted to see her before I left, to tell her I planned to ask for her hand. We were at one of the larger balls of the Season. She was with a friend, next to a large potted palm, and didn't see me." He stopped and took a breath. "Her friend asked her if it was true I was about to offer for her. She responded that she knew I was hopelessly in love with her. Her friend asked if she loved me. She said she did not, her tastes ran to gentlemen with dark hair and blue eyes. But . . . she would marry me because of my rank and fortune and—and, since I was so in love, I would be easy for her to manage."

Serena brought her hand to her mouth.

Robert took a large drink of his brandy. "As I stood listening in shock, she added that, once she had given me an heir, she intended to take a lover. Someone more to her liking."

Serena sipped the sherry, very glad that she had it. "I think her taste leaves much to be desired, not to mention her morals. What did you do?"

"I was mortified. I quit *ton* parties and began frequenting establishments that provide a different type of entertainment from those of the Marriage Mart."

"Did you ever see her again?"

His lips curled with disdain. "Yes, I saw her at one of the places I attended. She was looking for a lover."

Serena hid her shock.

"Her taste in men must have broadened, because she invited me to join her for an evening. I agreed."

Robert stopped and glanced uncomfortably at Serena. "Do you truly wish to hear this?"

"Yes, and I am equally sure *you* need to tell it."

Robert's eyes widened in surprise. "Perhaps you're right. I had a set of rooms that I used for the purpose. I gave her the direction and she met me." His note of derision was marked. "When we finally got to the deed, I felt nothing. She was nothing more than a light-skirt."

Serena remembered what Lady Beaumont told her. Her voice soft, Serena said, "A high-bred courtesan."

Robert glanced up suddenly. "Yes, that's it exactly. A high-bred courtesan."

What had he been like back then? So full of love and eagerness, then to have his illusions shattered and his heart broken. "Have you ever thought you were very lucky to have escaped her? Think what a misery she would have made of your life had you wed."

"I have tried *not* to think of her at all."

"But, Robert, you must. Don't you realize you've been trying to do to me what she intended to do to you? You want to use my love for you to control and manage me? Can you not see how that would make me feel?"

His expression changed as he grasped what she'd said.

Robert groaned and covered his face. "Serena, I—I'm so sorry, I didn't think."

This was progress. Now she needed him to move a few steps further.

"Tell me, Robert, is that what you truly want from marriage?"

Robert stilled, a myriad of emotions sweeping through

him, as he searched Serena's earnest face. Her beautiful amber eyes sparkled with unshed tears.

Impulsively, he took her hands and held them to his cheek. "No, that's not what I want. I want a marriage where there is love and trust, but . . . I'm not sure I am capable of either. I know this means I should release you from our betrothal, but, Serena, I—I cannot see my way clear to a life that doesn't include you."

Robert kissed her hands, not passionately or with practiced expertise, but with the desperate need that filled him. "When I left for Newmarket after that first evening with you, I swore I'd forget you. I thought you'd marry someone else, or I would eventually tire of you. It never happened."

Hope lit her face at his admission. "Could it be, Robert, that you do love me and will not allow yourself to admit it? If—if you don't want to be without me, and you've not tired of me, is that not love?"

"I wish I could tell you, but I don't know," he said truthfully. "I don't feel the way I felt when I was in love all those years ago."

"Well, I am very glad of that, Robert! I do not want the passion of a young man, almost a child. I want the passion of a man who knows his worth and the worth of what he has to give."

Serena stood, with a trembling smile. "I shall leave you now. Think on what was said here to-day. I will not wait forever, Robert, but I'll wait a little while longer."

She left the room.

Robert flinched as the door closed behind her, and he clutched his tumbler of brandy so hard, his knuckles went white. *He was going to lose her.* If he couldn't say the damned words she needed, she would be gone. What kind of hell was this?

After draining his glass, Robert went in search of Evesham and Rutherford, needing advice . . . and a miracle.

"Well?" Lady Beaumont asked Serena, who had come directly to her after leaving Robert.

Serena's face flushed. "Robert told me what happened."

"All of it?"

She nodded. "He didn't want to, but he finally did and very shocking it was. He held nothing back. Actually, I think he was amazed I'd listen to it all without having vapors."

"Gentlemen are always worried about our delicate sensibilities. Did he admit that he's in love with you?"

"No," Serena said sadly. "He said that he would offer to release me from our betrothal, but he cannot live without me."

"Heaven save us from foolhardy men."

Serena laughed at Lady Beaumont's disgusted mien.

"What in the name of God does he think love is, if not—" Lady Beaumont scowled. "I am about ready to wash my hands of him. He must be the most stupid man on Earth."

"Oh, not *the* most stupid!" Serena smiled in spite of herself. "He was very hurt by his first love, and he is afraid to try it again. I told him I would wait a little longer."

"Serena, you are a brave woman to go through all of this."

Serena said ruefully, "Not brave, ma'am, just a woman in love. Now if that great noddy would just bring himself to admit he loves me, it will all have been worth it."

Lady Beaumont smiled sympathetically. "You go on, dear, and rest. Come get me when it's time to meet the others in the drawing room. We'll go down together."

Serena blinked back her tears and bent to kiss Lady Beaumont's cheek. "Thank you. You've been so kind to me. I don't know what I would have done without your help."

Lady Beaumont's eyes grew misty. "Go along now."

Serena nodded and went to her chamber. She sat on the window seat gazing out, thinking of Robert's story. How could any lady, worthy of the title, have behaved that way—especially one so young?

Serena wanted to take Robert and comfort him, but even as contrite as he'd been, that path would lead her only to further ruin. She closed her eyes to hold back the tears that threatened. What if she didn't marry Robert? Somehow she knew there was no other gentleman she could love. Serena had given her heart—and more—to Robert.

She supposed she had enough money to live on her own. Perhaps she could involve herself in charitable works and find a new purpose to life. Yet where would she live? Not London, Yorkshire? A town by the sea?

Serena shook herself from the melancholy and prayed Robert would come around soon. Waiting was far too painful.

Robert finally found Marcus and Rutherford in the library.

"Serena wants me to tell her that I love her. How can I do that when I don't know if I am capable of the emotion?" he asked, both frustration and anguish in his voice.

"You have all the symptoms of being in love," Rutherford offered helpfully.

Robert regarded him crossly. "That may be, but I don't know if I *am* in love. I don't even think I know what it is. I certainly didn't see it when I was growing up."

"Did you ask what Serena desires from a marriage?" Rutherford inquired. "That's something Anna and I discussed."

Robert frowned. He'd been too busy trying to make her

his to think that far ahead, but perhaps Rutherford had an idea. "Marcus, did you and Phoebe have the same conversation?"

"Yes," Marcus responded thoughtfully. "Though I'd already told her I loved her, I wouldn't have won her hand if we hadn't come to an agreement on the major issues."

St. Eth knocked on the door, entered, and glanced at Robert with expectation. "So, young man, has there been any progress?"

The devil. Compromising a woman into marriage was supposed to be a simple affair. This was anything but, and his grandmother was not helping. "Were you aware, sir, that my grandmother told Serena she did not have to marry me?"

St. Eth's lips tightened. "No, but I cannot say it surprises me. Lady Beaumont is an original. Serena's remaining a spinster is not my preferred outcome. Unlike her ladyship, I do care if there is a scandal, and I do not wish to see Serena barred from the *ton.* You must find some way to convince her to wed you."

Robert agreed. Perhaps Serena just didn't know what being Viscountess Beaumont entailed. Many women wanted to marry him simply for the status it would bring. Unfortunately, he suspected Serena was not among their number. "My lord, to-morrow I would like to speak privately with Lady Serena."

St. Eth nodded. "Join us for luncheon. There will be time afterward."

Robert left the Hôtel Charteries determined to find an argument—other than lust—to gain Serena's promise to marry him and make her happy about the decision. He never wanted to see such misery in her lovely amber eyes again. It was as if her sadness pierced his very soul, and he was afraid, if he lost her, he might not even have that left intact.

* * *

Serena and Lady Beaumont joined the other ladies in the drawing room before dinner.

"Well?" Phoebe asked.

Serena related Robert's story, then sat down on the sofa, sadness sinking in. "So that's it. I told him I'd wait a short while more for him to reconsider."

"Well, I can understand why he would be wary of loving again," Phoebe mused, frowning. "But how can he equate that jade with you? That makes no sense."

Anna knitted her brows. "Robert is clear as to what you need?"

Serena smoothed her gown, hesitating. "Yes. He says he does not know if he is capable of love, yet he cannot give me up."

"I don't understand men," Anna said testily. "Why can't he see that everything he's doing *shows* he's in love?"

Serena shrugged. She'd been asking the same question since he left.

The door opened and the gentlemen entered.

"We have been with Robert," Marcus said.

"Was it instructive?" Phoebe asked, handing her husband a glass of wine.

"Not very," Marcus responded. "It's not that he doesn't want to come to the point, but for some reason, he simply cannot admit his feelings."

"Just like his grandfather." Lady Beaumont tapped her cane on the floor.

All eyes turned to her.

"All this time, until Robert tried to trap Serena into marrying him, I've been thinking it over." Lady Beaumont fixed her sharp eyes on Serena. "His grandfather had a devil of a time loving anyone. He considered it losing control. Love made him feel vulnerable, and it was Sisyphean labor for him to finally accept his feelings for me. Robert may not be cognizant of it, but, my girl, that is what he's afraid of."

Uncle Henry's lips twisted into a strange smile. "All men in love with their wives live under the cat's paw. It's not how we plan it, but it happens all the same."

Marcus and Rutherford glanced at their wives and nodded.

Chapter Eleven

The next day, Robert was shown to a parlor. Alone, Robert sat back and stared at the ceiling. Very French, nicely molded and patterned. He appreciated the subtle stripes of the wallpaper. Finally he got up and stared out the window overlooking the garden. The old wall with the espaliered trees reminded him of his kitchen garden at Haythrope Hall. He could imagine Serena walking in it, consulting with the cook and gardener. When Robert closed his eyes, she smiled at him as he approached, her eyes filled with love. He remembered how she'd tasted when he kissed her. How she felt soft and warm in his arms. How her breasts . . . enough of that. He already knew he wanted her. That part was uncomplicated.

He cursed under his breath. Why couldn't they have just let him carry her off? He'd have made it work. Robert shook his head. No, Serena had been too hurt by what he did. He ran his hands through his carefully arranged locks and down his face. Why did he feel like this? As if Serena held his life in her hands. If he couldn't give her what she wanted, then what? Robert's hands clenched and his jaw hardened at the thought she would be some other man's wife. Never. Not while he had breath.

He paced the room to calm himself. There must be a way to keep Serena. Robert turned back to the window. She was walking to the fountain and looked back as if someone had called her, then turned back to the house. There was a knock on the door and a footman stepped in to inform him luncheon was being served on the terrace.

After luncheon, he took Serena's arm and guided her away from the others. "Will you take a stroll in the garden with me?"

She raised her gaze to his. "Yes."

They walked along the path to the fountain. "I'd like to have a private conversation with you, if I may."

"There's an arbor with a bench toward the side wall," Serena said. "We may speak there."

She led the way, then gracefully lowered herself to the bench.

He sat next to her, reveling in her nearness. It was the first time he'd been alone with her since that day at Merton . . . if he could call having everyone in the house, gathered on chairs and sofas, watching them from the terrace, being alone.

Serena gently took his hands. "What do you wish to speak about?"

Robert had planned what he would say, but as he searched her face, he knew his prepared argument would fail. Instead, he said, "I know you want love in your marriage. We've never discussed what else you desire. Your dreams. Your expectations."

Serena dropped her gaze for a moment. "I've run a large estate and did it well. I want respect for my abilities. When my brother returned from the war, the property had not merely survived, it had prospered. I would not like to be left out of the management of my husband's estate. I have skills to offer, and I want an equal partnership with my husband, where I have an opportunity to use my knowledge and experience to make a positive difference."

Robert hid his surprise. It had never occurred to him that she might want to actually take part in running his land. He didn't even enjoy doing that. Intrigued, he shifted slightly and focused on her. "What types of things do you have in mind to help the estate's people?"

An excitement, like he'd never seen on her before, crossed her face.

"A school, if there is not one already, and perhaps an orphan house, if there is a need. Ensuring that the tenants' houses and outbuildings are maintained in good condition. I suppose I wouldn't know everything that needed to be done until I saw it.

"And I'm used to being in charge," Serena said, smiling wryly. "I don't take orders well. Of course, I understand there is give and take in any marriage, and I'm willing to do my part."

Robert tried to keep his countenance even. Ceding control to anyone had never sat well with him. He'd always thought Marcus and Rutherford besotted fools for having a partnership with their wives, but with Serena's excitement about caring for an estate, Robert wondered if his friends were not so idiotic after all. It was a revelation to hear Serena state her desires so simply. It shouldn't have been. She'd always been direct.

Increasingly, Robert understood how important having her as an integral part of his life would be. "Where would you like to live?"

Serena gave a small laugh. "Well, it's impossible not to

be interested in politics after staying with Uncle Henry. I'd want to be in London for the parliamentary sessions and would like my husband to take his place in the House of Lords. Other than that, I'd prefer to live on the estates, where the work is. What do you want, Robert?"

Suddenly what he wanted seemed to coalesce into an urgent need. Robert captured Serena's gaze and told her his dream, the old one he'd thought long dead, of what he hoped for in his future. "I want a lady, a wife who will stand beside me. Who will help me to make my people's lives better. One who is not so high in the instep that she cannot rub shoulders at a local fete. She will love my house and work to make it a home. I want a woman who'll not pine for London whenever she's in the country, yet will be happy there during the Seasons."

Serena stared at him and worried her lip.

Had he asked for too much? He regarded her intently. "Would it bother you to mingle with the local folk? The farmers and tradesmen?"

"You're funning." She gave him an exasperated look. "Robert, I've mixed with local people all my life, which you would know if you'd spent more time talking to me about topics other than the weather and babies."

"Serena, although I regret my mistakes, I cannot change what I've done in the past. I do promise to endeavor to do better."

She nodded and her jaw firmed. "Go on. What else is important to you?"

Robert heard Serena's strength, her steel, in the question. He would have liked to have said *"you,"* though that was an answer she wouldn't accept at present.

His voice became low and rough as he reached deeper into his heart. "I want a woman who will warm my bed, because she wants to be there, not because she must. A wife who desires me as much as I do her. A woman who will bear my children and love them."

She blinked back the tears that filled her beautiful eyes. Her voice was heartbreakingly sad. "And love between you and your wife, Robert? Do you not desire that?"

He couldn't lie, even though he knew his answer was going to disappoint her. "I know you love me, but I don't know if I can ever promise you love. I care deeply for you," he said earnestly, "more deeply than I ever have for any other woman, and I want you to be part of my life."

Serena started to protest, but he went on. "No, listen to me, please. I know passion is not the same as love, but I vow never to be unfaithful to you. I'll stay by your side." He stopped, afraid it wasn't enough. "I'm sorry," he said softly. "More than that, I cannot promise, and I'll not make promises I cannot keep."

He raised her hands to kiss them—first one, then the other, and saw the sadness in her face.

"I must think about what you've said," Serena began.

He tightened his grip. "I'll come to-morrow . . ."

"No," Serena interrupted. "I will send for you . . . when I decide."

That was not the answer he'd wanted. Shaken, Robert stood and bowed. "As you will, my lady."

After Robert had gone, Serena sat in the arbor contemplating what Robert had told her. She understood why he'd spurned love for so many years, and he'd offered everything except what she needed most. Could she be happy, living with him, never knowing if he would return her affections? Could she still have a full life? A meaningful life? Would the love of their children be enough to ease her heart? What would be better? This half-life he proposed, or the life of a spinster? She would never love another man.

She'd seen him with the Eveshams' and Rutherfords'

children. Robert was gentle and playful. He'd be a wonderful father and he'd keep any promise he made her. Maybe a marriage that began with mutual caring, respect, and passion would be enough for him to eventually understand what love between a man and a woman truly meant.

And if that never happened?

Serena stayed in the arbor for a long time, until the grief of her decision overwhelmed her. Marriage to Robert, under those conditions, would be too close to the lonely life she'd had at Castle Vere. She could not go back to that again.

Robert walked slowly back to his *hôtel*. Serena's somber demeanor hadn't given him much hope. He'd been such an idiot to have ventured to manipulate her into marrying him, and a sapskull not to have gotten to know her better.

To have never noticed the fine-tempered steel within her. She'd come alive when discussing the estate. That was his first hint that she had been, if not out of her depth in London, at least not in a world she understood well. Robert was certain she'd refuse his offer. She didn't know him well enough to trust him without a promise of love. His fault as well.

If only he could get her to Haythrope Hall, he could show her what her life could be. Robert stopped himself from smacking his head. What a fool he'd been, he thought in disgust. That was his answer—convince her to visit Haythrope Hall and *show* her what he was offering.

The following morning, rain pelted the windows. The gloom matched Serena's mood. She'd tossed and turned most of the night with visions of standing distraught before an altar, unable to tell Robert she'd marry him, or him saying he would never love her.

Tears stung her eyelids as she rang for her maid.

"Mary, please send a footman to go round to Lord Beaumont's hotel and ask him to join me in an hour."

"Yes, my lady. Do you want breakfast brought to you?"

Serena's stomach roiled. "No, I can't eat right now. I'll have something later."

Mary bobbed a curtsey and left to deliver the message.

Serena's heart cracked. With her refusal of marriage, she condemned herself to a solitary life without love and children. Still, a lonely marriage would be far worse. She blinked back tears.

Her back was to the door when Robert entered the parlor.

Serena turned. He strode to her and took both her hands. She looked down, uncertain how to tell him.

"Don't say anything, please," Robert asked. "Allow me to speak first."

She nodded.

He continued. "I've given this much thought since yesterday. It wasn't fair of me to ask you to make a decision about your future when you do not know the whole."

Puzzled, she lifted her eyes to his.

"You've not seen my home. How could you know if you'd like it or my people? I propose you visit for a few weeks. If you agree, I'll not press you for marriage during that time. Afterward, if you still don't wish to marry me, I'll release you."

Serena searched his face. Optimism and fear warred in his features. Hope crept into her heart. If she went, then she'd soon know what her life would hold, whether she would marry or not. "I cannot go with you alone. Who would accompany us?"

"Anyone you wish," Robert said rashly. "We can take everyone here, if you'd like."

Serena grinned slightly. "That's a lot of people."

He smiled. "I've noticed."

"Let us ask who wants to come," she suggested.

Robert held the door to the morning room open for Serena to pass through. The Eveshams and Rutherfords had their babies, Arthur and Ben, on the floor playing. Ester and Catherine sat with Robert's grandmother. All eyes turned to Robert and Serena as they entered.

Serena went to her aunts and Lady Beaumont and said in a subdued voice, "Lord Beaumont would like me to visit his home before I make my final decision. I agree that I should. I don't wish to be a bother, but someone must accompany me as a chaperone. Is anyone willing?"

"Robert, when do you plan to leave?" Lady Beaumont asked.

"In the next day or two. We can make the trip to Calais in three or four days, and if we travel quickly, in two or three more days we'll reach Haythrope Hall."

Lady Beaumont glanced at her daughter. "Freddy, come here."

She joined them. "Yes, Mama?"

"Are you holding out for that *comte* to make you an offer, or have you done flirting with the poor man?"

A smile flickered in Freddy's eyes. "No, Mama. I am quite finished. We were merely engaging in a light flirtation. I had no serious intentions."

"Minx," Lady Beaumont said fondly. "Would you mind playing propriety and escort Serena to Yorkshire?"

"Not at all." Freddy glanced at Serena and Robert. "When would you like to leave?"

"Would to-morrow be too soon?" he asked hopefully.

Freddy shrugged. "It will make for a busy day to-day, but, yes, to-morrow suits me."

"Serena?" Robert asked.

The sooner the better. She could not continue to live like this. "I can be ready to leave to-morrow."

"I will accompany you as well, my dear," Catherine said.

"Aunt Catherine, are you sure you wish to leave Paris?"

"Yes, I only planned to be away until the end of the Season, and that's almost over."

Phoebe looked up. "Robert, you may take our ship, the *Lady Phoebe,* for the crossing. It will be more pleasant than the packet."

That was a generous offer and more than he would have asked. "You're sure you don't mind?"

"The crew is merely awaiting our pleasure. It will give them something to do," she said. "I take it you'll wish to make an early start?"

He nodded. "Yes, as early as possible."

"Fine. I shall have François make you an early breakfast and pack something for the trip. You may take my carriage and one of the baggage coaches to Dieppe. I trust you can arrange passage from Newhaven?" Phoebe pursed her lips. "You should send a courier to have your traveling coach brought to Newhaven."

"Thank you, for everything," Robert said, stunned by her generosity.

"You still need lodging arrangements." Phoebe went to the desk. "I'll take care of it now."

Robert was amazed that Phoebe had planned the entire journey with the ease of a minor outing.

"Robert, you may escort me to my room," his grandmother commanded. "I wish to rest."

"Yes, ma'am." He helped her from her chair, then met Serena's gaze. "I'll return shortly."

Once they'd ascended the stairs, his grandmother stopped. "I am very pleased to see you finally acting like a man of sense. That was a good idea you had, inviting Serena to Haythrope Hall, for I will tell you, she was not going to accept you."

"I know. I could see it in her face yesterday."

"When you get her to Yorkshire, give Lady Serena her head. Don't try to rein her in. She will make you an excellent wife, *if* you can bring her up to scratch. Go on back down to her now. I can make my way from here."

"No, Grandmama, I'll escort you to your door and ring for Skinner," Robert said. "I have some questions."

"Harrumph."

Once she was settled on a sofa, Robert asked, "What do you know of Vere Castle?"

"Only what I've been told. Lady Ware said it was a great sprawling place, a large acreage, herds of animals, and several hundred dependants."

Much larger than the Hall. "Do you know how long Lady Serena managed it?"

"Since before her father's death. That brother of hers displaced her pretty quickly when he returned, although I think it had more to do with his wife. In my opinion, he managed it badly. You are not the only one to have treated the girl ill."

On the one hand, Robert would like to plant her brother a facer. On the other, if Vere hadn't made Serena leave, Robert would never have met her. "Do you think she'll like Haythrope Hall?"

"Robert, Lady Serena is country bred. I think you'll find a very different lady there than you've seen thus far. Now go, I need my rest."

He returned to the morning room and took his leave of Serena and the rest of the company. Marcus and St. Eth walked him to the door.

St. Eth slapped his back. "Beaumont, I hope to hear of a satisfactory resolution."

Robert flushed under St. Eth's penetrating stare. Robert knew he was being given a second chance to prove he was worthy of Serena, and that her uncle expected him to succeed. "Thank you, sir. It has taken me some time, but I think I can see my way through now."

"If your plans prosper, send me a message at St. Eth House. Lady St. Eth and I will take our leave from here in a few days."

"I will, sir. Everything will be in order for you to review." Marriage settlements were the last thing on his mind. First Serena had to agree to marry him.

Chapter Twelve

Serena, more cheerful than she'd been in weeks, practically flew to her room. If Robert wanted her to see his home—a place he hardly spoke of—perhaps they still had a chance to work things out. It could still turn out badly, but at least she would have tried.

Serena rang for Mary and told her to begin packing.

"Lor', my lady, we've never been so many places in all our lives as we've been in the past few months. Where're we going this time?"

"Yorkshire. We are visiting Lord Beaumont's estate."

Her maid stared at the wardrobe. "I'll start packing, but don't you have a gown with the modiste still?"

"I do, and that is not all I must fetch." Serena left the room.

Less than an hour later, Serena and Freddy sallied forth to do the last of their Paris shopping, collecting items previously ordered and added to their wardrobes.

"We'd best shop now," Freddy advised. "Who knows when we'll be back in Paris again?"

They paused for tea in one of the cafés lining the street.

"Freddy," Serena asked, "will I like Haythrope Hall?"

"Lord, dear, I can't tell you. I enjoyed it as a child. My mother never liked Yorkshire. She did her duty, but was always happier in London or in Bath, which was the fashionable resort at the time." Freddy patted Serena's hand. "You'll have to see for yourself if Haythrope Hall is the right place for you."

Robert arrived at the Hôtel Charteries early the next morning to find the coaches being loaded.

He walked in the house and discovered Serena in the breakfast room, munching François's croissants. He wanted her to always be as merry as she was now, but what if he was making another mistake? Or worse, making the same mistake his father had made in bringing home a wife who was never happy. The only time there'd been peace was when one or the other of his parents was gone.

Serena waved Robert to a chair. "Help yourself. I'll ring for more tea."

"Thank you." He sat next to her. "When will you be ready to leave?"

"Oh, probably in about a half an hour. It depends on how quickly the coach can be readied. Phoebe told us whatever did not fit she'd have sent by courier."

"Where are Aunt Freddy and Lady Ware?"

"Breakfasting in their rooms."

It was more than half an hour before they departed. They made good time through Paris and on to the road to Dieppe. Other than a stop for luncheon, they continued until it was dark. Three days after leaving Paris, the carriages pulled up outside the inn, Coq d'Or.

Once their rooms were arranged, Robert took Serena for a walk. She showed him some of the town and pointed out the schooner, *Lady Phoebe*. When they returned to the inn, she went to her chamber and he to the private parlor. Their aunts lambasted him when he entered.

"If this mad pace is the one you mean to set all the way to Yorkshire, Robert," Freddy said acerbically, "I shall take leave to tell you, it will not do! In two days, we've accomplished what would normally take four or five."

Robert gave her his most amiable smile. "Aunt Freddy . . ."

"No," Freddy snapped. "Use your considerable charms on someone else."

Robert turned to Lady Ware, who held up her hands. "Oh, no, I quite agree with your aunt. You've pushed us as fast as we can go. I insist on a more decorous pace for the rest of the trip."

He kept himself from scowling. Getting on their bad side would not help his cause. "We shall discuss the rest of the journey this evening. First, I must speak to the captain of the *Lady Phoebe* regarding our passage."

Robert had no trouble locating the ship. Captain Benedict greeted Robert, informing him Lord Evesham had sent a message, and the ship was standing ready to ferry Lord Beaumont's party across to Newhaven.

"How soon can we sail?" Robert asked.

"We can load your trunks to-day, but it looks like a squall will be coming through either tonight or to-morrow," Benedict said. "I won't know until later if it is possible to sail with the morning tide."

"I'll await word from you then and have the baggage brought round." Robert thanked him and returned to the inn, trying to think of a way to convince the aunts to maintain their current traveling pace.

Serena, wisely, he thought, chose to stay out of the conversation.

Freddy was uncompromising. "My dear Robert, it may do very well for *you* to travel in such a rough and ready fashion. But it will not do for us. Count yourself well served that we have agreed to travel directly from Newhaven to London and spend only two nights on the road to Yorkshire."

The only good news he received was that they'd be able to sail with the morning tide. The passage was rough but swift. They arrived in Newhaven in time to enjoy luncheon at the inn. Robert had arranged for his coaches to meet them. After eating, he excused himself to supervise the packing.

Freddy raised her brows as he reentered the private parlor. "That was fast. Are the trunks loaded?"

He shook his head. "Pitchley called me *Master Robert* and asked me if I didn't have somewhere else to be. Apparently, he thought my 'suggestions' were hindering progress."

Freddy laughed. "That is the problem with servants who have known one since childhood. Every time Nurse became irritated with me, she'd call me *Miss Freddy*—even long after I had married."

Catherine and Serena entered the room to find them both chuckling and demanded to be let in on the joke. Catherine, Robert, and Freddy exchanged funny and exasperating stories, while Serena looked on bemused.

"Serena, have you nothing to share?" Freddy asked.

"No, none of my old servants tried to put me in my place once I took over the castle."

"Ah, a formidable woman. Count yourself fortunate," Robert said. "Shall we look around the town while they're packing?" He glanced at their aunts. "Would you like to accompany us?"

"No, you two go on ahead," Catherine said.

Freddy made shooing motions and Robert and Serena left the room.

They walked out of the inn and crossed the street to the dock area. Newhaven was the cleanest port he'd ever seen. He took Serena to the end of a pier for a better look at the lighthouse.

"It's a magnificent view," she said. "The last time I was here, it was too dark to see anything."

Robert thought now might be a good time to ask the questions that had plagued him after his discussion with his grandmother. "How old were you when you took over Castle Vere?"

"Seventeen when I took over the management of the estate," Serena replied. "My father had a stroke and died less than a year later. But I became responsible for the castle proper at fourteen."

"Fourteen?" Robert could not imagine anyone being responsible for such a large property at that age. Now he knew where the steel in her came from.

To both of their detriments, he had greatly underestimated her. "Serena, why you?"

She shrugged. "My aunt, my father's youngest sister, had been responsible for castle management, when she left to marry, I took over."

Robert walked Serena back to the main dock area and down to the empty beach, where seagulls dove for fish.

"What of your mother?"

Serena shook her head. "Mama died when I was twelve, but she had not been herself for a few years before then." Serena shivered and pulled her cloak around her. "Come now, my life is not that interesting, and I will probably never see Vere Castle again. Tell me about Haythrope Hall."

Robert stared out at the Channel before glancing at her. He wanted to know more, such as why she was left alone for so long, but her lips were set in a thin line, so he acquiesced. "I'd rather tell you about the people and the town."

Her amber gaze sparked with curiosity. "Very well."

"Most of the senior staff has been with me since I was born, and the rest are either from the area or are relatives of other servants. Haythrope is a busy market town that lies just beyond the western border of the estate."

The wind whipped up and he turned her back toward the docks. "The Hall owns many of the town's stores and the church is within my living. When the old rector retired, I brought in a friend, John Stedman. He and I were at Eton and Oxford together. He's very modern and has a number of reformist ideas, which took some people aback."

Robert grinned wryly. "Of course, it's always hard, particularly in the country, to make changes. John is making steady progress. He married about a year ago to a lady from his home county . . ."

Robert heard his groom call and turned to see Pitchley hailing him. "I think we're ready to leave."

Robert, Serena, and their aunts arrived in London at his grandmother's residence, on Upper Brook Street, in the early evening.

Freddy descended from the coach. "Catherine and Serena shall spend the night here, Robert. You do not have to tell me you want an early start in the morning. We will be ready."

"Aunt Freddy?"

"What is it?"

"May I dine with you this evening?"

Freddy heaved an exasperated sigh. "Robert, I don't know what we have to eat. I assume there's something in the larder, but as neither Mama nor I wrote the staff, it may be bread and cheese."

Robert grinned. "I took the liberty of sending a message from Newhaven."

Freddy glanced at the sky. "Yes, all right then. You may dine with us. We'll keep an early evening, and I do not plan to dress."

He kissed her cheek. "Thank you. I'll see you in an hour."

Shaking her head, she went inside, while he took his leave of Serena.

Needing to stretch his legs from being cramped in the coach, Robert walked the few blocks to his house. A junior footman opened the door.

Robert handed him his hat and greatcoat. "I take it this means Finster has posted north?"

"Yes, my lord, he left as soon as we received your instructions to make Haythrope Hall ready, and he took most of the rest of the staff with him."

"Good. I'm dining at Upper Brook Street and shall leave for the Hall first thing in the morning."

His aunt hadn't misspoken when she'd said they'd have an early evening, by nine o'clock he was in his room. Robert thought back to his conversation with Serena before they'd left Newhaven. For at least the twentieth time, he berated himself for what he'd done. How brave she was for standing up to him after Merton and in Paris.

Robert grimaced. No lady, other than his grandmother, had ever done so. Nor had another woman captured him. If Serena but knew it, she'd trapped him quite effectively.

More than he'd trapped her. Serena had a way out, thanks to his grandmother, whereas he wanted no other and was caught forever.

That night, though tired by the travel, Serena lay awake. She looked forward to being in the country. She closed her eyes but his unique male scent lingered in her consciousness. Her body tingled. She had no resistance to Robert, none whatsoever. For the brief moment they were alone tonight, his gaze had dropped to her lips. Even now, they throbbed for him. If Freddy and her aunt hadn't been there this evening, Serena would have gone to him. She didn't know how she would keep her distance once they arrived in Yorkshire, yet she must.

Dawn was barely breaking over the streets of London as their carriages arrived at the first toll on the Great North Road. Robert had the coachman spring the horses, intending to make as many changes as necessary to get Serena to Yorkshire as quickly as he could.

Freddy quizzed Robert during a halt at one of the busy posting houses. "Robert, you're making good time. The roads are clear and dry. There's no reason for you to be prowling like a caged animal. You won't get home any faster."

It didn't matter. He wanted Serena in his home, and he wouldn't be satisfied until they'd reached Haythrope.

On the third day, Robert hired a horse and rode ahead only to meet Serena's coach three hours later in his curricle at a crossing several miles from Haythrope.

He smiled broadly. "Serena, come with me. You'll have a better view of the Hall than in a coach."

"What he means," Freddy said in an undertone, "is he wants to show you his estate without us around."

Serena laughed. "I'll come with you."

Robert helped her transfer from the coach to the carriage and gave the horses their office. "We shall approach through the town if you'd like."

"Let's do." She'd heard so much about it, she felt as if she'd know the town on sight, but its size still surprised her.

Haythrope was impressive. It boasted several shops, a blacksmith, bakery, and two inns. More than a few good-sized houses were situated around a common green and smaller, picturesque cottages lined the road. A large church and rectory stood at the other end.

As they passed, Robert was hailed by a man in his early thirties walking with a pretty, fair-haired woman.

"Robert," the man said, "it's good to see you back."

"It's good to be back, John. My dear, allow me to present the Right Reverend John Stedman and his lovely bride, Lora. John, Lora, Lady Serena Weir."

Serena smiled. "I am so pleased to meet you. Robert has told me about you both."

There was a quizzical look in Mr. Stedman's eye as if he was wondering what exactly was going on. Was he wondering where their chaperones were?

Robert must have seen the rector's look as well for he added, "My aunt and Lady Serena's aunt are following in the coach. I wanted to bring Lady Serena on ahead to show her Haythrope."

Mr. Stedman bowed. "I see."

"Lady Serena," his wife said, "we look forward to a longer visit with you once you've recovered from your journey."

"Thank you. I shall look forward to furthering our acquaintance," Serena replied.

"We'll stop by in the next couple of days." Robert set the horses to a trot.

She resisted the urge to glance back and wondered at the concerned look in the rector's eyes.

Robert stopped the curricle on a rise and directed Serena's attention to a view through the trees. "Haythrope Hall."

Serena took in the pale gray building with fancifully shaped gables, tall semicircular bay windows, and a Georgian portico in the center. It was a wonderful old house, the kind that had stood for centuries. The Hall was set in a park with an expansive lawn, and a lake stood off to one side. She could see an indication of extensive gardens in the back. Against her will, she envisioned children playing and fetes for the estate's dependants. Opposite the water, lime trees lined the drive to the house.

The Hall and town were almost more than she'd hoped for. Serena smiled. "Robert, the property is beautiful. I can't wait to see the inside and tour the grounds."

The front door opened before the carriage came to a halt. A footman ran out to assist Serena, but Robert bade him hold the horses and handed her down himself.

As they entered the large, airy, two-story front hall, an older woman waited with ill-concealed excitement.

Robert glanced up. "Ah, Lady Serena, may I present Mrs. Norton, my housekeeper."

Mrs. Norton bobbed a curtsey.

Serena extended her hand. "I am very pleased to meet you, Mrs. Norton."

The housekeeper beamed. "As am I to meet you, my lady. No doubt you'll want a tour of the house and to make an inspection. I shall hold myself ready for you."

Serena couldn't help responding warmly to Mrs. Norton, but this was not a good sign. Serena glanced at Robert and tried to give him some sort of signal that they needed to speak privately about the staff's expectations.

"Mrs. Norton, Lady Serena's aunt and my Aunt Freddy will arrive soon. I'm sure Lady Serena would like to freshen up before touring the house."

Serena tried to keep her tone light. "Lord Beaumont, before I do that, I believe I would like to take a turn in the garden. Will you escort me?"

He turned a concerned face to her. "Yes, indeed."

Robert led her out through a room in the back of the house to the courtyard garden beyond. She stopped by the fountain where the sound of running water would prevent anyone from overhearing them.

"The last time you spoke with your staff was before you arrived in France, wasn't it?" Serena began carefully. "From what Mrs. Norton said, they think I am here as a prelude to the wedding."

At least Robert had the grace to look guilty. "So it seems. I didn't think about their assumptions when I made the invitation for you to come here."

Well, neither had she. "How do you wish to handle this? It's not only the staff. Everyone in the area will expect to have the banns read now that we have arrived." Serena paced.

Small lines formed around Robert's mouth. "Yes, of course you're right. Serena, I'm sorry . . ."

"There is no point in that now." She briefly put her head in her hands. What an uncomfortable situation. "We cannot tell them the truth. It would be too awkward for everyone. We'll have to allow them to think what they will. Which means I shall inspect the house and, in general, carry on as if I shall be the Hall's mistress." Serena waved a hand, encompassing the property.

Robert caught her hands and held her gaze in his warm one. When he looked at her like that, with such caring, she'd do anything for him.

"I'm here for you," he promised. "No matter what you decide, I'll support you."

Serena searched his eyes. Yes, he would. She took a breath. This may not be as bad as she thought. "Well, let's get on with it. What shall we do to-day?"

His expression cleared and his lips tilted up. She really did not need to focus on his lips.

"First, you freshen up," he suggested. "Your maid and clothing should be here. Later we'll tour the house. That will be enough for to-day. We keep country hours here."

That was a relief. It would be nice to retire before one or two in the morning. "And to-morrow?"

He tightened his grip on her hands. "Would you like to meet some of my tenants?"

"Yes, let's do that. I'll plan to meet with Mrs. Norton the day after to-morrow." Serena sighed. "I hope I'll be able to hold her off that long."

Robert grinned. "I'll see what I can do to distract her. She's known me since I was a child and I have had considerable experience."

Chapter Thirteen

Serena was shown to an apartment overlooking the east garden, with a view of the ornamental lake and the wood beyond. Mary had already unpacked and had Serena's wash water ready.

Once Serena had completed her ablutions and changed, Mary said, "My lady, Mrs. Norton asked if I knew when the wedding would be."

Serena sucked in a breath. "What did you tell her?"

"I told her you and Lord Beaumont were discussing it. *Is* there going to be a wedding?"

"That's what I am here to decide," Serena said firmly. "We'll not say anything to Lord Beaumont's staff. There is no reason for them to know I have not made up my mind."

Mary glanced at her doubtfully. "As you wish, my lady."

Serena was turning from the corridor to the main staircase as Freddy and Catherine arrived. Stepping back so she wouldn't be seen, Serena watched the housekeeper greet their aunts.

Mrs. Norton greeted Freddy enthusiastically. "Miss Freddy." The housekeeper blushed. "I'm sorry, *my lady*. You're a sight for sore eyes."

Freddy hugged the housekeeper. "Norry, you never remember to call me 'my lady' at first. It's so good to see you. Come greet Lady Ware, Lady Serena's aunt."

"Welcome to Haythrope Hall, my lady." Mrs. Norton thought for a moment. "Don't you own the property next to here on the north?"

Catherine replied, "Yes, I moved there about five years ago after my eldest son married."

"Then welcome to Yorkshire as well. It'll be nice for you to have your niece living so close and all. We've been in a bustle getting ready for her. Such a good sweet lady she seems. It'll be wonderful having a mistress at the Hall again."

Catherine and Freddy exchanged brief glances.

Serena's stomach churned and she took a few deep breaths in an attempt to calm herself. It was time to make her presence known. "You certainly took your time arriving. We've been here for an age."

"Yes, well," Catherine said, "Freddy remembered an inn she wanted to stop at for a nuncheon. It was very pleasant." Catherine smiled meaningfully at Serena.

Clearly, they'd wished to give Robert and Serena more time together.

"Mrs. Norton," Serena said, "if you will escort Lady Stanstead and Lady Ware to their chambers, we shall have tea after they've refreshed themselves."

"Yes, my lady, it will be my pleasure."

"Freddy, Aunt Catherine, please meet me in the back parlor that leads to the garden. Freddy, do you know the room?"

"Yes, my dear, we won't be long."

Serena started to leave the hall, then stopped to address the butler. "Finster."

"Yes, my lady?"

"Please find Lord Beaumont and ask him to join me in the . . . what *is* the name of that room?"

"The Ladies' Morning Room, my lady."

"Thank you, Finster. Please have him attend me there."

Serena was pacing when Robert entered.

He walked quickly to her. "What is it?"

"Oh, Robert, I was about to descend the stairs when Aunt Catherine and Freddy arrived. Mrs. Norton was so happy when she told them I was to be the mistress here. I stayed in the upper corridor until she stopped. I couldn't face her. I feel like such a *fraud!*"

It was on the tip of his tongue to tell her if she would agree to marry him she wouldn't feel so badly, but that wouldn't help him. "No, you're not to feel that way. This situation is entirely my fault, and it's not as if you have made a decision *not* to marry me."

Serena breathed in. "No, that's true."

Robert raised her right hand to brush his lips across the back of it. She shivered. He met Serena's eyes, then dropped his gaze to her lips and stepped closer. "I've missed being alone with you."

She backed away. "No! That is what got us into this mess. Robert, I will not kiss you again unless I decide to marry you."

Damn, he'd done it again. "Very well, if that's what you wish."

"It's not what I wish," she said ruefully, "but it's how it must be."

A few minutes later, Catherine and Freddy arrived, their expressions serious.

"Well, nephew." Freddy's lips formed a moue. "I take it the staff still thinks you are marrying?"

"Freddy, it was something neither of us thought about," Serena said. "You know he'd told them we were before he came to France."

"And notice of the betrothal was in the *Morning Post*," Catherine added.

Mrs. Norton brought in the tea. "My lady, when would you like to meet with me?"

Robert answered, "Norry, I'd like to take Lady Serena riding around the estate to-morrow and then tour the house with her. She's been sitting in a carriage for the better part of a week. Can you wait until the day after to-morrow?"

Mrs. Norton's jaw dropped, and she narrowed her eyes at Robert. "*Master Robert,* do you mean to tell me that you dragged poor Lady Serena back from France and directly here?"

"Yes," he said, wondering why she'd care.

Mrs. Norton heaved a large breath. "Well, that was a hea-thenish thing to do if I ever heard of one." Mrs. Norton turned to Serena, all solicitude. "My poor lady, you take some time to rest from your travels. We can make the house inspection in two days. You just get used to being in one place again. I'll tell Cook she should give you another day before she sends you the menus."

Serena suppressed a giggle. "Thank you, Mrs. Norton. Two days would be wonderful."

After giving Robert a scathing look of disapproval, she left.

Serena collapsed onto the sofa, and gave herself over to the laughter she'd been holding in.

"You see, Robert? I'm not the only one who thinks your mode of travel excessive," Freddy said.

Serena glanced up. *"Master Robert."* And went off again.

"You may think it funny, but I don't! Every time I do something they think I shouldn't, I am reduced to the status of a six-year-old!"

"Heathenish travel." Serena giggled.

Robert smiled. "Oh well, at least I bought you a few days of peace."

"Since we are keeping country hours, it's time to dress for dinner," she said. "Robert, lead on."

Robert waited at the top of the grand staircase. Serena appeared dressed in an aubergine silk evening gown with a low V neckline and short gathered sleeves.

He tried to breathe. "You look lovely."

Serena swept him a graceful curtsey. "Thank you, my lord."

This is what he wanted, to see her every evening. "Come. I'll show you to the drawing room."

"House tour to-morrow?"

He held out his arm. "Yes. It is not a difficult house to navigate, even though it has a lot of rooms."

"I shouldn't complain. Vere Castle is a warren. One could become permanently lost with no trouble at all."

They entered the drawing room to find Freddy and Catherine already partaking in sherry.

"Freddy, how does it feel to be here?" Serena asked. "Does it feel like home?"

"Different. As if I've stepped back in time." Freddy pursed her lips. "I no longer feel as if it's *my* home, though I have a sense of well-being here. I may have to visit more often."

"Please do." Robert poured a glass and held it out. "Sherry, Serena?"

"I'd love some." She took the glass from him. "Thank you."

He and Freddy told Serena about the surrounding countryside and the neighbors they remembered.

When Finster announced dinner, Robert gave Serena a wry smile. "Cook is good, but as I recall, she doesn't do much with vegetables."

Taking a sip of sherry, Serena paused for a moment. "Let's see how it goes."

Dinner was well cooked and presented, but Robert had been correct. There was a dearth of vegetables and those on offer were covered in heavy sauces. That would never do. Her old cook at the castle was a wonder with vegetables and Serena always looked forward to them. Robert's cook needed her attention sooner rather than later. To-morrow she'd brave the kitchen.

Later that evening, as Mary was combing out Serena's hair, her maid paused. She hoped it wasn't going to be bad news. "You have something to tell me?"

"Yes, my lady. I was given a house tour by the housekeeper, and Will was shown round the stables. Mrs. Norton's doing the best she can, my lady, but it's all a bit shabby." Mary pulled a face. "I was seated at the table where I would be if you were married, and I heard that his lordship's started to redecorate the viscountess's rooms."

Serena briefly closed her eyes. Mary continued, "He told the staff you'd be married, and they're as happy as grigs. Mrs. Norton asked all manner of questions about Vere Castle. I said you'd been mistress for many a year, and knew what it took to hold house and keep the land in good order. Cook asked what you liked to eat, so I gave her some of your favorites."

Mary teared up. "Oh, my lady, I'll feel so sorry for these poor folks if we leave. This place isn't like St. Eth House, where everything is as it should be. They need a mistress here."

After dismissing Mary, Serena stood looking out at the lake. Almost June. She could hardly believe it, yet the moon rising before the sun set didn't lie. Was coming here really a good idea?

She hadn't thought his home could capture her so quickly. All afternoon, servants, such as the tweenie, Lolly, had smiled at Serena and welcomed her warmly. Serena had noticed their surreptitious glances as they wondered what sort of mistress she'd be, and she wanted to comfort them.

Guilt at the pretense clawed at her. Serena knew herself well. She'd been out of her depth in London, yet with her family surrounding her, she'd slowly made her way. Running a large house and an estate was what she knew best. She would not be able to hide her knowledge, or be willing to wait for Robert's approval to make the changes she'd seen the need for.

Serena slowly shook her head. As hard as it would be, she must guard her heart, knowing from experience that even the devotion of the tenants and staff would not make up for the lack of love.

The next morning after breakfast, Serena changed into her riding habit and placed the few lumps of sugar she'd taken from the table into a pocket. When she arrived at the head of the grand staircase, she found Robert waiting for her.

"Come." He grabbed her hand, and she had to lengthen her stride to keep up with him. "I'll show you the quickest way to the stables."

Tingles ran through her fingers, where he touched them.

It was always like this with him. "Why are you in such a hurry?"

Robert smiled. "You'll see. Would you like a good gallop?"

He pulled her down a passage and out a side door.

"Yes, Robert, I would love a gallop. It has been so long since I've been able to do that."

"Yes, one cannot properly give a horse its head in London or Paris."

They entered the stables, and Serena gazed at the well-kept stalls. A horse started to kick in a way she knew well. "Shamir!"

Following the noise with her gaze, she saw him looking out from one of the end stalls and hurried forward. "Oh, how I've missed you."

Serena took his large head in her hands and kissed his nose. He nudged her, then lipped her pocket. Laughing, she pulled out a piece of sugar.

"Robert, how did you get him here?"

"When we decided to come, St. Eth agreed to have Shamir sent ahead. We'll probably spend a great deal of time riding. So, I thought you'd like having your horse here."

Serena released her grip on Shamir. Her heart filled with love for Robert. If only he knew how much having Shamir meant to her. "Robert, thank you. That was so thoughtful."

She kissed him on the cheek. He tensed. She knew avoiding physical contact would be better, less dangerous, but how she longed for his touch.

Robert helped her onto Shamir and mounted Démon.

Once clear of the stable yard, they let the horses have their heads. Robert glanced at her occasionally as they rode, as if to assure himself she was still there.

Serena tried to focus on her surroundings. The cool crisp air, too cool for the end of May, had had an effect. The crops were not as far along as they should be because of the weather, but also, she thought, because of neglect. There was an air about the place that spoke of an absent landlord and a lazy steward. She'd have to talk to Robert about it. Even if Serena didn't stay, Robert needed to come here more often and take better care of his land. They skirted cultivated fields and crossed fallow ones before a group of cottages came into view.

"Your tenants?" Serena asked.

"Yes, this family has been here longer than I can remember. The lease is passed to the oldest son."

Long leases, that was good. "What happens to the younger sons?"

"Most of them go off on their own." He knitted his brows. "Why?"

"Having children far away is hard on families. Something should be done to provide employment for them in the area."

She decided to act as if she would be the mistress here, and to test Robert's sincerity in his offer of a partnership as well.

They reined in the horses and tied them off on a tree. A thin wiry man with grizzled hair and a deeply lined face came to greet them.

"My lord."

"Johnson."

Robert turned to her. "Lady Serena, allow me to introduce Mr. Johnson. His family has been at Haythrope Hall for as long as the Beaumonts have been here."

Mr. Johnson's face creased into a smile. "How de do, my lady. I suppose you'll hear this all day long, but we're happy to have you here."

Serena offered her hand. "As am I happy to be here, Mr. Johnson."

He looked a little flustered and glanced at Robert, who nodded. After wiping his hands on his shirt, Johnson took one of her fingers and shook.

"Marthy, come out here and meet her ladyship."

A voice came from inside the cottage. "You wait just a bit. I've got my hands in the dough."

"I'll just go in, shall I? There's no point in disrupting her kneading." Ignoring the men's shocked faces, Serena entered the cottage. One small room housed the kitchen, eating, and living area. A ladder led to a sleeping loft. This cottage hadn't been renovated in years, long before Robert was master.

Mrs. Johnson's eyes grew wide. "Oh, my lady, I would've come to ye!"

"No, no, Mrs. Johnson. I have enough experience with dough to know it can be very touchy. Why should you stop when I am quite capable of coming to you?" Serena smiled. "You certainly would not welcome my visits if I always interrupted your work."

Serena squatted down to a little girl and held out her hand. "Is this your daughter?"

"No, this is my youngest grandbaby. Tansy, make your curtsey to . . ." Mrs. Johnson looked up.

"Lady Serena."

Mrs. Johnson pushed the little girl forward. "Now ain't that a pretty name."

"I think Tansy is a pretty name as well," Serena coaxed.

Tansy approached her shyly, a thumb in her mouth. "Thas a pretty dress."

"Thank you. I'm glad you like it."

Serena reached into her pocket, took out a piece of hard candy, and gave it to Tansy, who looked ingenuously up at her grandmother. "She's a nice lady."

Mrs. Johnson nodded.

"May I sit down?" Serena asked.

"Oh, my, yes, my lady," responded Mrs. Johnson quickly.

Serena put Mrs. Johnson at ease, while she began to knead again. It didn't take long for Mrs. Johnson to become comfortable enough with Serena to tell her about the Johnson's children and grandchildren. The lack of space for everyone, the leaky roof, and her wish that her older children could live closer to home.

Serena waited until the dough was set to rise before she stood. She left the cottage with Mrs. Johnson and Tansy in her wake. "Are you ready, my lord?"

"Yes." After tossing Serena up and mounting, he looked back over his shoulder. "I'll look into the drainage problem, Johnson."

"Thank ye, my lord. I wish you a good rest of the day."

Robert and Serena waved and rode off to the next tenant's plot.

Mrs. Johnson turned to her husband. "Well I never in my life expected to have a real lady sittin' at my table talkin' with me like she was regular folk. His lordship's done a good job pickin' her out."

"Sittin' at our table?" Mr. Johnson asked, shocked.

"That's what I said. And askin' about all of us and how we was doing. What did you and his lordship do whilst we was in there?"

"Talked about some of the drainage problems we've been hav'n," he said.

"And when was the last time you did that?"

"Never," he responded a little thoughtfully.

The rest of the morning was spent in much the same way. Serena entered larger and smaller cottages, making mental notes of the families, their concerns and needs. Robert, because he could do nothing else while waiting for her, spoke to his tenants and discovered that his light hand on the estate had perhaps been too light, and his father's old steward no longer as capable as he'd thought.

They returned to the Hall in time for luncheon, but rather than having it in the dining room, Serena asked that it be brought to the study where she and Robert could discuss what they'd discovered and how to begin the repairs.

"There are several roofs with leaks," she said between bites. "And really, Robert, some of those cottages should be enlarged. As I suspected, there is a good deal of concern about their children's futures. Some of them have had to move far away to find work because they have no education, and their families never get to see them. That cannot continue."

"We can talk about solutions later. All morning I've been hearing about a drainage problem in the west field. I'd like to take a look at it," Robert said. "How much do you know about drainage?"

"Usually enough to spot the problem." Serena worried her lip. "I wish I could put off the house tour and ask you to take me to the rectory, but I really need to learn my way around."

"I'm perfectly happy to escort you until you become used to the Hall."

"Thank you. There is a lot of work to be done here. When will you speak with your steward? Some of what we've seen should not have been allowed to happen."

"When we have a complete list. There's no point in piecemealing it out."

Serena glanced up from her plate. "How long has he been with you?"

"He was old when I was a child. At least I thought he

was." Robert grinned, then spoke seriously. "I may have to try to convince him to retire."

"We need to discover why he's no longer doing his job."

"You're right. Much of the equipment is also old. Johnson and Armstrong mentioned a new type of plough."

Serena swallowed. "Is it the one with the self-scouring moldboard?"

Robert regarded her intently. "How do you know about ploughs?"

Though her expression was severe, her eyes twinkled. "While you have been doing the pretty in London, my lord, I've been farming."

It was clear Serena was determined to have the repairs made. "Let's write these lists so you can change for your house tour."

He sharpened a pen for her and placed the standish in the middle of his desk. Serena finished before he did and left him still writing.

After the door closed behind her, he leaned back in his chair. He'd have to buy a partner's desk like Phoebe and Marcus used. He liked working across from her. She hadn't been here for one day and she'd already begun making a change for the better. If it'd not been for her speaking with the women, Robert would never have discovered the problems some of his tenants were having. The men were far more reserved.

He'd been shocked when Serena walked into the Johnsons' cottage this morning. But he admired her knack for making the women and children comfortable, and her ability to draw them out so they'd tell her their problems. He laughed at the idea of either his mother or his grandmother doing the same. In London, Serena had always been a little shy, still feeling her way. Here she was a different woman, even more intriguing than before and much more capable.

His father had schooled him about the estate's management, but Papa had always been an absent landlord. There'd been no passion for the land and its people. That was what Serena had. Could Robert learn it from her? He'd let her do whatever she thought necessary to bring the Hall back to order.

Her joy in seeing her horse, Shamir, had been akin to giving another woman expensive jewelry. When she'd kissed him on the cheek, he'd itched to take her in his arms and hold her. Robert felt a tug on his heart. She was so special and made him want to trust her and protect her. The feelings were unfamiliar and unsettling.

Serena returned to the study holding several sheets of paper.

"What are those?"

"Menus. Please, look them over with me. I don't recognize some of these dishes." Serena handed him the lists and stood gazing over his shoulder. "What is a Parkin?"

"It's a type of ginger cake."

He quickly perused the other menus. "It looks as if Cook is making all my favorite childhood dishes." He glanced up at Serena. "Is there something you would like particularly to add?"

"Haggis, but I'd have to have the recipe sent to me." She went to the door. "I think we need a few more vegetables. I'll be back in a few minutes."

Robert rose. "Where are you going?"

"To the kitchen," Serena said as she reached for the door latch.

He caught up with her and handed Serena the lists. "I'll go with you. I don't want you to lose your way." Or run away.

Chapter Fourteen

Robert guided her through the baize door to Cook's domain. Mrs. Redding was a good Yorkshire woman, born and raised in the immediate area. She'd worked for the Beaumonts as long as Robert could remember. After introducing her to Serena, he lounged against a wall and watched Serena wrap Cook around her little finger.

Cook bobbed a curtsey. "My lady, I would have come to you. There's no reason you had to come down here."

"No, no, Mrs. Redding." Serena's tone was pitched perfectly. Friendly but not familiar and showing the proper amount of concern for Cook's travails.

Robert focused his attention more intently on what Serena was saying.

"I wanted to see the kitchen. It is so important to the comfort of everyone here at the Hall. Please let us sit and be comfortable. You can tell me if there is anything you need or would like to have."

Serena's attention was so focused on the older woman she didn't appear to remember Robert was present.

"Well, my lady . . ."

Before Serena addressed the menu, she asked for a list of all the problems with the kitchen and explored Cook's wish for one of the new closed stoves that she'd seen when visiting another house in the area.

Why hadn't he been told there were things needed in the kitchen?

"Where would we buy one of the stoves?" Serena asked.

Cook clasped her hands to her breasts. "They can be ordered in York, my lady, and the firm comes in and sets it up."

"Very well," Serena nodded, "would you like to make the arrangements?"

Cook breathed in. "Oh, yes, my lady, I have *all* the information."

His possibly future wife hadn't even glanced at him before agreeing to the repairs, replenishment of the kitchen, and a new stove. It dawned on Robert that she was testing him. He smiled, wondering if the new stove would cost more or less than the emerald necklace he'd bought her.

"Good," Serena said. "I'll leave you to it. We need to take care of the rest of the list as well. I have the menus and some questions, but first I wish to thank you for serving porridge at breakfast. It's what I am used to having, and I appreciated it. You will, of course, have to guide me concerning the local dishes. I have heard Yorkshire food is tasty. I'd like to see a few more vegetables on the menu if you wouldn't mind, and maybe not so many sauces."

All his life, Robert had dreaded eating the vegetables at the Hall.

"The old lord didn't like his vegetables. We got out of the habit. I'd be happy to add them for you, my lady," Cook said, still in a state of bliss over the stove.

Robert was stunned. He had no idea the problem was something he could have easily remedied.

"I've heard that you're from Scotland," Cook said. "I have a cousin there. I shall write her for recipes and add the dishes you're used to as soon as I receive the information. Just give me a list of what recipes to ask her for."

Serena smiled. "Thank you so much, Mrs. Redding. How very kind of you."

"You just call me Cook, my lady. Everyone does. Now next time, you let me come to you. It's not fitting for you to be coming to me."

Serena laughed lightly. "I hope you know I will come to see the new stove."

Cook beamed. "Oh, my, yes, *that* will be something special."

Robert had never seen his cook so happy. What did the cost matter, when the Hall was becoming a home?

Serena walked with Robert through the ground floor, then up the back stairs to the first floor, waiting for him to say something about her ordering the stove and the other things. When compared to horses and carriages, they were not expensive, but she doubted he'd have any idea what they cost.

Well, if he didn't bring it up, she certainly wouldn't.

His voice intruded on her thoughts. "Mrs. Norton can tell you how many the Hall sleeps."

They peeped in rooms and Serena listed more questions to ask the housekeeper.

He pointed out the folly that stood at one end of the lake and told her that beyond the wood was the stream where he fished.

Serena was falling quickly in love with the Hall and its people. Even with their undeserved hardships, they'd been warm and welcoming. She'd do what she could to help them while she was here.

"There are still the orchards to look at," he said, "but we won't have time to-day. Would you like to see the kitchen garden?"

Serena brightened. "Of all things!" She'd seen the high stone wall that she thought might be part of the garden—something she'd always wanted.

"Come this way."

They entered through a back gate. The garden was larger than she'd expected and completely walled in. She happily noted the fruit trees trained along the walls and grapes growing up arbors. Neat paths bisected the beds that had already been planted with vegetables and herbs.

His face lit up as he took her around. "It's my favorite garden."

"I can see why. How lovely. Ornamental and functional." And exactly what she'd always dreamed of having. Robert was making it harder for her to leave.

There was nothing of the sophisticated rake in his mien when he pointed out the trees against the wall at the far end of the garden. "We have the best peaches and pears in the area, without the use of succession houses."

"Would succession houses be of benefit here? I think the wall would keep the garden warm enough."

"I believe that is how it works. You can ask the head gardener."

"I shall put him on my list of people to speak with." At this rate she would probably end up adoring the gardener.

Later that afternoon, Freddy glanced up as Robert and Serena entered the Ladies' Morning Room for tea. Freddy handed Serena her cup. "I expected to see you at luncheon."

Serena took a sip. "We had a lot to discuss after going around to the tenants this morning, so we ate in the study."

Robert frowned. "The steward hasn't been keeping up with things as he ought. While Serena spoke with the women in the cottages, I had an opportunity to talk with the men, and none of them are happy."

Serena worried her lip. "Yes, we found everything from houses that need renovation and repairs to out-of-date ploughs."

"Therefore," Robert continued, "we're making lists to present to Foster. Once we've completed them, we'll call the steward in and have a discussion."

Freddy smiled and caught Catherine's eye. Serena and Robert seemed perfect together. She already had her hand on the pulse of the estate and commanded the respect of the servants. Not an easy accomplishment for a lady new to the house and area.

Serena sipped her tea and put down her cup. "I've told Cook to order the new stove she wants. Though it will probably mean picnic dinners for a couple of days, the result will be worth it." Serena glanced at Robert. "What are we doing to-morrow?"

"There are a few tenants yet to see, and we still must visit the rectory."

Serena rubbed a finger over her bottom lip. "Since I was in the kitchen to-day, I shall have to spend time with Mrs. Norton to-morrow, else she'll feel slighted."

"I suppose you're right," Robert said. "How long will it take?"

"She'll want me to inspect every room, the cellars, servants' quarters, as well as the linens, silver, and plates. I can put off the attics until later. She will probably be happy to have the linens left to her, so long as she can buy what she needs." Serena tilted her head as if in thought. "The inspection will take most of the afternoon, if not all of it, I suspect. I'm afraid the rectory will have to wait until the following day."

Robert nodded, "While you're with Mrs. Norton, I'll educate myself on self-molding ploughs."

Serena smiled widely. "Self-scouring moldboards."

Robert grinned. "Yes, those."

"Why don't you take one or two of the tenants with you?" she suggested. "It will give them a sense of ownership over the project."

"That's a nacky idea."

"We've only a few tenants left to visit," Robert said. "We can look at the drainage problem on the way back."

She tried to hide a yawn. "I am going to retire. We have a full day to-morrow."

Robert stood. "I'll walk you up."

They bid their aunts a good evening.

Freddy waited until she thought they were out of hearing and laughed. "Oh, my, I almost didn't make it through the stove. Was anything *so* funny as listening to them? As though they'd been doing this all their lives."

Catherine agreed. "In a way, Serena has. This is where she feels most comfortable."

"But, Robert," Freddy said. "I have never seen him so engaged with the farming aspects. I know he wasn't taught to talk to the dependants. My brother would never have dreamed of doing it. Catherine, what is this about Serena going *into* the cottages?"

"Serena has a way of making people feel at ease so they tell her their problems. If Robert allows her to do as she wishes—and it appears as if he is doing just that—Serena may stay because she'll have a hard time leaving the Hall."

"My mother advised him to let Serena have her head. For once, he's following sound advice." Freddy took a sip of tea. "We may have a wedding yet!"

"I can't think of a better place for her than here. She is so obviously needed," Catherine said, her tone serious. "Whether she'll stay without a declaration from Robert, that is another matter."

"Very true, I agree with you. Robert better step up soon." Freddy smiled impishly. "Because at this rate, Robert will have to find a way to keep Serena, or the staff will turn him out of his home."

Serena and Robert rode out after breakfast the next morning to visit the last of the tenants. She reined in first and was greeted by the men standing outside. Robert lifted her down and began a discussion with them, while Serena entered the first cottage. This one was much older and in far worse repair than the ones she'd seen the day before.

A slight dark-haired woman greeted her without a smile. "My lady."

"May I sit down?"

"I don't know as you want to. We've fleas and other bugs everywhere."

Serena frowned. "Did you tell Mr. Foster?"

"Yes, my lady. We told him last year. Ain't nothin' for it. Look it here at my girls."

Serena inspected the three small girls pushed toward her and saw bites all over their bodies. "Let me see your eyes."

The children opened them.

"Please give me a few moments." Serena walked out and into the other cottage. When she'd finished, she went to Robert and took him aside.

"Robert, these cottages must be burned and rebuilt. They are infested with bugs. The children's eyes are running because of it and they have bites all over their bodies."

"Drat Foster, what has he been doing?" Robert brought himself under control. "How do you suggest we go about doing this? Their belongings need to be dealt with as well."

She explained her plan, but could not keep the fury out of her voice. "I do not know how Foster could have let this go!"

"Let's visit one or two of the other tenants on the way back, and I'll have the carpenter in. Do you wish to be here for it?"

"I think I must."

"Very well." He rubbed her back. "We'll make it happen. Have you told the tenants?"

"Not yet." Serena glanced to where his dependants were standing. "I'll need your help."

"What do you want me to do?"

Her eyes danced. "Nothing much. Just stand there looking fierce, while I get the women on my side."

Serena went back to the group of men and women standing before the cottages.

Robert did as she asked. At first, the men looked angry, but the women gathered closer to her. Serena said something and one glance at Robert's countenance brought the men around.

"What was the problem?" Robert asked when she returned to him.

Serena tried not to laugh. "Only about the baths. Thank you for your dire scowl."

His lips twitched. "My pleasure."

They stopped at the Johnsons and the Armstrongs, the two most formidable of his dependants. Serena asked the women for their help and recommendations. Robert explained the problem and their plan to fix it to the men. He also asked both men if they would like to accompany him to York to purchase new ploughs. They accepted gladly.

"A good half day's work," Robert said, as they rode toward the Hall.

"Yes, the changes we planned will be good. Don't you think?"

"Yes, I do. Serena?"

"Yes?"

"Thank you. I never knew before how much there was to be done here," he said thoughtfully. "I like the challenge of solving the problems and knowing my dependants' lives will be better for it. It's rewarding, gratifying."

Serena nodded. "Because you're helping the people, the families who depend upon you. Is there a greater joy?"

Robert studied her. He'd been so stupid dealing with this woman. He'd used his knowledge of the women he bedded to try to understand her; however, she was unique. How very wrong he'd been. "Come, I'll race you back."

Robert urged Démon into a gallop.

Serena's laughter trailed on the wind as she passed him.

By the time he rode into the stable yard, she stood next to Shamir with a wide smile on her face. Robert swung down from Démon and grabbed her around the waist.

Smiling provocatively, he said, "What do you deserve for beating me as thoroughly as you did?"

"Ah, my lord, you were forewarned."

"I should kiss you," he said, "to assuage my battered ego."

Serena's eyes grew wide with apprehension.

He released her abruptly. "But I won't."

"Thank you." The tightness left her face and she gave him a small smile.

How much more of an idiot could he be? Flirting would

not win her over to him, but it seemed as if he couldn't stop himself from responding to her. He wanted her. Her laughter, her serenity, her gentleness and beauty. She soothed his soul, but if he couldn't give her what she wanted, all would be for naught.

Serena ordered luncheon to be served in the study before escaping to change. When she returned, the carpenter was with Robert.

"Good, show me the plans by the end of the day," Robert said.

She added, "The new cottages must be completed before the first frost sets in."

"Yes, my lady." The carpenter bowed himself out.

"Shall we make our final lists and then call in Foster?" Robert asked.

"Yes, I think we must, don't you?"

He frowned. "I'm not looking forward to it."

She took his hand. "No, how could you? He's an old and trusted retainer, but you've seen what's happening. Ou— people cannot live like that."

Robert heard her. She'd almost said "our people." Two days and she was already part of the Hall and even more a part of him.

Once Serena finished eating, Mrs. Norton came to fetch her.

He met Serena's gaze. "I'll see you later."

"Yes. Mrs. Norton, shall we go?"

"Just come with me, my lady, we need to look at all the hangings . . ."

Robert stared as Serena walked away, her head tilted to listen to Norry, giving the housekeeper her complete attention, just as she had with Cook. As she once had with him.

Yearning filled him as he remembered the joy and trust she'd given so easily until he'd betrayed her.

He went to see if Johnson and Armstrong had arrived. They awaited him in the stable yard and all three of them set off in the wagon to York.

"My lord, have you looked at the drainage problem yet?" Armstrong asked.

"No, we were going to look at it to-day, but the other cottages took our attention. We'll go out first thing in the morning. Do you have any idea what's causing it?"

They shook their heads. Robert encouraged them to discuss the farms and what had been happening since his father died, especially anything concerning his steward.

"He just don't seem interested," Armstrong said. "Not like he was afore."

"How long has that been going on?" Robert asked.

Armstrong replied. "Oh, I'd say the past three or four years. Don't you think, Johnson?"

" 'Bout that. After his wife died."

Foster's wife had died, and Robert hadn't even known about it. He needed to talk with Serena.

After he returned, he sent a message to her to meet him early in the drawing room. When she entered, he handed her a glass of sherry.

Serena took a sip. "What is it?"

"It's Foster. His wife died three or four years ago. That's when the estate began having problems."

Her eyes widened. "You didn't know?"

"No, no one told me. I've spent so little time here." His voice faded. "I didn't have many happy memories here for most of my life."

"That would certainly explain the lack of interest in the estate." Serena looked at him over the rim of the glass. "What to do is still a problem. I can feel compassion for

Foster. However, the neglect cannot be allowed to continue."

"No," Robert said sadly. "Maybe now there's a better chance he'll agree to retire."

Serena put her arms around Robert. "We'll speak with Foster to-morrow."

He wished he could kiss her, seek comfort from her as a man does with a woman. So many of his beliefs about himself were changing.

Serena brought his head down and touched her forehead to his. Then, as if she understood, lightly—very lightly—she kissed him. Robert struggled not to take her lips and her mouth. If there was a hell, he was in it. His life was changing, what of hers?

He stepped back.

Fortunately, their aunts entered the room just ahead of Finster announcing dinner.

"Serena, my dear," Freddy said, "I don't ever remember having such a fine meal here. What did you do to Cook?"

Serena chuckled. "We agreed meals did not have to be as the old lord wanted them. She appears to be very interested in trying new dishes."

"I shall send my compliments to her," Freddy said.

"Please do. It will make her happy."

"My dear, didn't you inspect the house to-day?" Catherine asked.

"Yes, I did." She turned to Robert. "I found the same types of problems, but easily fixed."

He nodded. "What needs to be done?"

"Many of the hangings need to be replaced, as well as some rugs. We will need to paint, of course—it has been years since it's been done. Some of the windows are loose and a few of the fireplaces smoke. Nothing more than I expected," she said. "I was extremely pleased to find everything clean and polished. Mrs. Norton is an excellent house-keeper. She is to give me a list of the linens to be replaced. I've given her carte blanche to purchase what is needed. I'll have to visit a warehouse to select fabrics soon. Would you like to come with me?"

Robert was inordinately pleased that she wanted him to accompany her. "Yes, we can make a day of it, and I'll show you some of the sites in York. Freddy and Catherine can help you shop for materials."

"That sounds delightful," Catherine said. "I know just the warehouse you should visit."

"I wonder if the Black Swan or the Lamb and Lion are still there," Freddy mused. "If they are, we could select one for luncheon."

"Ask Finster to make the arrangements," Robert said.

"Yes, I will!" Freddy grinned. "What are you going to do to-morrow?"

"We were going to visit the rectory," Serena replied. "We've had to put our plans off again. Two of the cottages must be burned and replaced. We will begin that to-morrow. I've already spoken with Mrs. Norton and Cook."

"Burned? Whatever for?" Freddy asked, aghast.

Serena explained what she'd found.

Freddy glanced at Robert. "Where was Foster while all that was going on?"

"His wife passed and it devastated him. He became quite reclusive. We're hoping he'll agree to retire."

"How sad," Freddy said. "He and his wife were very much in love. I can see how he would be lost without her."

Robert had just put more peas on his plate and lost his appetite. A chill of foreboding went through him. What if Serena didn't stay? How long would it take him to recover from losing her? Or would he?

Wanting to change the subject, he said, "It was interesting watching Serena tell the tenants their cottages must be burned." He forced himself to chuckle. "Apparently, the men almost mutinied at being told they'd have to bathe."

His aunt grinned. "Serena, how did you convince them?"

"I didn't have to do anything. Their wives were so happy to be getting new homes they forced their men to agree."

Robert glanced at Serena. He'd been so proud of her today. "It was touch and go for a few minutes. I was just about to step in when I saw the women haranguing their husbands."

Freddy was clearly impressed. "How very brave of you, my dear."

Serena's cheeks turned a lovely shade of rose. "It had to be done, and the women knew it. I truly think it was Robert's intimidating scowl that carried the day."

"I refuse to allow you to underestimate yourself," Freddy said. "Just say, 'Thank you, ma'am.' "

"Thank you, ma'am."

"Aunt Freddy is right. You've been working wonders." Robert met her gaze. She smiled in gratitude and his chest tightened. He wanted to wrap his arms around her and hold her close. He stifled a groan. He wanted to ravage her mouth, make her his, as she, in her innocence, was claiming him.

Instead, he smiled.

After escorting Serena to her room, he forced himself away from her door and back downstairs to have a brandy. His need to touch her was becoming entirely inappropriate. He could barely keep from kissing her now, even in front of others. He could lie to her and tell her he loved her. But she'd know the minute she saw his face. He had a whole new appreciation for the predicament of the men in Aristophanes's play *Lysistrata*.

* * *

Serena sat at the dressing table while Mary pulled the pins out of Serena's hair. The maid had been going on about how welcoming the staff was and how they had taken great pains to make her comfortable.

Serena smiled and nodded at the appropriate times, but inside, sadness overcame her. Everything Mary said was true. The dependants here were hard working and caring. Serena loved the Hall. Leaving would rip her apart.

"We are staying, my lady, aren't we?" Mary asked.

Serena tried unsuccessfully to smile. "I don't know yet, Mary. It depends upon Lord Beaumont." And whether he could offer her the love she so desperately needed.

Chapter Fifteen

Robert and Serena rode out the next morning to supervise the cottage burnings. Some of the other tenants had agreed to take in the newly homeless families until temporary houses could be built. Their meager possessions were already in carts by the time Robert and Serena arrived. She saw to the last-minute questions and instructions, while Robert supervised the structures for the fires.

Mrs. Norton arrived with soup and sandwiches, then ran Serena and Robert off before the bathing began. They galloped over to the field with the drainage problem, and Robert soon found the cause.

"I'm glad to see this can be easily fixed." Robert turned to Serena. "What do you want to do next? Visit the rectory or speak with Mr. Foster?"

She pulled a face. "I choose the rectory. I am not looking forward to our discussion with Mr. Foster."

"Nor I," Robert agreed. "Race?"

She laughed. "You know I always win."

"Give me a five-minute head start?" he asked hopefully.

"Not a chance, my lord." Serena spurred Shamir and was quickly across the field.

"You're a miserable witch, and I love you," he shouted after her.

She was already too far away to hear him, but his heart buoyed. *He'd said it and he'd meant it. He loved her.* His shoulders felt lighter, lighter than he could remember. He urged his horse after her. She and Lora, the rector's wife, were in conversation when he reined in.

"I told her you would be along soon," Serena said saucily.

Lora's eyes danced. "Does she always beat you?"

"Always."

She held back a giggle. "Come in and drink some tea."

John met them at the door. "You've finally made it, I see."

"We have been rather busy," Robert retorted.

"So I've been hearing. Burning down houses, shopping for ploughs, a new stove. You have the whole town talking."

"Does everyone know our business?" Robert asked aghast.

"Robert, it *is* the country. News travels quickly," Serena reminded him.

He shook his head. "I'd forgotten."

Lora smiled knowingly. "News travels especially quickly when it's a new lady causing the changes."

Serena shook out her skirts, but a betraying hint of pink rose in her neck. "I do not understand why so much is being made of doing one's duty."

"It is because you do it so well, my love. Will you excuse John and me for a few moments?" Robert asked. "I'll be right back. I promise."

She nodded. "Yes, of course,"

John led Robert back to the study. "What is this all about?"

"Serena hasn't decided if she'll marry me or not."

"Robert, we saw the announcement in the *Morning Post,* and then you dashed up here and told everyone you were marrying." John looked at his friend. "What did you do?"

Robert paced the room, stopped, and met John's eyes squarely. "I trapped her into marrying me." Robert flung himself into a chair. "Go ahead, tell me I am a fool. I know it."

"You compromised her? Robert, why?"

"I wanted her. She drove me insane, though she did nothing obvious to try to attract me. I went back into the *ton* for her. But she said she wouldn't marry me unless I loved her."

"And?" John asked.

"And now, I love her. I told her so to-day, but she was already too far ahead of me to hear. Now I'm trying to get up my courage to say it to her face. I'm a wreck, what if she changes her mind?"

John gave a short laugh. "Robert, you've found someone to love you, that you love, and who is good for you, and the Hall and Haythrope. Find a way to tell her you love her fast. Otherwise, you'll lose her, then you really will be a fool."

"Yes, you're right." He stood. "Let's go back to the ladies. I told Serena I'd not be long."

"Wait a minute. This is Thursday. I'll announce the banns on Sunday. You have two days."

"I thought you were my friend."

John smiled wryly. "I am."

Serena sat in the cozy parlor, discussing the town and its residents with Lora. "Is there a school?"

"Not as such," Lora said. "Once or twice a week, one of the ladies teaches the children reading and writing. It is very informal and not consistent. They only take the town's children."

Serena frowned. "So none of the estate's children are included?"

"No." Lora tightened her lips. "The feeling is that if the Hall wishes to educate their young, it is their responsibility."

Serena had never confronted this problem in Scotland. "If the estate provided some of the funds, would the town help to support a proper school that included the Hall's children?"

Lora was quiet for a minute, thinking. "Yes, I believe so. You would have to discuss it with the council, but yes, I imagine they would."

"Is there a suitable building in town or must we construct one?"

"Actually, there is a house in the center of town that would support several classrooms. The old lady who lived there died. If her heirs would be willing to sell . . ."

"Will you take me to see it?" Serena asked.

"Now?"

"Yes, why not? I can at least look at the outside."

"Oh, the inside is not a problem either. Hardly anyone locks their doors here. Do you wish to wait for Robert?"

"I don't want to interrupt him."

Lora rose. "Let me tell John where we're going."

She knocked on the door of her husband's study and peeked in. "I'm taking Serena to see old lady Crenshaw's house."

"I think we are finished here," John said.

Robert walked to the door. "May we accompany you?"

"Yes, yes, of course you may," Lora assured him. "I am just going to fetch my hat."

When Robert entered the parlor, Serena smiled at him.

"Why do you want to see the Crenshaw house?" Robert asked.

She told him about the lack of a proper school and the problem with the estate's children.

His eyes twinkled. "So, we'll start a school?"

"Yes."

"I am pleased to see you don't do things by half-measures, my dear."

The kiss he gave to her cheek stunned her into silence.

Serena approached the front door of Crenshaw House and paused.

"Allow me." Robert opened the door and surreptitiously brushed her cheek again as she entered and followed around as she made an inspection.

Despite her broken concentration, she nodded. "I think this would work."

"With space to grow," Lora said.

Serena worried her lower lip and looked at Robert. "I think the Hall should own it. I would not like to be always quarrelling with the council over the building's use. The council should help pay for the teachers, of course."

"I agree," John said. "With the arguing that goes on at council meetings, it's a better idea for the Hall to own the building."

Robert looked thoughtful for a moment. "In that case, I'll look into the purchase without involving the council."

The four of them were on their way back to the rectory when two women came up to John. One of the women supported an obviously distraught friend.

"Mr. Stedman, you must help! I don't know what to do. A man came and took Silly's son yesterday. He said he had the right to do it. She finally came to me to-day in vapors."

"Someone took her son?" John asked. "Where was he?"

"Well it's hard to get anything out of her," the woman replied. "She's been crying so much."

Serena stepped forward. "Let me talk to her." Putting her arm around Silly, Serena bent her head, and set herself to calming the woman as she walked toward the rectory. "You must tell me what happened so we can help you."

Haltingly, Silly said, "He were a big hulking man. He come out of the woods and saw my Jemmy and grabbed him and I screamed and tried to pull Jemmy back. And the man told me he had the law on his side to take my Jemmy to work in the mines. Jemmy, he's my oldest." She sobbed. "He does odd jobs and helps with the young'uns. Oh, I don't know what I'm going to do without him."

Serena's heart contracted. What could be worse than losing a child? She looked back over to John, Robert, and Lora. "What do you know about this?"

John pressed his lips together. "It is common enough farther south, but we're so remote we've not seen it here. They must be desperate if they are coming this far north."

"*Do* they have the right to take children?" It would be infamous. "I can't imagine that they could. That's barbaric."

"I agree," Robert replied. "We'll have to consult a solicitor."

Serena couldn't believe something like this was happening. "Is he the only one who has been taken?"

John shook his head. "I have not heard of any others. However, children disappear from time to time. It's possible someone's been poaching them."

"Well, they're not going to poach the children here." Robert's countenance hardened. "When we go to York tomorrow, I'll stop by the solicitor's office to learn what the law is. But no matter what, I'll not stand for it. Where exactly was the boy taken?"

"Do you remember that group of cottages bordering the wood at the other end of town?" Silly asked.

"That's Hall property. I'll tell my gamekeeper to keep an eye out for any strangers. You'll need to spread the word in town. Serena and I shall speak with the squire. He's been acting as magistrate in my absence."

Robert and Serena rode back to the Hall in a subdued mood.

Robert cursed under his breath. "I've clearly not been spending enough time here, if someone thinks they can take the Hall's children with impunity."

"You are here now. That's what is important. Robert, we must stop this outrage."

He glanced at her, his eyes burning with anger. "We will."

The squire, Sir Baldwin, and his lady were in the small drawing room with Freddy when Robert and Serena returned. They'd missed luncheon, were hungry, and had work to do, but now, Serena and Robert had no choice but to join their guests. At least, Robert wouldn't have to spend time chasing Sir Baldwin down to discuss the abductions.

"Sir Baldwin, Lady Harriman, how nice to see you." Robert bowed to Lady Harriman and shook the older gentleman's hand. "My dear, allow me to present Sir Baldwin and his wife. Sir Baldwin is the squire and the master of the hunt. Lady Serena Weir."

"Lady Harriman, Sir Baldwin, what a pleasure it is to meet you." Serena shook their hands and took a seat.

"Well," Sir Baldwin said, "as we've been telling your aunt, we wanted to stop by and welcome you to the county, Lady Serena."

Lady Harriman curtseyed. "Indeed. We would not want to be backward in welcoming you to the Hall, my lady."

Robert smiled with pride as Serena artfully drew Lady Harriman out concerning the families in the area while he spoke with Sir Baldwin about the kidnapping. It occurred to him that Serena was nothing like his mother and grandmother who favored London. Serena already loved the area and its people and she glowed with a confidence he'd not seen in Town.

Sir Baldwin promised to make inquiries about the missing children and have his servants keep an eye out for Jemmy. A half an hour later, Robert walked them to the door.

"That," Freddy sapiently observed, "will be the first of many visits you may expect to receive."

"I must change now." Serena darted out the door of the drawing room.

Robert caught up with her on the stairs. "Meet me in the study. I'll have Norry bring us a nuncheon."

"Thank you. I'm so peckish."

Serena slipped into the study just as a footman was leaving. She surveyed the feast set out on the desk. "Oh, this is wonderful."

Robert held the chair for her as she sat to the side of his desk. They ate in silence, while Robert tried to find the perfect way to tell her he loved her. He'd put Serena through so much, she deserved that it be special.

Sitting back, she wiped her fingers on a serviette. "You're very quiet."

She was beautiful and everything he could ever want in a wife and lover. And now, she'd stay and love his home and their children. Robert felt almost giddy at the thought of his life with this magnificent woman. "I'm merely thinking."

He'd wait until they were finished with their repast.

A few moments later, Griffin, the head gardener, came in wishing to speak with Lady Serena.

"Mr. Griffin, I will be with you shortly." She turned to Robert. "I forgot I am to meet with him to-day. I have no idea how long this will take. He plans to discuss the formal gardens with me. They've not been replanted in many years."

"Yes, that's fine." It wasn't, but what was Robert to say? "If you don't mind, I'll speak with Foster while you are with Griffin." Robert came out from behind the desk. "Serena, there is something I wish to tell you."

Finster knocked and opened the door. "My lady, Cook is awaiting your pleasure in the Ladies' Morning Room. I take it the matter is of some urgency."

Serena sighed. "I'm sorry Robert, can you tell me later?"

"Yes, we'll take a stroll after dinner."

"I'll see you in the drawing room." He kissed her hands and she left.

Robert scowled at the closing door. He hadn't wanted to wait until this evening. Damn it. He loved her and she deserved to know. The suspense had him in knots.

Robert glanced up as Serena descended the stairs, dressed this evening in a bronze silk trimmed with a cream lace. A shard of sun coming through the window struck her hair and made it shimmer. His gaze focused on the large amethyst drop that hung down, almost touching the gathered silk of her bodice, and on that infernal curl caressing her breast. Tonight, he'd tell her he loved her. He'd wrap the curl around his fingers, draw her close, and kiss her senseless. All he had to do was make it through dinner.

Excited at the prospect and on the verge of making his

and Serena's excuses to their aunts, Robert stifled a growl when Finster entered and announced the arrival of Lord and Lady Bell, Miss Bell and Mr. Bell. Robert and Serena's eyes met. Another delay. They rose and greeted their guests.

Although the Bells stayed for only thirty minutes, Tom Rush, an old friend of Robert's, and Tom's wife were announced as the Bells were leaving.

"I tried to get her to hold off"—Tom grinned with good humor—"but once she'd heard that Sir Baldwin and his lady had come by, there was no stopping her."

Holding back a curse, Robert shook Tom's hand. "After the squire visited we knew we'd have the whole county upon our doorstep. Lady Serena, please allow me to introduce Mr. Thomas Rush and Emma, his wife. Tom and I grew up together."

Serena greeted them. "Mr. and Mrs. Rush, how pleased I am to meet friends of Robert's."

Mrs. Rush curtseyed. "Please, call us Tom and Emma. We do not stand on ceremony with anyone at the Hall."

Serena smiled. "Thank you. You're very kind."

The ladies quickly became involved in a comfortable coze. Serena seemed to be immediately drawn to Emma, who was about her age, but had been married to Tom for several years.

By the time their guests finally left, Serena looked done up.

She glanced at Robert. "May we speak to-morrow? I'm too tired to think."

"Of course." Robert's plans for the night vanished. He silently cursed. "I like my neighbors, but this evening I could have happily consigned them all to the devil."

Serena's lips curved up. "How many more visitors may we expect?"

"Several, I should imagine." Somehow, he'd have to find

time alone with her before Sunday and the announcement of the banns; otherwise, she'd never forgive him.

The following morning, Serena, Robert, and their aunts gathered for their trip to York. Catherine and Freddy chose to ride in the carriage. Robert enticed Serena to take his curricle with a promise that she could handle his high-couraged grays.

Her eyes sparkled with mischief. "How very brave of you to allow me to handle the ribbons, my lord."

"Not at all. You are an excellent whip." He handed her up. "While you and our aunts are at the fabric warehouse, I'll go round to the solicitor. Where did Freddy finally make reservations for luncheon?"

"The Lamb and Lion. It's closer to the warehouse."

While the ladies spent all of the morning selecting fabrics for new bed, chair, and sofa covers, hangings, as well as drapes, Robert had a good visit with the solicitor and then made his own purchase. He was already in the private parlor in the inn when they arrived.

Robert smiled smugly and waited.

Serena removed her hat and gloves. "You must have good news."

"Yes, indeed, the best. That villain cannot legally take any of the children without their parents' permission. If we find him, we can hold him for kidnapping."

Serena hugged Robert. "I knew his claim couldn't be true. Now we'll have to let everyone know that that beast is lying. Then, we must think of a plan to catch him."

Robert resisted the urge to pull her closer, their aunts be damned, but he hadn't told her he loved her yet. "We'll find him. I promise you, I shall not allow this to continue."

Serena's face glowed with happiness. "I know you won't."

Grinning, he said, "I also made a purchase of my own."

"What is it?"

"Patience, my love. You will have to wait until to-morrow to see it. It's being delivered before noon."

"Is it for me?"

"Partly," he teased. "You'll just have to wait."

Freddy had been right—the social floodgates had opened. That evening, others of their neighbors presented themselves at the Hall to meet Serena. Freddy had just said good-bye to Mrs. Edgecombe, when Lord Malfrey was announced.

She looked around, stunned, unable to believe her eyes. Her heart slammed in her chest. "Edward? Is it really you? You haven't changed a bit."

"Freddy?" His gray eyes darkened and he came to stand in front of her. "I—I didn't know you were here. You're as beautiful as I remember. How have you been?"

They gazed at each other, and she felt the familiar warmth of her hands being engulfed in his. It had been so long since she'd last felt his touch. She'd missed him so.

By the time Robert and Serena reached them, Freddy had re-collected herself. "Serena, Robert, allow me to introduce Lord Malfrey. He used to be Mr. Timmons and was raised near here. Edward, my nephew, Viscount Beaumont, and Lady Serena Weir, who is visiting."

Edward bowed. "I apologize, my lord, for not making myself known to you earlier. We never seem to be here at the same time."

"No matter. I remember old Lord Malfrey. I thought his heir had some sort of outlandish name."

"Yes, I daresay you are referring to Cosmos, my cousin. I was next in line to the title after him."

Freddy's heart thudded. "When did you become the heir?"

"Shortly after you left."

She struggled to school her countenance into something resembling a smile. "How—how nice for you." She couldn't think of anything else to say or do, but she daren't remain standing there, or she might burst into tears.

They were silent for a few moments and Robert said, "Lord Malfrey, do you know everyone else here, or shall I introduce you?"

"Thank you. I know everyone."

Edward was staring at Freddy like he used to and she felt warm and flushed. What a shock to see him after all these years.

Serena touched Freddy's arm. "Freddy, it is such a warm evening. Would you like to go out to the terrace with me?"

Thank the Lord for Serena's quick wits. "Yes, yes, I would."

Edward still had hold of Freddy's hand. "May I join you ladies?"

"Of course," Serena said.

Lord Malfrey offered his arms to them and they walked onto the terrace.

Once there, Serena directed their steps away from the doors. "If you'll excuse me, I must attend to our guests who are just leaving. Enjoy the night."

Chapter Sixteen

Freddy stared out over the garden. Her throat tightened and tears threatened. Edward stood close behind her. She closed her eyes as his heat radiated through her. Twenty-two years. Yet she'd never forgotten him.

"Freddy?"

She turned and gazed up into his warm gray eyes. Her body thrummed, and she leaned toward him, wanting his arms around her.

"Lady Serena is a very astute young lady."

"Yes, we have hopes she'll marry Robert." Freddy's voice hitched. "Edward."

He reached out and with one long finger caressed her jawline. When he reached her chin, his hand cupped her face and his lips brushed softly against hers. His tone was rough. "Freddy."

She reached up and clasped her hands around his neck.

The years fell away as she returned the pressure of his kiss. "Oh God, I've missed you."

The next morning at the breakfast table, Serena handed Robert a cup of tea. "How was your meeting with Foster?"

"He wants to retire. One of his daughters lives in Harrogate, and she's been after him to come live with her. He looked so down in the mouth that, coupled with his desire to leave, I didn't think there was any reason to discuss the estate problems with him."

"I agree. I'd like to check on the tenants' temporary houses. I understand they've been completed."

He smiled. It was due to her they'd been finished so quickly. "I'll meet you in the stables."

Robert rose from the table and called to Finster after she'd left the room. "I have a new desk for my study arriving to-day to replace the old one. If I've not returned by the time it's delivered, supervise the placing of the desk yourself."

"Yes, my lord."

Robert attained the stables just as Serena was about to mount.

She shivered when he placed his hands on her to toss her onto Shamir. He almost told her that he loved her. But he wanted them to be alone, not in the stable yard with a curious audience.

They'd barely cleared the fence to the meadow when they gave their horses their heads. Galloping through the clear morning air, he saw the joy in her face at being free to ride as she wished, not hemmed in by London's proprieties.

They didn't slow until the new buildings were in sight. Serena greeted the women and children who came to meet her and accompanied them into their temporary homes. Robert stayed by the horses until Serena returned.

"How are the women and children doing?"

"Much better. Nary a bug bite present. They are so much happier."

"Good. I'm glad it worked."

When they arrived back at the Hall, he lifted Serena down and led her to the study. He stopped at the closed door, and she glanced at him curiously. Reaching around her, Robert threw it open to reveal his surprise.

Serena glanced from Robert to the room and could barely believe what she saw. "Oh, Robert, a partner's desk. This is what you bought in York?"

"Yes, and I think it's even better than the one Marcus and Phoebe have."

"Much better."

Serena turned and found herself in his arms; her heart fluttered as his hands framed her face, and his lips moved softly on hers.

"Serena," Robert murmured. "I have been trying to tell you for two days that I love you and each time we've been interrupted. Serena, I love you and I can't live without you. Please say you'll marry me before I go mad."

"Are you sure you want to marry a miserable witch?" She teased, recalling his words.

"You heard me?"

She tried to maintain a slightly haughty expression, but lost the battle when he drew her closer. "I have very acute hearing, my lord."

He placed soft kisses beneath her ear and down her neck. Every nerve in her body came alive. "You haven't answered me."

Someone knocked on the door. "Go away!" Robert shouted.

"But, my lord."

Robert stalked to the door and opened it, startling the footman standing on the other side. "I don't care who wants what or whom. No one is allowed to knock on this door for the next thirty minutes. You may stand here and guard it."

"Yes, my lord. Of course, my lord."

Robert closed the door, locked it, and took her in his arms once again. "Now, where were we, my lady? Ah yes, I remember. You owe me an answer."

She could have cried with happiness. This was everything she'd wanted. He was everything she wanted. "Yes, I will marry you, my lord."

He claimed her mouth, scattering her wits, demanding she respond. Robert's tongue teased the seam of her lips and she opened them, allowing him to take possession. His kisses encouraged her to respond to him as she had before. Serena tried to keep up with him, but succumbed to the pleasure he gave her. He slid his hands, heavy and possessive, down her back and over her derrière. As he molded her to him she felt the proof of his arousal and shivered under his touch.

He was no longer the experienced rake tempting her to go beyond where she should, but the man who would love and keep her. The man who would be her husband and the father of her children. The man she'd not been able to resist. The man she loved to distraction.

Serena stretched her arms up to clutch the back of his neck, letting her fingers play with his blond curls. Robert responded with almost frightening intensity. His hands continued to roam as if he had to touch all of her to make her his.

She pressed herself into him, craving his touch. When he pulled back, she tried to draw him close again.

"Serena, my love," he mumbled into her mouth. "If we don't stop, your first experience making love will be on top of our new desk."

She pulled back and looked into his moss-green eyes, warm with passion, and tried to think, unable to take in what he was saying. Making love? *On the desk?* Would he really take her here, now? "Oh."

Robert smiled down at her. "That is not how I've planned it."

Serena was finally able to emerge from the haze his kisses caused and curiosity took over. "You have a plan?"

He kissed her deeply, and when he lifted his head, his smile was different, wolfish.

"I most definitely have a plan."

Robert's voice mesmerized her as he caressed her again. His hands moved with a feather-light touch slowly up over her waist and under her breasts. Little fires danced beneath Serena's skin, her breasts tingled, and her nipples hardened. Robert gently touched the curls at her neck and a sensual shiver ran through her.

She could barely breathe. "What . . . what is your plan?"

His voice was deep and soft as velvet. "To make you want me as much as I want you. That's not something you can understand now, but you will. Soon."

"Soon?" Serena swallowed. "Don't you want me to be a—a virgin on our wedding night?"

"No, most emphatically, no. I want you to be my partner on our wedding night."

She searched his eyes and a slow wicked smile played on his lips.

Trembling, she said, "I think our thirty minutes must be about up."

"We have a little more time." He captured her lips and her senses and she let him sweep her away. His hands never stopped and her body learned to anticipate each touch and crave the next.

When he finally lifted his head, and held her closer, she framed his face with her hands and, for the first time, she murmured, "I love you."

Robert reveled in her breathy kisses, her love, and her body responding to his touch. But he kept tight control over the part of him that wanted to take her now. He tensed as he fought urges stronger than he'd ever experienced before. How could he want this woman so badly? This was so much more than mere lust. He needed her like he needed to breathe—and her first time making love would be painful enough—and he'd be the cause. For that, he'd need a bed. The desk would have to wait.

He unlocked the door and asked the footman to have luncheon brought to them. While they ate, Robert sent a note to John and penned quick letters to St. Eth, Marcus, Rutherford, and his London solicitor. His letter to his grandmother was even shorter.

Dear Grandmama,
You were right. The wedding is in just over two weeks.
Yours,
Beaumont

Serena enclosed notes to St. Eth, Phoebe, and Anna, and wrote a postscript on Robert's letter to Lady Beaumont.

My Dear Ma'am,
Thank you for your help and advice.
My love,
Serena

Robert raised a brow in enquiry.

"I'll tell you some day," she promised.

"I'll need to write to your brother asking permission, or at least informing him we are marrying." Other than telling Robert how her Season had come about, Serena had not mentioned her brother.

Her chin firmed. "No, I'll write him."

"My love, won't he think it odd?"

"Robert, I really do not care what he thinks. He could not have known sending me to London would turn out well. He did it to get rid of me. I have been my own mistress for many years now. You need have no one's permission to marry me other than mine. I'll write and inform him of our marriage."

He pulled her to her feet, into his arms, and kissed her. "It shall be as you wish."

Serena returned his kiss. "Thank you."

On Sunday, Robert met Serena coming from the corridor where her chamber was located. "Are you ready to hear the banns read and face everyone in the area wishing us happy?"

She smiled calmly. "Yes, I am."

He wished he could be so composed, but his heart tightened with anticipation. If anyone made an objection, he'd beat them to a pulp. "Well then, we should go."

Placing her hand on his arm, she said, "We cannot leave without Freddy and Catherine."

Freddy joined them moments later. "Serena, you look perfect."

Robert took Serena's hands and kissed them. "You always look perfect."

She glanced around. "Where is Aunt Catherine?"

"I am right here. Shall we leave?" Catherine squeezed Serena's arm reassuringly.

They arrived at the church even earlier than Robert planned, but in the indefinable way of country life, word had gotten out that the rector would read the banns and the wedding date would be announced. The church was already full and spilling over.

Robert escorted her as they made their way to the family pew. Needing to touch her, he held her hand tightly while John read the banns. After the service, Robert stayed by her side as they ran the expected gauntlet of well-wishers. It seemed like everyone from the town, the Hall, and most of the countryside had come to congratulate them.

His heart filled with pride as Serena met the locals and made a point to discover something about each one of them. She took the time to mention the school, probing the feelings of the town's citizens.

"It looks like your betrothed has come off fine."

Robert turned to Tom Rush. "She has, hasn't she?"

"I'll tell you, we've been a little concerned about who you would finally bring home, but you've done a good job."

A joy Robert hadn't known before settled over him. He had picked the right woman. After years of fearing marriage and love, he'd found exactly the right female to spend his life with, and he couldn't be happier. "I know."

Sunday dinner at the Hall was served after church. As he took his place at the table he glanced around. Only Serena and their aunts were present.

"Do my eyes deceive me, Freddy? Malfrey's *not* here?" he asked in a teasing voice.

Lord Malfrey had joined them for luncheons and dinners so often, Robert was expecting to find him at breakfast one day.

Freddy, without coloring even a little, retorted, "I didn't

think he would be interested in helping with your wedding plans."

"Oh my," Serena said. "We have only two weeks to arrange the wedding. I didn't even think to ask Phoebe and Aunt Ester to come up early."

Catherine smiled. "I don't think you need worry, my dear. I expect to see them within a week of receiving your letters."

Nodding, Serena replied, "You're right. They'll naturally expect to help."

Soon his house would be overrun with her relatives, and their peace cut up. Robert groaned and received narrow-eyed looks from the ladies.

"It's not that I don't want to see them," he made haste to explain, for being in bad loaf with Serena was not what he wanted. "I only expected to have a little more time for us to be alone."

His plan to seduce her slowly as well as his desire to have her closer would have to be moved up. Robert flashed a glance at his betrothed. "I received word that the viscountess's chamber is done."

Serena nodded, but her attention was distracted by her aunt.

Catherine's eyes sparkled. "We should make a guest list and begin arranging the wedding breakfast. How many will the Hall sleep?"

Serena's jaw dropped. "Why does that matter? I thought we could have a small wedding, just family and a few friends."

Freddy looked up. "Serena, you will not be allowed a small wedding."

Robert reached out to cover her hand. "Freddy's right, my love."

This time Serena groaned. "I don't understand why not."

Catherine gave her a sympathetic look and explained, "The St. Eths and the Beaumonts are among the oldest and most prestigious families in England. Both lines can be traced back to the Conqueror. It would not do to cause talk by having what would be seen as a shabby wedding."

Robert felt remorse at Serena's distress. What Catherine didn't say was that if he hadn't done what he did at Merton, Serena might have had a small wedding. Perhaps it was good that her family would be here. "I'm sorry, my love."

Serena made an attempt to smile. "No, no, I quite understand."

Catherine glanced at them all. "Well, if no one minds, I would like to go home for a few days before all the excitement begins. I've had a letter from my steward and there are some problems I must address. I'm not far, if you need me."

Assured they would be fine on their own, Catherine left the table to make her travel arrangements.

Robert glanced at Serena. "Have you noticed a change in the staff? They seem to have closed ranks around us. I heard a tweenie tell someone to-day after the service that she didn't comment on anything that happened at the Hall. By the other girl's expression, I gather that has not always been the case."

Serena glanced up at the ceiling. "*I* would be amazed if the staff is not expecting an *interesting event* in nine months, considering you locked the door and set a guard."

"Robert." Freddy laughed. "When did you do that?"

He hadn't thought of what anyone would think. Robert gave them a sheepish smile. "When I asked Serena to marry me. I'd been trying to do it for two days, and we were constantly being interrupted. I became a little desperate, I'm afraid."

"As your chaperone, I should be appalled. As your aunt, I find it very funny. Edward is coming for me soon. I shall see you this evening, my dears." Freddy rose from the table and left.

Robert gazed at Serena. "I haven't shown you the wood or the folly yet."

"No, do you think we'll be left alone?"

"Yes, Sunday is a true day of rest here. No one will come for us unless it's a crisis."

They walked hand in hand through the woodland path to the folly, which was in the style of an old cottage. Robert opened the door for Serena to enter.

A fireplace stood at the end of the room, opposite the door. The inside was clean and well furnished with a table and four stools, a couple of comfortable chairs, and a chaise. Large windows looked out over the lake, with a view to the front of the Hall.

Serena walked around and halted at the windows. "Robert, how lovely. Is someone using this place?"

"I had Norry fix it up for you. There might come a time when you want a little peace and quiet, away from everyone. Until then . . ."

Robert came to a stop behind Serena and put his arms around her. He loved the way she reacted when he touched her. A little pause, an intake of breath. Playing with the curls at the back of her neck made her pulse race. Robert relished her innocence and looked forward to teaching her how much pleasure she could find in his arms, in his bed.

Serena leaned back against him and sighed. Moving his hands in concert, he caressed the sensitive area under her breasts. Her nipples tightened in response. She arched as he gently kneaded the two perfect mounds. When Serena's legs gave way and she started to slide down, Robert, chuckling, picked her up and lowered them both onto the chaise. Loosening her laces and stays, he gently pushed them down.

Shuddering breaths escaped her as he stroked. Serena

gave him so much satisfaction with her ingenuous, uninhibited responses. Robert's chest swelled with the knowledge she was finally his. Drawing her against him, he fluttered kisses against her jaw and neck. When her lips opened on a soft moan, he possessed her mouth as he intended to possess her body, running his tongue over her teeth, exploring until she responded in kind. Robert cared so much about the pleasure he could give her. This was what love was.

Serena stroked his back and chest, greedily feeling the muscles under his shirt. He moaned. Lying on his side, Robert pulled her closer, once more molding her bottom to his body. The ridge of his erection rode against her stomach. One hard thigh moved to settle between her legs.

She was on fire and frissons of pleasure raced through her. How did he do that? Robert held her to their kiss until she had no choice but to breathe through him. The laces on the back of her gown and stays loosened. Before she understood what had happened, her breasts were bare against his jacket, her bodice around her waist.

Serena gasped as Robert pressed light kisses down her neck and over her breasts. Her nipples ached with need. His tongue licked one nipple then took it into his warm mouth. She made a thin keening noise and pressed into him. More, she needed more.

One moment Robert was kissing her then the next his mouth and tongue were like butterflies teasing her neck and breasts. His hard leg pressed against the apex of her thighs made her ache for something, but what? When he took her nipple into his mouth, waves of intense pleasure shot through her. The tremor took her by surprise. Her whole body shook with a wonderful relief, and she sank against him. He pulled up a warm blanket and held Serena until she awoke.

"Robert."

"What, my love?"

"What was that . . . that trembling I felt?"

"That, my sweet, was an orgasm."

Serena was silent for a moment. "What is an orgasm?"

Robert shifted her and met her eyes with a frown. "Has no one ever discussed anything sexual with you?"

"No. I know about breeding, of course. I mean I had to. We had cattle and horses and the like, but they didn't appear to me to be enjoying it overmuch. What I felt was definitely enjoyable."

"An orgasm is what happens when a gentleman properly pleasures a lady. I promise you'll have many more."

He settled her back against him, closer than before. He'd had no idea she was such an innocent. All the women he'd been with had been experienced, but Serena was a blank sheet, a woman he could mold into his perfect lover and mate. Robert pressed his lips tenderly against her temple and smiled.

Chapter Seventeen

They remained wrapped in each other's arms until Serena heard a carriage.

She nudged him. "My love, someone is here."

He stood and looked out the window. "I don't recognize the carriage. Turn around, I'll help you dress."

Robert quickly tied her stays and gown and straightened her hair. They walked hurriedly to the house through the back garden, holding hands.

Finster, his habitual aloofness fraying, met them as they entered the morning room. "My lord, my lady, Mr. Stedman is here. Another child has been taken."

Robert tightened his grip on her. Glancing back over her shoulder, Serena called, "Finster, where have you put him?"

"In the front parlor, my lady."

Not that she needed to ask as Robert bellowed, "John!"

John stepped out of a room near the front hall.

"Tell me what's happened," Robert said.

"Mrs. Brown came to me not more than twenty minutes ago, and told me her younger son came running in saying some large man took his brother. Hugo is about ten years old."

"It sounds as if our friend is still here," Robert growled. "Finster, find everyone you can. We need to begin searching."

"John," Serena asked, "where was he kidnapped?"

"On the stream bank, near the cottages at the end of town. Near where the first lad was taken."

Serena pressed her lips together. "That is Hall property, is it not?"

John nodded.

Robert would have to show his dependants he could protect them. "Robert, you take the curricle and I'll drive the gig. I'll be fine. My groom shall come with me. We need to have as many people searching as possible, and, if we find Hugo, Will can help me bring the boy back."

"Serena, instead of your groom, take Pitchley. He knows the land. I'll ride Démon. It'll be faster, and I can get into more places."

She nodded and turned to the stables. Robert grabbed her waist and pulled her to him. "Be careful, my love." He kissed her and let her go.

Serena blushed.

John smiled and turned his head.

Serena reached the stables just as the gig was being brought out. Will approached. "Pitchley shall accompany me," she told her groom. "He knows the area better. Right now that's what we need. You go with someone local who can show you around. The more people we have looking, the better chance we'll have of finding the child."

Will had protected her since she was little and so now he narrowed his eyes, but finally nodded. "Yes, my lady."

Serena squeezed his arm. "Thank you, Will."

"Up with you, my lady." Pitchley handed her into the carriage.

She glanced at Robert's groom. "Hugo went missing near the stream, by the cottages at the end of the town. Tell me where we should go first."

"There is a shortcut back o' the town. We'll go that way."

She gave the horses their office.

Pitchley directed her over to a lane on the other side of the stream. She dropped the horses to a walk while he searched through the trees and underbrush. Suddenly, a boy darted onto the path, being chased by a burly man.

"You come back here, you scamp," the man shouted, "or I'll have the law on you."

"Hugo," Serena called, "this way."

The boy stopped and stared at her.

"Pitchley, quickly, help him."

The groom jumped down to intercept the kidnapper, now within an arm's length of the child. Serena moved the carriage forward and struck the man across the face with her whip. He bellowed and fell back, giving Pitchley time to grab the lad's thin arm and toss him into the gig. The blackguard caught the side of the carriage, and, her heart in her throat, she whipped up the horses. Finally, he fell behind.

After they left the lane and Pitchley directed her toward town, she spoke to the boy. "Hugo, isn't it?"

"Yes, ma'am, but how'd you know?"

"Your mother went to the rector, who came to the Hall to tell us. There are a lot of people looking for you."

"Lor', ma'am. Lookin' for me?"

Pitchley cuffed the lad lightly. "That's *my lady,* to you, young scallywag,"

"Lor', my lady," Hugo obediently repeated.

The groom grinned. "You'll do."

"Hugo, do you know where that man was taking you?" Serena asked.

"Aye, my lady. Had me tied up at some sort o' camp."

"Could you find it again?"

"We can go there now, if you want."

"No, we'll send some of the men."

Pitchley directed Serena to turn down yet another lane. In short order, they arrived at the rectory. Hugo's mother stood with Lora. Hugo scrambled down from the gig, ran to his mother, and hugged her.

"Pitchley, you may go find his lordship now. I'll be fine by myself."

"No, my lady. His lordship would be reet upset if I left you."

"Lora, Hugo knows where the man's camp is. We need to send a message to Robert or someone to go after the kidnapper."

"John is here with some of the others," Lora said. "The rectory has become the search headquarters."

"Show me, please." Pitchley helped Serena down.

She turned to the child. "Hugo, come with me."

The boy followed in Serena's wake.

Lora knocked on the door to her husband's office and walked in. "Lady Serena is here. She found the lad."

"Lady Serena!" John exclaimed. "Thank the Lord."

"Hugo saw the villain's camp. He may have left it already, but these men here can search for the site."

She turned to walk out, but when she didn't hear them following, she glanced back and fixed them with a look.

They glimpsed at each other and John, but none of the town's men would meet her gaze.

Did they not want to follow a woman? That would have to change. She raised a haughty brow. "Gentlemen, *now,* if you please! This blackguard is kidnapping our children. If you are *afraid*"—she let the word hang in the air—"I will go myself, and you may explain yourselves to his lordship."

They muttered, stirring.

"Which is it to be?" She turned and walked out the door, hesitant footsteps followed. Taking Hugo and Pitchley with her in the gig, Serena led the men to the wood.

"You will know the blackguard by a recent slash across his right cheek."

Minutes later, Robert rode up to Serena, where she waited.

"What's happened?" he asked.

"We found Hugo. He'd escaped from the kidnapper and he's now leading some of the townsmen to the outlaw's camp."

Robert drew his brows together. "Were the men searching near here?"

"No, I found a group of men in the rectory."

An enigmatic smile played on Robert's lips. "How did you convince them to join the search?"

"I told them they must help and if they were afraid, I would go myself, and they could explain that to you. Why are you grinning?"

"My love, they were explaining to John why *they* could not look for the boy."

"Oh . . . oh, my." Serena laughed.

"You should'a seen her, my lord." Pitchley said proudly. "It was the prettiest piece o' work I ever seen. Her ladyship led them here and pointed them to the woods. Told 'em to look for a man with his cheek laid open. Her ladyship did that herself."

"Maybe I'd better go and find out how they're doing," Robert said. "I'll meet you back at the rectory. Pitchley, stay with her."

"I'll stay reet here with her ladyship, my lord." The groom told Robert where they had rescued the boy.

Serena turned the gig, drove back to the rectory, and assured Hugo's mother that his lordship was with the other men. Once inside with a cup of tea, Serena yielded to the entreaties of the other ladies to tell her tale.

Over an hour later, Robert returned without the culprit. Though disappointed, Serena wasn't surprised. The man had probably made himself scarce after they'd saved Hugo.

Hugo, whom Robert had brought with him, was in high ropes. The boy had ridden on his lordship's horse which was slap up to the echo.

Only Lora, John, and Hugo's mother remained in the rectory when Robert returned. "The scoundrel wasn't there, but he did leave some items behind." Robert turned to Serena. "We don't know where the villain has gone but he'll be dangerous. He'll not soon forget you whipped him."

"No, I daresay he won't." Serena sighed. "If your game warden takes a look at the camp, he should be able to tell us something more."

"I like the way your mind works." Robert grinned. "I've already had my game warden out there. He's the reason we found what we did."

"Did you find any trace of the other boy, Silly's son?"

"No, which means they're collecting the children and taking them off."

This was the worst possible news. "Silly will be heartbroken."

"We'll stop them." Robert gazed at Serena. "Can you doubt it after our success to-day? Come. Let's go home, my love."

Robert lightly caressed her cheek and she smiled. "Yes, Robert, let's go home."

As she rode beside him, Serena realized she really was a part of Haythrope and the Hall, and she was very glad she was staying.

A large man with a lacerated cheek sat at a table tucked in the back of a hedge tavern, a few miles from Haythrope, nursing an ale. He looked up as another man sat down. The newcomer, obviously a gentleman, was dressed in a many-caped drab coat and wore a hat with a large brim pulled low, shadowing his face.

The large man shifted in his seat and tried not to meet the gentleman's eyes.

"I told you, did I not," he said, clipping his words, "to leave Haythrope when the cry was sent up after you grabbed the first boy?"

"Aye, but I saw the other one and thought he'd be easy pickings," the man said, trying to defend himself.

"You are not paid to think. It is, obviously, a skill you've not developed. Leave Haythrope and its environs. The people there do not take kindly to their children being taken."

"What about that bitch that done this?" He pointed to his face.

The gentleman's voice turned to ice. "You'll certainly not approach that *lady*. If any harm were to come to her, I could not ensure your safety. Indeed, I would not even try. You brought this on yourself. Live with it and move on to a different area."

The man watched the gentleman go and said in an under voice, as if the gentleman could still hear, "The trouble with bloody toffs is they got no loyalty. Never want to get their precious hands dirty. But I'll get my revenge."

* * *

The next day, Catherine handed two full sheets of paper to Serena. "Here is my list. Have you taken care of your father's side of the family?"

Serena took the foolscap and was relieved to find the roll of names was not as long as she'd thought. "Not yet. I'll include it when we send the letter to Robert's secretary."

Catherine embraced Serena. "I'll see you in a few days, my dear."

Lord Malfrey pulled up to fetch Freddy as she was waving to Catherine.

Robert turned to Serena. "No one is around to play gooseberry." He sighed, his smile wicked. "What shall we do?"

She laughed, playing along. "If we remain here, we will be at everyone's beck and call."

"You're right." Robert told the footman that if anyone asked, they were going for a walk and pulled her around the side of the house. "Folly?"

"Yes." Serena had to run to keep up with him. "Robert, you are walking too quickly."

Rather than slowing down as she'd wished, he threw her over his shoulder and strode off.

"Robert!" Serena tried to protest, but began to giggle. She was still laughing when, moments later, he placed her carefully down on the chaise, her laces and stays already loose. How had he done that so quickly and without her feeling a thing? He kissed the side of her mouth. When she opened her lips to speak, he captured her mouth, teasing her to answer. His taste was musky and sweet and tempted her to want more.

Flames leapt at his touch and the feelings she had before, the ones only his kisses drew forth, threatened to overwhelm her. She wanted more, wanted him to touch her as he had before, and she wanted to feel the explosion that showed her the stars.

Holding to the kiss, Serena shook loose her already un-buttoned sleeves, allowing her bodice to drop to her waist as he claimed her swollen mounds. His thumbs grazed them lightly. Serena moved her hands to his shoulders, then around his neck.

Robert tilted his head, possessing her mouth even more fully. Lost in the kiss, she was barely aware of his hand until he stroked the inside of her leg. Through the thin muslin of her skirt, his touch elicited a tingling that followed his caress.

She shivered and held him tighter. Each touch set her skin alight. When his hand covered her mons, her breath became ragged. Robert held her to the kiss as he played. A throbbing need filled her.

She was on fire. He deepened their kiss until she pressed against him. Slowly, he moved one hand over her stomach to her hips, thighs, and legs and then down to the hem of her gown. He lifted it, moving his hand caressingly up her leg until he reached her garter. Serena moaned when he touched her inner thigh. She had no idea it was so sensitive. When he reached her curls, Serena felt a dampness. He stroked slowly and gently, and she thought there could be no better feeling in the world, until he inserted one long finger. A second finger joined the first, and he thrust into her. Serena's hips arched against him, in what must have been an age-old signal for wanting more.

He moved his lips and tongue lightly down over her throat and breasts, until he took one nipple fully into his mouth and suckled. Serena threw her head back and almost didn't recognize the high, breathy cry she made as wave upon wave of pleasure allowed her to touch the sun.

Someday, she'd learn to give him the same joy he was giving her.

* * *

Robert inwardly crowed when he brought her to completion. *Serena was his.* He'd kill anyone who tried to take her from him now. He needed her like he needed his next breath. He'd felt that insatiable hunger almost from the beginning, and it had terrified him. His desire for her was only growing stronger. He looked down at her, slumped in his arms, and softly nuzzled her hair. He'd make his idiocy up to her. Show her how much he loved her. Robert wondered how he could keep her with him every night in his bed.

Serena protested when he removed his hand and smoothed her skirts.

He kissed her. "Finster will be looking for us."

"I don't know if I can stand."

Robert smiled. He'd never before known a female whose legs turned to jelly because of his attentions, but he liked the way it made him feel. "I have noticed the first thing to go is your legs. I'll help you dress."

"I wonder if Mary has noticed the difference in the way my laces are tied."

Robert gave a shout of laughter. "If she has, I doubt she'll say anything, my lady. You'll be married in two weeks to the only person who'll be retying them. Are you ready to stand?"

"Yes, I think I can manage it now. Robert, will it always be like this between us?"

"Don't you like it?"

"I do, very much. I didn't know anything could feel that way."

"You will enjoy it even more later, I promise." He touched the curls at the back of her neck, and she leaned against him. "Come, we should go."

"Yes, they'll be looking for us and I'm hungry."

The plates were set out on their desk when they returned.

They ate and worked on the accounts for the rest of the afternoon.

A knock sounded on the door.

"Yes, come," Serena said.

"My lady, my lord, a letter from the solicitor in York," Finster announced.

"It must be about the house in town." Robert extended his hand, took the letter, and broke the seal. He perused the contents before handing it to her.

She read it. The house was theirs. None of the heirs lived in the area and they were happy to sell it. "I think the price you offered may have had something to do with how quickly the sale went through."

Robert grinned. "But you wanted it, my love, and I wish to please you."

"Thank you." She gazed at his warm moss-green eyes. Robert was so handsome and everything was going so well. Surely nothing could ruin their happiness now. "Lora is working on finding an administrator. We must bring the search forward and make a firm count of the number and ages of the children who will attend. Would you like to ride out with me in the morning?"

He nodded. "Yes, then we'll go to the rectory."

Serena reached for a piece of paper. "I'll send Lora a message asking if it's convenient. Or do you think they'd like to dine with us this evening or drink tea?"

"We can certainly send a note asking."

Serena scribbled a short letter, sealed it, and rang for Finster.

He opened the door.

"Please have this taken to the rectory and wait for an answer."

"Yes, my lady."

"Thank you, Finster."

A half an hour later, a footman came in with a missive. Serena took it. "It's from Freddy, she and Malfrey have decided to dine in York. Let's finish these ledgers and then dress for dinner."

Serena was changing when a note confirming that Lora and John would dine with them was delivered.

Robert was already in the drawing room when she arrived. He drew her into his arms and enveloped her in his strength. "I love you."

Serena put her hands on his cheeks. "I love you, too. I've never been happier."

He bent to kiss her and someone coughed from the door behind him. Robert put his forehead against hers. "Yes, Finster?"

"Mr. and Mrs. Stedman are here."

"Show them in."

A few moments later, Finster opened the door again to announce John and Lora.

Serena greeted them and took Lora's hands.

When Serena was young, this was how she thought her life would be. Having a house of her own, a husband, and entertaining their friends. She'd lost a good part of her dream after her mother died and her father had needed her so badly. The rest disappeared when her brother failed to return and take his place as earl.

Now her dream had come true. "I am so glad you could come on such short notice. I shall not make a habit of it."

Lora bussed her cheek. "There was no bother. It did not inconvenience us at all, and we are happy to join you."

Serena led Lora to the small sofa near the fireplace. "We have wonderful news. The building for the school is ours. We received the solicitor's letter to-day."

"Serena, that is good news. We shall have to bring our

plans up then. When will you have the numbers for the Hall?"

"We're riding out to-morrow. I can bring them to you in the late morning. Will you have the town's information by then?"

"Yes."

Robert strode to a sideboard. "Lora, would you like a glass of sherry?"

"Yes, please. That would be lovely."

They discussed the school until dinner was served.

Serena was happy to see that Cook had risen to the occasion. For the first course, they enjoyed a fresh pea soup removed with poached salmon, and lobster patties. The second course consisted of roasted chickens, rabbit in currant sauce, French beans tossed with mushrooms, a salad, and asparagus. Creams and a blackberry trifle were served for dessert.

Afterward, Serena rose from the table, and to her delight, the gentlemen decided to join them in the drawing room rather than stay to drink their port. Robert handed the glasses to John and brought the decanter with him.

"Serena, did you replace your cook?" Lora asked.

"No, she is really quite good when left to her own devices. Would you like to take a turn around the garden?"

Lora grinned mischievously. "What I would love to see is your kitchen garden. It's quite famous."

"And beautiful." Serena turned to her betrothed. "Robert, we are going to the kitchen garden. Would you and John like to join us?"

"Yes." Robert gestured to John. "We'll take our port."

The ladies walked ahead, while Robert and John ambled in their wake.

"I like her," John said. "She seems to be perfect for you."

"She is." Robert couldn't imagine a life without Serena. "I didn't know what was so special about her, but from the moment I saw her, I couldn't get her out of my mind."

"I haven't seen you this content in many years."

"As always, you're right and that's a very annoying habit of yours. Serena is making the Hall a home again. Even as a child, I don't ever remember being so comfortable here. I have no desire to return to London."

John chuckled. "But Robert, what took you so long to see what was under your nose?"

He shook his head and glanced at Serena. "Fear, I suppose. For years I was afraid to fall in love, believing that I'd be betrayed again. I couldn't bring myself to admit that I'd fallen in love with Serena almost from the first moment I saw her. Certainly after the first evening we spent together at the theater. Women are easy to deal with for a couple of weeks. But a lifetime is another story. And I felt if I admitted my love, I'd lose the control I had. I would no longer be a strong man like my father."

"Has it occurred to you," John asked, "that autocracy is not the same as strength?"

"It should have. That's most likely what drove my mother away. I wonder if she would have loved it here if my father had been different."

They were interrupted by Lora exclaiming over the garden, "What a bright thought, placing a table here."

Robert looked around to see a large, rectangular wooden table with four chairs set on flagstone. Other chairs were stacked off to the side. He glanced at Serena. "When did you arrange this?"

Her amber eyes lit up. "The other day. Do you like it?"

He put his arm around her waist. "I do. May we take tea here?"

She leaned against him. "I've already ordered it."

"My love, what made you think of this?"

"You adore this garden so much. I thought it would be pleasant if we could sit out here and enjoy it together."

Robert pulled a chair out for Serena. Once she and Lora were seated, the gentlemen took their places.

Lora looked around and said, "Serena, you will start a new fashion, taking tea in one's kitchen garden. For once, Yorkshire will lead London."

She shrugged. "I only hope I am not thought too eccentric. Yet it is so much warmer here than on the terrace."

"This summer we need a warm place out of doors," John said. "It still feels like spring."

Serena nodded. "The weather has been unseasonably cool. We're lucky the wall keeps the enclosure fairly warm. Still even in here, the fruits have not ripened as quickly as usual."

After tea, Robert and John once again walked behind the ladies to the Stedmans' carriage.

"This was a most enjoyable evening," John said.

"Thank you. One of many, I trust."

"Robert," John said and stopped.

Robert frowned. "John, I asked you to come to Haythrope because you've never shied from telling me what I don't want to hear. If there is something on your mind, say it."

"Very well. Robert, I want you and Serena to be happy, and you have a tendency to ride roughshod over people, even when you have their best interests at heart. At times you think only of what you, as Viscount Beaumont, want and how to get it. In a marriage, that way leads to great unhappiness."

The muscle ticking in his cheek was all Robert would show of his irritation. John was wrong. This time he was wrong. Robert had been giving Serena what she wanted, encouraging her to make the Hall her own. "I am not going to do anything to destroy what Serena and I are building."

"I hope so, Robert. I sincerely hope you are a different man than your father. His autocracy destroyed his marriage. Yes, well, enough of your rector's advice."

Somehow the evening seemed a little darker than before.

Chapter Eighteen

The next morning, Serena woke to the weak sun and Mary making the wash water ready. Stretching, Serena rose, grateful for the fire. "Good morning. I don't think we will ever have a proper summer this year."

"Good morning, my lady," Mary said listlessly. "It has been a bit chilly."

That was odd. Mary was usually full of energy in the morning. Serena hoped that Mary wasn't sickening. "I'm riding out after breakfast."

"Yes, my lady."

Serena watched as Mary moved slowly around the room. "You know I never interfere, but if something was amiss, you'd tell me, wouldn't you?"

Mary sighed, blinked a few times, and glanced out the window. "It's nothing for you to worry yourself about. I got a letter from the castle, is all."

Serena's heart stopped for a moment. "Is everything all right?"

Her maid hurried over to Serena. "Oh, there's nothing to worry you. Everyone is fine. It's—it's, well, do you remember the man I told you about before we left Vere?"

"The one who asked you to marry him, and when you told him you'd promised to come with me, he said he'd give you a year to return?" The first man who'd ever proposed to Mary.

Her eyes filled with tears, and she sniffed. "That's the one. He's up and married Sukey."

Serena jumped out of bed and hugged her maid. "I am so sorry. I know this is hard for you. Perhaps I should not have allowed you to accompany me."

"No, my lady, you are not to be taking the blame. If he couldn't make it six months, he'd have been faithless in a marriage. I'm much better off here and I like it. I'm glad we're staying." Sadness fringed her words.

"If you're sure? You can take a holiday if you'd like."

Mary scoffed. "With your wedding in two weeks and all the guests from London, I wouldn't leave you now for anything. Here, you need to get dressed. His lordship will be waiting."

Serena put her hand on Mary's arm. "You'll tell me if there is anything I can do?"

"Yes, my lady. I'll be fine." Mary took out a morning gown and suddenly grinned. "I have a bit more news. It appears your brother's wife, Lady Vere, is not as happy with you gone as she'd thought. She didn't have a good idea of how much you did."

Serena shook her head. "Well, she's got no one to blame but herself. I tried to tell her."

Mary nodded sagely. "Yes, my lady, and you weren't the only one."

* * *

Robert was at the top of the grand staircase, waiting for Serena. She loved that he always met her.

They entered the breakfast room to be greeted by Freddy as she took a bite of toast. After swallowing, Freddy said, "Good morning. I hear I missed the Stedmans last evening and tea in the kitchen garden."

"Good morning." Robert walked to the sideboard where the breakfast dishes were set out. "That is what happens when you dine away from home."

"Robert. Behave." Serena pinched him, before taking a piece of bacon. He'd been perfectly happy to have been alone with her and their guests last night.

Freddy took a bit of egg, swallowed, and waved her fork. "Do not let it worry you, my dear. He can't help being over-bearing. It's in his blood. My brother and father were just the same. Nephew, for your information, Edward will be dining with us this evening."

Serena saw Robert's shoulders tense and wondered if it was because of Edward.

A footman placed porridge before Serena and handed her some papers. "From Cook, my lady. She asked you to take a look at the menus before you go out to-day."

"Thank you."

Finster came into the room. "Lady Stanstead, Lord Malfrey is awaiting you."

"Thank you, Finster. Please tell him I'll be with him shortly. Serena, I'll see you at dinner if not before."

"Have a good day."

After they'd eaten, Robert said, "Serena, my love, there is something I'd like to discuss with you."

Serena poured another cup of tea. "Yes?"

He searched her face. "I've been wondering."

What could he be thinking and why was he so serious? "Go on."

"Do you think it would scandalize anyone if you moved into the viscountess's chambers before the wedding?"

Serena's jaw dropped. "I think it would scandalize anyone who heard of it."

"But we have only a week at the most until our respective families descend upon us."

"That soon?" Serena held her hand to ward him off. "And you want me to move into the rooms next to yours. You've taken leave of your senses."

"No, I *want* you to move into my room. I'll settle for the viscountess's."

Serena shook her head and took his hand. "We need to go." She tugged.

He stood and whirled her into his arms. "Shall I persuade you?"

"No." She infused her tone with a conviction she didn't have. "Now come."

Before she could stop herself, she tilted her head up for a kiss. That was the problem; he likely could talk her round. She had no sense at all when it came to him. "No seduction to win your point."

Robert heaved a sigh and followed her to the stables.

Once on their horses, they didn't stop until the outermost cottages came into view. The tenants' questions regarding the school ranged from the hours to transportation. The survey concerning the number wanting to send their children to the new school took all of the morning and then some.

When they returned, Serena divided the children by age and gender. She gave him the list and sat back with a satisfied smile. "What do you think?"

He perused the list. "I have to say, I'm quite impressed. I had no idea our tenants wanted a school. I'm glad you thought of it." He stood and held out his hand. "Now, my lady, I have something to show you."

"What is it?"

"Come with me." He led her up to his wing of the house and opened a door, standing aside for her to enter the redecorated viscountess's chambers.

Afternoon sun spilled in, warming the large room. Serena wandered around, glancing occasionally at Robert. He'd put so much effort into this and it was beautiful, exactly as she would have done it. Previously, the chamber had been hung with dark blue drapes and bed hangings and the walls covered with a blue printed wallpaper. It was now decorated in pale, earthy greens, warm blues, and cream. The wallpaper, patterned with birds, trees, and flowers in a large and well-spaced print, gave the appearance of more light. The drapes had small stripes in the same colors as the walls.

"The muslin bed hangings are for summer," he told her, "to be replaced in autumn by warmer velvets."

"Robert, it's beautiful, perfect. How did you know these were my favorite colors?"

"They're the colors you wear most often."

Tears of joy started in her eyes as the realization set in. He'd begun this before when he was here the first time. While she was running off to Paris.

He truly had loved her, even then, and wanted to make her happy. "Thank you. I never would have done this for myself."

Robert took her in his arms. "It took me a while, but I figured that out. Let me show you the rest."

He walked behind her as she surveyed the rooms which would comprise her apartment. Their chambers, built in an inverted U, occupied half of the west wing. The viscountess's bedchamber, located on the west side of the wing, joined a large dressing room with cupboards built into the walls and three doors. The first led to her bedchamber, the second to a shared sitting room at the end of the wing, and the third to a bathing chamber situated between the two dressing rooms.

A wide corridor separated the viscountess's chambers from the viscount's on the east side. A large rectangular sitting room, only accessible from their chambers, spanned the width of the wing at the end of the building. Mullioned windows formed three sides, the only break being the large Norman-style fireplace. The room reminded Serena of an ancient solar.

When they returned to the bedchamber, she slid her hands over his shoulders. "I love it. The rooms are all perfect."

Robert bent his head and kissed her.

Serena shivered as he swept his hand over her back, drawing her closer to him. Moments later, her bodice sagged. He'd done it again. One of these days, she'd feel it being unlaced. Serena pressed against him. His lips claimed hers, their tongues danced, and the kiss heated. She clung to him as the kiss swirled out of her control. He raised the bottom edge of her skirts and cooler air touched her legs. A pooling of warmth, then a deep yearning filled her as his hand cupped her bare bottom and settled between her legs. Then, her skirt dropped.

Robert pulled back from the kiss, his eyes warm and intense. "I want you."

"You have me." She reached up, to draw him back to her.

"I want to make love to you, here, now!"

Serena's breathing quickened. "Are you sure?"

Robert searched her eyes, the beautiful amber eyes that had haunted him since they'd met. "I've never wanted anything more. We'll take this one step at a time. First you'll tell me what you want. If you want me to stop, you have only to say 'no.' " He paused and prayed she would not tell him no. "Are you ready?"

Her breasts rose and fell and she nodded. "Yes."

"Do you want me to kiss you, to touch you?" Robert kept his voice soft. He'd waited for this day for so long.

"Yes."

Forcing himself to breathe, he smiled. "That is what I want as well, but I want you to kiss me before I kiss you."

"Me?" Serena flushed. "You really want me now?"

Oh God, if she only knew how much he needed her. "Always." His voice was gravelly and deep. "Serena, my love, show me you desire me."

She swallowed, placed her hands on his face, and touched her lips to his, kissing him lightly, as if it was their first time. When he responded, she felt a thrill of feminine power and boldly ran her tongue across his lips. His mouth opened and she slipped her tongue in. He tasted of blackberries and something uniquely male. His tongue joined hers. She tilted her head more, deepening the kiss. He clasped his arms hard around her, she felt his urgency.

Serena sighed as her caution fled, and she moved her hands greedily over his linen shirt, feeling his hard muscles. Tugging at his shirt, she freed it from his breeches, then rubbed her palms over his bare skin, across his back and up the sides of his chest. When he swept his fingers down her back and caressed her derrière, she moaned and sent her hands more purposefully down his body to his hard buttocks and pulled him closer, his desire evident against her. He shifted rhythmically against her.

Serena was panting with need. This was so unfair that she didn't know what to do next. "Now what?"

His voice was low and seductive and his eyes smoldered. "What do you want? Tell me what you want me to do."

What did she want? "Touch me here. My breasts."

He cupped her bosoms, softly kneading them through the light muslin of her gown, and played with her nipples. Serena moaned with delight and kissed him more deeply. Her body was on fire as he ministered to them, and the throbbing in her chest eased, but if she wanted more, she'd have to tell him.

"Take them with your mouth, please."

She gasped as he twirled one nipple between his fingers and gently squeezed. Her body grew hotter under his touch. He slowly pulled down her bodice and stays. Her chemise still covered her. Robert took one breast in his hand and licked the other through the light muslin. When he took it in his mouth and gently sucked, she knew her knees would soon cease to support her.

He fluttered kisses up her neck and whispered wickedly against her ear.

"Do you want more?"

This was torture. All of her yearned for him. "Yes, I want what you did before. I want your fingers—your fingers inside me."

"Very well, my lady."

The room was warm, but cooler air wafted around her legs as Robert rucked up her skirt, placed his hand on her wet curls, and stroked. A soft sigh escaped her. He sank into her mouth and slid one long finger into her tight, scalding heat. He held her against him. With each slow thrust of his fingers, Serena tensed and trembled more. He held her to their kiss until she shuddered and convulsed around him, then Robert picked her up in his arms and took her to the bed.

He held her in his lap and stared at the smile playing

around her lips; he pressed light kisses against her temple. Serena glanced at him from beneath her long, thick lashes. It was a gesture so sultry he tensed as his need for her surged. When she reached up to kiss him, he fought his urge to take her swiftly.

There was only one first time. And Robert would use all his skill to make hers as perfect as possible. He opened his mouth in response to her and groaned. Her bodice and chemise were around her waist, her stays somewhere on the floor. He was still fully clothed. "Tell me, do you wish for more?"

"Yes." Serena tugged at his shirt. "Off, take this off."

"As you wish, my lady." He released her long enough to pull his shirt over his head before returning to her. Robert stood her up and pushed her gown over her hips. The garment fell in a soft *whoosh* to the floor.

Her eyes glazed with desire; she swayed slightly, then tensed. He held her to him and stroked her back until she relaxed again.

"Robert . . ."

"Don't think. I love you. I love your body. Let me look at you. Touch you."

A deep pink colored her breast and face. "But I'm . . ."

"Yes, my darling, this is how you should be before me and I before you. Look at me."

Serena's gaze soaked in his broad chest, heavy muscle covered by springy blond curls that tapered down to only a thin line to his breeches. She reached a hand out and lightly touched his chest.

"I won't break."

Spreading both hands on him, she ran her fingers through his curls, over his muscles and found his nipples, squeezing them as he'd done to her. Robert's jaw clenched. He reached for her.

"No, wait." She unfastened the buttons on his breeches, and her hands moved over him as she pushed them down. His erection sprang up between them. Her gaze lowered. His shaft stood in a bed of more blond curls. He was more well-endowed than the Greek statues in the museum. Serena lifted her eyes to his. "You're beautiful."

He pulled off his boots, stockings, and breeches and threw back the bed coverings, then laid her carefully on the sheets. Slowly he untied her garters and rolled down her stockings, caressing her legs as he did. His tongue created a light path from the back of her knee to her ankle. She craved each touch, each light lick. When he stretched out next to her, his body was like a furnace. Robert removed her pins and spread her hair over his hands, then down over her breasts to her waist.

He buried his face in it and kissed the soft place under her ear. "This is all you need to wear."

She yearned for him to touch her.

"I'll show you how nice being naked can be," he whispered, intending to learn all of her, bit by bit. Using his tongue, he traced the side of her neck and paused at the pulse. He moved down and circled her breasts then lower over her slightly rounded stomach to her hips, licking, suckling, enjoying her musky taste. He settled at the apex of her thighs, then shouldered her legs apart. With his hands under her buttocks, holding her steady, Robert covered her mons with his mouth. Serena gave a small cry of protest.

"Do you want me to stop?"

"I—I don't know." She panted. "What are you doing?"

"I'll show you. Tell me if you don't like it."

"All right."

He licked her swollen nub. Serena writhed with pleasure and cried out his name. He reveled in her slippery heat. Her breathy cries and moans drove him on. Holding her down when she'd tried to thrust, he drove his tongue into her sheath and tasted her nectar. She shuddered as he moved over her, the head of his erection at her entrance. "Are you sure you want this?"

He stilled. If she told him no, he'd stop.

Her eyes were glazed with desire and she gasped as if she'd been running. "Yes, I want this. I want you."

Robert slowly entered her, drawing back and pushing in a little farther each time. He'd never taken a virgin before, but he knew, no matter what he did, he would cause her pain. "Look at me."

Serena glanced up, her gaze so full of trust his heart clenched.

"This will hurt. It will be the only time. Keep your eyes on mine."

She nodded and fear lurked in her eyes.

He kissed her. "Don't be afraid, my love."

Robert kissed her again, then held her gaze, searching her face as he slowly filled her and stopping when she tensed. He took her mouth and plundered as he thrust sharply through her maidenhood and stopped when she cried out.

God, he hadn't wanted to hurt her. Placing soft kisses on her face, he wished he could take away her pain. "Are you all right?"

"Yes, the pain is going away."

A tear slipped from the corner of her eye and he thought his heart would break. "You're crying."

She brought his head down to hers and kissed him. "It's because I'm happy. It's a strange feeling, having you inside me."

Kissing her gently, Robert caressed her cheek and hair, anything to keep her happy and not crying. "I'll wait for a bit. There is no rush."

Serena nodded. "Kiss me."

He captured her lips and mouth and when she relaxed he started thrusting again, slowly, until he was deeply in her and she responded to his long unhurried strokes. "Put your legs around me."

Serena did as he asked and held him tight. Her every moan, her every cry, became a symphony to him. For the first time, Robert had to fight to maintain command over himself. When she climaxed, his control broke. He pumped his seed into her before pulling her, sated and limp, against him. Lying back against the pillows, holding Serena close, he marveled at the intensity of his love for her. His strong desire to protect her, even from the fleeting pain of their first mating, surprised him. The need to make her his wife had never been stronger. Why hadn't he insisted on a special license? The wedding was much too far away.

Serena's heart swelled and threatened to burst with happiness. Robert held her so intimately, his heart pounded against her cheek, yet she burrowed closer to him. Telling him what she wanted somehow increased her anticipation and her need. When Robert had said he wanted her to be his equal in this sensual sphere, she'd thought it ludicrous. He had so much experience and she, none. Yet what they did made her feel more his equal. She'd wanted what he would give her, and he'd found joy in their lovemaking. Her body ached with a need she couldn't deny, frissons of pleasure shot through her and still her senses led her on.

Remembering what they'd done, there'd been a little pain, but it was not stronger than the waves of pleasure that racked her body. Then there was . . . only him.

The fires within her flared and she turned toward Robert as he reached for her. This time, when she lifted her hips to greet him, he didn't stop, and soon a maelstrom sent her spinning, and she flew apart as waves of delight and happiness consumed her. She'd never known anything could be this wonderful.

Serena awoke cradled against him, his arm heavy around her. Somehow he'd pulled up a sheet to cover them. Robert was right, being naked did feel good. Serena stretched a bit and felt small twinges in her thighs, then rolled and found him regarding her under his thick lashes. A question hung between them.

"I'm fine."

He grunted.

She explored his chest and was fascinated to find that his nipples tightened at her touch. Curious, she grazed them lightly with her teeth. He stirred like a sleeping giant. She caressed him down over his hard taut stomach to his shaft and took it in her hand. The skin was so soft. It grew and hardened. She wondered how many times a day that happened and thought back. When he'd held her before, she'd noticed there was frequently a hard ridge riding against her.

"Serena, love, are you sure you can take me again?"

She met his gaze, licking her lips and looking back down at his now straining erection. "How many times a day does it . . . ?" she asked, waving a hand.

Robert broke into laughter. "With *you,* I don't know. You have a definite altitudinal effect. We'll have to experiment, but not to-day or to-morrow. If you're not sore now, you will be."

"Will I?" Her voice was low and sultry. She found his nipple again.

Robert closed his eyes and drew a ragged breath. Teaching her about sexual pleasure might be the death of him. He couldn't imagine why he'd ever wanted a marriage of convenience. He groaned deeply, rolling her under him and spreading her legs.

Robert kissed her lightly, and captured her mouth. Serena's answer was desperate and needy. Her body readily responded to him. He entered her slowly, trying to sense any pain she might have. But her low keening urged him on. He kissed her deeply as her skin dewed.

Rolling to his side, Robert held Serena so that there was no space between them. His world shrank to her. Serena pressed against him. He lost his control, lost himself. When she cried out, he poured his seed and his love into her. Robert loosened his grip and pulled the cover back up over them. He kissed her hair and stroked her.

Fierce possessiveness surged through him. The last time that had happened, he'd tried to force her to marry him. He vowed not to make important decisions without her full consent. He'd not risk losing her now.

"Sleep, my love."

Suddenly, she was aware of Robert as never before, warm and strong, holding her to him. Loving her.

A light tap sounded on the door. "My lord?" Henley, his valet, inquired.

Robert blinked and glanced around the room. It was still light, but it had to be close to dinner time. They must have been here for hours. "Yes, I'm here."

Henley cleared his throat. "My lord, can you tell me if her ladyship is with you? Her dresser is looking for her."

Good God. At least Henley and Serena's maid were discreet. Robert gazed down at Serena, a warm feminine bundle cuddled next to him.

"Yes," he answered. How many others knew? Why couldn't he have waited until tonight?

Next to him, Serena stirred. Her eyes wide, she glanced

up at him. Robert put a finger to his lips. "Henley, how many are searching for us?"

"My lord, most of the servants think you and her ladyship have gone out," Henley said with dignity.

Robert shifted higher onto the pillows, bringing Serena with him. "How exactly do they have that impression?"

A soft-voiced consultation took place on the other side of the door.

"Ah, Miss Mac Duff, her ladyship's dresser, may have mentioned that you and her ladyship had taken a walk."

Robert's shoulders shook with barely suppressed mirth. "Well done, Miss Mac Duff. I commend your quick thinking. If you will bring her ladyship's clothing and whatever else she needs to the viscountess's dressing room, I believe we will manage to overcome this potential contretemps."

"Yes, my lord, right away."

His valet and Serena's dresser must have decided to abandon whispering. Robert listened to the conversation taking place on the other side of the door.

"If they've been in there all afternoon, they'll need a bath. Mr. Henley, if you order water, I shall gather her ladyship's things."

"With the greatest pleasure, Miss Mac Duff."

One pair of feet faded and a door closed across the corridor.

Serena raised her eyes to Robert's amused green ones, and grinned. "Oh dear. I am very glad for Mary's quick thinking."

"Mmm." He swooped down to kiss her.

Serena laughed as he drew her under him again.

"Do we have time?"

"If you are able, we have time." He rolled her onto her stomach.

Serena descended into bliss. "Oh, *Robert.*"

*   *   *

Water being poured into the copper tub woke Serena. They must have had both the doors open for her to hear that.

"We can only have one tub filled," he whispered wickedly. "We could, of course, bathe one at a time. I would insist that you go first, or we can share the bath."

What an interesting idea. "Won't we scandalize Henley and Mary?"

Robert rolled on his side to face her. "I doubt anything could scandalize Henley. He's been with me much too long. I can't answer for your Miss Mac Duff."

Serena couldn't either, but it wasn't as if she was taking a lover. Husbands are allowed to do what they wish. "Is bathing together an indulgence you plan to continue after we are married, my lord?"

"Most definitely one of the many indulgences I plan to continue, my lady." He reached out to caress one breast.

She wanted to purr. Now she knew what a cat must feel like.

"My lord, your bath is ready," Henley said through the door.

"Thank you, Henley. You are dismissed."

"As you wish, my lord. Ah, about her ladyship."

"She'll manage without Miss Mac Duff."

"Yes, my lord."

Robert rose from the bed. "Come, my lady." He held his hand out to her.

They walked through her dressing room, into the bathing chamber. The room was almost completely covered in blue and white tiles, including the large stove that stood in one corner, warming the entire area. Steam rose from a copper tub set in front of a fireplace. The room had a distinctly Continental feel.

"My grandfather designed it and had the chamber built after a visit to Baden-Baden. Allow me to hand you into the tub."

Serena sank gratefully into the warm water. Robert followed with a linen cloth and soap. He washed her slowly, careful not to dislodge the cloth holding her hair up. When he reached between her legs, she winced.

"You're sore. Why did you allow me to enter you the last time? I would have stopped."

She took the cloth from him and scooted closer to wash him. "I didn't stop you because I knew the pleasure would overcome any pain."

Robert drew her near, unheeding of the water splashing onto the floor. "I love you with my heart and body and soul. More than I ever imagined I could love anyone."

"And I love you. I never want to be parted from you. If you want me to move into the viscountess's chambers, I shall and—and damn propriety!"

Robert chuckled deeply at her fierceness. "I wish to God I hadn't insisted on the banns being read. We could have been married by special license, but our aunts are right, a large wedding is for the best."

A knock sounded on the door. "My lord—" Henley began.

Mary interrupted. "My lady, you've got to come now or you'll be late."

"Been with you long has she?" Robert whispered.

"Long enough, though she's never spoken to me in *that* tone before."

"Possibly because you've never done anything to warrant it." Robert rose to hand her out of the tub, then carefully dried her. "We did well. We managed not to wet your hair."

"That would have truly delayed me." Serena wrapped the towel around her and entered the dressing room.

* * *

An hour later, Mary and Henley watched as Serena and Robert descended to the drawing room.

"They're a pair, Mr. Henley," Mary said, shaking her head. "Reckless is what she is. Spent years taking care of everyone else with not a thought for herself, and you see where it's led. If they keep on like this, I don't know how we are going to manage to keep this a secret."

"I agree, Miss Mac Duff. With two weeks until the wedding, we might have to put our heads together. I never thought to see his lordship so besotted, not that I in any way disapprove," he added hurriedly. "But it does seem to be making him imprudent."

"Aye, and I've never seen either of them happier."

Chapter Nineteen

Freddy and Lord Malfrey were already in the drawing room when Serena and Robert entered ahead of Finster.

"Malfrey, has Freddy told you that we've had a few children taken by procurers for the mines?" Robert asked. "Serena saved the last child."

"Abductions here?" Lord Malfrey's eyes narrowed. "When was that?"

"Late last week. Why, do you know something about it?" Robert asked.

"I'm not sure and I don't wish to say anything until I know I'm right." He frowned. "Is the kidnapper still around? I'd like to ask him some questions."

"He escaped. I've got my gamekeeper watching likely places for him to hide. He may have left the area."

"Lady Serena rescued the child?"

Robert smiled broadly. "Yes, she found the boy running away from the lout and struck him with the carriage whip so that my groom could grab the child from him. He apparently has a very noticeable slash across his face. He'd be foolish to remain here."

Lord Malfrey inclined his head. "Well done, my lady. Well done indeed."

"Thank you, my lord. I am only sorry it was necessary to take the action." She turned to Freddy. "The sale on the building for the new school has been completed."

"Wonderful. When do you propose to begin the term?"

"I hope we can commence in a few weeks."

"A school for the estate, my lady?" Lord Malfrey asked.

Serena nodded. "For the Hall's children and the town. Now that we own the building, we'll present the council with a complete plan soon. I suspect we'll start evaluating apprenticeship programs as well. The mothers I've spoken with want to keep their children nearby and out of dangerous mines and factories."

Lord Malfrey remained for tea, then took his leave. Freddy walked him to the door.

"Edward, do you really think you know who is behind these kidnappings?"

"Unfortunately, I think I have a very good idea who may be causing it. I sincerely hope I'm wrong."

"I won't press you, of course. You'll tell Robert if you discover anything?"

"Most definitely. Shall we meet to-morrow?" he asked.

"With Catherine away for a few days, I should really remain here. There was a slight problem to-day when Lady Montrose stopped by and neither Serena nor Robert could be found. Lady Montrose is the biggest gossip in the area. I would not want her to attempt to sully Serena's reputation," Freddy said. "You may join us for tea, if you'd like."

"I'd love to drink tea with you. I understand your concern, though I doubt Lady Montrose could harm Lady Serena. The whole county is infatuated with her." He raised Freddy's hand to his lips.

Her fingers tingled as his lips grazed her knuckles.

"Robert could not have made a better choice than Serena. Nevertheless, we still have almost two weeks until the wedding and with Catherine gone, I am their only chaperone." She glanced from her hand to his strong handsome face and smiled. "I expect St. Eth to arrive by the end of this week or the beginning of the next. With a house full of Serena's relatives, I'll have more time for you."

Edward grinned. "I'll look forward to that. Until to-morrow then."

Freddy stood in the doorway as he walked down the stairs to his waiting carriage. Their days together had been halcyon. Much as they'd been before she was sent off to marry old Lord Stanstead's heir. Recently, she and Edward had discussed bits and pieces of the past, but she still hadn't told him all of it. She must tell him soon, and she prayed he would understand her decisions.

She closed the door and returned to the drawing room where Serena and Robert were deep in conversation. Freddy was suddenly struck by how much they behaved as if they were already married, even more so now than before. She studied Serena. There was nothing overtly different, yet she was more relaxed, more in tune to Robert, and he to her. They looked almost like lovers. Is that what they were doing all afternoon?

Freddy coughed. They didn't jump apart as she expected. Serena merely looked up and calmly smiled at her.

"How was your day?" Serena asked.

"It was lovely. I heard Lady Montrose came by." Freddy raised a brow.

Serena shook her head. "I don't believe I've met her."

"She is the area's gossip."

"Then I can't say I'm sorry to have missed her."

"Do you want to tell me where you were all afternoon?"

Serena and Robert silently consulted each other.

It occurred to Freddy she may not be ready for the response. "Robert, before you deign to answer, please pour me a glass of sherry. I think I'll need it."

Robert poured two glasses of sherry and a brandy for himself.

"We were together, but neither Serena nor I will discuss where we were or what we were doing. We are now considering Serena moving into the viscountess's apartments. The redecoration is complete and with the corridor between them, they are not directly connected."

Freddy took a rather large swallow of sherry and wished she drank brandy. What would they do if she said no? "The chambers are a little close together. However, that's preferable to your tripping over a maid, or anyone else." She gave an arched look to Serena, who didn't even blush. "Keep it quiet. Be discreet, and I'll have no objections."

"We'll bid you good night." Serena kissed her on the cheek.

Robert's eyes were smiling when he kissed her cheek as well.

"Devil," she said quietly to him before they left the room. Now if she could just get her own love life straightened out. She would give anything to be as happy.

As Lord Malfrey rode home, he couldn't shake the feeling of impending doom that hovered over him. He didn't know why he suspected his heir was in some way involved with the kidnapped children, but he felt it strongly. He left his horse to the footman at the front door. His butler bowed him into his house.

"Have you seen Mr. Aubrey?" Malfrey asked.

"No, my lord, not this evening."

"When you do, tell him I want a word with him before he goes anywhere in the morning."

"Yes, my lord."

Malfrey was reading the *Morning Post* when Aubrey knocked.

"You wanted to see me, Edward?"

Edward took his time folding his news sheet. "Aubrey, have you heard about the children who've been kidnapped?"

His cousin rubbed his quizzing glass with a handkerchief as if he'd not a care in the world. "No, why? Is it important?" He glanced up with an impassive look on his face. "Are they children of anyone who matters?"

Edward's jaw clenched. "All children are important. The station of their parents is not the issue. Are you, or are you not, aware of the kidnappings?"

"No. Then again, I really do not spend much time around the locals. I prefer York."

Edward tried to make out if his cousin was telling the truth. Even as a child, Aubrey had always been a proficient liar. Edward was afraid that Aubrey hadn't changed since his youth. "I hope you are being truthful with me. If you are not, and I discover you're in any way involved in the kidnappings, I'll have no compunction in turning you over to the authorities and giving evidence against you. I'll not have this family's name besmirched any more than necessary."

Aubrey's gaze reminded Edward of an adder.

"Really, Edward, I don't know where you get such fanciful ideas. What use have I for a pack of underbred brats? I shall see you when I am next forced to ruralize." Aubrey turned on his heel, and glanced back over his shoulder. "Do not forget you have no other heir."

Edward stared after his cousin and wondered if he should

voice his suspicions to Beaumont. *Damn.* Malfrey threw his paper down and stood. If there were any more kidnappings, he'd have to say something. Until then, he'd keep his own counsel and watch Aubrey's every move.

After being informed the previous evening that Serena would now occupy the rooms that had been redecorated for her, Mary saw Henley in the corridor between the bedchambers and gave him a speaking look.

"I am to move her ladyship's clothes." Mary pressed her lips tightly together.

He raised his brows. "Indeed."

Mary nodded. "It would be best if both beds looked slept in each night."

"Yes, I understand." He bowed. "You may rely on me, Miss Mac Duff, to do my part."

"Thank you, Mr. Henley. I knew I could."

Serena awoke in Robert's arms, not to the early morning sun she was used to in her previous room, but to a slow changing from dark to light. The summer solstice was in a few days. She sighed contentedly. How quickly she'd gotten used to sleeping not wearing a stitch and to having him large and warm next to her. She traced his chest and ran her finger through the hair. Her gaze slowly rose to his face that seemed so innocent in repose. Small bits of blond stubble covered his cheeks and chin. His lips moved as he snored softly. Serena wondered if she'd wake him if she ran a finger over his lips.

At the first touch, Robert's eyes opened. He gazed back at her and smiled before gathering her in his arms. Serena never knew she could be this happy. As if their being together was meant to be. Was this why she'd spent so many years alone? She snuggled into him and drifted back to sleep. Two hours later, they awoke together.

Obeying her body's prompting, she rolled to face him and rubbed sinuously against him. Robert looked his question.

"I'm fine. A good night's sleep was all I needed."

"Humph." He captured her eyes and searched her face, then reached down to gently touch her.

Serena smiled and tried to hide the twinge of pain.

"That hurt, didn't it?"

"No, not at all," she lied.

"Serena, we've had this discussion before. Do not lie to me. Ever," Robert said without humor.

Her eyes narrowed at him, ready to protest.

He pulled her closer, keeping his gaze locked on hers. "I understand you want to give me pleasure, but what pleasure could I possibly have knowing I was hurting you, even for a moment? Give yourself time to heal. We have the rest of our lives to make love."

She flopped back on the bed in disgust and he grinned. Giving her a light kiss, he got up and reached for his dressing gown. "I'll wait for you in the corridor."

He left, going through the dressing room into the bathroom, then to his chamber. Henley stood waiting for him. Robert was surprised to see his bed had, apparently, been slept in. He glanced at his valet.

Henley stared into the space beyond Robert's right shoulder.

"Remind me to raise your salary, Henley." Laughing, Robert turned to the washbasin as a maid entered to stoke the banked fire.

"Miss Mac Duff's as well, my lord."

* * *

They were eating breakfast when Serena suddenly remembered they'd had an engagement yesterday that they'd missed. She glanced at Robert and shook her head. "I've lost my mind. We were to have gone to the rectory yesterday afternoon. I didn't even send a message."

"I had one sent."

"Why? You could not have possibly known . . ."

He smiled wolfishly.

Heat infused Serena's face. "Yes, well, maybe you did know. When are they expecting us?"

"This morning."

"We may leave after I change into my habit."

Without looking up from his plate, he said, "We're taking the gig."

They never took the gig when they could ride. "Whatever for?"

"Trust me. You'll be much more comfortable in the gig than on horseback."

Serena tightened her lips. Why did he think he always knew better? This would have to change. "I shall meet you in the stable yard."

"I've ordered the carriage brought to the front."

Serena inclined her head and rose. "I shall meet you in the corridor."

"As you wish."

What was he about, telling her when she could ride or make love?

By the time she opened the door to leave her new chamber, Serena had worked herself into a high dudgeon. She stepped out into the corridor and bounced off Robert.

He took her hand, kissed the inside of her wrist and, with a naughty-little-boy look on his face, said, "You didn't specify which corridor. I chose the closest one to you."

"Of course you did." She hadn't meant to sound like a shrew, though she knew she did. How could he be so completely loveable one moment and so domineering the next?

"Don't be angry. I am only trying to take care of you."

"Indeed."

A smile entered his eyes, but he kept his lips straight. "Tell you what. If you still wish it, we'll ride this afternoon. But since you're dressed for the carriage now . . ."

Mollified, Serena said, "Very well, we shall take the carriage, this once."

Lora met them when they drove up to the rectory. "Welcome. You look as if you have good news."

"Yes," Serena said. "We've got the school numbers from the Hall."

Serena gave her cloak and gloves to the maid. Lora led them to the parlor and Serena took a seat on the sofa. "Over sixty children from the Hall shall attend. Not one parent of a young child declined, and if we can insure classes appropriate for the older children, we may have more."

"Serena, how wonderful. I have twenty-two from town. Some of the parents decided to either keep them in the other school or not send their children at all. I do wish they could understand the value of even a rudimentary education."

Serena leaned forward to pat Lora's hand. "More may come once they can be brought to understand the benefits."

"Yes, well, there is no use repining. I contacted the headmistress of my old school, who is a native Yorkshire woman. She just retired and is willing to help us set up our school *and* act as administrator for at least the first year or so. She will be the best person to decide how many teachers we shall need."

"Set up a meeting and tell me when we can speak with her. I'd like to begin classes in the next few weeks."

Tea was brought in and Lora poured.

Serena continued, "My cousin, Phoebe, will probably arrive early next week. She set up schools on all her husband's estates and may have some ideas as well." Serena sipped her tea. "In the meantime, we will need to have the house cleaned and the locks changed. Tables, benches, and supplies should be ordered as well."

"I can arrange to have the house cleaned."

"Good. I'll have Robert attend to the locks, and perhaps you and I can make a trip into York to look at desks and other furniture we might need."

"What a good idea. I've not been to York for ages. We shall make a day of it."

The proposed trip to York took place three days later. Robert, having other business, declined to accompany her.

Serena was surprised and amused to find he'd ordered the traveling coach with two coachmen and four outriders for her trip.

"Really, Finster, I don't think I need this type of an entourage for a shopping trip to York. It is not above an hour away. Please dismiss everyone but one coachman and two footmen."

"My lady," Finster said apologetically, "his lordship particularly insisted upon this arrangement."

Serena bit her lip. "Very well." She tried not to feel controlled and smothered. Surely his extreme protectiveness would wear off. Or would it?

Lora greeted Serena when the coach pulled up.

An outrider helped Serena down and she accompanied Lora inside. "I wish I knew what he thinks could possibly happen to me between the Hall and York."

Lora patted Serena's shoulder. "Knowing Robert, I am not all that surprised he sent people to guard you."

Serena's gaze focused on her. "What do you mean?"

"From all John told me, Robert's father and grandfather

were autocratic despots. They expected everyone to follow their dictates without question. I understand that even their wives could not gainsay them. He would, naturally, be influenced by their examples."

"Are you saying Robert is like that?" Serena exclaimed.

"John says you have done wonders with him, my dear."

Serena bit her lip. "I thought his behavior before was an aberration," she said softly, then remembered the carriage incident the other morning, and when he announced their marriage.

Serena tried to tamp down the distress flooding her.

After everything she'd accomplished at the Hall, how could he not trust her to make her own decisions? How long would it take before he never took her desires into consideration and began making all the decisions, even ones about her body? But he'd already tried that . . .

"Serena, are you all right?"

"I don't know." She rubbed between her brows, fighting sudden panic. "And I don't know in whom I can confide my misgivings."

"John," Lora replied firmly. "He knows Robert better than anyone."

"But he is Robert's friend."

"He is also the rector. He'll not betray your trust. Come. I've known him for a long time. He is much wiser than his years and will know what to do."

Lora took Serena by the arm to her husband's office. "My love, Serena needs to discuss something with you. Serena, I'll be in my parlor when you've finished." Lora closed the door behind her.

John motioned Serena to a comfortable chair near the fireplace before taking the one opposite her.

Agitated, she played with the fringe on her shawl.

"Is this about Robert?" he asked gently.

Serena glanced at him. "Yes, it . . . it may be nothing. On the other hand, it may be a very large problem for me."

"Start from the beginning. I find that's easiest. What may be a problem?"

She bit her lip. She had to talk to someone. "Did Robert tell you how we happened to become betrothed?"

"He told me he trapped you."

"Yes, he did. As bad as that was, it—was not the worst of it." Serena told him what Robert said on the trip from Merton to Mayfair. That she must marry him and he wouldn't give her up.

When she'd finished, John leaned back in his chair. "He told me he was a fool, but I'd no idea he'd been *such* a fool." John fixed his eyes on her. "What occurred after that? I know you fled to Paris—what did Robert say that made you decide to come to the Hall?"

Serena told John of the partnership Robert promised, and her decision not to accept him unless he could admit he loved her. Then she related his offer to release her from their betrothal if, after two weeks at the Hall, she still believed she could not marry him.

"I have recently had reason to suspect that, in spite of his promises, he may be reverting to type. That perhaps the fashion in which he's been treating me, of late, is the deviation," she said with a frown.

"Yes, I see your point. Robert had a disastrous affair when he was younger . . ."

"I know. He told me about her."

"What you may not know," John continued, unperturbed, "is afterward, he decided to marry only for convenience. I always thought it a bad idea. A marriage of convenience could only exacerbate his autocratic tendencies. Then he fell in love with you, Serena, deeply in love. I've never before seen him willing, indeed eager, to join in a partnership with another person, never mind with a woman. I think he knows that, were he to try to rule you, he stands in great danger of losing you altogether."

Serena twisted the fringe more urgently and a warmth rose from her neck, infusing her face. "Yet, in the past few days, he's said and done some things that make me fear he *will* not take my views into consideration."

John's voice was still gentle. "Such as?"

"Well, refusing to allow me to make my own decision regarding something personal and now saddling me with guards for the drive to York, when a coachman and two footmen would have been sufficient. Orders that I was not allowed to countermand."

John frowned. "You've discussed this with him?"

"I discussed the first problem, or rather he noticed I was concerned and he told me he would not become a tyrant with me. But, I walked out to-day to discover I am surrounded by guards, and he was not at the Hall."

"Serena, do you wish to cry off?"

She tried to keep her voice calm, but her throat closed. "I cannot. Even if I wanted to, I cannot."

She blinked back her tears.

John handed her his handkerchief and waited for her to control her countenance once more. "Will you trust me with this?"

"Do you mean to speak with Robert? I—I don't think he would react well to your . . ."

"Interference?"

Serena nodded as she wiped her eyes.

"You have a good time in York and leave Robert to me. If there was ever a bigger chucklehead, I have yet to meet him."

Serena rose. "Yes, I'll do that. Thank you."

John stood and opened the door for her. "Try to have fun,

Serena. I have it on good authority shopping is good for the soul."

Serena tried to smile.

He escorted the ladies to the coach. "Will you have luncheon in York?" he whispered in an aside to Lora.

"We shall if you'd like." Lora's eyes twinkled mischievously. "Is there any particular inn you'd like us to visit?"

"Have I ever told you, you make a wonderfully perceptive rector's wife?" he asked. "The Cock and Bull, I think."

"We'll see you there around one o'clock?"

"That should give me enough time."

Chapter Twenty

John fixed Robert with a hard look as Robert entered his study.

"I've spoken to the council . . ." Robert met John's gaze and broke off. "What is it? Nothing's happened to Serena, has it?"

"To the best of my knowledge, no one's hurt Serena other than you," John responded drily. "What on earth were you thinking? Sending her off to *York* with an escort more appropriate to a trip to London *and* not discussing it with her first or allowing her to change your orders?"

Robert frowned, clearly confused.

"You are the most idiotic man I know," John said exasperated. "How exactly did you behave and what did you say to Serena after you trapped her?"

Robert looked warily at John. "I—um—I told her she had to marry me."

"You played the tyrant."

"I suppose my words could have been . . ."

"Cut line, Robert." John pinched the bridge of his nose. "You acted autocratically then, and stupidly did the same just recently. And"—he paused to ensure Robert was listening—"you did it again to-day. Will you never learn? Do you want to lose her?"

Robert's jaw tightened. "She can't leave me, not now."

"I don't even want to know your reasoning for such a stupid remark." For all his good qualities, Robert was one of the most difficult men he knew. "Good God man, don't you know that even if you get her down the aisle, you will never have the marriage you want unless you change your ways? There is more than one way a wife can leave her husband."

Robert collapsed onto the chair. "I wanted to keep her safe."

"Robert, she is a grown woman, not some young chit. She is quite capable of arranging her own travel for a shopping trip to York. For you to have behaved in such a high-handed fashion, without your history, is outside enough. With the way you've behaved in the past, it is more than enough to cause her to worry about how you'll treat her in the future."

Robert covered his face with his hands. "I didn't think."

"I'd say that was fairly obvious," John replied brutally. "Honestly, Robert, I'd expected more of you. Where is all your famous address?"

"With her? I never had it." He groaned. "The only time I thought I had the upper hand was the day I . . ."

"That did you a lot of good, didn't it?"

"What do I do now?"

John smiled. "It just so happens, I have a line on where our ladies plan to take luncheon. What say we join them, and you may make your apologies?"

"Not with you standing there, I won't."

John closed his eyes in frustration. "Robert, I'll take Lora for a short walk."

Robert smiled. "Oh, in that case, lead on."

John heaved a sigh. "If for no other reason in my life, I will warrant a place in heaven for having had to deal with you."

When the landlord opened the door to the private parlor, Serena saw Robert and stopped.

Lora gave her a little push forward. "It will be fine. Now give him a chance to explain, but don't be too willing to forgive him."

Serena glided into the room, her head high. Robert looked miserable. John glanced at his wife, who motioned for him to leave.

"John," Lora said. "I would love to look at the garden. Serena, you will excuse us, won't you?" Lora whisked her spouse out the door.

Serena glared at Robert.

"My love." Robert walked toward her. "Forgive me."

She narrowed her eyes. "I'd like to forgive you. I don't know if I can trust you."

He started to take another step closer.

"No, no, no, don't come closer." She looked around, saw a table and took refuge behind it. "You cannot continue making decisions on my behalf without at least discussing them with me first."

Robert eyed the table between them with disgust. "All right."

"I have never given you reason to suppose that I was anything other than capable." She raised her brows. He eyed her and she fought not to blush. Damn the man. "Other than allowing you to kiss me."

He replied slowly, "No, other than with me, you have not."

"Good." Serena stood straighter, and tried to steady her pounding heart. "I wish to make a proposal."

Robert eyed her warily. "And that would be?"

"If, in the future, you feel the need to protect me, you will agree to discuss it with me first."

Therein lay the problem. He always needed to protect her. Robert glanced at the table again. If he could just get his arms around her—no, that wouldn't be the answer. Should he tell her?

"Robert, what is your answer?"

Did all men have to go through this? "There is never a time I don't feel the need to protect you." He searched her eyes. There. It was out, and it didn't seem to help. Damn it, what did she want?

"Robert," Serena said. "I need you to treat me as an adult. I am perfectly capable of ordering my own carriage for a shopping trip."

"You're right. I overstepped my bounds."

"So you agree—the next time, I shall order my own carriage?"

"Yes, you may order your own local travel." Happy that he'd cleared that fence, Robert smiled charmingly and took a step in her direction.

Serena's eyes widened. "No, not yet. Stay where you are."

He raked a hand through his hair. "What do you want from me? I agreed you could order your own travel. Isn't that enough?"

"I want you to treat me as an equal. I want you to honor the promises you made. You cannot do that if you try to wrap me up in cotton wool. Would you treat John or Marcus the same way you are treating me?"

"I'm not married to either of them."

Keeping the table between them, Serena paced.

"Serena, please, my love. I want to make you happy. I just don't know what it is you want."

"This isn't working," she muttered.

Robert shoved the table aside and hauled her into his arms. "Don't say it's not working."

He ruthlessly kissed her.

Serena returned his kisses. Just what she didn't need to do. Regathering the wits that had fled under his onslaught, she struggled not to sink against him.

"Robert, listen to me."

"Serena, I love you. I won't let you leave me."

She leaned back and captured his gaze. "I cannot live feeling as if I am not in control of my life. Don't you understand? That's what made me so afraid of you after Merton. You disregarded me, my desires, only so you could order my life the way you wanted it. You're doing it again."

"My love, it was all for your own good."

"Whether you were right or not isn't the issue. My point is that *you* made the decision. You didn't allow me to make my own choice. You treated me as if I was incapable of acting for my own good. It's very likely I would not have been able to—to make love, but *you* refused to allow it." Did he understand at all?

Robert pulled her back into his arms as if he was afraid to let her go. "I don't know if I can do everything you want. I promise I'll try. If I backslide, and I probably will, you have my permission to call me to account."

Oh God, she wanted to trust him. "I don't know. I don't know if I can believe you."

He touched his forehead to hers. "Please, I need you. I promise I'll tell all the servants your orders must be obeyed. I love you. Serena, don't leave me."

Love, fear, and desire mingled in his beautiful green eyes. He did love her and he wanted her. "In that case"—she put her hands on his face and kissed him—"I'll agree."

"You'll be the death of me."

His thumbs skated over her breasts, singeing her. Lighting her fires. Serena moaned as the need for him exploded through her. He was an addiction. All he had to do was touch her and she was ready to offer herself to him. He lifted her derrière against him. Pressing her to the hard bulge in his pantaloons.

"Serena, I need you now."

"Here?"

Robert kissed her deeply. "Here"

She panted and her heart raced. His hand moved between her legs, stroking. "How much time do you think we have?"

In two long strides he'd reached the door and locked it. "Enough." Robert flashed her a wicked smile. Her heart missed a beat.

"Bend over the table."

The throbbing that started in her breasts shot straight to her core. Serena did as he asked.

"Spread your legs for me," he whispered, stroking between her thighs. He lifted her skirt up over her back.

Cool air swirled around her legs as he lifted her gown. She sighed as he slowly filled her. Robert held her hips, anchoring her to him as he drove deeply into her. She shivered.

This was the first time they'd made love outside of her bed. The elicit excitement heightened her pleasure. The knit of his pantaloons rubbed against her. His musky scent, his hands gripping her, caused her body to spin out of control. Robert thrust harder and deeper as she contracted around him. Serena sucked in a breath to cry out.

"Shush—you can't make any noise."

Robert's deep, soft voice caressed her. Serena shook as her need built again and mewed. How did he do this to her?

"I'm going to come into you," he said, his voice sinfully wicked. "I want you to feel me spill my seed. While we're having luncheon, as my semen runs down your legs, you'll feel me still in you. I want you to remember this."

Serena exploded again just before the warmth he'd promised spewed into her.

Robert quaked violently, possessing her in the only way he was sure she'd allow. When he withdrew, he smoothed her skirts back down and helped her to a chair. Her eyes were still glazed with desire when he poured her a glass of water from the carafe on the table.

"Serena, my love, drink this and sit up. You must behave as if nothing occurred."

Incredulous amber eyes lifted to him in disbelief. "You must be joking. How am I to do that, pray?"

The corners of Robert's lips lifted slowly. He moved behind her. Ah, yes, he enjoyed teaching her. No missish resistance. Just questions. Questions were easily answered. The tips of his fingers ruffled the curls on her neck and his teeth grazed her ear. "You'll limit yourself to our bed, if you can't learn."

Her breasts betrayed the quickening of her breath. Perfect creamy mounds. Ones he would taste again soon.

Serena licked her lips. "Where else?"

"I can think of any number of places," he purred. "A pleasant interlude at a ball. An escape from the young ladies exhibiting their accomplishments at a musical." He cupped her breasts. "Being married doesn't mean we can't slip off to indulge."

"Oooh," she breathed.

* * *

Pressing his advantage, Robert retained his sensual hold on her during the meal. He sat beside her, making her feel his gaze wander over her body, resting on her breasts or lips. He touched her legs under the table and, under the guise of conversation, played with the curls at her neck. When he lifted her skirt and stroked her leg, she had trouble maintaining her conversation with Lora.

By the time they'd finished eating and talking, Serena was ready to do violence. It had taken all the control she could muster to keep her face calm under his sensual onslaught. She'd begun to think there was nothing he would not do, no place he would not touch her, as she was forced to maintain a steady stream of polite conversation. He was sinfully wicked.

She couldn't understand how he could laze in his chair speaking so calmly, talking with John as if his devilish hands weren't driving her mad.

By the time Serena sank back into the plush cushions of the carriage, her pulse was beating rapidly and her skin so sensitive that one touch would push her over the edge. Perhaps he'd give her some relief in the coach, but she'd have to wait for what she really wanted.

Robert followed her in, gave the order to start, and lowered the shades.

His chuckle was slow and sensual. "Let's see how ready you are for me, my lady."

Her bodice and stays were free and dropping and, before she could ask what he planned, he'd lifted her and pushed her gown down over her hips. She was clad only in her chemise and stockings, and he possessed her breasts. She reached out to untie his cravat, but he held her hands away.

"I cannot easily retie my neckcloth. You, I can have re-dressed in a trice."

Robert lifted her, placing her back on the seat, and picked up her gown. After spreading it carefully on the other bench, he released his erection.

"Robert, you cannot mean to do it *here?*"

"I plan to have you everywhere and in every way." He lifted her over him and lowered her carefully onto his member.

"Oh, I like that." Serena sighed as he filled her.

"I rather thought you might." He thrust up, seating himself deeper. Hot wet silk covered his shaft. Thank God she came at once. He was never so close to losing control. Robert had tantalized other women as he had Serena, but he'd never before become so achingly aroused while playing his game.

Sated, Serena collapsed against him.

Her skin was still flushed when he helped her dress and neatened her hair. He held her against him as the coach turned into the drive. "Are you all right?"

"Yes, I'm hungry again."

"Then it's good that we are arriving in time for tea. My love, in the interests of holding up my end of our bargain, I should tell you I sent for Charles Mariville, my secretary. Aside from the fact we'll need his assistance, he is bringing a special license."

"A special license? For what purpose?"

"Your protection. In the unlikely event something happens to me before the wedding, I cannot—will not—leave you as you are—unmarried. I've spoken with John about my concerns and he's agreed."

Serena frowned.

"Please allow me to do this, my love. You may already

be carrying my child. If something were to happen, as my widow, you'd be protected. If not . . . you understand the consequences as well as I."

Her face softened. "Yes, of course, I'll agree. But I must tell you, Robert, you are the most thorough, tyrannical rake I've ever met." She kissed him softly. "When did you decide we needed the license?"

He glanced at her, chagrined. "The moment you told me you'd marry me."

Chapter Twenty-one

Charles was waiting for them outside when they pulled up to the Hall's portico.

Robert shook Charles's hand. "I'm glad you've arrived. How was your trip?"

"Fast, my lord, very fast." Charles grinned and bowed. "My lady, it is my great pleasure to finally meet you."

Serena shook his hand. "Thank you, Mr. Mariville. Tell me, who is coming and when should we expect them?"

"Lord and Lady Evesham will start out to-morrow," Charles said, "as well as Lord and Lady St. Eth and your grandmother, my lord. They are all traveling together."

"Charles, you have the license?"

"Yes, my lord, of course."

Robert's shoulders lightened. He'd never before felt his own mortality so keenly. "Good. Let's go in."

"Charles, will you join us for tea?" Serena asked.

"Thank you, my lady. Tea is just what I need." His gray

eyes danced. "I hear you've been making some changes around the Hall."

"Not only around the Hall." Robert gestured. "Come and we'll tell you all about it. Finster, please send someone to the rectory and ask Mr. Stedman to attend me. When he arrives, I shall want Lady Stanstead as well."

"Very well, my lord."

"Charles, while we wait, I'll tell you what we've been doing . . ."

An hour later, after being apprised of all the changes taking place, Charles gave in to a long whistle.

"You two have been busy, and you are about to be a lot busier. All the invitations have been sent out and accepted."

Robert scowled and cursed the need for a large wedding again.

A look of interest appeared on Charles's face as Serena reached out and patted Robert's hand. "It will be fine," she said. "We'll manage. Let's focus on the Hall. There are enough people engaged with the wedding, it will work itself out."

Finster announced the rector.

John greeted them. "I take it the special license has arrived."

"Indeed. I'd like to complete what we need to now, so that you only have to sign it, if necessary."

"Serena?" John asked. "Are you in accordance with this?"

She took Robert's hand. "Yes, I've agreed."

"Charles, will you act as a witness?" Robert asked.

"With pleasure, my lord."

Freddy opened the door. "Robert, what do you want?"

"Ah, Freddy, we'd like you to act as a witness."

"For what?"

Robert explained about the special license.

"Yes, I'd be delighted."

It was the work of only a few minutes before the license was signed and witnessed. Robert heaved a sigh of relief.

John placed the document in his notebook and glanced at Robert. "I'll keep it with me and in the event of your untimely demise prior to the wedding, I'll sign it."

"Freddy," Serena said, "we expect Phoebe, Marcus, Uncle Henry, Aunt Ester, and your mother in a few days."

"Someone will need to tell Catherine," Freddy said.

"No one's declined an invitation," Robert added.

"That doesn't come as a shock," Freddy replied. "Even Rupert is attending."

"My cousin, Rupert?"

"Do you know another one? My son has curtailed his Grand Tour to attend your wedding."

"I haven't seen him in years." Robert turned to Serena. "Rupert must have attained his majority by now. I remember him being full of pluck as a little boy."

Freddy smiled fondly. "Yes, pluck to the backbone, that's Rupert."

Finster opened the door to announce Lord Malfrey and Freddy's face lit.

She took his hand. "Edward, you know John, but have not met Charles Mariville, Robert's secretary. Charles, Lord Malfrey is an old friend of mine."

Edward greeted Charles and accepted a cup of tea, which Lord Malfrey drank quickly. "Freddy, will you walk out with me?"

"Yes, of course." She turned to Serena. "Please excuse us."

Freddy placed her hand on Edward's arm, and they walked outside to the folly. She stood looking out over the lake as Edward wrapped his arms around her. "Edward," she began, "there is a matter I need to discuss with you."

"There is something I need to discuss with you as well, but first . . ." He bent his head, placing soft kisses down her neck. Soon afterward, Freddy was sprawled naked next to him on the chaise, sated.

"Edward, I need to tell you, when I was sent to marry Stanstead's heir . . ." Her voice was quiet and she couldn't keep it from trembling. What if he took what she was about to tell him badly? What would she do if he never wanted to see her again?

"Here." He tipped her chin up with the crook of his finger. "Look at me."

She blinked back the tears that threatened. She'd never told anyone. "I was pregnant when I was sent away."

His eyes widened, and Freddy searched his face before continuing. "I don't know if my husband ever knew whose child it was. He was never really interested in—in me. After the wedding, I told him I was breeding, he never touched me."

Edward's voice was strained. "The child?"

Freddy smiled softly. "His name is Rupert. He's a strong, intelligent, normal young man. He has the look of the Beaumonts, except for something about his face and, Edward, he has your eyes."

Edward's fingers caressed her cheek. "Did you ever tell him?"

"What would have been the point? Legally, he was my husband's son and now he is the Earl of Stanstead. I only wish I could have told you sooner, that things could have been different. He'll be here for the wedding, and he's not at all stupid. When he sees you, he may well put it together." Freddy searched his face.

Edward's voice caught. "Thank you. Even if I can never claim him as mine, thank you."

"I love you, Edward. I always have. There has never been

anyone else for me. Having Rupert is the only thing that made my life without you bearable."

Edward kissed her gently. "If only your father hadn't sent you away so quickly. If only I'd known . . ."

Freddy held him close to her. "What did you want to say to me?"

He kissed her again. "Freddy, I want you to marry me more than anything in my life. I've always wanted to marry you. Will you agree to be my wife?"

She nodded, overjoyed. After all these years, they could finally be together. "Yes, after Serena and Robert marry."

Edward frowned. "I don't want to wait. We can marry by special license."

"But, my love, I'll be needed at the Hall to help with the wedding preparations."

He placed light kisses down her jaw. "I have no objection to your spending every day, every evening at the Hall, as long as you spend every night with me. We've waited so long already."

"Very well. Shall we go back and see if John is still at the house?"

Edward smiled.

They arrived as John was making his excuses.

"John, we'll walk you to the door," Freddy said. Once they reached the foyer, she told him she and Edward had decided to marry by special license.

He nodded. "Well, this is my week for special licenses. Bring it to me and I will be happy to leg-shackle you."

"Who else has married by special license?" Edward asked.

"Serena and Robert. It was more of a precaution than an actual wedding," Freddy explained.

Edward grinned. "Shall we tell them our news?"

"Yes, let's do. I'm sure they'll be happy for us."

They bid John adieu and walked, hand in hand, back to the morning room.

"Do you want to tell them or shall I?" Freddy asked.

"I'd like to make the announcement."

They walked in together. Robert's lips twitched and Serena smiled expectantly.

Edward put his arm around Freddy. "Lord Beaumont, I wish to inform you Lady Stanstead has agreed to be my wife."

Robert gave a bark of laughter. "I wondered if you were ever going to . . ."

"We are so happy for you," Serena interrupted. "This calls for champagne. Robert, would you please?"

"Yes, my love." Robert reached for the bell pull and ordered champagne.

Freddy took a seat on a chair next to the sofa. "We'd like to marry quietly."

Robert exhaled a frustrated breath. "Would that *we* could marry quietly and not raise everyone's hackles."

"Why didn't you marry when you were young?" Serena asked the pair.

"We wanted to." Freddy glanced at Edward, standing next to her. "We were very much in love. But my father wouldn't allow it. I was sixteen and Edward was still up at Oxford. He was second in line to the title at the time. Edward had been promised a position in the foreign office. I begged my father to let us wait, but he packed me off to Kent, where I was made to marry Stanstead's heir."

The champagne arrived and Robert poured the glasses. He handed one to Freddy. "Didn't Grandmama help you?"

"She tried, but my father would not be swayed. He'd received the offer just a week after my presentation. He and old Lord Stanstead had been great friends. After we were married, I discovered his son had no interest in me, or indeed any woman. We were rarely in each other's company."

Edward picked up the story. "My cousin died shortly after Freddy married and my grandfather arranged a match for me. At the time Freddy was widowed, I was still married. Ellen, my wife, died several years ago, but I knew Freddy had a child, and I couldn't ask her to leave him."

"I don't blame you at all for not wanting to wait now," Serena said. "I think it's wonderful that you found each other again!"

"I still plan to be here to help with the wedding preparations," Freddy promised.

Edward smiled wryly. "That was her only concern. She originally wanted to wait until after you married, but I dissuaded her." He glanced at Robert. "Now if someone could tell me how I go about obtaining a special license, I'd be grateful."

Charles came forward. "My lord, if Lord Beaumont permits, I'd be happy to help you."

"As long as you don't mind another fast trip, Charles," Robert said, "I give you leave to post to London to-morrow. You may change horses as often as necessary."

Edward bowed. "My thanks to you, Lord Beaumont."

"Malfrey, if you're going to be my uncle, you can stop calling me Lord Beaumont. Gives a rather off appearance, don't you think?"

"Then you'd better call me Edward."

"Done. You'll dine with us, of course," Robert said.

Edward grinned. "My pleasure."

Robert turned to his secretary. "Charles, you'll dine with us as well. We have a lot to discuss if you're to hie back to Town to-morrow."

"Of course, my lord."

"With everyone arriving soon, I'd better send a note to Aunt Catherine. She'll want to be here when Uncle Henry and Aunt Ester arrive." Serena sat at the small desk. She finished the note in short order and rang the bell for a footman to have the missive taken to her aunt. "Well then, let's retire to dress for dinner."

Serena met Robert in the bathing chamber. "I feel sorry for poor Charles, having to post back to London almost immediately after he's arrived."

"If I know Charles, he'll drive straight through and back again. I have a feeling he's taking a good deal of pleasure in all of this."

"Is he not always so cheerful?"

"Charles's father, my dear, is a rector. I've always suspected he disapproved of my way of life."

"Ah, and now that we're marrying, he's much happier."

"Yes, and speaking of marrying, come here." Robert held her to him. "Maybe we should have John finalize the license."

"Then there would be no need for a large ceremony."

Robert considered. "I suppose I can wait. It's not that far off now, and I want everyone to watch us say our vows."

Serena grinned. "So there will be no mistake that we are actually married?"

"So there will be no mistake. You realize that as soon as the words are spoken, I've no intention of sharing you with anyone for hours, if not days."

Mary was in the corridor when Henley came out of the bathing chamber carrying several wet towels.

"Mr. Henley, please allow me to help you with those."

"Thank you, Miss Mac Duff," he responded with a slight bow.

"Were all these towels from this afternoon?" Mary asked with widened eyes.

"Yes, Miss Mac Duff, all of them."

"Oh, my." Mary took part of his load. "I wonder what they were doing."

"I would not like to hazard a guess, Miss Mac Duff."

Mary blinked. "No, indeed, Mr. Henley, nor would I."

Robert waited for Serena when she entered the corridor between their bedchambers. "What would you think of combining our bedchambers after the wedding?"

"If you'd like to do it, I have no objection. I do rather like my room. It's warm in the afternoon."

"I rather like your room as well, much better than mine. We can have it done when we're in London for the Little Season."

"What a good idea. I'd also like to add a door from the main corridor to our foyer."

"I'm afraid we'll also have to order a new bathtub," Robert said, a little guiltily. "That one is just a bit small."

Serena smiled slowly. "We did make quite a mess."

"So Henley pointed out to me."

"Henley? But he's so—so . . ."

"Staid, proper, and discreet? That's the reason I hired him."

Serena's smile deepened. "What did he say?"

A look of unholy amusement entered Robert's face. "He said, 'My lord, might I suggest you obtain a larger bathing vessel.' "

Serena choked on a giggle.

Just at that moment, Mary entered the corridor, gave Robert a narrow-eyed look, dropped a stiff curtsey, sniffed, and entered Serena's bedchamber.

Robert's eyes widened. "What was that about?"

"That, I suspect, my lord, was about Henley and Mary having difficulty protecting my reputation, due to our bad behavior." Serena finally went into a whoop of laughter.

Robert tried to scowl and failed. "I take it I'll be in their black books until the wedding. I was a fool to have had the banns read. This waiting is killing me."

"If we were in Scotland, we could be handfasted."

"What's that?"

"A couple exchanges vows that are valid for a year. If at the end of the year's time they decide to part, no one is held at fault."

"What if one of them wanted to remain married?"

"It must be mutual."

Robert growled. "Stupid law. We shall not be handfasted. I'll be dam—darned—if I'd give you the option to leave after a year. Not at the rate I make a mull of things."

Serena went off into a fresh peal of laughter.

The sight of her happy and laughing caused his chest to tighten. How he could have been so stupid as to have hurt her, he didn't know. "Come, my lady. They'll be wondering what happened to us."

Charles handed the wedding guest list to Serena, as Robert looked aghast at a dish offered by one of the footmen and asked, "What is that?"

"Cook said it was haggis, my lord."

"Haggis?"

Serena looked up. "Cook must have received the recipe from her cousin. Please give it to me. I don't know if his lordship will like it."

"I remember the conversation about the recipes, but what exactly is this dish made of?"

Serena replied airily, "Oh, a little of this and a little of that, although each recipe differs. Try a small bite. I assure you, I shan't be upset if you do not like it."

Robert tasted it. "Not bad, not bad at all."

Serena grinned. "I'm glad you like it, as I am quite partial to haggis. Although, similar to sausage, one does not always wish to know what is in it."

After dinner, they sorted through the lists Charles had brought.

"We're going to have *how* many guests staying here?" Robert asked for the second time.

"Robert," Serena said, drawing her brows together, "it doesn't do any good at all for you to keep repeating yourself. The number will not change. Every bedchamber will be in use."

Serena pushed back a curl that had escaped and turned to Robert's aunt. "Freddy, you know most of these people. Are there any particular arrangements we'll need to make for anyone?"

Freddy told Serena which elderly guests would have problems getting around and which of their guests had aversions to others of the guests.

For the fifth or sixth time that evening, Robert burst out with frustration, "We should have married by special license."

Serena rounded on him. "Do give over, Robert! We are not having this wedding to please ourselves. Our people would feel cheated if there was no celebration. Speaking of which, I must talk with Cook. We'll have to set up tables on the lawn for everyone who is not attending the wedding breakfast."

Robert clamped his mouth shut. She was right. Besides, he was so happy when she said "our people."

"Beaumont," Edward said, "let's leave the ladies to this. I've been wanting to try my skill at billiards against yours."

"Good idea, Malfrey. What stakes will you give me?" They walked out of the room and Robert turned to Edward. "Thank you. I have a feeling I was about to get myself in trouble. I've not got the hang of this marriage thing yet."

Edward gave a bark of laughter. "There will be a prize for you if you figure it out. Most men don't. My best advice is to agree with your wife more often than not."

Robert stifled a groan. "That is easier advice to give than to follow."

"Most assuredly, but the benefits are more than worth it."

Chapter Twenty-two

"My lady," an urgent voice whispered from behind the dressing room door.

Serena rubbed her eyes.

"My lady!"

"Mary? What is it?"

Mary's voice was soft but insistent. "His lordship must leave. The maid and footman are coming with your wash water."

Serena moved to wake Robert, but an iron band masquerading as an arm clamped down on her. She twisted around to face him and he brought her flush against him.

"Robert you must go. Now!"

When he tried to slide her beneath him, Serena freed one arm and shook him hard. "Robert, you must go. The footman!"

He opened his eyes and blinked.

"My lord, please hurry," Mary pleaded.

"What time is it?" He reached for his dressing gown, patting around the bed.

"Stay where you are, I'll get it." Serena disentangled herself from him and sat up. She was stopped by Robert's dressing gown landing on top of her head. Mary must have found it.

He quickly donned it and hurried out the door.

Robert entered his bedchamber and was met by Henley's look of long suffering. His valet glanced at him and smiled smugly for a moment, before resuming his impassive mien. Robert looked down. The fabric of the gown tented out. He snarled and climbed into bed. "It pleases me to no end to think I have humored you."

Henley continued to set out his master's clothing. "Not at all, my lord."

Lying back against the pillows, Robert swore and stayed in bed until he heard the footman come with his wash water. He tried to remind himself it was only for another week. After that, he could damn well stay in her bed as long as he liked.

Tim, the footman, regained the corridor in time to see Daisy, the maid who'd delivered the water to Lady Serena. They had recently been stepping out, and he volunteered for any job that would bring him in contact with her.

Daisy smiled. "Did I tell you I saw his lordship kissing her ladyship in the corridor before he left yesterday?"

"No. I hope it didn't shock you."

She shook her head. "Oh, no, how could it? They being so much in love, they can't help themselves. I hope when I get married, I love my husband and he loves me as much. Mrs. Norton says as how such love was, was . . ." She scrunched up her face, trying to remember the word. "Well, how it was not in the common way with the lord and lady's set."

"I'm sure your husband will love you just as much," Tim replied.

Daisy's skin turned a pretty shade of pink and she continued, "And Mr. Finster said, as how when all the nobs get here how we'll have to all be protecting them like. So's no one gets the wrong idea," she said importantly. "He says as how them nobs *and* their servants love a scandal and just try to make trouble. And Mr. Finster should know, him spending so much time in Lunnon." Daisy nodded her head emphatically.

"We'll need to be real careful so none of them Lunnon servants gets to talking. We protect our own."

Serena met Robert in the corridor. "I need to speak with Mrs. Norton about the guest arrangements. Why don't you go fishing?"

He'd go fishing when he could take her. "No, I'll go over the stabling with Pitchley."

"That's something I'd not thought of."

They entered the breakfast room, and Robert held out Serena's chair for her before he noticed there were three people at the table rather than two. Malfrey had joined them. "You're here early, Malfrey. Did you miss us?"

Serena pinched him. "Good morning, Edward."

"Good morning, Lady Serena, Beaumont."

"Please call me Serena." She bid everyone a good morning and took the bowl of porridge and the baked egg Finster offered her before pouring tea.

"Are you here to provide us moral support?" Serena asked Edward.

He took a piece of ham. "I think that's the reason. I wasn't told. I tend to come when summoned."

Robert, unable to help himself, grinned. "Like a well-trained dog."

Edward's lips twitched. "Be careful. Even well-trained dogs bite."

"That is quite enough you two." Freddy said tartly. "Neither of you seem to behave at all."

"I'm sure you will be a great deal of help, Edward" Serena said, amused. "Unlike some, who shall not be named."

"I am pleased to see the four of you having such a wonderful time," Catherine said dryly. "I, on the other hand, am in a panic over what St. Eth will say about the questionable sleeping arrangements."

Robert glanced at Serena, seeing her not at all concerned, but instead brimming with merriment.

Finster, who fixed his eyes at a point on the wall, unexpectedly said, in his customary aloof tone, "It is well known that, although Lady Serena is occupying the viscountess's apartments, nothing untoward is occurring. I might add, there is not a member of this household who would say otherwise."

He bowed. "Now if you will excuse me?"

Grinning, Robert waved him off. Finster left, closing the door behind him.

"Well, that was interesting," Freddy said, laughing. "I don't think I've ever heard him say so much at one time."

"You have very well-trained servants, Beaumont," Edward said.

"You wouldn't think them so well trained if you'd heard them call me *Master Robert,* in a way to make me feel six years old again." His brow furrowed for a moment. "Come to think of it, none of them has called me that for a while." He glanced at Serena.

"Well, Robert, there was nothing for it. They couldn't continue calling you *Master Robert* when you are their lord. After I explained my reasoning to Mrs. Norton and Finster, they understood perfectly."

"I'll wager they did. They know on which side their bread is buttered." Robert smiled. "It appears the entire staff has closed ranks, and it's not me they're protecting. Well done, my love."

Serena's eyes were soft. "It is both of us."

"If you have duties to attend to to-day, I suggest you do them quickly," Catherine said. "Henry travels fast. It would not surprise me to see him here by luncheon, and I predict we will have a test of the staff's loyalty."

Serena was hurrying down the back corridor, glancing through her lists, when she ran into a wall of solid muscle. "Oh!"

Robert caught her from bouncing off him. "Finally. I thought I wouldn't see you until luncheon."

She put her arms around him and tilted her head up for a quick kiss. "Where were you going?"

"To check the fishing rods."

"My lord, what makes you think you'll have time to fish this week?"

"They're not for me. For St. Eth and Marcus," he said. "I'd like to keep St. Eth occupied, and I'll sacrifice Marcus to the cause."

His hands skated over her shoulders to her buttocks. Serena swallowed and a tremor slid through her. Her voice was low and sultry. "Do you have some time?"

Robert smiled and swooped to kiss her. "I thought you'd never ask."

"We can't be long. I'm on my way to see about the flowers."

He steadily walked her back toward a door to an unused parlor, reached around her, and opened it. "We won't need much time. I missed you this morning."

Serena was coming to enjoy that aspect of Robert quite a bit. "Did you? You should have awoken earlier."

"After last night, I'm surprised you didn't sleep until noon. When we're married, don't expect to escape me in the morning."

"I never want to escape you."

Robert captured her lips. His tongue caressed hers and her breasts swelled and ached. Frissons of delight stroked her. She knew she was wet and ready for him. Serena couldn't understand how he so expertly managed to ravage her mouth and steal most of her senses while at the same time whisking her into the room so smoothly. It must be one of the benefits of marrying a rake.

He lifted her and held her against the wall. "Put your legs around me."

The next sounds out of her mouth were breathy moans and a cry as he took her hard against the wall. He'd never lusted after a woman like he did her.

Every day—no, every minute—he wanted to be with her, inside her, listening to her sweet sighs and moans and the low keening sound when she came for him.

Robert chuckled deeply as she sunk against him, complaining once more about her wobbly legs. He lifted her off him and pulled out his handkerchief to clean them up before sitting in a chair and holding her tightly.

He gazed at her with pride and possession and love. A love he never thought he'd experience. So all encompassing.

Serena opened her eyes and frowned. "Is something wrong?"

"No, God, no." His voice was gravelly. "I love you."

Serena lifted one hand to his face and cupped it. "I love you, too, and I love what we have together." She pulled herself up to kiss him. "Now, I must go."

"The gardener?"

"Yes, among the many matters we must deal with this week."

"How are your legs? Can you walk yet?"

"I don't know."

He set her on her feet and she took a step. "Yes, I'll be fine. You go to your fishing rods, my lord, and I'll see about the flowers."

Robert's gaze followed her. Should he have told her he liked her wobbly legs because he was the cause? Maybe another time. He'd have the rest of his life with Serena to tell her.

Yet how long would that be? His father and grandfather both had died in their prime. He remembered his grandmother's grief. Had his grandfather run out of time to say the things he wanted to say? Life had never seemed so precious.

The Hall was in a hum of activity as everyone prepared for the first guests since the old lord's funeral. Freddy assured Serena the new hangings and coverings were in place. Serena was in the main hall, speaking with Finster, when the coaches drove up.

Finster bowed. "I'll send for his lordship, my lady."

"Please do." She stepped out onto the porch stairs.

Marcus jumped down from the first of the two vehicles, then turned to help Phoebe.

Serena went forward to greet them. "Phoebe, Marcus, welcome to the Hall."

Marcus bowed. "Thank you. I'm glad to be here and very glad to be out of that coach. I thought I traveled quickly. St. Eth sets a murderous pace."

Robert strolled up from the side of the house. "Phoebe, don't tell me you left your blacks on the road?"

She shook out her skirts. "I had no choice. They'll be brought up in a day or so." She hugged Serena. "You look wonderful. It's plain to see this part of the country agrees with you."

"Yes, it does." Serena smiled widely before turning to welcome her uncle.

"You're in good looks, Niece." Henry cast an assessing glance around. "You're to be congratulated, Beaumont, on the condition of your property. If the rest looks half as good as the house and the gardens, I shall be well pleased."

Robert stood a little stiffly, and Serena felt an overpowering urge to protect him from her formidable uncle. Taking her place next to Robert, she took his hand, squeezed it, and squarely met her uncle's eyes. "Uncle Henry, welcome to the Hall. I believe you'll find the estate, as a whole, in excellent order."

Henry's lips twitched a little. "Good. You may take me round in the morning."

Robert bowed. "With pleasure, my lord."

Frowning, Serena glanced around. "Uncle Henry, where are Aunt Ester and Lady Beaumont?"

Marcus uttered a short laugh. "After the first few hours, they decided the pace St. Eth was setting did not meet their notion of civilized travel. I expect we'll see them late to-morrow."

Henry had the grace to look a little chagrined. "There is a lot to do and not much time to accomplish it. Have the two of you decided on your marriage settlements?"

Glancing quickly at Robert, Serena shrugged. The only

settlement they'd discussed was which bed to sleep in. "No, we've discussed everything except those."

St. Eth pressed his lips together. "Well, if you'll have someone show me to my room, you may get on with it then."

Troubled by her uncle's abrupt manner, Serena called for Finster. "Lord St. Eth would like to be shown to his chamber. Uncle Henry, I'll send tea up. Luncheon will be served at one o'clock."

Robert was in conversation with Marcus and Phoebe. Serena joined them. "Why was Uncle Henry upset?"

Phoebe glanced skyward. "Allow us to clean off the dust, and we'll explain."

"Come, we'll show you to your chamber." Serena took them to a suite of rooms at the opposite end of the wing in which the viscount's chambers were located.

A half hour later, the two young couples were seated in the morning room, drinking tea.

Robert passed a hand over his face. "I knew your uncle and I would discuss the settlements, but I didn't expect to be clouted with it the moment he arrived. What's got him so out of sorts? Tell me it's not me this time."

"No. It was a letter from Castle Vere," Marcus said. "St. Eth was so aggravated, he practically flew out of London. The *only* reason we kept up with his breakneck pace was to be here when he arrived in order to help."

"Tell me the worst," Serena said.

Marcus glanced at Serena. "Henry wrote your brother asking for the details of your portion. St. Eth received a very impertinent letter from Vere concerning the settlements. He said as no one thought to consult him about your marriage— which he was not happy about—and since you were long past your majority, you could handle the settlements on your own. He also thought you could do better than a viscount."

"That letter shows Mattie's influence," Serena said sadly. "I wish I'd thought of this earlier. I'll have to send to my solicitor in Edinburgh and to my man of business in London for the documents we'll need. Robert, I am sorry. I'll write the missives immediately and have them sent by express post."

"There's no reason for you to apologize. You've had more than enough to keep you busy since you arrived. All my information is ready." Robert's brow furrowed and he looked at Phoebe and Marcus. "Marcus, didn't I hear that you settled Phoebe's property on her?"

"Yes, I'd no need of it," Marcus said, and playfully added, "and she had no intention of giving it up."

Robert turned to Serena. "There's nothing stopping us from doing the same, is there, my love?"

Serena shook her head. In fact, it was a very good idea. "Do you know, I've never given the settlements the least bit of thought? If I'd considered it at all, I would have insisted on keeping my personal possessions, but the rest, if I am to keep it, how does it work?"

"Quite easily." Phoebe put down her cup. "A trust is set up to hold all your property. The only provision is that Robert must agree to the trust before the wedding."

"I will agree."

"Good. You'll make Uncle Henry much happier. Once he has a look around and goes over your financial records, he should be in a very good mood. Now, tell us what you've been doing since you got here. Everything looks in such good skin."

They spent the time until luncheon discussing the changes wrought at the Hall.

"I would've never thought to burn down the cottages." Robert proudly praised Serena's skills. "If you ride out with us to-morrow, you'll see all she's accomplished."

"I can't take all the credit. You allowed me to do as I wished. No matter what it cost you." Serena smiled.

Other than the brief problem with the coach that day, he really had encouraged her to take charge whenever she'd seen a need. "Phoebe, I'd like you to come with me to the rectory to-morrow. We have a meeting with the new school administrator later in the afternoon and, of course, you have much more experience than I."

"I'd like nothing better," Phoebe said. "Is Mrs. Stedman the former Lora Ashhurst?"

"I believe she is," Serena replied. "Do you know her family?"

"I know Lora. I remember when she came out," Phoebe said. "Even though she'd told her father she'd already made her choice, he insisted she have a Season. Lora took quite well, but none of the gentlemen could hold a candle to John. I'm delighted to hear Lora is doing so well. Where are Catherine and Freddy?"

Robert's eyes sparkled with undisguised glee. "They'll be here in time for luncheon, along with Lord Malfrey, I imagine. Freddy is marrying him as soon as my secretary returns from London with the special license. They left early this morning to inspect the Grange, Lord Malfrey's estate. I'm not the only one sporting his blunt on his property."

Finster announced luncheon.

Serena rose. "We should go."

The two couples were walking down the corridor to the family dining room as Catherine, Freddy, and Edward arrived.

"You're cutting it close," Robert remarked. "St. Eth is here."

Catherine's eyes opened wide. "Oh no, maybe I shall take a tray in my chamber."

"Why would you want to do that?" Phoebe asked. "Don't you want to see Uncle Henry?"

Catherine pinched the bridge of her nose. "He is the best of brothers, but he is going to be so upset with me."

"Just don't mention any potential problems unless he asks. I cannot think he would be so indelicate," Freddy said.

Catherine shuddered. "He would. The man doesn't care a fig for delicacy if one of his family is involved, and I'm not sure he'll agree with your decision." She frowned at Serena. "He hasn't asked you, has he?"

"No, he was too upset over my marriage settlements."

Phoebe knitted her brows. "I have no idea what you are all talking about, but if it will upset Uncle Henry, don't, I pray you, say anything about it until we've discussed Serena's settlements, and he's in a better frame of mind. We already had to leave Aunt Ester and Lady Beaumont on the road to appease him."

Freddy's jaw dropped. "You left Mama on the road?"

While the ladies huddled in the corridor together discussing the trip from London and the reason for Henry's bad humor, Marcus leaned close to Robert. "What is it Catherine doesn't want St. Eth to discover?"

Robert said, chagrined, "It seemed a good idea at the time, and we do have a special license." Trying to change the subject, he said, "By the by, where's Arthur?"

"He'll be along in an hour or so." Marcus's eyes narrowed. "What have you done?"

"Serena is in the viscountess's chambers."

"Wha . . ." Marcus quickly turned Robert away from the ladies, his voice a harsh whisper. "Are you out of your mind? What the devil did you think you were doing?"

Robert looked around to insure no one was listening "It wasn't my decision alone. Serena agreed and we asked Freddy. She agreed as well, and if something were to happen to me, we've signed a special license, so Serena is protected."

"That's something at least," Marcus grumbled. "Why did you think you needed to protect her?"

Despite all his efforts not to, Robert smiled.

"Ah, I see."

"I rather thought you would. What do we do about St. Eth?"

"Keep him involved in the settlements until your grandmother and Aunt Ester arrive. I have great faith in the ladies to come up with something."

"My lord," Finster said, bowing. "Lord St. Eth asked that you begin without him. He will be down directly."

"Thank you, Finster." Robert turned and addressed the ladies and Edward. "St. Eth will be a little delayed. Shall we go in?"

With the table in the small dining room now full, Robert led Serena to the foot of the table where Finster held the back of the chair.

Catherine's brows came together and she had a worried look. "Oh, my dear, do you think you should? With your uncle here?"

Suddenly unsure, Serena glanced at Robert.

He smiled charmingly. "Do as you wish. Everyone at the Hall, including me, thinks of you as its mistress."

Serena nodded. "Aunt Catherine, I shall go on as I have done since I've arrived, and how I intend to go on. Uncle Henry will just have to accept it."

Chapter Twenty-three

While touring the house, Henry stopped a footman to inquire about luncheon. Informed that the meal was about to begin, he made his way to the front of the house and was close enough to hear Catherine's dismay at discovering he was at the Hall.

He backtracked and, thanks to a very good sense of direction, regained his chamber without too much of a problem. "Griffin," Henry said to his valet. "Find out for me what is going on here."

Griffin bowed. "Yes, my lord."

"Tell whatever footman you find I have been delayed and will join them presently."

"Certainly, my lord."

Griffin returned about twenty minutes later.

"Well?" Henry asked.

Griffin fixed his eyes above Henry's head and began sonorously. "It appears, my lord, much refurbishing has gone on in the past two weeks—to include new hangings, a new stove, and new tenants' cottages, as well as other items that needed to be replaced or repaired. There is talk of a new school, as well, my lord. The changes, my lord, are attributed to Lady Serena. Lord Beaumont encouraged her to do as she saw fit. I was attempting to question a parlor maid, when the housekeeper, a Mrs. Norton, appeared. A most formidable lady, my lord, however, not quite what we are used to dealing with . . ."

"Griffin, get on with it," Henry said. "There is nothing in what you've related that would cause me concern."

"No, my lord. As I was about to say, the only unusual occurrence is that Lady Serena has taken over the viscountess's chambers. I was assured by Mrs. Norton, who then summoned Miss Mac Duff, Lady Serena's dresser, and Mr. Henley, Lord Beaumont's valet, that nothing untoward has occurred. It was made plain to me that Lord Beaumont sleeps in his bed and that Lady Serena has not seen the viscount's chamber at all."

Henry pursed his lips thoughtfully. "What does the staff think of Lord Beaumont and Lady Serena's arrangement?"

"The staff is most attached to Lady Serena and thinks of her as their mistress, my lord. They are very much looking forward to the nuptials. Mr. Henley also made mention of a special license, although I was not made privy to the details."

"Very well. Excellent job, Griffin."

Griffin bowed. "I am always happy to be of service, my lord."

Henry entered the dining room and did not, by so much as the flicker of an eyelash, betray that he found anything odd in Serena's sitting at the foot of the table. Between the butler hovering solicitously near her and Beaumont's proud grin when he glanced at her, it was plain Serena had found her home.

She smiled, genuinely happy to see Henry.

He fixed his gaze on Beaumont. "Have you discussed the settlements?"

Robert met Henry's gaze, and nodded toward Serena. "*We* have decided Serena will keep what is hers. I understand it must all be put in a trust."

"Settlements on girl children and younger sons?"

Robert inclined his head. "Whatever you deem fit. The bulk of the estate is entailed. However, I have private funds left to me by my mother and an aunt."

"Are you prepared to discuss your financial details?"

Robert smiled politely. "At your pleasure, my lord."

Henry was pleased. Beaumont was behaving exactly as he should. "After luncheon then."

"Good." Serena turned to Henry. "Now, if you are finished for the moment, we may continue this discussion later. Uncle Henry, try the fish. Cook has a way with it."

When they'd finished eating, the entire party, with the exception of Freddy and Edward, repaired to the study. Freddy whispered to Serena that she and Edward were off to Yorkshire to visit his solicitor, who, she said, would no doubt be shocked at her being present.

"You've given us some food for thought, my dear. I congratulate you on handling St. Eth so well. We'll see you before dinner." Freddy hesitated and her eyes filled with sudden tears. "You fit perfectly here at the Hall."

Serena hugged Freddy. "I feel right here. It feels like home. Now go or we shall both be crying and our gentlemen will think we mean to run away."

* * *

Lord Arthur, Phoebe and Marcus's eleven-month-old son, arrived and had to be admired before they finally made their way to the study.

Phoebe exclaimed at the large partner's desk. "How beautiful and how enormous."

Serena was delighted. "If you look on the sides you'll see how the spaces for the ledgers are fitted in. It makes it so much easier."

Marcus stood next to Robert. "You spared no efforts."

"Once she was here, I had to find some way to convince her to stay."

Robert opened the files containing his accounts and placed them before St. Eth, already seated at the desk. "Would you like a sherry, sir?"

"Please." St. Eth glanced up at the group. "You may all sit while I review Beaumont's information."

The room became quiet as five pairs of eyes focused on him. Although Robert knew his accounts were in order, having St. Eth study them made Robert feel like a callow youth.

Finally, St. Eth pushed back the chair. "This is better than I expected. Beaumont, if you tell me who your solicitor is, I shall instruct mine to contact him. Serena, I'll need a letter from you, authorizing me to act on your behalf."

"My solicitor is Mosley, sir," Robert said.

St. Eth chuckled. "That will make things easier. Mosley represents our family, as well. Now," St. Eth said and stood. "I'd like to see that great-nephew of mine again."

Beaumont reluctantly gave Serena's uncle the baby and wondered how long it would take before Serena was increasing. Robert hoped it would be soon.

After dinner and tea, Serena and Robert showed Phoebe and Marcus into the viscountess's parlor. Upon entering the room, Serena directed Phoebe's attention to the view from the windows. It was nine o'clock and weak light still poured in from the west.

The room was furnished with an old French secretaire, two sofas, a number of chairs, and two large, soft armchairs, a daybed, and a few marble-inlaid tables. Bookshelves covered the inner wall. Bright Persian rugs overlapped on the floor. Very improperly, the ladies, after having been given glasses of brandy, had taken off their slippers and curled up next to their gentlemen.

"This is a lovely room," Phoebe said. "Do you use it much?"

"No, it's actually the first time I've been in the room," Serena replied. "I like it. Who decorated it? Do you know, Robert?"

"We'll ask my grandmother when she arrives." He drew Serena closer. "I can't tell you how relieved I am St. Eth is no longer upset."

"The only person who could bear to be around him on the trip was his valet," Marcus said. "I've never seen Henry as exercised as he was after he received Vere's letter." Evesham glanced at Robert and Serena. "You two seem happy."

Robert looked at Serena. "We are."

Phoebe studied them for a few moments. "Do none of your servants think your living arrangement a little precipitant?"

"Phoebe, are you being impertinent?" Robert joked.

"No, I am being shamelessly curious."

Serena chuckled softly. "Henley, Robert's man, and Mary, my maid—though I've been informed I must call her my dresser now that I am to be a *viscountess*—took it upon themselves to insure Robert's bed is slept in every night. He must leave me in sufficient time to prove he's in his own bed when his morning wash water arrives."

Marcus frowned at her. "I don't understand what being a viscountess has to do with it. You're already an earl's daughter."

Serena widened her eyes, and assumed a prim demeanor. "Ah, but I'm not an *English* earl's daughter."

Robert, who had been languidly stroking Serena's shoulders, suddenly sat up, dislodging her. "Who said that to you?"

Serena shook herself and met Robert's frown with one of her own. "Who said what to me?"

He growled. "Who said a *Scottish* earl's daughter was not equal to an *English* earl's daughter? That is not a distinction you would have thought to have made."

"Ah." Serena started to rearrange herself comfortably against Robert again, but he held her off, capturing her gaze. *"Who?"*

"I don't even know who they were. I was in the ladies' retiring room at Almack's when I heard them. They were bemoaning the way you looked at me, my love. What does it matter?"

Robert settled her next to him again, holding her protectively. "Harrumph. Spiteful cats. Is it any wonder I eschewed the *ton* for years?"

Serena cuddled into him. "There is no point in thinking of it now. All of it is long past. Where do you plan to take us for the picnic to-morrow?"

"The ash grove."

"With the stream?"

"Yes, that's the one."

Phoebe smiled at Marcus, then looked at the clock. "Oh my, look at the time. We must be off, else I'll not be up to nurse Arthur and accompany you to-morrow. Serena, would you mind showing me your bedchamber before we leave?"

Marcus said, "Robert, let me see that bathing chamber you told us about."

Once they'd gained Serena's bedchamber, Phoebe took her hand and towed Serena to a small sofa against the wall. "Everything is good? I see that you look happy, but I need to ask." Phoebe searched Serena's face. "You cannot think how many times I've blamed myself for introducing the two of you."

Tears of joy filled Serena's eyes. "Everything is wonderful. He was so funny when he finally told me he loved me . . ."

Phoebe laughed. "How typically Robert."

Once in the bathing chamber, instead of admiring it, Marcus regarded Robert for a few moments.

"Marcus, if you want to talk, we'll have to go into my bedchamber. This room echoes."

"Very well." He followed Robert.

"What's on your mind?" Robert asked.

"Not mine so much as Phoebe's. She's been worried since you left France. You do love Serena?"

"Do you know, Marcus, you are the only man I know who would ask me that question? Yes, I love her. I more than love her. I can't imagine my life without Serena."

"Good." Marcus started toward the door.

Robert stayed him. "Wait. There is something I need to know, and I don't know who else to ask."

His friend turned.

"You know how uncertain life can be. I thought of something this morning I wanted to tell Serena, and I didn't. Then I thought, what if I never have another chance to tell her?"

"Tell her when you think of it. For as much as she didn't quite have her feet under her in London, she does have them here. Consider how she handled Henry. Serena is a strong woman. I'm not saying you won't need to protect her in London. But, with you, here she can be herself."

"Thank you."

Robert walked Marcus out to the corridor where Phoebe and Serena were talking.

Phoebe grinned at Robert and Serena. "We'll leave you here. I think we can find our way to our chambers."

Serena laughed. "I have no doubt, considering you're just down the corridor."

Robert stood behind her as Phoebe and Marcus left. "I have something to tell you."

Turning, Serena glanced up at him. "What is it?"

"I love it when your legs give out."

Serena carefully removed Robert's arm and climbed out of bed. They needed to start betimes to-day if Uncle Henry wanted to see the estate.

Mary was in the dressing room. "You're up early."

"Yes. Please tell Henley he may fetch his lordship. I'll dress in here."

Her maid set up the wash basin and slipped out of the room. A little while later, Henley's voice reached her.

"My lord, I was instructed to wake you."

"Where is . . . ?" Robert groaned. "Very well."

The door to the bedchamber closed.

Serena finished dressing and met Robert in the corridor.

When they arrived in the breakfast room, Finster held her chair. "We'll have a warm day to-day, my lady."

"Thank you, Finster. That will be welcome after all the cold weather we've had."

Robert's eyes narrowed at her seated at the far end of the table. "I don't like you sitting so far away."

Serena tried to keep from laughing. "You told me to do as I wished."

Robert scowled. "Can't you sit next to me at breakfast?"

Well, it was breakfast and they were the only ones there. "If you desire it, my lord."

"I do, my lady. Finster, please help her ladyship move."

Finster's lips twitched, but he contrived to maintain his countenance. "Yes, my lord. My lady?" Finster led Serena to the chair next to Robert's.

Before Serena could sit, Robert fixed his butler with a look. "Finster, don't you have something to do in the corridor?"

"I believe I do, my lord. I shall attend to it at once."

Robert stood, drawing Serena to him. She tilted her head up as he captured her lips. "You're mine. For the rest of your life, you're mine."

"I'm yours, as long as you're mine."

"Do you think I'd ever want another woman?" Robert asked, surprised.

"Not now, no. Yet, I know I'm not as experienced . . ."

Robert kissed her again. "You're mine to teach, and I'll teach you everything you need to know. I'll never stop wanting you."

Serena sighed. She didn't know from where her sudden uncertainty came. She kissed him as if it was their last kiss, desperately, greedily. Robert responded. His hand on one of her breasts, he backed her up to the wall and rucked up her skirt.

Someone knocked and Serena pushed him away. "Robert!"

With great effort they regained their places before the door opened.

Serena bowed her head over her plate, taking deep breaths and calming herself.

"Good morning." Robert greeted Phoebe and Marcus. "We were wondering when you'd join us."

* * *

Serena rode ahead to gallop the fidgets out of Shamir. Robert had taken care of hers after breakfast, when she'd gone to change. She'd die a slow death if ever he went to another woman.

Uncle Henry made comments here and there as he surveyed the fields and was clearly impressed. "You've done a good job, Beaumont."

"I'd like to take the credit, but it was Serena who showed me what needed to be done. I'd never really talked with one of my tenants until she entered their cottages and left me to fend for myself. It was not the way my father taught me."

Robert and Serena took Henry, Phoebe, and Marcus to the Johnsons' farm so that St. Eth could see the renovations and the new cottages. It pleased Serena that he was so impressed.

Afterward, Robert led the way to the ash grove where Freddy and Edward waited for them.

Freddy searched their faces. "How did it go?"

Serena handed her reins to Robert. "I think it went well. Uncle Henry was pleased, wasn't he, Robert?"

"I think so," Robert replied.

Uncle Henry had dismounted and Robert turned to her uncle. "Here, I'll take those, sir."

Robert took Henry's reins and tied them to a tree.

Serena spied the long trestle table set up with plates, cutlery, wine, and platters of food. It reminded her of a London party. "Oh my, this wasn't exactly what I had in mind when I asked for a simple picnic to be set out."

Robert's lips twitched. "No, nor I."

"Cook certainly outdid herself." Serena would have to make a point of complimenting Cook. "How much will you wager that this is puffing off our consequence to Uncle Henry?"

He grinned. "Not a groat."

They took their places at the table, and Serena signaled for the footmen to begin serving.

A smile hovered around Uncle Henry's lips. "Do you always picnic in such splendor?"

She was about to admit it was not what she had planned, when Robert held up a glass of well-chilled wine to Henry in a toast.

"It is in your honor, my lord."

St. Eth saluted Robert and Serena with his glass. "This was very well done. You are to be congratulated."

She glanced at Robert and a sense of pride at all they'd accomplished came over her. "Thank you, Uncle Henry."

After the meal, Phoebe and Marcus, along with Edward and Freddy, went to explore the grove.

"Tell me," Henry said. "Catherine mentioned to me a problem with missing children?"

Serena pressed her lips together. The horror of that missing child was never far from her mind. "A thug has been taking them, we think, for the mines."

"Serena saved one of the boys," Robert said. "I've had my gamekeeper searching for campsites."

A scream from off in the woods on the other side of the small stream rent the relative quiet. Serena glanced toward the trees.

Robert ran toward the cry, and a young boy, of about eight years, tore out of the wood. A large man with a thin scar on his face followed.

Chapter Twenty-four

"Robert, that's the man who's been taking the children!" Serena cried, quickly running toward the lad.

"Serena, stay where you are." Robert bounded across the stream. He grabbed the youngster, and returned to give the child to Serena, before Robert, followed by Marcus, took off after the kidnapper. Just a few seconds after the men had left, there was a sound of horses.

Serena held the shivering boy to her, calmly cooing to him. "There now. He won't touch you again. Tell me your name and how you came to be taken by that villain."

The youth sniffed and nodded. "Me name's Arch. Me and my brothers was fishing, and he come up and grabbed me. He tried to get my next brother, but they took off."

"Your next brother? Do you mean the brother closest to you in age?"

"Yes, ma'am."

"How long have you been with the kidnapper?" Serena asked.

"It were the day afore yesterday he took me."

"Can you tell me where you are from?"

"Wood Hill."

Serena glanced at Phoebe. "Catherine's property."

Phoebe nodded slightly.

Freddy and Edward came rushing up. "What is it?" Freddy asked.

"It's the kidnapper," Serena replied, and then turned her head to see Robert, looking murderous, come crashing back through the woods with Marcus.

"I think we can catch them if we take the path through the forest. What's the lad told you?" Robert asked.

Arch cowered and sidled against her.

"It will be all right, Arch. His lordship isn't angry at you, but at the man who took you." Serena tightened her hold on the boy. "Did the blackguard steal any other children?"

Arch nodded. "He had five others. They was all tied up, but he thought I was too little to get away. When he stopped to take a leak, I jumped down and ran as fast as I could from the wagon."

"You did a very good job," Serena said with approval. "Now, do you know where he was taking you?"

"No, ma'am. He just said he had a place he'd keep us and it weren't far."

"Good. I'm going to leave you with these men." Serena pointed at the footmen. "They'll feed you and give you something to drink before they take you to my home. Lady Ware is my aunt, and she's staying with me."

She signaled to the older footman. "Feed him and then take him to the Hall. He's one of Lady Ware's dependants. We will try to find the other children."

"Yes, my lady."

Henry touched her arm. "I'll go back to the Hall and notify the magistrate. Do you want me to send round to the rectory as well?"

"Yes, thank you. I don't know how long this will take." She glanced up. "Robert, are you ready?"

His lips formed a thin line. "You're not coming."

"I most certainly am." Serena looked pointedly at Phoebe and Freddy, already mounted. "Don't waste time trying to argue with me."

"It is too dangerous," he said, clipping his words.

"These are my people too." Serena clenched her jaw. "I am going and unless you plan to tie me up, you can't stop me. You have no right to stop me."

With a growl, he tossed her up into her saddle, mounted, and rode off before she could settle her skirts.

"What was all that about?" Phoebe asked.

Serena gritted her teeth. "Robert's autocratic nature. Let's go before he gets too far ahead. I don't want him to lose us."

Ahead of them, Robert scowled at Marcus. "Why are you allowing Phoebe to come?"

Marcus raised a brow. "Even if I wanted to, how do you propose I stop her?"

"Isn't there something in the marriage vows about obeying?"

Marcus glanced at Robert as if he'd lost his mind. "Yes, and you'd be well advised never to mention it."

Robert turned at the tattoo of hooves behind them. "We'll discuss this later. Our ladies are almost upon us."

They were riding in a lane just wide enough for two horses side by side. After a little bit, Serena looked around. "I don't remember this being Hall land. Whose is it?"

"Mine," Edward scowled.

A few minutes later, Marcus rode up to Serena. "We've

picked up the kidnapper's trail. Is there a building out here where children could be hidden?"

"Yes, an old barn," Edward replied tightly. "I know a shortcut through the woods that is much faster than the trail. If there are children being kept there, I'll be able to get them to safety before you and Robert arrive via the road."

Marcus nodded at Edward, then turned to his wife. "Phoebe?"

"I'll go with Serena. You and Robert take care."

"Always, my love. You as well." Marcus rode back to Robert.

"Edward, we'll follow you," Serena said.

Freddy rode up next to Edward. "Darling, what is it? You look so distraught."

"My cousin and heir, Aubrey, swore to me he was not involved in the kidnappings. I didn't believe him and warned Aubrey I would see him transported. It appears my fears were correct. No one else would know about the barn."

"Oh, Edward, I'm so sorry."

"We'll deal with him later. Let's worry about the children now."

Shamir seemed to sense Serena's urgency and tried to outpace the other horses, but Serena held him back. "It won't do you a bit of good. I don't know where we're going."

He tossed his head.

Edward slowed as they arrived on the outskirts of the clearing around the barn. He lowered his voice. "I'll go on ahead. If there is no one else around, I'll wave for you to approach."

"I'm coming with you," Freddy said.

"Freddy . . ."

"No. I'll not debate this. If we're caught, we can say you

are showing me around the property. Besides, you'll look less threatening if I'm with you."

Phoebe nodded. "Edward, she's right. Couples always look more innocent than single men."

He sighed. "Come then."

As they rode forward, Serena kept her eyes on the barn searching for any indication another villain was there. "My guess is that the path leads up to the door."

"I think you're right," Phoebe responded.

A few minutes later, Edward and Freddy waved. He led them to the door, which had a new lock. Rage infused his face. He stepped back to kick at it when Phoebe stopped him.

"Here, let me try." She took out her dagger and poked around the large iron padlock. Soon, a satisfied smile appeared on her face and the lock released.

"Lady Evesham, where did you learn to do that?" Edward asked, impressed.

Phoebe smiled smugly. "I have a husband with a great many unique talents and, please, call me Phoebe."

"Let's see what we have." Serena pulled open one half of the large door while Edward opened the other. Light flooded the immediate inside of the barn and there was a rustling. No fewer than fifteen boys ranging in age from seven or eight to young teens peered out from the back of the barn. That villain had been busy.

"You're safe. I'm Lady Serena from the Hall. We've come to take you home." How could anyone do something so evil? She fixed her eyes on one of the older boys. "Are any of the blackguards around?"

The boy shook his head.

"Good."

Serena approached the children. They were restrained

with metal cuffs attached to chains. She followed the chains to some iron rings set into the ground. Serena trembled in fury. "What kind of monster does this? How do we get these things off them? Phoebe, can you use your knife?"

"I'll certainly try." Phoebe inserted the point of her dagger and twisted it. "There's the first one."

Serena and Freddy helped each boy to his feet while Edward kept watch.

"I hear the wagon," he said.

Phoebe glanced up. "I just need a few more minutes."

Serena took a breath. "Edward, close the doors and relock them. You, Robert, and Marcus can come in once the wagon is inside."

When the doors shut, the barn darkened. A tingle of fear ran down Serena's back as the lock clicked. She moved the boys to the wall near the door. "We have two men following the wagon. Once the doors are open and he drives in, very quietly leave the barn and go to the gentleman who was just here. Do you understand me?"

The boys nodded.

"Good. Don't go anywhere else. Once we've dealt with the monster who put you here, we'll make arrangements to send you home. Is there just the one villain, the one with the slash on his face?"

"No, my lady, there was another. A nob, by the looks of him."

"Can you tell me what he looks like?"

"Looked a lot like that other gent'man which helped us."

Serena turned to Freddy, surprised.

"It must be Aubrey Malfrey, Edward's cousin and heir. He's been staying here. Edward suspected, but hoped . . . Oh, poor Edward."

Serena spoke calmly. "There's nothing we can do about

it now. We must concentrate on the children. Where's Phoebe?"

"I'm here," Phoebe answered from above.

"Phoebe, what are you doing, and how did you get up there?"

"All barns have lofts. I just found the ladder. There is a small window up here overlooking the path. Once our villain gets near the doors, I'll try to signal Marcus and Robert."

Serena turned back to the boys. One of the smaller ones began to weep and she took him into her arms. "You mustn't cry now. I'm here to care for you. Tell me your name and how long you've been here."

"My name's Ben. I don't know. A long time."

"My lady," an older boy said. "Ben was caught the same time as me. I make it to be 'bout two weeks."

"What's your name?"

"Erasmus, my lady."

"Erasmus, do you know where they were taking you?"

"No, my lady, but I heard somethin' about some ship."

"Serena," Freddy said, "I'll wager you it has something to do with slavery of some sort."

"I'd hate to believe it," Serena said, "but I cannot think of what else it could be. Thank the Lord we were able to find them in time. Is Jemmy here?"

"That's me, my lady."

"Be quiet now. I see him," Phoebe called down.

"All right, boys, hug the wall so he can't see you when he drives in and be silent. No noise at all."

The wagon stopped and the door unlocked and opened. Serena's heart pounded so loudly, she was sure the man could hear it.

She, Freddy, and the boys were plastered against the wall

on the opposite side from where the boys had been chained. As soon as the wagon cleared the door, Freddy pushed the children out. A slight rustling of hay told Serena that Phoebe was back.

As the last boy left, a large shadow fell across the open door.

The man untied one end of the ropes holding the boys from something fixed to the bed of the wagon. Serena stood on tiptoe, but still couldn't see what it was. He lifted them down one by one, keeping hold of the loose ends of rope.

The shadows shifted. Robert and Marcus entered, walking toward the man.

Robert scowled with rage. Not the cold anger she'd seen in him at other times, but something infinitely more dangerous. *Primitive.* A word she'd never before associated with him. Robert grabbed the villain as he set the last child on the ground, twisted him around, and hit him squarely on the nose.

"That's for stealing children on my land."

Robert hit the man again. "That is for threatening my wife."

Robert punched him in the stomach. "And that is for causing the parents of these children worry."

Serena's heart swelled with joy, watching Robert defend them. "Robert?"

"Yes, my love?"

"Might I please have one for scaring the children?"

Robert's lips tilted up. He bowed. "Of course, my love."

He turned back to the thug, who was still doubled over. Grabbing his hair, Robert pulled the villain's head back and let go as he drove his fist into the man's face. "That is for scaring the children."

The blackguard fell to the floor.

Serena glanced at Robert and pointed to the chains. "You can secure him to those."

After the children were unbound, Freddy took them to Edward.

Serena went to Robert. "The man has an accomplice. Freddy thinks it may be Aubrey Malfrey, Edward's cousin. The children also mentioned a ship."

Robert's jaw clenched. "Slave trade of some sort, no doubt."

"Yes, that's what we think."

"We need to summon the magistrate." Robert turned a basilisk eye on the culprit, his smile anything but nice. "Those chains will give him a taste of his own medicine."

"What if his partner returns while we're gone?" Serena asked. "They'll only continue their perfidious acts."

"A rider approaching," Phoebe called softly.

The three moved quickly to the side of the barn. Phoebe slid in next to Marcus.

They waited until the rider entered and dismounted. The man was tall and slender, with light brown hair. He glanced around and stared at his henchman, chained and gagged.

Robert stepped forward. "Aubrey Malfrey."

"I'm afraid you have the advantage, sir."

"Viscount Beaumont, at your service."

Malfrey executed a slight bow and charged Robert.

Robert deftly stepped aside and hit him on the back of the neck. Malfrey went down. Robert glanced at Serena, but she saw the movement behind him and screamed, "Robert, Malfrey has a gun!"

Beaumont turned quickly and attacked. As Robert kicked the weapon out of Malfrey's hand, it discharged.

Robert dropped to the floor, blood flowed from his head. Marcus punched Malfrey, who crumpled to the ground.

Blood! There was so much blood. Serena rushed to Robert, lifted his head to her lap and sobbed. "No, no, no!"

Phoebe tried to pull her away. "Serena, love, let Marcus look at him. He knows what he's doing."

Serena allowed herself to be drawn away.

"He'll be fine," Marcus said. "The bullet grazed his temple, but didn't go any deeper."

She couldn't draw a breath and shook uncontrollably.

Marcus placed a hand on her shoulder. "Serena, listen to me. He'll be fine."

"Then why did he pass out?"

"The ball hit his temple. He'll come around in a bit. Serena, I wouldn't lie to you."

Impatiently, she pushed her tears away. "Why is he bleeding so much?"

"Head wounds bleed. We should find something to bind it with."

Serena tore off the flounce of her petticoat, and used it for a pad, saving a piece to wind around his head. "There."

Robert's lids fluttered as he came around.

"Robert Beaumont, you stupid, wonderful man! *Thank God you're alive.* Don't ever again tell me I must keep myself from harm, while you . . . you . . . endanger yourself. Don't ever do that again! I couldn't bear to lose you."

"Come here, my love." He pulled her head down and kissed her. "Now you know how I feel."

Serena returned his kisses. "I'm sending you with outriders everywhere you go."

His laugh rumbled against her. "Yes, my lady."

Marcus grimaced. "You're going to have a devil of a headache."

"I already do. My head feels like it's been trampled by horses. What's happened to Malfrey?"

"I have him," Edward replied.

Robert tried to rise and fell back with a moan. "I do seem to be having more of a problem than I thought."

Marcus shook his head. "Give it a few minutes. We've trussed Malfrey up."

Edward's eyes were hard pebbles. "Well, Aubrey, I thought you didn't know anything about this. I meant what I said. You will be prosecuted."

Aubrey gave Edward a haughty look. "You wouldn't risk a scandal."

Edward scowled. "If you don't agree to transportation, they can hang you for all I care."

"What about the title?" Aubrey countered. "I'm the last Malfrey."

Edward's hands clenched. "I would rather have the title escheat to the Crown then have you hold it."

"Where are Freddy and the children?" Serena asked.

Phoebe responded, "The children are still outside, and Freddy has gone to the Hall for help. We really have nothing more to do until someone arrives."

Serena glanced at Edward. "I'm so sorry this has happened."

"No, there was always something unsavory about Aubrey. Word had gotten back to me about some of the characters he'd associated with lately. When I heard about the children, my first thought was that he was in some way involved."

Robert insisted on going outside to wait. Not an hour had passed when they heard carriages.

St. Eth rode with Freddy into the clearing and raised a brow. "I hear you have been having an interesting time of it."

Serena nodded. "Interesting indeed, but we've all come off well. Although Robert was injured."

"Not enough to force him to forego his wedding, I trust."

It was the first time since Robert had been hit that she felt like smiling. "No, not enough for that. He'll need a day or so of rest. Marcus said it's not serious, but Robert has a dreadful headache."

"Who was the second villain?" Henry asked.

"Edward's cousin."

"I'm sorry to hear that."

Freddy dismounted. "Edward?"

"Here, my love." He caught her up into his arms.

She kissed him fiercely. "Are you all right?"

"Yes. It looks as if the title will end with me. I shall recommend transportation for Aubrey."

Freddy regarded Edward intently. "I wasn't going to tell you yet, but the line may not end with you."

He lowered her to the ground. "What do you mean?"

"It's early days yet, but I think I may be breeding."

Edward shook his head as if trying to clear it. "Freddy, how could you know so soon?"

She flushed. "I've only felt the way I do now once before, when I was pregnant with Rupert."

"Freddy, if you're right . . . Oh, my love!" Edward kissed her again. "We must marry immediately."

"Lord Malfrey, I don't think there will be a problem." Henry grinned. "Mr. Mariville was arriving when I left. He said to inform you he had your special license."

Edward twirled Freddy around in his arms. "To-morrow?"

"If not to-day."

"I've notified the magistrate that the kidnappers have been caught," Henry said, "and the children rescued."

Edward went to Robert, who still lay on the ground, his head in Serena's lap. "Tell Sir Baldwin, they can hang Aubrey if he won't agree to transportation. I'd rather risk the scandal of a trial than leave him free in England."

"You can tell Sir Baldwin yourself," Robert said. "He's right behind you."

"My lord, what's happened?" The magistrate rapidly walked to Robert and Serena.

"I was injured. Nothing really, but I've a devil of a headache."

"My lady, you have blood all over you. Have you been injured, as well?"

Serena glanced down at Robert. "No, it is all Lord Beaumont's blood. He was hit in the head."

Switching his attention back to Robert, Sir Baldwin asked, "Are you well enough to tell me about all of this?"

"I'll let Lady Serena and Lord Malfrey tell you." Robert closed his eyes. "My head feels as if horses are running through it."

Serena told Sir Baldwin about the men who were kidnapping the children.

"Lord Malfrey, will you sign as a witness?"

"Of course."

"Very well, I'll take them to the inn. If you remember, we use the cellar there as a jail and afterward, I'll draw up the transportation papers."

Edward agreed. "If you need anything else from me, send someone round. I'll have the statement to you within a few days."

With that settled, Serena turned to Henry. "Uncle Henry. Do we have enough conveyances to transport the children to town?"

"The wagon ought to be large enough."

"The ones from here shall go to the rectory until their parents can fetch them," Serena said. "The others shall go to the Hall. Uncle Henry, did you send the message to the rectory that the school meeting would have to be postponed?"

"I sent for the rector as soon as I arrived and informed him of the circumstances. I am sure he sent a message to his wife."

When they arrived at the Hall, Serena helped Robert to her room and attended to his wound and changed his bandage.

Sitting back, Serena looked at her handiwork. "There, that looks better. At least now, you aren't wearing a bandage decorated with whitework." She kissed him on the cheek. "I must speak with Catherine."

She found her aunt in the morning room. "Aunt Catherine, what do you want done with the children from your estate?"

Catherine thought for a moment. "Let's get them cleaned up and fed before they go anywhere. We will send them to my home, then if one of your grooms can take a message, their parents can meet them at Wood Hill."

An hour later, Catherine left with the children. No sooner had the wagon driven out of sight, when a cortege of coaches heralded the arrival of Lady St. Eth and the Dowager Lady Beaumont.

Chapter Twenty-five

Five large carriages arrived, one after the other, to the front entrance of the Hall, and a footman was dispatched to find Lord and Lady Evesham and Lord St. Eth.

Serena and Robert descended the Hall's outer steps, as Lady St. Eth and Lady Beaumont were handed down from the coach. Serena flew into her aunt's arms.

"Serena, what is this? Am I to take you away?" Ester teased.

"No, never. I'm just so happy you're here!"

"Well, girl?" the older lady asked.

Serena turned to Lady Beaumont and, smiling broadly, embraced her. "Ma'am, thank you. I've never received better advice. There is so much to tell you."

The dowager chuckled. "You'd better call me 'Grandmama' now. Robert, what's happened to you?"

Robert grimaced. "I had a slight accident. We'll tell you about it later."

Serena's smile faltered a little when she glanced at Robert. How close she'd come to losing him didn't bear thinking of. She turned her attention back to her aunt and Lady Beaumont. "Oh, but what am I doing keeping you out here? I'll show you to your chambers and after you've rested, we'll have tea. Or, would you rather have tea served in your rooms?"

Lady Beaumont smiled. "I'll drink tea with you, my girl, if you'll give me a half an hour. Robert, come to me in a few minutes."

"Tea will be set out on the terrace, outside the morning room," Serena said.

"A good choice with this wonderful weather," Lady St. Eth remarked. "Serena, don't worry about me, Henry is here."

He bowed to Lady Beaumont and greeted his wife. "I'll show you to our chamber."

Serena twined her arm with Lady Beaumont's and led her into the house.

Once Henry and Ester were in their bedchamber, he took his wife in his arms and kissed her.

"Henry, you are much more relaxed than when I last saw you." Ester searched his face. "Did you accomplish what you'd hoped, my love?"

"Even more. I'm extremely pleased with the way it has all turned out. Serena is so accepted here that the servants are almost militant in their protection of her. I sent Griffin about and this is what he was told . . ."

As he related the story to her, Ester's eyes widened in shock. "In the viscountess's chambers!"

Henry gave a bark of laughter. "Yes, and Griffin was assured that it was all very proper."

"I don't believe it."

Henry chuckled. "Nor do I. But they insist Beaumont sleeps in his bed every night and Serena has not seen the inside of his room."

"So there is nothing to do?"

"No, nothing, Serena is mistress of the Hall and everyone supports her. You would have been very proud to see her with the tenants."

Ester smiled softly. "Oh, Henry, I'm so pleased she has found her place. You remember how unhappy she was when she left Scotland? And Beaumont loves her?"

Henry took her hands. "Unreservedly. He turned into a much better man than I thought possible. Very different from his father or grandfather."

Ester frowned. "Why was Robert wearing a bandage?"

Henry's eyes sparkled. "It's their story. I'll let them tell it. I was only minorly involved."

"Let's join them. I want to hear all about what happened to-day."

"Well, Robert?" his grandmother said, once she'd settled onto the chaise in the large chamber with south-facing windows. "I suppose you'll tell me what happened to you. First, I want to hear how you and Lady Serena are doing."

He grinned. "I took your advice and gave Serena her head. She's worked wonders."

"She's only been here three weeks."

Robert sat next to his grandmother and covered her long thin hands in his. "Grandmama, I can't explain to you how Serena took to the Hall and the Hall to her. It was amazing to watch her with the staff and our tenants. Of course it was touch and go that first week before she decided she would marry me. We had to pretend to everyone that there would be a wedding, and Serena wasn't at all happy about that."

"No, she wouldn't be. Serena is not a dissembler. You're happy?"

Robert met her gaze. "Yes."

"Well, my boy, you certainly took the hard road to get here, but I'm pleased you made it. Now, give me a bit of time, then you may come back to take me to my tea and tell me about your head and this wedding you have planned. Which, from what I've been hearing, is going to be the most well-attended event in quite a while."

Robert groaned. "God help us."

Freddy and Edward were kissing, when her mother and Robert walked into the morning room.

Lady Beaumont narrowed her eyes. "What on earth is going on? Edward Timmons, is that you?"

"It's Lord Malfrey now, my lady." He bowed.

"When did that happen?"

"I became heir to the title shortly after Freddy left to marry."

Lady Beaumont sat on a sofa and shook her head sadly.

Freddy sat next to her mother. Something was wrong, but what? "Mama, you know we've never discussed my marriage."

"No, dear, you never wanted to."

"Mama, Rupert is Edward's son."

Lady Beaumont's lips firmed. "We knew it. That was the reason you were married off so quickly."

Freddy's eyes flew open. This couldn't be happening. "No, oh no! You *knew?* And you made me marry anyway?"

"Your father wouldn't hear of your wedding young Timmons. Lord Stanstead knew his son was unlikely to get an heir . . ."

Freddy interrupted her mother. "Mama, how could Father condemn me to a marriage where I could never be happy?"

Lady Beaumont embraced her. "Your father wanted an advantageous match for you. Stanstead was one of his oldest friends. They both knew the son liked men, and Stanstead desperately wanted an heir. The two of them hatched the scheme."

She glanced at Edward. "I begged your father to contact Malfrey here. But their minds were made up. He thought he was doing what was best for you. Old Lord Stanstead's only regret was that you didn't have more children."

She couldn't believe what her mother had said. "Under the circumstances, how did they think I was going to? My husband never touched me."

"You must remember, my love, they came from an older school. Stanstead thought that you'd have discreet liaisons and become pregnant again."

Freddy suddenly sat back. "And he would have accepted the children?"

Lady Beaumont's lips formed a thin line. "Looked forward to them."

Freddy gasped. "I have never in my life had hysterics, but I may very well have them now!"

Her mother settled back against the pillows. "I may as well tell you the rest. Your father knew you were unhappy and was concerned you'd run off to Timmons. He told old Lord Malfrey, and to avoid a scandal, Malfrey arranged a marriage for Edward. There you have it all."

Edward stood frozen. "We were all pawns in their game. Nothing more."

Lady Beaumont pinched the bridge of her nose. "You

may regard it as that, of course. You may also try to see it from their points of view. Stanstead had no heirs other than his son. The title would have ended. Freddy, your father thought you'd be much happier not having to make and scrape. You hadn't been raised to it. Edward . . ."

"I know, my lady, my grandfather worshiped respectability. He would have done anything to stop a scandal."

Lady Beaumont glanced from her daughter to Edward and back again. "Rupert looks more like you, Freddy, but his eyes and something about the face . . ." She studied Edward more closely. "His shoulders and I think something of his manner resembles Malfrey. Will you tell Rupert?"

"Only if he asks," Freddy said. "I don't think it would do any good otherwise."

"No, probably not," her mother responded.

"Mama, Edward and I will be married to-morrow."

Lady Beaumont's eyes misted, and she smiled. "Freddy, I—I couldn't be happier. I only wish I could have kept you from suffering for so long."

Freddy blinked back her tears. "Shall we just say *all's well that ends well?*"

"Yes, we shall say just that." Her mother squeezed Freddy's hands.

"Malfrey, what do you have to say for yourself?" Lady Beaumont said bracingly.

"Just that I love her, ma'am, and I'll make her as happy as I am able."

"Well, it seems as if Serena will have another party to plan," Lady Beaumont said as Serena walked back into the room.

Hearing the older woman, Serena glanced at her, startled. One party was all that she could manage. "Another party?"

"A tea for Freddy and Malfrey," Lady Beaumont said. "It's too late to plan a breakfast."

Serena grinned. Perhaps Robert's autocratic nature was not all from his paternal side. "Yes, ma'am."

As Serena was pouring tea, Charles, Robert's secretary, who had been resting, entered the room. She handed him a cup. "Charles, you should really not be up."

He took the tea. "Thank you, my lady. There is something I must do first."

"Mariville, you look like H . . . the devil," Robert said.

"I'll be fine with a good night's sleep. I wanted to give this to Lord Malfrey." Charles took the special license from his coat.

"How did you get back with it so quickly?" Edward asked.

"We didn't stop. I drove straight through, arriving in London about midday, procured the license, and began our trip back."

"That was beyond the call of duty. Thank you, Mr. Mariville." Edward executed a short bow.

"Anything to further the cause of true love," Charles said, grinning. "I knew once I was here I could sleep."

"True love? Charles," Robert drawled, "has anyone ever told you, you are impertinent?"

Charles's smile widened. "Yes, my lord, you have."

"You may help the ladies with the wedding breakfast and the tea."

"Tea, my lord?"

"Our lives are changing, Charles. We no longer have a bachelor establishment. Her ladyship will give you the details, and she will decide how you may assist. Now go rest before I'm accused of working you to death."

Robert walked over to Serena. "Where is Aunt Catherine?"

"She's gone to take the children from her area home." Serena took his hand. "She'll be back to-morrow for Freddy's wedding. Where is Edward?"

"Charles gave him the special license and he's ridden to the rectory, he and Freddy both."

Serena nodded; she wouldn't be surprised if they held the marriage to-morrow. "We will need to compile an invitation list for the wedding tea. I've met a great many people locally, but not everyone."

Phoebe said, "Lora can help us. She will know everyone in the immediate area and beyond."

"Of course. I'm so glad you thought of it," Serena said. "You've wanted to see her anyway. Let's ride over."

"No," Ester said firmly.

Serena stared at her in surprise and saw an identical look on Phoebe's face.

Robert chuckled and was quelled by Aunt Ester's quick, narrow-eyed glance. "I cannot keep up with all the comings and goings as it is. I'll not allow you two to disappear as well. We have lists to make. Send a servant to the rectory asking them to join us for dinner."

"But, Aunt Ester," Serena protested, "the tea is to-morrow. We need to send the cards round this evening."

"When you send the messenger, ask Lora to write down the names and send it back with him. There cannot be that many families. This is Yorkshire, not London."

"Yes, ma'am," she said. "I'll send a footman right away."

Robert placed his hand on her shoulder. "I'll do it. You stay and make your plans."

Serena placed her hand over his and smiled up at him. "Thank you, my love."

* * *

The next morning, a small group gathered in the church of Haythrope Hall for the wedding of Frederica, Countess of Stanstead, and Edward, Baron Malfrey. The only surprise was the early arrival of Rupert, the Earl of Stanstead, late the previous evening.

Freddy walked into the breakfast room to find Rupert in the company of the other younger people.

Rupert turned to her. "Mama, I hear I'm just in time to give you away. Do I have a choice? I'm quite fond of you, you know, and I'm not sure I wish to let you go."

Rupert grinned merrily as Freddy flew into his arms.

Tears pricked her eyes. "Rupert, I'm so happy you're here. When did you arrive?"

"Last night." Rupert gave a short laugh and handed her his handkerchief. "There's no reason to cry, you know. You don't have to marry the rogue. I'll protect you. Give you my word."

She chuckled wetly. "You're a silly boy. I want to marry Edward. He should be here soon."

Robert coughed. "Malfrey was here earlier and went away."

Freddy's mouth opened, as she took in their mischievous looks. "Whatever for?"

Serena's eyes twinkled with laughter. "I have it on good authority that it's bad luck to see your betrothed the morning before the wedding."

What was this nonsense? Freddy frowned.

"Rupert," Serena said, "please help your mother sit, while I fetch her a plate and some tea."

Freddy toyed absently with the food on her plate before focusing her narrowed eyes on Beaumont. "I can't believe you sent Edward away. You know, Robert, what's sauce for the goose is sauce for the gander."

"It wasn't Robert," Serena said. "Your betrothed stopped

by to see that all was in order. Robert invited Edward to breakfast, and he refused."

Freddy closed her eyes and slowly shook her head. "I had no idea he was superstitious."

"He probably didn't want to tempt fate," Robert said sagely. "I know how Malfrey feels."

Rupert, all good humor, said, "Mama, what's it to be, shall I take you away or give you away?"

Freddy looked up at her tall, handsome son and smiled. Rupert had all the Beaumont height and bright curls. But his shoulders were slightly broader, his face had more angular planes and his eyes were Edward's calm gray. "You may give me away."

It was hard to say who smiled more broadly during the ceremony—the bride or the groom. The party had already returned to the Hall before Edward and Rupert were introduced.

Edward bowed to Rupert and looked into the mirror image of his eyes. "My lord, I'm very pleased to finally meet you."

Rupert returned his gaze curiously. "I don't think you need to call me 'my lord.' You're my papa-in-law now. You'll take care of her, won't you?"

Edward stood stock still, afraid, with his rush of emotion, he'd give himself away. This young man was everything he could have wanted in a son. "Always. I love your mother very much."

Rupert's forehead wrinkled. "Have we met, sir?"

Edward's jaw clenched. Adhering to Freddy's wishes that Rupert not be told unless he asked was harder than he'd thought it would be. "No, we've never met."

His son studied Edward. "How long have you known my mother?"

"For many years. We knew each other well before she married."

Freddy came quietly up to stand behind and off to Rupert's side.

"You loved her back then as well." It was not a question.

Edward nodded and responded gruffly, "Yes."

Rupert's brow cleared, and he smiled. "Then I think you are rather more than my papa-in-law."

Edward's jaw dropped, and he had trouble getting his reactions under control.

His son laughed easily at Edward's shock.

"Freddy, you were right. He is very quick." Edward turned his gaze back to Rupert's. "How did you guess so swiftly?"

"I've known for years I was none of Stanstead's get." Rupert flashed a grin at Freddy. "I thank you for that, Mama. I knew about my father's proclivities, and I knew I'd been born early. Occasionally, I'd ask Grandmama, but she'd just tell me Beaumonts breed true. Still, that didn't explain my eyes and my face. I just didn't know who, until now. I suppose at some point you'll explain how it all happened."

"Your mother and I were told the whole story only yesterday."

"Come, let's find someplace quiet," Freddy said firmly. "Too many secrets have been kept for too many years."

"My love, the tea."

"The tea is not until this afternoon, and I've been told I have nothing to do but appear. Serena has things well in hand."

They walked out to the other end of the terrace where

some chairs and a chaise had been set up. Freddy told Rupert what her father and old Lord Stanstead had done.

"I was raised without a father, you without a husband, and you, sir, without a wife, all to save the earldom," Rupert said thoughtfully. "You have no heir?"

Freddy and Edward told him about the kidnappings and Aubrey's part.

"I thought Yorkshire was supposed to be dull. I'll have to visit more often. It sounds as if you have been having a busy time here. Will your estate escheat?"

Freddy blushed. "Perhaps not. You might have a brother in a few months."

"You *have* been busy," Rupert exclaimed good-naturedly. "Well, I've always wanted a younger brother or sister. What shall I call you, sir?"

"Other than Lord Malfrey, anything you'd like."

"I think 'sir' will do for to-day, after that I'd like to call you Papa."

Edward's chest swelled. "If you're sure. I wouldn't like you to be put in an embarrassing situation."

"If anyone comments, I'll just tell them I like my mama's new husband very well."

This was more than Edward had hoped for. "You'll come and stay with us at the Grange?"

"I'd like that. I'll remain here tonight and come to you to-morrow. You are newlyweds, after all." Rupert smiled as Freddy's face grew red. "I'm going in now to find Robert." Rupert bowed to them both and departed.

"I seem to be tearing up quite a bit to-day. Edward, I'm so happy."

"I'm in shock. I had no idea he'd take it so well."

"I knew he wouldn't be that surprised, though, I agree, he took it a great deal better than I thought he would. He's actually happy about it."

Edward gazed down at her. "I want to kiss you—*now*—and we have no place we can go."

Freddy stood and held out her hand. "Come with me. I know exactly the place."

Rupert lifted a glass to Robert. "I never thought I'd see you married. How did she catch you?"

"She didn't. Gave me a devil of a chase, and I almost didn't catch her. It was a near thing, I'll tell you." Robert's gaze followed Serena on the other side of the room. "Grandmama showed me the way."

Rupert gave a bark of laughter. "Beaumont, you're in love!"

Robert scowled. "You don't have to shout it."

His cousin doubled over in laughter. "If I hadn't seen it, I wouldn't have believed it. The rake has been well and truly hoisted by his own petard."

Chapter Twenty-six

They were gathering in the drawing room for the wedding tea when Robert glanced up to see his grandmother enter the room. For the first time since he was a child, she was not in black bombazine, but in a pearl dove gown of obvious Parisian origin. "Grandmama, you look wonderful and years younger."

She rapped his knuckles. "After you left Paris, there was little to do but shop, and the modiste there was extremely persuasive. I do think I look well, though."

He chuckled. "You do indeed."

"Mama, you'll take the shine out of us all." Freddy kissed her cheek.

Robert, Serena, his grandmother, Freddy, and Edward made up the receiving line. In addition to the neighbors Serena had met previously, she was introduced to Mr. and Mrs. Calverton, Lord and Lady St. Quentin, and their daughter, Miss Quentin. Serena noticed the measuring look Lady St.

Quentin gave her as she moved through the line. Serena smiled politely and raised a brow.

Lady St. Quentin's countenance cleared. "I have it now. I saw you in the Park driving your curricle. You are St. Eth's niece."

Serena's smile became genuine. "Yes, although I don't believe we've met before, have we?"

"No, I was visiting my sister-in-law to arrange a house for next Season, when our Eliza will make her come out. My sister told me you were the catch of the Season. We are very pleased to welcome you to our little area of Yorkshire, my lady."

She passed on to Lady Beaumont, continuing her theme. "Lady Beaumont, I suppose you're happy to have Robert settled."

"Yes, Lady St. Quentin, we are all very happy Lady Serena is to join our family."

"She's so beautiful and well connected," Lady St. Quentin enthused before congratulating Freddy and Edward.

Lady Montrose arrived to cast a disapproving eye on the receiving line. She greeted Serena civilly, but with no warmth, and said to Lady Beaumont, "Well, she certainly is very forward. I've heard all the stories. I'm sorry for you, my dear Lady Beaumont. Your nose must be sadly out of joint."

Lady Beaumont's smile did not reach her eyes. "You are doing Lady Serena an injustice. She has allowed herself to be led by me and is doing precisely what I advised."

Lady Montrose nodded. "She probably needed to be told how to go on, being from *Scotland*." As if Serena had been from Spittlefield. "And she's so old as well. I'm told she trapped Lord Beaumont into marriage. I'm glad to see him making the best of it."

Before his grandmother could utter the set-down Serena

knew was on her lips, Robert leaned over Serena to address Lady Montrose. "You have your story sadly confused. It is *I* who trapped Lady Serena into marriage. A circumstance you would do well to remember. I will allow no criticism of my affianced wife, nor shall I take lightly any aspersions on her character."

Lady Montrose turned a bright red and went off in a huff, forgetting to congratulate Freddy and Edward.

"As nice a squabash as I've ever seen anyone give her," Edward said.

Serena bit her lip and tried not to worry about what Lady Montrose said.

Lady Beaumont smiled reassuringly. "Don't let what an ill-bred fishwife says fret you, my girl. You have Robert and the rest of us for support."

"We'll help as well." Tom Rush had walked in behind Lady Montrose.

"Yes, indeed. I don't know anyone more unpleasant than Lady Montrose," Emma concurred. "Lord and Lady Malfrey, we are so pleased to be able to wish you happy. Tom, tell them your news." Emma went on excitedly. "He's been asked to run for Parliament!"

Tom laughed. "She's my most enthusiastic supporter."

Robert chuckled. "Not a bad thing to have in a wife."

Lady Beaumont declared it was time to join their guests and herded them into the drawing room and out onto the terrace, where long tables had been set up with food and drink.

The malevolent Lady Montrose, unable to draw any of the other guests into her vicious gossip, decided to take her leave.

Serena was with Lady St. Quentin when Lady Montrose approached. Whatever she was about to say died on her lips, and after a few moments she wished Serena a courteous adieu.

"I wonder what that was about," Serena said. "I was sure she'd planned to say something cutting."

Lady St. Quentin's eyes sparkled with amusement. "I think it was your guardian angel—or should I say devil? I don't think I've ever heard Robert described as an angel."

Serena grinned. "No, not even his grandmother has ever called him an angel. Where was he?"

Lady St. Quentin's lips curved. "He appeared behind you as Lady Montrose began to speak."

"Are there many more like Lady Montrose?" Serena asked.

"No, thank the Lord. She has nothing good to say about anyone. The fit she threw when I married St. Quentin was something to see. You'd have thought he was marrying a weaver's daughter."

"Are you from here?"

"Heavens, yes, I'm Tom Rush's sister, which is the reason Tom was selected to run for Parliament. St. Quentin held the seat for years and is now ready to hand it off to someone younger. Lady Montrose married and moved south. Unfortunately for us, her husband didn't live long and she returned. Tom claims Montrose died to rid himself of her."

Serena couldn't stop her lips from curving up. "You must know Freddy, Lady Malfrey, quite well."

"We are much of an age, but no. I was sent away to school, and she was kept home. By the time I returned, she was gone and married. We're happy to have her back. It's past time we had some new blood in this area of the county. Now, tell me, if you will, about this new school you and Lora have begun."

By late afternoon, the ladies were deep in discussion concerning the new school. Phoebe, who had the most experience, outlined what their immediate needs would be and which issues to discuss with the administrator. A committee was formed and each lady tasked with a job. By the time her guests took their leave, Serena was delighted that so many of the local gentry were involved. Now if she could only forget what Lady Montrose had said.

Robert walked into Serena's chamber late that evening, expecting to find her already in bed. Instead she was staring out a window, her white night rail glowing in the soft candlelight. Serena's long tresses glinted in the flickering flames. Night had fallen so darkly, he could make out her concerned countenance reflected in the window.

Clearly lost in thought, Serena gave no sign she'd heard him enter. Robert moved behind her and studied her face before putting his hands on her shoulders.

"A penny for your thoughts?"

Serena raised her eyes. Robert met her gaze in the window's reflection.

"Lady Montrose."

"It's a shame I didn't know about her earlier. We wouldn't have sent her an invitation."

Serena sighed. "I do not know how we can avoid inviting her. Despite her delight in attempting to make everyone miserable, she appears to be received everywhere."

Robert searched her face in the window. "You're concerned about what she said."

She frowned. "I am concerned others will think the same."

"You can't allow them to worry you overmuch."

"No, I suppose I should not," Serena said quietly.

"It'll take some time for you to grow a thicker skin." He'd never really appreciated how isolated Serena had been before she came to London. "I'll be with you and any gossip won't last long. The *ton* has a very short memory."

He gently moved her hair aside and kissed her neck.

Serena reached back to stroke him, and turned into him. "I have you, my family, and some friends to get me through."

"I'm sorry. I haven't made it easy for you." He bent his head to kiss her sweetly and lingeringly. Robert smiled possessively before divesting her of her nightgown.

Later, she lay boneless beside him as Robert arranged her back against his chest. He nuzzled her ear. "Have I told you I love you?"

"Not to-day."

"I do, you know. Love you." He invested the word with all the joy and fear welling up in him. Joy that he'd found her and made her his. Fear that somehow she might be taken away from him. Robert gently brought her closer to him and held her tightly as he drifted to sleep.

For the first time since they'd begun sleeping together, Serena awoke alone. Troubled, she sat up to see Mary lay out her riding habit.

"Oh, good, you're up. I was just about to wake you, my lady. His lordship said you must hurry as you've much to do to-day."

It was on the tip of Serena's tongue to ask why his lordship hadn't woken her, but that was a question for Robert. One he'd better have a good answer for.

"I've got your wash water ready."

Serena rose quickly, washed, and sat while Mary dressed her hair.

When Serena was ready, Mary shooed her out the door. "He'll meet you in the breakfast room."

Robert was already consuming his customary large breakfast when she entered. He looked up, smiling, and rose from the table.

"What is it?"

"This." He kissed her and took her right hand and slipped a ring over a finger. "Grandmama brought it with her, as well as the rest of the Beaumont jewels. I wanted to give it to you before, but when I didn't know if you'd marry me, I left it in London."

The ring was of gold filigree set with emeralds, diamonds, and tourmaline. Serena studied it before lifting her eyes to Robert's. "It's beautiful. I love it."

"I rather thought you would. It's the first piece of jewelry I've ever selected for a lady."

Serena didn't believe him.

Robert held the chair for her. "It's true. I always had Charles to go round and buy whatever was appropriate."

She'd heard he was cold to his paramours, but . . . "You didn't."

"Indeed, I did. Eat. We must be off on our rounds."

Though happy about the ring, she was still upset he'd left her alone this morning. Particularly since he didn't want her to leave him. Was this another case of do what I say? "Why are you in such a rush?"

Robert's demeanor was innocent. "The morning is slipping by. I want us to be on our way. Eat."

Taking a bite of her eggs, she said, "I would have been up and about earlier if you'd wakened me," she said.

He laughed. "No, you wouldn't."

Serena huffed and applied herself to her breakfast. As soon as she was finished, Robert pulled out her chair and took her hand.

"Robert, must you tow me behind you everywhere?"

He looked back over his shoulder and frowned. "I don't always. Walk faster."

Giving it up for a lost cause, Serena tried to keep up with his long stride.

"Where do you want to go first?" she asked.

"To the outer cottages."

Robert tossed Serena onto Shamir, and after he mounted, she sent Shamir clattering out of the stable yard, jumped the fence, and flew over the meadow. Breathing the fresh morning air deep into her lungs, she urged her horse faster. She was halfway to the cottages before she reined in to wait for Robert to catch up.

They arrived at the site where the cottages had been burned to find the foundations for the new houses already laid and one of the walls begun.

"This is wonderful. Robert, you knew. Is this the reason you wanted to ride out here to-day?"

"I thought you'd be pleased and for some reason, I didn't want the rest of our families with us."

"I understand," she said, softly. "This is our first project. But," she added tartly, "I did not like waking up alone."

Robert lifted her off Shamir and kissed her. "I'll make it up to you this evening."

The women and children came to meet them. "Yer lordship, yer la'yship."

The women curtseyed, and the children surrounded them.

Robert reached into his pocket and held his hand out to the children.

"Ohh, sweets," one little girl cried.

Robert grinned. "There, take them, then off with you."

They briefly inspected the foundations before riding back to the Hall.

Serena glanced over to see Robert deep in thought. "Serena, despite the weather, the crops look appreciably better this year than in the past. How much of it is due to our tenants' new living conditions, I wonder."

She met his gaze. "A great deal, I should think. Feeling

comfortable in one's home, knowing one's children are well—it is all of a piece."

"Let's go round to some of the other tenants as well. I wish to look over the repairs on the other houses."

"A good idea."

They returned to the Hall and entered the study. Charles rose and bowed. "I've just sorted the correspondence and other documents. They're on your desk. Lady Evesham's sisters and their husbands have arrived."

"Charles, you are invaluable. That's half of our task," Serena said.

"Why don't you join the others for luncheon," Robert suggested. "We will be eating in here."

"As you wish, my lord. My lady."

Robert closed the door and in two long steps had Serena in his arms. "I'm finally alone with you."

She put down the letter in her hand and returned his embrace.

Serena chuckled and Robert began a low-voiced tirade. "There are getting to be entirely too many people in this house. And don't tell me it's my fault, because I know it is. Another example of my high-handed, autocratic disposition. If I hadn't had to have everything my way, we'd be married by now and left alone. But no, *Viscount* Beaumont had to—"

Serena stopped him with a kiss. "Robert, think. If we'd been married by special license, Rupert wouldn't have met his father until much later. Our staff and tenants would have nothing to be excited about. None of them have been to a party in years. Who knows what else would have happened? There is no point in bemoaning it now."

"What about you? How do you feel about the prospect of so many guests?" he asked with concern.

Serena leaned her cheek against his broad chest and listened to his heart beat. "I'll muddle through. I'm happy my family is here to help me. Now I'll know how to go on when we return to London for the Little Season."

Robert opened his mouth to speak.

"No, no, we must go. You know Uncle Henry expects you to take your place in the Lords, and really, my love, it's your duty."

They worked until reminded they needed to dress for dinner. Robert leaned back in his chair. "I would never have gotten through all of this alone."

"Charles is a great help. We must go, or I shall be in Mary's black book. She told me I need to bathe before I dress for dinner."

"I wasn't talking about Charles, I meant you. Without you I could not have done it."

She slipped onto Robert's lap. "Thank you."

A gleam entered Robert's eyes. "I'm sure I need to bathe as well. Perhaps I'll help you."

He escorted Serena to her room, went to his own, rang for Henley, and waited. He took so long arriving and preparing Robert for his bath, that by the time Robert entered the bathing chamber the only thing left of Serena was her scent. Disgusted, he climbed into the tub and gave Henley a black look for his efforts.

This evening he'd seduce her until she could think of nothing but wanting him.

As was his custom, he met Serena in the corridor between their chambers. He leaned against the wall, bringing her with him into a shadow. "I wish this were over."

Serena drew his head back down. They kissed deeply. "Soon, my love. We need to go down."

Robert kissed her one last time, running his hands over her. Her nipples hardened, and he smiled.

Serena's body tingled at his touch. It was a good thing they were still in their area of the wing. She inhaled sharply. "Robert, you devil. Why did you do that?"

A wicked smile played on his well-molded lips and flames seemed to flicker in his moss-green eyes. "Because I wanted to."

He was pure seduction and every part of her body took notice. "I shall never make it through dinner if you keep this up." She tried to make her tone tart, but, even to her, it sounded low and breathy.

Robert caressed her derrière. His chuckle was deep, seductive. "I'm giving you something to think about."

She gasped. "You'll crush my gown."

His hands skated over her body, sensitizing her skin and setting her alight. When he stroked between her legs, wetness pooled.

"That should do it." He smiled wolfishly.

She knew that he'd spend the evening using small touches to keep her desire stoked. She would have to appear calm when every part of her body screamed for him to take her.

Serena's skin was flushed as they descended the stairs. How the devil was she to get through this evening?

Chapter Twenty-seven

Although she was able to maintain her outward calm, Serena trembled with his every touch. Even at dinner, when she'd glance down the increasingly larger table, she remembered what he'd done. Robert, the fiend, smiled and held up a wine glass to her before turning to respond to a remark Aunt Ester made.

Serena tried not to look at him or react to his gaze. Yet, his expression heated her. When his wicked, wicked eyes rested on her breasts or on her lips, her body longed for him. She prayed for immunity and turned to answer her uncle.

In the drawing room, he was worse. Without the table between them, he could caress her. Endlessly. Her hands, the small of her back, her neck.

His breath tickled her ear when he whispered, "You may dismiss your maid early, I'll undress you tonight."

Her mouth was so dry she couldn't answer, and she hoped no one had heard him.

Once in her bedchamber, she flew into his arms before
he'd closed the door. Desperate and needy, she took his head
in her hands and claimed his lips, her tongue surging into his
mouth as they struggled over who would lead. She tried to
stay in control, but he waltzed her over to her dressing table
and turned her to face it.

"Robert, what? I want you now. You've been playing
with me all evening."

He removed his jacket and shirt. "And I'm going to play
some more. Look at me in the mirror."

Serena met his gaze and shivered. He was darker and
larger behind her. Like a silhouette for her body.

"Now watch."

His mouth moved over her ear and down to her neck. She
sighed and closed her eyes.

"No, keep them open."

One hand caressed her jaw while the other loosened her
bodice and stays.

His lips tilted up. "That was easy. You must have gotten
this in France."

Robert kissed her neck, running the tip of his tongue to
her throat.

Serena shivered and followed his hands with her gaze as
they roamed her body.

He lowered her bodice and tossed the stays aside. She
wanted to close her eyes again when he lifted her breasts as
if weighing them.

"Look. Watch me touch your breasts."

Her mouth was so dry she couldn't swallow. "Robert,
why?"

"I want you to watch me possess you. Put your hands
over mine. Feel how I knead your breasts."

She did as he asked and marveled at the strength of his

hands and how gently they touched her. Slowly, he lowered her gown until it finally slid to the floor. His hands made the journey back up her body, cleverly touching her in all the places that made her shiver. When she tried to sink against him, he held her up, chuckling.

"Not yet, sweetheart."

He pressed his knowing fingers into her wet curls. Serena struggled to stand. She caught his gaze in the mirror. His face was all lean, hard planes. Nothing soft. No hint of the *tonnish* gentleman. This was a lord used to ruling. His muscles flexed against her back. Serena's breath hitched. She finally understood the man behind the charming demeanor and how much power he'd ceded to her. She wanted to weep with joy.

When the understanding of what he wanted to show her dawned in Serena's eyes, he used his foot to move the stool closer to her. "Place one foot on it."

He held her gaze as she did as he asked. He nudged the stool out a little, then released his shaft, lifted her, and, placing it at the entrance of her body, he slowly entered her.

"What do you see, my love?"

"I see my lord taking me, making me his."

Robert plunged deeply into her, his soul exposed to the one woman who had finally seen and understood him and loved him.

Serena shuddered in ecstasy and her knees gave way.

Robert laughed, sweeping her into his arms. "That's further than I thought we'd get. Your legs must be getting stronger."

He lowered them onto the bed and shifted her under him. Robert groaned as she took him into her body—and into her heart.

* * *

"Mrs. Norton, here are the details of the guests arriving this afternoon and their room assignments." Serena gave her housekeeper one of the many lists on her desk. "Please ask Mr. Mariville and Finster to attend me. I need to go over the dining room seating."

"Yes, my lady. Will there be anything else for now?"

Serena pursed her lips. "Has all the new linen arrived?"

"Yes, my lady. Got in the day before yesterday, as well as the new soaps and the like. Addie's got a way with the flowers. We'll have fresh ones in every room. Don't you worry yourself about any of that. You've got enough on your hands with the fine London guests coming. I know how persnickety they can be. We haven't had a crowd like that in many a year, but we're ready for 'em."

"Thank you, Mrs. Norton."

Mrs. Norton bobbed a curtsey, and left to soon be replaced by Charles and Finster. "Charles, what have we for a seating plan?"

"We're only concerned about the dinner this evening?"

Serena nodded. "Yes, to-morrow we'll dine in small groups and the wedding breakfast will be set up on the terrace."

"I'll have the list to you for your review in a few minutes." He sat down at the desk.

"Finster, the footmen?" she asked.

"All ready. Even the under footmen are on their best behavior."

Good. There had been a slight battle for position the other day. "I'm glad to hear it."

Charles handed her the seating chart and she perused it. "Please make a copy of this and give it to Finster."

"Yes, my lady. Once that's completed, is there anything else you'd like me to do?"

"I am sure there will be something. It seems there always is."

Serena was in a back corridor when someone's arm grabbed her around the waist. She let out a shriek as she was pulled into a room and roughly kissed. "Robert?"

"I'd better be the only one kissing you, my lady."

She would dearly love to enjoy one of their short interludes. "Here?"

"Not that I haven't thought about it. Unfortunately there's no time and little privacy. How are you doing?"

"I am fine. All I am doing is organizing. I could do that in my sleep. It's this evening that has me in a quake. I've resolved not to think about it."

"Very well, call me when the first guests get here. We'll greet them together." He kissed her again and left.

The London guests arrived and were directed to the drawing room with a view to the lake and encouraged to take a short stroll while their luggage was taken to their rooms. If anyone thought it odd to be welcomed by Serena and Robert, rather than Lady Beaumont, not a widened eye betrayed them.

After all the guests were ensconced and had the opportunity to wash off the dust of their travel, Serena had tea served.

Mary fumed. "I'll tell you, Mr. Henley, I have never met with such impertinence. One of the ladies' maids had the gall to ask *me* if her ladyship was sharing his lordship's bed. I told her I would not stoop to gossip about my mistress and for her information, my lady has not seen the inside of his lordship's bedchamber!"

"It's worse than that, Miss Mac Duff," Mr. Henley responded. "One of the tweenies was approached by a servant and offered a bribe. She reported it to Mrs. Norton, who gave the servant an earful. The *ton* thrives on gossip of the most vicious sort. I assure you, Miss Mac Duff, none of our staff will encourage this type of curiosity."

"I have been very impressed by the loyalty of all our household staff, Mr. Henley," Mary said.

"If you will permit me to say, Miss Mac Duff, you have integrated into the staff quite as well as her ladyship has into the Hall."

"Thank you. It is very kind of you to say so." Mary blushed.

"Perhaps, once the wedding is over, you would consider taking a walk in the garden with me?"

Mary smiled shyly. "Why, Mr. Henley, nothing would please me more."

Serena left her chamber wearing a gown of gold tissue over a Pomona green underskirt embroidered in gold thread. The bodice was cut low and square. An old filigree necklace set with emeralds and pearls adorned her neck. Curls danced from the knot at the back of her head. One lay on her breast.

Robert caught his breath and slowly reached out. Touching the curl, he twined it around his fingers and kissed her. "This enticing curl and your eyes haunted me."

Her lips lingered on his, before she said, "For me it always was your eyes."

He held his arm out to her. "Come, my lady, let us brave the horde."

The number of guests staying at the Hall required that the large reception rooms be opened, as well as the state dining room that hadn't been used since Robert was a child.

A footman stopped with a tray full of champagne. Robert took two glasses and handed one to Serena. He stayed by her side as they mingled with their guests before dinner was announced.

"My love, you've done an excellent job, and I know this was your doing, not Phoebe's or Lady St. Eth's."

"I won't deny I did it. But it is too early to declare a success."

"Who am I leading into dinner?"

"Aunt Ester is the most senior peeress. The Duke and Duchess of Huntington are with relatives and will drive over in the morning."

Finster announced dinner. Robert watched St. Eth as he escorted Serena to the foot of the table. Soon she'd be his wife.

Later that night, after their houseguests had retired, he joined Serena and their families and the Rutherfords in the Ladies' Morning Room.

"The dinner could not have gone better," Ester said. "We are very proud of both of you."

Lady Beaumont grinned. "I've never had an easier time hosting a dinner in honor of an engaged couple."

"Indeed, Mama. The only finger I saw you lift was the one holding your wine glass." Freddy's lips curved up. "Serena, you did a wonderful job."

"Thank you, Freddy. I do think it went well."

Robert lifted his glass. "To my lovely affianced wife."

"To Serena," St. Eth added.

Rupert grinned. "Beaumont, I think you used that term just so you could say 'wife.' I've never seen a man so eager to marry."

Freddy rose. "I think we shall go home. Don't forget we must all be in church to-morrow." She glanced at Edward. "Our first time as a married couple."

"You're right. I feel as if I've been married much longer than a few days."

He caught her fingers as she went to pinch him. "Enough of that, my lady."

Edward kissed the offending fingers and Freddy leaned against him.

Rupert smiled affectionately at them.

"Do that a lot, do they?" Lady Beaumont asked.

"Yes, ma'am. It's no bad thing to see one's parents so much in love. It gives me hope."

"Watch who you say that around."

"Yes, Grandmama."

The next afternoon, Serena and Robert were called to greet Lord and Lady Elling, a tall, well-rounded woman who could not seem to stop her gaze from wandering over Robert.

"Lord Beaumont, how delightful to see you again," she purred.

He bowed. "My lady."

Lady Elling's gaze seemed to covet Robert.

Serena tried to control her temper. She'd be very happy to relieve the woman of her eyes. She must be one of Robert's old—old—whatever they were called. How was Serena supposed to compete with—that?

With great difficulty she maintained her countenance. "Lord Elling, Lady Elling, this footman will show you to your chambers. Please tell him if you require anything."

Now the woman was staring at Robert's groin, and Lord Elling didn't even seem to notice. Serena dug her nails into her hands as the Ellings were escorted upstairs.

"My lord," a footman said. "There are some gentlemen wishing to fish."

"I'll come now." Robert turned to Serena. "I'll return as soon as I'm able."

She smiled and nodded. No hurry. Serena didn't even want him in the same house with that woman. She'd seen bitches in heat act with more decorum.

Serena and Robert had greeted the last arrival almost an hour ago. She was in the main hall with Finster, going over the guest lists. "Lord and Lady Worthington were the last of them."

"Yes, my lady. I do not think the Hall has ever been so full of people."

She sighed. "Well I'm glad they're all here and we can get on to other things. Do you know where his lordship is?"

"I last saw him go toward the study, my lady."

"He'd better not be hiding," Serena said tartly. Her tension level had risen with the number of guests arriving.

Finster's lips twitched. "No, my lady."

"I'll fetch him. Our guests will be down soon for tea."

Making her way down the corridor, she heard voices coming from behind the closed door of the study—their study—and froze as she recognized Lady Elling's voice. Serena's hands curled. She'd scratch the lady's eyes out, then murder Robert. How could he? He'd promised!

As she put her hand on the latch, Robert spoke.

"*Leave now.* I have nothing to say to you. I cannot imagine what you hoped to accomplish by following me in here."

"Can you not, Robert? A leopard does not change his spots." The lady laughed. "Just because you're marrying doesn't mean we can't pick up our love affair."

"You are mistaken, my lady." Robert's voice had hardened. Even when they'd driven back from Merton, it was not so chilling, so deadly cold. "*We* did not have a *love af-*

fair. I swived you and you returned the favor. Do you think I could ever want a wh . . . ?"

Serena quickly opened the door and made herself smile. "There you are, my love. Lady Bellamny is asking for you." Serena stopped and turned as if she had just noticed Lady Elling. "Oh, you must be lost. This room is private, and I assure you there is *nothing* for you here. I shall have a footman guide you back to the main area of the house."

Serena tugged the bell pull, took the lady by the arm, and walked her out of the room. "Ah, Frank, please take this lady back to the main hall or escort her to her room. She got lost."

"Yes, my lady."

Serena met Lady Elling's eyes squarely. "You might want to restrict your wanderings to the main areas of the Hall. You may also mention to any other interested parties that Lord Beaumont is no longer available."

Serena returned to their study and locked the door.

Robert was standing, his face flushed and hands clenched. She wrapped her arms around him. His body radiated anger. His muscles bunched. She'd never seen him so enraged.

"Robert, my love, take me. Here. Now."

Robert lifted his eyes to hers. "I can't. How can I after that whore was here, sullying our room?"

"Because she was here, saying what she did. We need to take the room back. Reclaim it as our sanctuary. I want you, Robert."

Serena grabbed his hand and tugged him to the desk. "Show me how much you want me." She shoved aside the files and raised her skirts.

Robert growled and lifted her onto their massive partner's desk. He claimed her lips and took all she willingly gave. Their tongues tangled. He tilted his head and devoured her. Serena struggled to keep up. She speared her fingers through his soft curls, pressed her breasts into his chest, and moaned when he claimed them as well. Pure lust lanced through her. She reached down to unfasten his buttons, and his erection sprang into her ready hand.

Serena caressed the soft skin. "This is mine. You are mine."

Robert pressed her back onto the desk. No sooner had she spread her legs then his hard shaft nudged against her entrance.

"Now!"

He held her hips and with one hard thrust buried himself deep within her. Serena wrapped her legs tightly around him and urged him on. Never had their mating been so fraught with primitive need. Serena gasped and fought for control.

"Serena, my love, I never thought to bring this to you. Forgive me."

Her voice was low and fierce, her possessiveness showing. "There's nothing to forgive. You are mine now, and I won't let you go."

Robert plunged into her again and again. "Promise me."

She arched up, trying to take him deeper. "I promise. No other woman will ever have you."

Elation roared through him. He tightened his grip on her hips. Holding her, he thrust harder and deeper, faster. "Never?"

"Never. Never. Oh, Robert, now!"

He held her close as she shattered, convulsing around him, bringing him with her.

Sometime later, Serena could barely lift her heavy lids. She and Robert were on the floor, a thick Turkey carpet beneath them. Robert lay on top of her, his head next to hers, and they were still joined. She didn't spend time wondering how they got there. Serena wrapped her legs around him and rocked her hips up. Robert grew hard again. She increased her motion, moaning and kissing his ear—the only part of him she could reach.

He lifted his head. Serena's lips brushed against his and she ran her tongue across them. His mouth opened, and she surged in and captured him.

Robert seized control of the reins, claiming her as she'd claimed him, thrusting into her. Serena took his face in her hands, kissing him ravenously. Robert was as close to losing his wits as he'd ever been. Her love and possession radiated through him. Equals, they were finally equals in this sphere as well. Serena rolled to the side. He obeyed her and flipped them over so she was on top.

Serena lifted and plunged down on him so strongly he gasped. Her hair had loosened, wantonly and long, curling auburn tendrils brushed his face. Her skin was dewed and her breath came in short pants. Robert rose to kiss her, saw her breasts straining against her bodice, and took her lips as he began to knead.

She was struggling to reach the pinnacle, the one she couldn't quite achieve, when he found her pearl and circled it, rubbing slowly. Serena arched back and cried out as tremors shook her body; he joined her in release.

Chapter Twenty-eight

Robert didn't know how long they'd been in the study. No one had knocked. He lifted his head, bringing his eyes into focus, and groaned as he looked at the clock. It was past time to dress for dinner and she was still on top of him.

"Serena, my love, we have to get up."

"Mmm."

Nothing pleased him more than to see her unable to move because of him, but they must go. "Come, we must dress for dinner."

She opened her eyes slowly and blinked. "How long have we been here?"

"Long enough for people to know we are missing."

"Well, there's nothing for it then." Serena closed her eyes. "I'll just go back to sleep."

Robert's shoulders shook as he tried not to dissolve into laughter. "Come, my lady, I'll carry you to your chamber."

He picked her up and opened the door. A footman stood at the entrance of the corridor leading to the main rooms.

Serena was just coming round as Robert closed the door to her chamber and placed her carefully down on the bed. He tugged the bell pull. Mary appeared almost immediately.

"Where have you been, and what's happened to my lady?"

He struggled not to smile. "She overexerted herself and needs a few minutes."

Mary glared at him suspiciously.

Robert gave her his most charming smile.

Mary rounded on him, advancing. "Could ye not have waited till the marrow? Only the Good Lord knows how I'm to put her ladyship together now."

Robert quickly opened the door and made his escape. A few long strides had him safely in his room. He closed the door and laughed. Never, even in his career as a rake, had he been chased from a room by an enraged dresser.

Lady Elling returned to her bedchamber, angry and humiliated. Beaumont had been about to call her a whore and that chit he was marrying knew it. Or did she? Lady Serena had given no impression of having heard anything, though she obviously knew something was going on by the warning she gave. Robert had made no secret of the fact that he planned to marry for convenience. If that was the case, he'd expect his bride to be a virgin. What if her maidenhead was plucked by someone else before the wedding?

It wouldn't even have to go that far.

Beaumont would be magnificently enraged if Lady Serena was put in a compromising position. He'd still have to marry her, yet it would forever drive a wedge between them.

But who to do the deed? Lady Elling tapped her fan

against her fingers. She'd have to be careful in choosing her tool.

Due to the number of guests and the good weather, Serena had the tables set up on the terrace. They would dine alfresco. She was in a group talking with Phoebe and Anna when a footman walked up quietly to her and in a low voice informed her she was wanted in one of the parlors.

Serena excused herself to the others. "Who is it?"

"I don't know, my lady. Shall I accompany you?"

Serena knitted her brow.

The footman looked concerned. "You don't know who it is, my lady, and there are so many people here, you must be careful."

"Very well then, come with me."

He led her through a side door to one of the small back parlors and held the door open. Serena stepped in and he followed close behind.

She saw an elegantly dressed gentleman standing alone, with his back to the room, taking in the view out the window. He was one of the many guests with whom she had little acquaintance. But, thankfully, his name came to her.

"Lord Talbert, is it not? I was told you wished to speak with me."

Turning, he smiled seductively and took a step forward. Lord Talbert glanced from Serena to her footman and frowned. "My lady, I was told you wanted to meet privately with me."

Serena's frown matched his. "Indeed? I have no wish to be rude to a guest, but why would I wish to be alone with you?"

They turned at the sound of footsteps. Robert burst into the room, followed by four London ladies. His gaze alighted on the footman and Serena. "What are you doing here, my love?"

Serena shrugged. "Frank here"—she indicated the footman—"was given a message that there was some sort of problem."

Robert addressed his footman. "Who gave you the message?"

"I don't know her name, my lord. One of the ladies' maids."

Robert swung to the women who had followed him into the room.

Serena placed her hand on his arm. "Allow me." Serena raised a brow. "What brings you ladies here?"

"We were told Lord Beaumont would dash off, and we should follow him as something interesting would occur," one of the ladies said.

She glanced at Robert who was struggling not to scowl. Something interesting would have occurred if Frank hadn't insisted on accompanying her. "Who told you to follow him?"

"Why, Lady Elling, to be sure," another lady said.

Robert moved, but Serena tightened her grip and smiled graciously. "Thank you for your concern. I really do not think there is anything for you to see, do you?"

"No, my lady. We're sorry to have intruded."

Frank followed them and closed the door.

"Lord Talbert, please tell me exactly what was said to you," Serena said. "You obviously were not expecting to see me arrive with my footman."

Talbert smiled ruefully. "No, anything but. I believe, Lady Serena, that Lady Elling tried to arrange a compromising circumstance. Fortunately, you had the presence of mind not to come alone. I received a note, purporting to come from you, asking me to meet you here."

When Robert growled, Talbert gave a slight smile. "Had I known yours was a love match, I would not have come. I do try to avoid possessive husbands." Lord Talbert bowed, walked to the door, and stopped. "I beg you won't take it amiss, but if I happen to chance upon Lady Elling, I intend to warn her that she might want to leave your home before she runs into Beaumont. She doesn't deserve it, but I have had a rather long acquaintance with her, and she does prove useful at times."

Not understanding, Serena glanced at Robert.

He smiled humorlessly, his eyes hard as he returned Lord Talbert's steady gaze. "Rather less expensive than the alternative, I take it?"

Lord Talbert smiled. "Just so. Elling can keep her in jewels and I can provide the . . . other."

"Do as you see fit, but know that if I find her, I'll have my footmen throw her out. You might also tell her"—Robert's jaw clenched—"never to approach my wife again."

Talbert's smile widened. "I will mention it. I wish you a very happy day on the morrow. I don't think I'll be here to see you."

Talbert hadn't left the room before Robert drew Serena into his arms, nuzzled her hair, and kissed it. "I'm sorry, my love. You should not have had to be subjected to her sordidness. I thought I could promise you my past life wouldn't touch you, but I can no longer be certain."

Serena tried to move back a little to see his face. He held her tighter. "Robert, it doesn't matter if fifty women try to lure you back to them. It's taken me until to-day to understand that I can offer you more than they can. I know you are mine. I know I am yours. Together, we are a match for them and more."

Robert sucked in a breath. "I don't know how I was so lucky to catch you."

Serena smiled. "Come, we've been gone long enough."

By the time they reached the terrace, many of their guests had retired for the evening. Freddy and Lady Beaumont had acted as hostesses for the tea.

"You missed the excitement," Freddy said as they strolled up.

"What excitement was that?" Robert asked.

"Well, apparently Lady Elling was called back to Town and had to leave immediately. Lord Talbert escorted her."

Serena smiled. "I cannot think her absence will be a loss."

Freddy glanced sharply at her.

"Open your budgets, you two," his grandmother said. "What do you know that the rest of us don't?"

When Robert and Serena related a rather abbreviated version of the tricks Lady Elling had played that day, Lady Beaumont chuckled. "I always thought old Elling had lost his head when he married her. If he ever does have an heir, it will be none of his. Serves him right marrying a girl forty years younger than him, and a widow at that."

Lady Beaumont turned to Serena. "My girl, you need to be going to your chamber soon." The older lady turned a sapient eye on Robert. "Alone."

Serena blushed. "Yes, ma'am."

"Robert?"

He sighed. "Yes, Grandmama."

"I need a few moments with Serena, privately."

After he left, Lady Beaumont asked a footman to find Serena's female relatives, then took her aside. "I've not had a chance to talk to you alone, my dear. Though you're handling Robert well, I think you should know that his parents' marriage was not happy. It was my son's fault. He fell in love with a young woman who had no more sense than a peagoose. She couldn't stand up to him, and he made her life a misery."

This had been what was missing in Serena's knowledge of Robert. "I've heard that Robert is not as bad as his father."

"No, but I believe that is your influence."

Serena smiled. Freddy had been right that morning when she said it was in his blood, but Serena knew Robert wanted to work with her. She would make sure he did. "Thank you for telling me."

Phoebe, her sisters, and Anna arrived. Phoebe grinned and led Serena to the corridor outside her bedchamber, where Robert waited.

"You may have a few minutes to say good night," Phoebe said, before retreating to the grand staircase.

Serena put her hands on his shoulders. "I have no idea what they are doing."

"Nor do I, but I don't think I'm going to like it."

"Nor I."

Robert touched his lips to hers. She opened them and he entered. She tasted like wine and honey, with maybe a touch of orange. "I love you more than my life."

Serena pulled him closer. "I love you too. You are my life."

Robert groaned. "This is going to be the longest night of my existence. I swear to you—I give you my solemn oath—I will never spend another night away from you."

Serena chuckled. "Never is a long time, my lord."

He made a low guttural sound. "Nevertheless, never it is. No more talking."

He took her face in his hands and plundered. Serena met his tongue stroke for stroke. He reached down to cup her derriere.

"That's enough, Robert," Phoebe said from the staircase.

Serena was gently taken away from him. They held their hands until even the tips of their fingers were parted and the door to her chamber closed.

He turned to find Marcus waiting for him.

"Billiards?"

Robert glanced back at Serena's door.

Marcus shook his head. "It's no use. They'll never let you close to her until the wedding to-morrow."

Robert sighed. "No, I suppose not. Billiards it is. It's going to be a long night, isn't it?"

"I'm afraid it is." Marcus took his arm and led him down the staircase, where they were greeted by more of his soon-to-be-relatives.

When Serena woke, the cots her cousins and Anna had slept in were empty, and Mary had laid the table for breakfast. She went out into the corridor and returned with a large tray.

Serena watched curiously as Mary set the tray down, and returned to the corridor. A whispered conversation took place. Mary returned and set up breakfast.

That was no surprise.

Phoebe and her sisters had told Serena last night she could not leave her chamber until Uncle Henry came for her.

Before they'd settled down to sleep, they'd had a light repast of fruit and cheese with wine, accompanied by a very enlightening conversation about men and women and their desires.

After Serena finished her tea, another knock came. Mary went out and returned with a basket. She slipped through the dressing-room door. Serena followed.

Mary jumped. "Oh, my lady, you shouldn't be sneaking up on a person like that. You like to have given me a start."

"Mary, what *are* you doing?"

"Following my orders, my lady."

Serena shook her head. "Is my bath ready?"

"No, not just yet. You go back in your room, and I'll come fetch you."

This was all very strange. "Very well."

Mary came to get her a few minutes later. Serena sniffed and looked down at the tub. Lavender heads and rose petals floated in the water. "What in heaven's name is all this?"

"It's what Lady St. Eth said was to go in your bath water." Mary took Serena's nightgown and wrapper. "You just get in and relax. I'll get the rest prepared and come back for you."

Serena sank into the hot water, breathing in the myriad calming scents.

Mary came back just as the water was cooling, handed Serena a towel, and placed a jar of cream on the stool.

Serena glanced at her dresser.

"I was told you are to rub it on you. Like a salve."

"Where?"

"All over you."

Serena did and her skin was no longer tight.

"Well?" Mary asked.

"I like it. You'll have to get the recipe. It makes my skin so smooth."

Mary smiled. "Well, that's what I was told it would do. Come now, you need to start getting ready. The ladies will be here shortly."

Serena donned the new chemise Mary handed to her. Obviously from Paris, it was almost translucent and soft as the finest silk. "Mary, where are my stays?"

"You don't need them with your gown."

"Of course I do, don't you remember I decided to wear my yellow silk?"

Mary looked down and shuffled her feet before she raised her head and looked at something over Serena's shoulder. "Well, you see, my lady . . ."

"What she means to say is we arranged your wedding gown." Aunt Ester entered.

"Aunt Ester, I don't understand."

She smiled. "Well, we couldn't have you marrying in an everyday dress and we knew *you* wouldn't bother buying one, so we bought the fabric in France and Madame designed it especially for you. Phoebe?"

Phoebe was followed by Catherine, Freddy, Phoebe's sisters, Lady Beaumont, and Anna Rutherford. Serena's eyes misted.

"No crying," Aunt Ester ordered. "It will make your eyes red and we cannot have that."

Mary slipped the gown they'd brought over Serena's head. It was a deep cream, almost yellow. The low bodice was pleated in layers of lisse silk and the long sleeves were made of a single transparent layer of the same silk. Seed pearls were interspersed throughout the bodice and sleeves. The skirt was of thin silk with more layers of lisse over it to create a floating effect. Serena stared at her reflection. "Phoebe, Aunt Ester, it's—it's beautiful. I would never have chosen anything so fine."

Phoebe laughed. "We know. That's why we bought it. Now, for the rest." She stepped back.

Mary deftly twisted Serena's hair high, before pulling a few strands of curls down. Phoebe's sisters gave Mary a diamond comb to hold the knot.

"That is something new," Phoebe said.

Lady Beaumont placed a necklace of diamonds and peridot around Serena's neck. The setting was the same type of gold filigree as her ring. Freddy handed her the matching earrings. "These count for something old. They are part of the Beaumont jewels. They're yours now, my girl," Lady Beaumont said.

Serena grabbed her hand before the older lady could withdraw it. She met Lady Beaumont's eyes in the mirror. "Thank you, Grandmama."

Lady Beaumont sniffed and blinked. "You're a good girl, and you've done more than I thought possible. You take care of them and him, and I'll be more than happy."

"And this," Catherine said, holding out a diamond and sapphire ring, "is both borrowed and blue."

Serena threatened to tear up again, but she was hurriedly bustled into the hallway where Uncle Henry was waiting.

He beamed at her. "I don't know why it is that all my nieces always look so radiant on their wedding days. Serena, you are beautiful."

Serena smiled mistily. "Thank you, Uncle Henry."

"Come, my dear, you have a recalcitrant bridegroom who will not leave the Hall until he's sure you are under-way."

"Isn't he supposed to be at the church, or close to it?"

Uncle Henry chuckled. "He is, but he's not. As I said, he refused to leave until he knew you were ready to leave as well."

Phoebe's lips twitched. "Why anyone should expect Robert to be easy to manage, even on his wedding day, is a mystery to me."

She and the rest of the ladies descended the stairs ahead of them, to shoo Robert out of the Hall so he wouldn't see Serena.

Once Robert was safely away, Uncle Henry escorted Serena to the waiting carriage and raised a brow. "Outriders?"

Serena shook her head and grinned. "Outriders."

Once in the carriage, Henry assumed a serious demeanor. "Serena, you are sure this is what you want to do?"

Phoebe's eyes danced with laughter. "Don't worry. He asked me the same thing."

Smiling, Serena said, "Yes, this is what I want to do."

"Very well then, I'll take you to the church. I think you've made a wise decision, my dear. I'm not at all sure that if you'd changed your mind, I could have kept Beaumont from carrying you off. He's a very determined young man."

Serena laughed. "True, Robert is nothing, if not determined."

When they arrived at the church, Serena looked down the aisle toward the altar and placed her hand on Henry's arm. She began her walk to the man who would be her husband.

Robert stared at her. The expression in his face made her want to run to him. The tall, handsome, *tonnish* gentleman, whose cultured façade hid his real strength and who he really was. Kind and gentle, aggravating and difficult. All of him was hers and she loved him.

Robert stared at Serena, and his chest seized.

Marcus nudged him. "She's exquisite."

"She is indeed." At first, Robert thought he'd never seen her look more beautiful, but then an image of her in the morning light, her hair curling around her, made him think again.

She was beautiful no matter what she was wearing or doing, and she was his. He reached for her, only to be held back until Henry gave him her hand.

Robert gripped it firmly as they said their vows. When she promised to be his forever, he searched her face for any lingering doubts and found none. Joy filled him. Finally, John pronounced them man and wife.

Serena smiled and Robert loosed all the emotions he'd been holding in. He took her face, kissed her, then swung her up into his arms and proceeded back up the aisle to the door, ignoring the shocked silence and then the laughter.

Serena hid her face in his shoulder. "What happened to not making us the talk of the *ton?*"

"I couldn't wait any longer. Do you mind?" he asked, contritely.

"No. Not every lady gets to be carried out of church."

Robert smiled. "Serena, are you happy?"

She brought his head down and kissed him. "I am the happiest woman in the world."

Robert returned her kiss. "And I am the happiest man."

Lord Huntley sipped his champagne. "Who would've thought we'd be celebrating Beaumont's wedding and enjoying it so much. Typical of Beaumont to create a scandal by kissing her and then carrying his bride out of the church."

Lord Wivenly lifted his glass in salute. "How the mighty have fallen."

Mr. Featherton raised his quizzing glass. "I don't know about that, he looks happy enough."

Wivenly, taking a sip of champagne, regarded the newly married couple and scowled.

"Look at Evesham, Worthington, and Rutherford—they all look happy," Mr. Featherton complained. "They make being leg-shackled seem not so bad. Not good, mind you, but not as bad as I've heard."

Rupert joined them. "You look to be having a serious conversation at this table, unlike the rest of the company."

Wivenly made room for him. "We were discussing the merits of marriage."

Rupert chuckled. "Ah. Well, I know Robert's relieved to finally have the deed done."

"That, Stanstead, was rather obvious," Wivenly said

dryly. "Been to a good number of weddings. This is the first time I've ever seen the bride borne off by the groom."

Rupert smiled. "Couldn't get to the church fast enough this morning, until we reminded him he still had to wait for Serena. Then he wouldn't budge until he knew she was on her way. He even had outriders for her carriage."

Wively made a disgusted face. "He's lost his mind, the besotted fool. Never let a woman get her talons that far into one. It never ends well."

Rupert laughed. "I see some gentlemen here who'd beg to differ with your assessment."

Huntley scowled. "It's no laughing matter. With the three of them married, Beaumont especially, my mother will be after me to do the same. Don't know that I'll forgive him for this."

Wively nodded. "There must be some way to avoid the parson's noose."

Rupert smiled. "Anyone care to make a wager as to who'll be the next to fall prey to Cupid's arrow and wed?"

The men pulled out their notebooks and written bids hit the table. Rupert sat back, content with the furor he'd caused. When he lifted his drink in a toast, his attention was caught by a slender young lady with blond curls dressed in celestial blue standing with Phoebe's relatives.

"Stanstead, are you listening to me?" Huntley demanded.

"What? Oh yes, got all my attention." Rupert bowed. "I've just seen someone I need to speak with."

The Honorable Miss Charlotte Marling stood next to Lord and Lady St. Eth listening absently to their conversation with Lord and Lady Fairport. She surveyed the guests on the lawn, and her eye was caught by a tall blond gentleman standing in a group of other men. Charlotte saw him glance up and quickly turned her gaze.

Can a beautiful Worthington widow find love again?
Depends on who's asking . . .

Before he died, Patience was the Earl of Worthington's second wife. So why shouldn't Patience be allowed a second chance at marriage, too? Of course, finding a new husband was not something the mother of four had ever planned on. But a surprise encounter with her first love has suddenly made the impossible seem possible all over again . . .

It seems like a lifetime ago that Richard, Viscount Wolverton, was halfway around the world, looking for adventure . . . while Patience, at her coming-out, was left with no choice but to take old Worthington's hand. Richard never forgot the woman whose heart he yearned for—and now that he's back, he's not going to let her slip away again . . .

Please turn the page to begin reading
Ella Quinn's bonus novella
in her Worthington series,
THE SECOND TIME AROUND!

This book is dedicated to my granddaughters,
Josephine and Vivienne.

May all your dreams come true.

Acknowledgments

Anyone involved in publishing knows it takes a team effort to get a book from that inkling in an author's head to the printed or digital page. I'd like to thank my beta readers, Jenna, Doreen, and Margaret, for their comments and suggestions. To my fabulous agent Elizabeth Pomada for seeing the potential in my books. I'll miss working with you. To my new agents, Deidre Knight and Janna Boikowski, for their continued support.

To my wonderful editor, John Scognamiglio, who loves my books enough to contract them for Kensington. To the Kensington team, Vida, Jane, and Lauren, who do such a tremendous job of publicity. And to the copy editors who find all the niggling mistakes I never am able to see.

To my readers. Without you, none of this would be worth it. Thank you from the bottom of my heart for loving my stories!

Chapter One

Pulteney Hotel, London, 1815

"And this is Viscount Wolverton." Patience Worthington watched as Almeria, Lady Bellamny, smiled as she introduced the gentleman to the Duchess of Bristol. Almeria turned her black eyes on Patience. The smile didn't fade at all as she said, "Wolverton, I believe you have already met the Dowager Countess of Worthington."

What in God's name is he doing here? Patience inclined her head and held out her hand. "Indeed. The years have treated you well, my lord."

Bowing, he took her fingers in his. "As they have done to you, my lady."

His lips hovered over her hand and prayed he would do nothing more than kiss the air above them, but no. The devil pressed his warm, firm lips to her knuckles; even through her gloves she could feel his touch and fought the urge to suck in a breath. "Thank you, my lord."

One would think after all these years and his betrayal she would be immune to him. And one would be wrong. She held her breath, counting—*One, two, three, four, five. Thank God*—until he finally straightened and returned her hand to her. Patience let out the breath, yet she could not control the pounding in her breast. It took all the control she had not to make an excuse and leave the room. Yet, she could not do that to Dotty Stern, soon to be the Marchioness of Merton.

"He has been a friend for a very long time," Almeria continued, as if she had no idea of the havoc she had created by inviting Wolverton. "Though he hardly ever comes to Town."

"Well, my dear," Lord Bellamny said, "you couldn't be here so often if it wasn't for the help he gives me. Someone must assist me in my experiments."

"Very true, my dear."

Patience made the mistake of glancing up at the same moment Richard Wolverton stared down at her. His amber eyes smoldered as they had the last time she had seen him, only days before her marriage to the old Earl of Worthington. Had he finally decided to take a wife? If so, it was about time.

Her throat tightened as she thought of the young ladies who'd be happy to snatch up a handsome viscount. Well, it was no bread and butter of hers. He could wed whomever he wanted.

Well-bred chuckles by the other guests distracted her enough to drag her gaze from Wolverton's. She had to get away from him. Fortunately, the next guests to arrive were Lord and Lady Thornhill. Dressed for once as if they actually belonged in England. Normally, they wore the raiment of the places they had visited.

Drat him. He'd stopped kissing her fingers but still had not let them go. Patience jerked her hand out of Wolverton's grip and hastily made her way to her friends. "I am so glad to see you here." Her voice sounded as if she had been running for miles. "What a lovely gown."

"It is not in my usual mode, but I quite like it." A faint line appeared between Lady Thornhill's brows. "You seem a little out of sorts. Chaperoning young ladies can be very tiring, I'm sure."

"Not at all." Really, Patience had to calm herself. If only she had known *he* would be present, she could have prepared to see him again. "In truth, Worthington and his wife have taken them in hand. Which is a great relief to me as you must imagine."

Lady Thornhill's gaze did not leave Patience's face. "I had wondered how you would like their marriage. It must be a huge change for you. All of you."

"It is working out exceedingly well." She flashed the other woman a smile. "Particularly for the children." Her four girls and Grace's seven brothers and sisters had taken to one another like ducks to water. Patience had heard stories of children not getting on with each other. Then again, they had all been properly raised, and wanted the best for their elder brother and sister.

"The numbers are not even," the duchess announced, thankfully cutting short any further inquiries. Patience had barely had an opportunity to fully adjust to her new living arrangements in Stanwood House when Miss Dorothea Stern, the duchess's granddaughter and a friend of Grace's family, had come to visit for the Season. This evening was the betrothal ball for Dotty and the Marquis of Merton.

The duchess waved an imperious hand. "Some of you gentlemen will have to escort two of the ladies." Focusing on Patience's daughter Louisa, age eighteen, and Grace's oldest sister, Lady Charlotte Carpenter, also eighteen, Her Grace raised a brow. "I did not wish to give any of the young gentlemen the idea they were being singled out for you younger ladies. Make them work for your affections. It is never good for a gentleman to be too sure of himself."

Merton made his way quickly to his betrothed. Although he was a cousin of Worthington's, Patience had not cared at all for the young man until he had met Dotty. Perhaps in some cases it was true that the woman made the man.

Not that Patience would know about that. Nevertheless, the pair was obviously in love, and it had turned out to be a good match.

She shifted her gaze to her stepson, Mattheus, Earl of Worthington, only to find him staring at Wolverton then at her.

Well, fiddlesticks! There was no hope now that Matt would not ask about the man. She would love to be able to tell him it was none of his business, but that was not and would never be the truth. Not only was he the sole guardian of her daughters, his half sisters, but she was living under his roof, or rather Grace's. Which was the only way she could remain close to her children. Patience would never be allowed to remove the girls from his home.

Sometimes she wondered if her late husband had left the girls as wards of Matt so that Patience could never remarry. Yet, she doubted her late husband would have been deliberately cruel. His unkindness had been one of benign neglect, and an inability to love a woman other than his late wife, Matt's mother. If only she had known that before she had wed him her life would have been much easier.

The duchess's personal butler announced dinner, and Matt strode to his wife, who was standing not far from her. He took Grace's arm, and was about to offer Patience his other arm when Wolverton appeared next to her. "Allow me, my lady."

She could have screamed with frustration. His only purpose could be to complicate her life. "Thank you, my lord." She was going to murder Almeria. "What brings you to Town?"

He must have slid a glance at her because the side of Patience's face began to burn. As it had always done when he was staring at her. "You."

Patience gasped. Not loudly, she was much too self-contained to draw attention to herself. But Richard could feel her pulse jump, and he was pleased that he still had the ability to shake her calm, to make her react to him. He wondered if her old husband had been able to command her attention in the same way. The corners of his lips twitched. Probably not. Whether she knew it or not, she was his and always had been.

If only he hadn't been such an idiot. Who forgets the year of his beloved's come out? A young man who had traveled halfway across the world looking for adventure, that was who. By the time he had returned home, it was just days before her marriage to Lord Worthington. He had argued with her father to be able to see her, but it was as if her parents had locked her in the house. When they'd traveled to Town for the wedding, he had followed. However, his pains had been to no avail. Neither her mother nor father was going to let him ruin their plans for Pae. After all, an earl outranked the heir to a viscount. There was also the scandal that would ensue if she broke the betrothal just days before the nuptials. He would not have cared, but he was the only one. Even his parents would have been appalled if Pae jilted Worthington for Richard.

Too late. That is what everyone had told him. But he wasn't too late now.

Her startled blue gaze flew to his eyes. "In that case, you might as well take your leave."

"Can't." He pushed her chair in. "I rode up here with Bellamny. Doesn't like to travel alone."

"I am surprised he is here at all. He never comes to Town."

"There is a scientific meeting at which he is giving a paper." A footman poured wine and Richard searched for changes in her. There was no need to tell her the part he had played in arranging the scientific assembly. "He could not miss the opportunity to gather with fellow scientists."

Her long fingers, almost devoid of rings, wrapped around the stem of the wineglass, then slid up to hold the goblet between her thumb and index finger. "I assume it is a great honor."

"Indeed." If Richard had his way he'd drag her out of the room. Once he had her in his arms, he would convince her to marry him.

Several years ago, after her period of mourning had run, Lady Bellamny had taken Patience in hand, bringing her to Town and teaching her what she needed to know to go on as a widow. He had been surprised, and not at all happy about that turn of events.

As Patience had not given old Lord Worthington the second son he desired, Richard had assumed she would return home with her daughters. He would have pursued her again and this time no one would have talked her into marrying someone else. Then again, that she had wed his lordship was partly his fault. He never should have given in to the temptation to see a bit of the world. Yet what young man truly considers the disasters that can take place in his absence?

She turned her head, giving her attention to the gentleman on the other side and giving him a view of her glossy blond hair. Her skin appeared as soft and silky as it had when she was younger. He raised his hand and almost allowed his index finger to trace the line of her jaw.

Almost. Yet he noticed the current Lord Worthington glaring at him. Richard lifted his wineglass in a salute, but the younger man did not respond in kind. Instead, he canted his head toward his wife as she spoke in hushed tones, and nodded toward someone on his side of the table. If there was going to be trouble from Worthington, Richard should discover it as soon as possible.

After the second course was served, Worthington rose, holding up his glass. "To Miss Stern and my cousin Merton. May they have a long and happy marriage."

As she participated in the toast, Patience smiled, even though a tear hovered on her thick, dark blond lashes. Then she sniffed, and before she could reach her reticule, he had his handkerchief out, dabbing the corner of her eye.

"What are you doing?" she whispered fiercely. "Stop it this instant. You will draw attention to us."

"Why were you crying?" His tone was sharper than he'd wanted it to be, but he couldn't bear for her to be sad or in pain.

"Tears of happiness." Her fingers fluttered as if to wave him away. "What does it matter to you in any event?"

"You should know the answer to that question." He trailed one finger down the soft skin of her bare arm, causing her to tremble. "I want you, Pae."

Her spine went rigid. "Do not call me that."

He took a sip of wine. "You used to like it when I murmured it in your ear."

"That," she said in a cold tone most probably meant to put him in his place, "was a very long time ago."

Another toast was made, putting an end to their discussion . . . temporarily. "I understand there is to be at least one waltz at the ball this evening. I would like to reserve it."

"I am not dancing. I must chaperone my daughter."

Obviously, he had not done sufficient research into the guest list. "Why would your daughter be here?"

Her sigh was one of pure exasperation. "She and Lady Charlotte, Lady Worthington's sister, are friends with Miss Stern. She is also a cousin of Lord Merton. So you see, I have no time for your games." Pausing, Pae raised her chin in a somewhat pugnacious manner. "Whatever they might be."

What she said made sense, but something was not quite right. Naturally, one would think that a mother would chaperone her daughter. Yet, yet . . . "I never understood the reason you did not bring your children home."

"That was not an option open to me."

Why the devil not? The only time he had gone to her father after he'd returned to England, he'd been baldly told that she would be very well off if she survived her husband.

"Worthington is their guardian, and would not even entertain the suggestion that they reside anywhere but in his house."

Bloody hell! Why the deuce hadn't Richard asked Almeria Bellamny how things stood? *Because you are too damned proud to go begging for information.*

For years, he had listened eagerly to every tidbit dropped about Pae, and he had waited for her to have her fun and come home. To come to him.

He had also assumed she was still in love with him, as he

was with her. Well, she might very well be, but if she had to leave her daughters in order to marry him, courting her was going to be much more difficult than he had originally thought. And he didn't have forever. After all, neither of them was getting any younger, and he still had to produce an heir.

Somehow, some way, he must convince Pae to spend the rest of her life with him.

Chapter Two

Later that evening, Patience found a chair next to her old friend and mentor, Almeria Bellamny. "Why did you not tell me Wolverton would be here? He was not on the guest list."

"Neither was my husband." Her answer was typically cryptic.

"But you knew."

"Yes, I was aware that he planned to join George." She focused her obsidian gaze on Patience. "What I did not know was whether you still cared for him. You have never mentioned him."

Rather she did not allow herself to think of Richard. What good would it have done? She had her daughters and must be happy with them. Remarriage, even to a man she had loved, was out of the question. "I have no feelings for him."

One black brow rose. "You may attempt to lie to yourself, my dear, but do not try to lie to me."

"I do not wish to have any reaction at all to him." She let out a puff of air that made the feather hanging down along her cheek flutter. "One would think that after all this time I would not feel anything at all."

"Perhaps if your marriage had been better . . ." Almeria let the sentence hang in the air between them.

She was the only one who knew how devastated Patience had been at her husband's lack of affection. Matt had some idea, but she would never have confided in him about his own father. "He was extremely charming." And her husband had been a skilled lover. If he had not been so considerate of her in that way, she might not have fancied herself in love with him. "If only he could have got over his first wife's death."

Almeria's lips pinched together. "I tried to tell your mother that Vivers men mate for life. Even if he wanted to, he could never stop loving Elizabeth, and marrying you off to him was no good." Almeria gave a fatalistic shrug. "But she was too thrilled about the match to listen."

"Thrilled indeed." Patience remembered well the raptures her mother had been in when the offer of marriage had come. "Had I known, I would not have had hopes that we could fall in love." If Wolverton had not left her to go traveling around the world, if he hadn't broken his promise to come home before she had her come out, she never would have wed old Lord Worthington. Yet he had not arrived until the offer had been made and accepted, the settlement agreements signed, and the wedding was just a few days away. "There is no point in crying over spilt milk. I had Matt and the children to keep me company. He was more of a father to the girls than his own father was."

And still was. He had always been there for them. The only unfortunate part of it all was that it meant she would never know true love in a marriage. She had not missed it as much before he had wed Grace. Yet having to live in the same house with the couple who were so obviously in love, and to see what she had missed, it was becoming increasingly difficult to be sanguine. And now there was Merton and Dotty. Since the rift between both branches of the Vivers family had been healed, there would be frequent visits between them and Worthington and Grace. Nevertheless, there was nothing for it, and she could not truly blame him for wishing to honor his father's wishes. Patience sighed.

"You could have an affair," Almeria said casually.

Patience opened her mouth, then snapped it shut. How her friend could make the most outrageous statements in such a matter-of-fact tone, she had no idea. "I beg your pardon?"

"You heard me. As long as you are discreet, no harm will come of it."

Except that she had absolutely no idea how she would explain her absences to her stepson and Grace, not to mention her daughters. If they even noticed. Not once since Patience had moved into Stanwood House with the girls had any of them needed her in the middle of the night. There must be something about sleeping on a floor with six other children that was comforting.

Still, an affair was not the answer. At least she did not think it was.

Before she could respond to Almeria's suggestion, Worthington pulled up a chair and sat in it. "Was Lord Wolverton bothering you?"

Patience resisted the urge to pleat her skirts. "No, why do you ask?"

"I think I've known you long enough to recognize when you are upset."

"Well, you are out." She winced at the sharpness in her voice. "I simply did not expect to see him here."

"Then you know him?" Matt's intent focus made her feel like a deer being hunted.

"I knew him growing up." Not a total lie, yet not the entire truth. "But he left to travel before I came out. I did not realize he had returned."

"Harrumph. Let me know if I should put a flea in his ear."

"I assure you, I am perfectly capable of telling a gentleman that I do not wish his company." She raised one brow in what she hoped was an intimidating manner. "I do not require looking after. Your time is better spent chaperoning the girls."

"If you're sure?"

"I am."

Standing, he bowed and left.

"Ah," Almeria said, fluttering her fan. "I see your point."

"About what?"

"An affair, of course."

The skin on one side of Patience's neck began to warm again, and she glanced across the ballroom.

Wolverton.

She should have known. He turned to say something to a man standing next to him. His form was still muscular, with a trim stomach. At dinner she had noticed a few strands of silver mixed with the dark brown hair at his temple. His nose had a bump it had not had before. Most likely he had broken it, but when had he acquired it and how? At one point she had known everything about him; now she knew virtually nothing.

She gave herself a shake. She did not care. None of it mattered. And an affair was not any more possible than was marriage.

The following evening, Richard accompanied the Bellamnys to a select dinner at the home of Lady Jersey. Not long after they arrived, Pae was announced. As she stood briefly in the door, he was able to study her as he had not been able to the previous evening. She was more beautiful than she had been at sixteen. Despite her having given birth to four children, her figure was better than good. It was mature, with all the curves a man could wish for in a woman. He could almost feel her soft skin beneath his fingers, and he burned to touch her in ways he had never been able to before. He should have seduced her before he'd left rather than allowing her to marry old Lord Worthington. Hell, he should have found a way to seduce her after he'd returned.

It would have caused a scandal, but soon another scandal would have come along to dull the *ton*'s memory. And he would have spent the last nineteen years loving her and their children instead of waiting for her to come to him.

Lady Jersey greeted Pae, kissing her on the cheeks in the French style, then taking her arm. It was clear by the way in which she greeted the other guests that she knew them all. A few men looked at her appreciatively, but none of them appeared at all possessive. Were gentlemen of the *haut ton* all eunuchs? Or did they know something he did not?

He salved himself with the thought that they had not known her as a young lady. Had not listened to her dreams, and wishes, and desires as he had done, and, if the Fates were kind, would do again.

She and their hostess circled the room, approaching him from his right.

"Aside from Lord Bellamny, whom we do not see nearly enough of, we have a new gentleman in Town."

Lady Jersey's lips tilted into a polite smile, as Richard bowed. "My dear Lady Worthington, allow me to introduce you to Viscount Wolverton. My lord, Lady Worthington."

This was ridiculous. How many times was he going to be introduced to the woman he had known all her life?

She inclined her head as if she was not already on familiar terms with him. "A pleasure, my lord."

He reached for and took her fingers in his. "If I had known such beauty was hiding in Town, I would have visited earlier."

"I suppose I must be flattered, my lord." The smile she had pasted on her face did not reach her eyes. They were engaged in shooting daggers at him. Despite her cool outward demeanor, if he made her this angry, she must care at least a little bit for him.

He caught the tremor in her hand as he placed a kiss on her knuckles.

Lady Jersey's curious gaze swiveled between him and Pae. "You must excuse me. I have another guest who has arrived."

Making a point to keep a reasonable amount of distance between him and Pae, lest another part of her decided to attack him, he barely noticed her ladyship's departure. "We meet again."

"Apparently, we are destined to run into each other while you are in Town." Giving him a bland look, she fluttered her fan. "When did you say you were leaving?"

"I didn't." Nor would he. Not until she admitted she was his. Bellamny might have to ride home by himself. "But I wouldn't hold my breath if I were you."

The most mulish cast he had ever seen on her—and he'd seen a lot of them—settled on her chin. "You are impossible."

What the devil had happened to her? She used to be such a biddable girl. Opening his eyes wide and giving her the innocent look that had gotten him out of more trouble than he could remember, he replied, "But I haven't done anything."

"Yet." She clipped the word. "Did you not tell me that you had come to Town for me?"

"I did." That may have been a slight error on his part. "However, I am willing to be persuaded that I was mistaken."

She narrowed her eyes. Ah, God, the woman knew him too well. "Are you telling me the truth?"

Or perhaps not. The thought saddened him. "When have I ever lied to you?" Aside from a moment ago, that was. "We were friends. Can we not be friends again?"

Her azure gaze softened. "You would be satisfied with that?"

There was nothing for it. He was going to have to lie again. "Yes."

"In that case"—a tentative smile graced her lovely pink lips. Lips he had kissed only once—"we may be friends."

Richard sucked in a breath and gave thanks to several deities he had come across over the years. "Thank you." He made a show of surveying the room. "I am a bit rusty. Whom do I escort into dinner?"

Pae glanced around, and he could see her calculating the ranks. Then she seemed to slow. "Me." She stared at him as if she could hardly believe it. "You will escort me."

"Excellent." Suddenly she looked like a startled hare. He had to think of something quickly before she found an excuse to bolt. "At least I'll be sitting next to one person I know. I am out of the practice of making polite conversation."

"Oh, yes. Of course." Her shoulders dropped, and her expression returned to one of well-bred calm. "Why do I not introduce you to some of the other guests?"

Because he didn't care about any of them. "Thank you. I would enjoy broadening my acquaintances."

He spent an interminable half an hour being introduced to Lord and Mister this and Lady and Miss that. When all he wanted to do was talk to *her*. How the devil was he going to get Pae alone?

The answer it turned out was that he was not. He did, however, discover that she loved to ride in the Park during the Grand Strut. Not that she told him, but he'd become very good at listening to one conversation while engaged in another.

After dinner, when the gentlemen joined the ladies for tea, he took his cup and joined the circle of guests with whom she was standing. One gentleman, a latecomer to the dinner party, opened his mouth, and before the man could issue an invitation to Pae, Richard jumped in. "Lady Worthington, would you accompany me for a ride in the Park tomorrow?"

The other man glowered at him, and he resisted the urge to preen.

"Yes, that would be lovely." Again there was that disconnect between her words, mien, and her eyes. What had happened to the joie de vivre that had been part and parcel of Pae?

"It appears I must request the following day," the other gentleman said.

"Sir Grant," Pae responded gently, "I regret that I must refuse your kind offer. I am only accompanying Lord Wolverton because he is an old family friend."

"You may as well find out now rather than make a cake out of yourself," Lady Bellamny said in her usual acerbic manner. "Lady Worthington does not ride out with gentlemen."

"I see," the man said smoothly.

Yet it was clear that Sir Grant did not understand at all. Although Richard was beginning to, and it did not please him at all. Pae may have children, and position, but she had turned into a shriveled-up old maid. What had happened to the vibrant lady she had once been?

Chapter Three

Patience had never had such a horrible time at a dinner party in her life. There was Richard, who confused her to no end. First by saying he had come for her, which would have thrilled her beyond belief when she was younger, but could cause a plethora of problems in her current life.

Then he had said he would settle for being merely friends. That, she was almost certain, was an outright false-hood. Yet he had not said or done anything to distress her during the rest of the evening. That was something she should be grateful for, she supposed.

And there was that dreadful Sir Grant. Why Sally Jersey would have even invited the man, Patience had no idea. He was handsome to be sure, but the devil was a rake. She could tell by the way he had almost undressed her with his eyes when he thought no one was looking.

Well, if he thought to toy with her, she would quickly put him in his place. He would not be the first gentleman, using the term loosely, she had spurned. She had too much to lose. Her children being the most important.

Her exile to the country had ended five years ago when her year of mourning had concluded. During her marriage her husband had not allowed her to come to Town at all. It was definitely not the life she had envisioned when old Lord Worthington had proposed.

Since then, she had worked long and hard to be in the position she was now: respected and sought after for *ton* events. There was even a chance that she would be invited to be a patroness of Almack's. Considering that she had essentially disappeared from Polite Society during her first Season until after her period of mourning had ended, it was quite a coup that she commanded the respect she did. Never again would she allow herself to be left on the fringes of Polite Society. Nor would she allow herself to fall from grace. A scandal would destroy all she had worked for, not to mention harm her daughters' chances for a good match.

She gave herself an inner shake. There was truly nothing to be concerned with. Her life was perfect. Or had been until Richard Wolverton had shown up.

An urge to groan came over her. Why in the name of heaven had she agreed to a carriage ride with Wolverton? Just the thought of being next to him for an hour or so made Patience warm enough to apply her fan.

"My lady?" Wolverton's soft voice caressed her. "Would you like to step outside? It is quite warm."

It was, but not for the reasons he probably thought. "A stroll round the room will be sufficient. I would not like to catch a chill."

He placed her hand on his arm. "As you wish."

Thank God for gloves. At least no part of her flesh would touch his. That would have been her undoing. She would be fine as long as she did not allow him too close.

"Do you never miss home?" he asked in a conversational tone.

She did, yet that was not an admission she would make to him. "I have little time to miss a life I left so long ago."

"I thought of it often while I was away." Richard's tone was wistful, making her wish to visit her home county again.

"What did you do after—after I married?" Perhaps if he told her he'd chased women and gambled or engaged in other forms of low entertainment she would be able to ignore the tingling sensation in her fingers or the feel of his muscular arm.

"I left again." The corners of his lips turned down. "I had an uncle who was a botanist. I accompanied him on an expedition."

"I am surprised your father allowed you to go."

This time he smiled. "It was the lesser of two evils. I had threatened to buy a pair of colors. With my uncle, I would not be encouraged to take the sorts of risks war involves."

Patience could not have borne it if he had died. Where had that thought come from, and why must it appear now, exactly when she did not feel anything for him? "I can see how he would think traveling with your uncle was safer. I would love to hear about your journeys."

He told her about the new species of plants they had discovered, and of being chased by head-hunting natives in New Guinea. The skin at the corners of his eyes crinkled. "That was an adventure I was glad not to repeat."

"No indeed. I would imagine the thought of being someone's dinner is not pleasant." She repressed a shudder. Would anyone have even mentioned his death to her? Or would she have read about it in the news sheets? "When did you return?"

"Just over five years ago."

"Did your father not die around then?" Her mother had written to her shortly after she had been widowed, telling her of old Lord Wolverton's passing.

"About six months or so after I returned. It was sudden. He caught a chill that settled in his lungs. At the time I had my hands full running, or rather learning to run, the estate." Richard slid a glance at her. "I'd meant to come up to Town the following spring but was unable to leave due to my mother's illness."

That was the Season Patience had first come to Town after her husband had died. What would she have done if she'd seen him? "Lord Bellamny said you helped him."

"Although he would never keep Lady Bellamny from attending the Seasons, he becomes lonely. I visit with him, and we discuss not only his scientific experiments, but estate management as well as other topics." Richard was silent for a few moments. "He has been a good friend."

"As you have been to him I am sure." Patience wondered what it would be like to return to the place she had grown up in. She had never felt as if Worthington was truly her home.

When she had first arrived as a bride of seventeen and pregnant, Matt had been upset over the marriage, but they had soon become friends. He had been home for half term and had been the one to summon the midwife when Louisa was born. Her husband had been hunting, and when he discovered the child was a girl, sent her congratulations on her daughter and wished her better luck the next time.

"And you." Richard's low voice interrupted her musings. "How do you spend your time?"

She had never given it much thought before. "I attend the Seasons, and go to Brighton for several weeks in the summer. I am at Worthington the rest of the year, but there are always house parties to attend when things become dull." She gave him a slight grin. "Albeit lately, life has proven more exciting than I expected. My stepson"—a term she and Matt had always laughed over as there were only four years between them—"has married a woman who had custody of her seven brothers and sisters. Six of the children are still at home and none of them has reached their majority." She gave a little laugh. "While Worthington House is being remodeled to accommodate everyone, we are residing at Stanwood House. I feel rather like a gypsy at the moment."

"I should say so." Richard could not imagine living in a house with another married couple and ten children. Surely, Lord Worthington would be relieved to have his sisters taken off his hands. It was not as if he were their father, after all. Perhaps if Richard were to speak with his lordship, they could come to an agreement. "We have completed our circuit. Would you like to continue?"

"No, thank you." She removed her hand from his arm. "I shall call for my carriage."

"In that case, allow me to accompany you to the hall." He replaced her hand on his arm. Pae would not get away from him this time. "I predict Lord and Lady Bellamny will be ready to depart soon as well." He caught his friend's eye, as he and Pae made their way to Lady Jersey and bid her a good evening.

Once in the hall, he said, "I shall come for you at five o'clock. I believe I remember that being the correct time. Am I right?"

Her long, thick, blond lashes had lowered almost shyly. "You are correct."

Raising her hand, he pressed a kiss to her fingers. If only they were not wearing gloves. "I believe your carriage has arrived."

"I shall see you tomorrow afternoon."

She wasn't getting away that easily. He escorted her to her coach. "Good night. I shall see you on the morrow."

She met his gaze with a confused one of her own. "Good night."

He wanted nothing more than to bend his head and kiss Pae. Instead, he assisted her into the carriage. Once she was settled he slapped the side of the conveyance. "The lady is ready to depart."

Richard stood on the pavement for a few moments until she was out of sight, then returned to the hall. Lord and Lady Bellamny were already there.

"Did you have a good time?" Almeria asked. Her sharp, black eyes studied Richard as if she could read his mind.

"Better, much better than I had expected." He had been able to spend time speaking to Pae without interruption. He glanced to a man he'd met earlier. One who spent too much time watching Pae. "Who is Sir Grant?"

"A libertine and fortune hunter," Almeria replied. "He is safe enough for this type of gathering. The ladies here are completely up to snuff. He is not invited where there are young ladies present. I supposed it amused Sally to have him. He can be quite charming."

Richard wished Lady Jersey had not bothered to entertain herself in that manner. He did not like the way the man had looked at Pae, as though she were a beefsteak he'd like to eat. "I merely hope I am not required to be in his presence again."

Almeria chuckled knowingly. "I trust you to set him straight if his behavior becomes too familiar."

Damn right he'd set the man straight. With a bloody nose.

Early the next morning, Richard visited a carriage maker Almeria had recommended. As luck would have it, the craftsman had a curricle that the buyer had cancelled. It was not at all what he would have ordered. The color was Spanish brown when he preferred black, and thick gold paint outlined every curve as well as the wheels. But needs must. Thankfully, there was no crest on the side. He would add his later when he had the vehicle repainted. He gave the carriage maker his card with the Bellamnys' address written on the back. "Please deliver it to Green Street with the bill."

"Thank ye, my lord." The man tugged his forelock. "Glad to be able to help. It's a well-sprung carriage."

"A pleasure dealing with you, Mr. Hatchett. I was lucky to find you with an extra sporting carriage on hand."

Richard strolled out onto Long Acre Street where he found a hackney. "Tattersalls."

The coach lurched forward. It was a full half hour later before he entered the famous auction house. After inspecting several pairs of carriage horses, he made a bid on a matched pair of light Cleveland bays with white stockings and stripes on their faces. "Fifty quid."

"Sixty."

He glanced over and was not at all happy to see Sir Grant. The man inclined his head.

"Seventy," Richard countered.

"Seventy-five."

He briefly wondered how high the other man would go, when he realized that it did not matter. Sir Grant would no more get these horses than he would have Pae. "One hundred."

He raised his cane to the brim of his hat in a salute. "I believe you have won this round, my lord."

"Round?" Richard lifted one brow. "I believe you are under a misapprehension. I have no reason to be in competition with you over anything. Good day to you, sir. Better luck on your next bid."

He turned to go settle his purchase, when Sir Grant called out, "Convey my compliments to Lady Worthington and tell her I look forward to seeing her soon."

"If you happen to come up in conversation, I shall," Richard replied without turning. "However, I think that unlikely. In the event you have not noticed, she is hardly enamored of you."

"Ah, but ladies have a habit of changing their minds where I am concerned." Sir Grant's grin tempted Richard to wipe it off the man's face.

Bloody hell! That was all he needed to do. Pae would never allow him near her again.

He'd warn Pae, but chances are she would not appreciate it. He'd simply have to remain as close to her as possible. The corner of his lips tugged up. Which would suit his purposes precisely.

In the meantime, he really should plan to meet with Worthington soon. Richard would have to do it in a way that would not set his beloved's bristles up. Perhaps it was time to visit Brook's.

Chapter Four

Patience glanced at the clock for at least the hundredth time in the past hour. "I have changed my mind. I think the blue with the gold braid would be better."

Her lady's maid, Reid, turned back to the clothes press. "My lady, this is the fourth time you've changed your gown. It is five minutes to the hour, and I'd have to press that gown for it to be presentable. Are you trying to be late?"

"No." Patience resisted glancing in the mirror once more at the yellow lustring carriage gown trimmed with green ribbon. "I shall go as I am."

She added a pair of jade earrings, after which her maid set her bonnet on her head, tilting it slightly before tying the large silk ribbon rakishly under her left ear. Stopping herself from running her slightly damp palms down her skirts, she looked in the mirror. She was not as young as she had been, but her complexion was still good. She took a large breath and blew it out.

This was ridiculous. Why taking a drive with Richard Wolverton should make her so nervous she did not understand. She should still be furious with him for not returning all those years ago. Yet, even though she tried to hold on to the anger, she could not. He had been too much a part of her earlier life.

A shout came from below her window. Thank heaven the younger children were playing in the garden. She would not be forced to introduce Richard to any of them. In fact, she might be able to slip out of the house with no one knowing where she had gone.

After quickly donning her gloves, she picked up her parasol. "I am ready."

"Have a good time, my lady."

"Thank you, I shall." If she could justify meeting him at the curb or down the street, she would have done so.

She was halfway down the main staircase when the front door opened. At the same time, Daisy, the one-year-old Great Dane, dashed through the house followed by the youngest girls, her daughter Theo, and Grace's sister, Mary. Patience covered her eyes, waiting for the disaster that was sure to happen.

"Close the door, fast," Theo shouted.

The door slammed shut, shaking the frame.

"Done." Richard's jovial voice rang out.

Separating her fingers Pae peeped through them. One of the footmen was hanging on to Daisy's collar, and Theo and Mary had stopped running and were gazing up at Richard.

"Who are you?" Theo asked.

Patience wanted to sink into the carpet, or go hide somewhere. Now the whole house would know a gentleman had come to take her out. And there would be questions. Questions to which she did not even know the answers.

Straightening her shoulders, she finished descending the

stairs. "Lady Theo, Lady Mary, may I introduce Lord Wolverton?" Wide-eyed, the girls nodded silently. "My lord, my daughter Lady Theo and Lady Worthington's sister, Lady Mary."

The girls gave credible curtsies. Amazing really at eight and five.

"But *who* is he?" Theo persisted.

"His lordship is an old family friend who has come to take me for a carriage drive." Patience pasted a smile on her face. "Is that not nice of him?"

Mary glanced through one of the windows flanking the door. "You have very pretty horses. I am to have a pony when we go to Worthington."

"Yes, indeed." Patience grabbed on to the innocent statement. "And you know we cannot keep horses waiting."

"That is what Matt always says." Mary nodded sagely.

Making sure Daisy was still under control, Patience strolled to the door. "I shall see you later."

But fate was not with her. At that moment, Louisa and Charlotte entered through the front door.

They glanced around, and Louisa asked, "Did Daisy try to escape again?"

That was all it took for Theo to launch into the complete story of how Matt took Duke, their three-year-old Great Dane, to Worthington House across the square. "He should leave him here. Daisy misses him."

"She definitely behaves better when Duke is around." Charlotte stroked the dog. "I'll take her back for you."

Daisy's tail began to wag. Patience reached out to Richard, who was standing in front of the door watching the scene as if he had suddenly entered Bedlam, took hold of his arm, and pulled, moving him just before he would have been assaulted by the door as it opened.

Matt, accompanied by Duke, his Great Dane, at his side, entered the hall. "What have we here?"

Theo once again began to explain. Mary joined in, Daisy started to bark, and soon the noise echoed through the marble hall, bouncing off the walls, practically deafening her.

"We must go, now," Patience whispered in Richard's ear.

"Does this occur often?" he asked in a tone full of horrified wonder.

"All the time." She tugged his arm. If they were lucky, they would be out of the house before anyone noticed.

She nodded to the butler, who had appeared out of nowhere to open the door.

"Patience."

Sighing, she turned. "Yes, Matt."

"Have a good time."

"Thank you, I shall."

He lifted Mary in one arm and Theo in the other. "Duke, Daisy, come."

In mere moments, the chaos ended. Patience glanced at Richard. "Let us go quickly before anyone else decides to make an appearance."

He handed her into the curricle, and was silent for several minutes as they made their way out of the square. Once they were on the main street to the Park, Richard remarked, "That was interesting."

To put it mildly. "If the house is one thing, it is lively. Although, with ten children living in it full-time and one visiting on school holidays, that is to be expected."

Under his tan, his face paled. "You had mentioned that, but I truly had no idea what it entailed. Are you responsible for all of them?"

"Good heavens, no. Matt and Grace, his wife, have most of the responsibilities. She is a wonder. Before they met, she had guardianship of her brothers and sisters. Fortunately, she is extremely organized, and the governess and tutor she hired are exceptional."

"I would imagine you would rather live separately with your daughters, though." Richard feathered the corner into the Park. "Do they not become lost amidst the other children?"

"Actually, it is quite the opposite. The children have become very close, almost as if they had been raised together." This was the time to tell him how impossible it was for them to ever have a life together. "I would not remove them even if it was possible." She gave him a wry grin and tried for a bit of humor. "You saw Matt with Theo and Mary?" Richard nodded. "The girls are inseparable. I do believe Theo would run away if I moved her elsewhere, and Madeline, my twelve-year-old daughter, would go with her. She has formed a close friendship with Grace's twin sisters of the same age. It is as if we have triplets in the family instead of twins." Patience slid him a glance, but he was busy handling the horses. "Do you understand?"

"I do." Or at least he understood much more than he had before. This was not a case of taking Pae's daughters off Worthington's hands and being thanked for it.

As they made their slow way around the carriage drive, Pae waved to her friends and took the time to introduce Richard. When they had gone about halfway, he was forced to bring his carriage to a full stop.

Two barouches had pulled up alongside each other so that the ladies could more easily speak. A young buck shouted at them to move, and was pointedly ignored. That piece of impertinence would cost them several minutes at least.

Some may be in a hurry, but he was happy to be able to spend more time with Pae while he attempted to find some way of convincing her to be his. If she still loved him, surely they could find a solution that would work for him, her, and the children.

If she still loved him. That was the real question.

She had always reacted to his touch, but being older now,

he knew there were times lust had little to do with love. That then was his first task. He must discover if Pae felt for him as he still felt for her. Currently, she was staring off into the distance and not paying him any attention at all.

Another carriage rolled up, and after a few moments, the barouches were convinced to move to the verge.

He cleared his throat. "I have heard Richmond is lovely this time of year."

"Oh." She glanced at him, startled out of her reverie. "Yes, it is."

"As I have never been, could I impose upon you to show me the sights?"

Her brows drew down, causing a slight line to form between her perfectly shaped blond brows. "I suppose I could. Better yet"—she smiled—"you could make up a party."

That was not at all what he wanted. "If I knew anyone I could. The number of people I am on more than nodding terms with is pitifully small."

"Do you know no one in Town?" Her tone hovered somewhere between irritation and incredulity.

"Only the Bellamnys and you." She did not appear at all impressed by his social contacts, so he added, "It is possible that some of the older gentlemen I traveled with are about."

Pae stared at him for several moments before responding, "You really must begin to meet more people."

"I suppose that at some point I will make friends. Until I do, will you accompany me to Richmond?" Richard knew he sounded a bit pathetic. Yet, he really did need to be alone with her, and since carrying a lady off on a black charger was out of fashion, this was the best he could do.

"Very well," she replied slowly.

He sucked in a breath. One more hurdle to get over. "I shall pick you up in the morning."

Her eyes widened. "You want to go *tomorrow*?"

"Yes, of course. After all, I do not know how long I shall be in Town." Another partial truth. He could remain or depart whenever he wished.

"I'd forgotten you were traveling with Lord Bellamny."

Richard could tell nothing by her tone. Although if she did care for him, she would probably be happy for him to leave as soon as possible. He was clearly a complication to her well-ordered life, and his returning to Kent would make her life easier.

She would not have to face her love for him or what he wanted for them.

Two ladies hailed Pae. As had happened previously, the ladies' brows were raised until she once again introduced Richard to the women, Viscountess Pierson and the Countess of Hammersmith, as an old friend from home. After that, her friends appeared to lose interest in him.

"Shall I see you at Lady Featherton's ball?" Lady Pierson asked.

"Indeed. I would not miss it." Pae turned to him. "Lady Featherton always has the most ingenious decorations. Last year, the ballroom was made to look like a large tree. One would swear we were dancing among the leaves. Lady Bellamny will have received an invitation."

"I take it you are visiting Lady Bellamny." Lady Hammersmith suddenly appeared fascinated. But for the life of him he could not think why.

"Yes, I came to Town with Lord Bellamny. He is to give a paper at one of his scientific societies."

"Are you also of a scientific bent, my lord?" she asked, leaning forward as if to catch his every word.

Richard wasn't quite sure what to make of the woman. "I was part of a group studying the various flora in South America and the Pacific."

She smiled like his cat did when it had caught a particularly juicy mouse. "I am absolutely fascinated by travel. I must invite you to dine with me."

He inclined his head. "I would be delighted, my lady."

That should make Pae happy, yet when he glanced at her, the corners of her lovely lips were drawn in. Was she jealous? The thought pleased him enormously.

She quickly pasted a smile on her face. "We really must not hold up the traffic. I look forward to seeing you at the Feathertons."

A few minutes later, Lady Louisa and Lady Charlotte waved from a Prussian-blue high-perched phaeton pulled by the most beautiful pair of grays he'd ever seen. He brought his carriage to a halt.

"Mama, look at the new pair Matt bought us." Lady Louisa beamed.

Lady Charlotte nodded. "Such sweet goers as well."

Pae looked at the horses, then at the girls. "I can see. He always has had an eye for horseflesh."

"Is it safe for you to be driving that thing?" The words were out of his mouth before he could stop himself. Even Pae could not help but think he was being presumptuous.

Louisa's giggle reminded him forcibly of Pae's when she was younger. A sound he hadn't heard in too long a time.

"Matt said it is safer for us to drive a gentleman than for a gentleman to drive us. At least until we come to know the gentleman better." Lady Charlotte grinned. "He is very protective."

Richard was coming to have a great deal of respect for Pae's stepson, and he did not like it a bit. "I've never given it much thought, but I understand his thinking."

"Mama," Lady Louisa said. "Grace asked me to tell you she has some things to discuss with you when you return."

"Yes, of course." Even though Pae's tone was even, he sensed she was nervous about something.

The girls went on their way, and he started his horses again. "Is there a problem between you and the new Lady Worthington?"

Pae shrugged lightly. "It is nothing, really."

"It must be something. The request seemed to make you uneasy." He covered her hand with his, giving her as much support and comfort as he could. "I may not have seen you for several years, but I can still sense when you are unhappy."

"Not . . . unhappy. Never that. It is merely that . . . well, to be truthful, I have never learned to hold house, and at times I exceed my allowance."

Irritation that Lady Worthington would chastise Pae as if she were nothing more than an errant child surged through him. "I hardly think it is her place to correct you."

"Oh, Richard." She turned her hand and wrapped her fingers around his. "It is not like that at all. Please do not think it. Grace simply goes over the accounts with me, and if I require a loan, she makes the arrangements. She is never cross about it. It is I who am always mortified that I cannot keep my accounts in order. We even agreed that I should receive my money twice a month rather than quarterly to make it easier for me to keep track of it." She heaved a sigh. "You see, I have no head for numbers."

No. He did not understand. She had always been clever and quick-witted. She beat him to flinders at charades and other word games. However, an inability to perform accounting was no great thing, after all. One could always hire a secretary. Yet there seemed to be something else entirely going on with Pae's life that made him wonder if all was not right. If only he knew what it was.

Chapter Five

The following morning, Patience awoke much earlier than usual. The bed hangings were still drawn, and no sound of her maid could be heard.

What was she doing up so early in the first place?

Reaching out, she tugged the bellpull. Several minutes later, her maid arrived carrying a cup of tea accompanied by two pieces of toast and an egg. "Your wash water will be up in a moment." She arranged Patience's breakfast on the bedside table. "Did one of the girls wake you up?"

"No. I simply awoke. What time is it?" Patience picked up the cup and sipped, savoring the strong blend of Assam and Ceylon.

"Going on nine."

Goodness, she was up betimes. Then she remembered that Richard was coming for her. "I must hurry. I am to drive out to Richmond at ten o'clock."

Shortly before the hour, while she and her maid were

staring at each other in the dressing mirror after she had rejected yet another hairstyle, a footman came to announce that Lord Wolverton had arrived and was waiting in the front parlor.

"Now, my lady, you must decide." Reid's face was set in stern lines.

"A simple knot." Patience nodded. "I will be wearing a bonnet, so it will not matter."

Fifteen minutes later, she descended the stairs to find Richard pacing the hall. "Is something wrong?"

"Not now." He smiled. Taking her arm he led her to his carriage, and in a few moments they were winding their way through the streets of London. "You will be happy to hear I have received an invitation to dine at Lady Hammersmith's house two days hence. I know how much you wish me to begin finding my own way amongst the *ton*."

Perhaps, but *not* with Maria Hammersmith. The woman would have poor Richard for breakfast. "Charming. Have you sent your acceptance yet?"

"I haven't had time. I shall do so when we return this afternoon."

Patience stifled a sigh of relief. There must be another entertainment more suitable for him to attend. She searched her mind and had it. "What terrible timing. That is the evening of one of Lady Evesham's political parties." She slid a glance at him. "You did say you wished to become more active in the Lords."

"Bad luck, indeed. I shall send my regrets to her ladyship." The corners of his lips curled up slightly.

That could mean anything. Had he not wished to attend Maria's dinner, or was he pleased about meeting other peers? What a bother it was only to be able to see his profile. When she glanced up a large wagon was in the middle of the road. "Take care of that dray."

He skillfully maneuvered around the conveyance. "Thank you. I'm not used to all this traffic."

In no time at all, it seemed, they were out of the city and on the main road to Richmond, the vehicles and crowds left behind. Why had she not thought to come out here before? It was much more pleasant than being in Town all the time. "The weather is lovely."

"It is. I ordered it just for you. Thank you for accompanying me."

She smiled to herself, remembering other times he had claimed to control the weather. "Thank you for suggesting it. It has been an age since I've been out here."

An hour later, they arrived at the large park bordering the Thames, and Richard drew the carriage to a stop. Jumping down, he fetched a basket from the back of the curricle before lifting her from the carriage.

The moment his arms circled her waist, she caught her breath.

I should not be having this type of reaction to him. What we had was long ago. I'm too old to feel this way.

If only she could command her body to stop feeling anything for Richard, her life would be so much easier. "There is a lovely view where we may stop to picnic."

"Lead on, my dear."

Tucking her hand in his arm, she steered them down the main path. The woods were full of early spring flowers. Violets and lady's slippers decorated the forest floor. Massive rhododendrons showed off their colorful flowers. Richard, naturally, knew all their Latin names. "When I left, the bluebells were just beginning to cover that one area of land between your family's home and mine. Do you remember it?"

Patience did. The display used to be even better than Baroness Merton's famous bluebell garden. Albeit not as close to Town. "Yes. I can almost see it in my mind's eye."

She waited for him to renew his suggestion that she return home for a while and found she was disappointed when he did not. Although, to be fair, he had given his word he would be nothing more than a friend to her. It was what she wanted, after all.

Soon they came upon her favorite spot to picnic. Old trees provided shade but did not obstruct the view over the river.

"I couldn't have selected a more perfect place to enjoy our luncheon."

They laid out a heavy cotton blanket. While she unpacked the basket, he opened a bottle of wine. The Bellamnys' cook had provided the usual picnic fare: roasted chicken, buttered bread, fruit, and cheese. Richard dug into the food with a relish she did not usually see in older gentlemen. On the other hand, he was not *that* old, just past forty. Only five years older than herself.

As she placed a piece of chicken and some fruit on the plate, the memories of other picnics with him rushed back to her. None of them had been as elegant as this one. Usually, their meals consisted of sandwiches and apples begged from their cooks.

"You were right," he said, wiping his fingers on a serviette. "It reminds me a little of home. Shall we stroll for a while?"

A picnic and a stroll, perhaps a dance or two, that was all she would ever have with him, and suddenly her heart ached for its loss. She blinked back the tears that pricked her eyelids. "I would love to."

They ambled down toward the river, her hand tucked very properly in his arm, but when the path steepened a bit, he took her hand in his and didn't let it go. She felt like a girl again, walking with the man she had thought she would wed. How different her life was compared to what she'd thought it would be.

"You're very quiet, Pae. Are you all right?"

Ruthlessly shoving down her memories, she smiled. "I am fine. Need we speak?"

"No, not if you are comfortable with our silence."

They had always been able to be together without talking. It seemed that hadn't changed. "I am content."

He stopped, turning her to face him. "Is that enough for you, mere contentment?"

"It must be." Her throat closed painfully as she beat back a surge of emotion for him. "I do not have a choice."

Richard's lips formed a thin line and he nodded. They made their way back to where they had picnicked. A half an hour later they were in the carriage on their way back to Town.

A drop of water hit Patience's gloved hand. "Richard, I believe it is beginning to rain."

He glanced up at the sky. "It is probably only a sprinkle. However, I shall put the top up. I would not want your gown or that very fetching hat to get wet." After bringing the horses to a halt, he pulled up the convertible hood of the carriage. "That should keep you dry."

He started the pair again, and she settled comfortably back against the seat. They'd had such a lovely day. True to his word, he had not once mentioned his feelings for her. Although, she had caught him gazing at her in a way that warmed her from her head to her toes.

A very long time ago he had kissed her, and she wondered what it would be like to feel his lips on hers again. Her breasts began to swell and tingle. No other man had ever had the effect on her that he had.

She reached out for him but stopped herself. If only

things were different. But they were not, and no amount of wishing or sighing would change the facts of her life. Still, as long as they were together she could enjoy his company and the day.

A large, multicolored butterfly danced in front of her face, but Richard urged his horses to a trot and it left. Birds flitted around the hedgerow on the side of the road. If only the day could last longer, yet they were already halfway back to Town.

Soon the relative quiet of the country would be replaced by a house that was only quiet after the younger children were asleep.

Suddenly a strong breeze came up, seemingly out of nowhere, and the sky darkened.

Just as the rain started coming down in sheets Richard practically threw the blanket they had sat on during their picnic at her. "Cover yourself up. We're in for it. I'll stop at the first inn I can find."

"I don't know how you can see anything at all." She could see nothing beyond the horses.

Her half boots were already soaked. If they did not find shelter soon, they would both come down with influenza.

The carriage swerved, and she held on for dear life.

"Here we are." Richard had maneuvered them into the small yard of an inn. He glanced at her. "You'll be warm soon enough."

An ostler ran out, grabbing onto the lead horse's head. "I've got them, sir. Get you and your lady into the inn."

A moment later, Richard lifted her from the curricle and carried her into the inn. "Landlord," he bellowed unnecessarily as a man was already hurrying toward them. "I'll need a room for her ladyship and a private parlor."

The landlord wrung his hands. "Right sorry I am, my

lord, but I only got one chamber left. It has a parlor with a table fit for dining, and the fire was lit a few minutes ago, so it should be warmish."

Richard looked at her, then nodded. "That will do. Send a maid up as soon as may be."

"I'm that sorry, my lord, but all my girls are running their tails off. One of my lads can bring you tea, soup, a fresh loaf of bread, and wine right soon though."

Pae stood next to Richard, staring around and shivering in earnest now. If she did not remove her wet clothes, she would soon be ill. "That will do. Thank you."

He cupped her elbow, guiding her as they followed the innkeeper up a set of plain, wide stairs. She pressed her lips together but said nothing until they were in the room and the door had closed.

"I suppose I should be glad we are not in the common room." She pulled at the bedraggled ribbon of her ruined bonnet. "Oh, bother. I can't get this untied."

"Here, allow me to try." The ribbon was completely soaked, but he managed to tease out one end. "There, almost done." He lifted the hat from her head. "I don't suppose there is any chance of saving it."

The straw drooped and the artificial flowers looked as if they'd drowned.

She shook her head. "No, probably not."

With shaky fingers she unfastened the toggles on her spencer.

She should never have come with him. How on earth would she ever explain this to her family?

Chapter Six

"Let me help." Pae's fingers were cold to the touch. The cloth was drenched, and when Richard removed the garment her skin immediately pebbled into gooseskin. Her bodice was soaked as well and her skirts clung to her legs. "It must all come off."

Her eyes flew wide, and a lovely blush rose from her neck to her cheeks. "Richard, you know I cannot undress while you are here."

"I don't think you have much choice. I seriously doubt that you can get out of that gown by yourself." He purposely didn't mention that he must remove and dry his clothing as well. "Let's see what we have." Striding to the wardrobe, he found several blankets. "These should keep us covered and warm."

A knock came on the door, and he opened it.

A boy of about fifteen carried in a large, covered tray. "My da said to bring this right away, and ask if you need anything else."

"Towels would be welcome."

"They're behind the screen, my lord."

"Thank you."

Once the contents of the tray had been unloaded onto the sturdy wooden table set under a window, the lad bowed and left the room. Just as Richard was about to close the door, Sir Grant strolled by. A sly grin formed on his face as he looked in the room. The scoundrel could not have failed to see Pae standing before the fireplace trying to warm herself.

Richard shut the door with a snap. He had a few ideas what the other man would do with the information that he and Pae were in a chamber together, and none of them were good.

Turning back to the only woman he had ever loved, he prayed he was about to make the right decision.

"Stay where you are," he said, handing her a blanket. "I'll unfasten your tapes."

Her back was as straight as a poker and her shoulders inched up toward her ears as he slowly undid her gown. His fingers accidentally brushed the back of her neck, and she sucked in a breath. He fought the urge to caress her soft skin and press kisses under her ear. The gown dropped to the floor in a waterlogged heap. Her stays were only slightly less damp, but still wet enough to cause her to remain chilled. They too fell to the floor.

The last thing to go was her chemise. "If you wish, go behind the screen."

"Y-yes, I'll do that." She scurried away from him.

A moment later, the fine linen was draped over the wooden frame.

Richard quickly divested himself of his equally sodden clothing, wrapped one blanket around his waist, and waited. Soon the sound of small boots hitting the floor could be heard, and a pair of silk stockings joined the muslin.

His body tightened, and his blasted shaft decided it was being invited to play. He had not been a monk, especially after Pae had married and he'd thought he had lost her forever, but it had been a damn long time, and he wanted her as he had no other woman.

Patience remained behind the screen for several moments gathering her courage. After all, there was no point in staying there all day. She was no innocent miss, and Richard was merely a friend. Not to mention that she must spread her clothing out to dry, and she wished for a cup of tea while it was still warm. Thank the Lord no one had seen them enter the inn or knew they were sharing a chamber.

She made sure the edge of the blanket was tucked in securely before stepping out from behind the screen, and stopped. Richard sat in a chair next to the fire, naked from his waist up. All their garments had been hung over a sofa he had pulled in front of the fireplace.

He turned. His eyes widened slightly as he gazed at her. She pushed a strand of damp hair behind her ear, surprised to find her fingers trembling.

It had been so long since a man had seen her less than fully dressed. "I must look a fright."

"You look beautiful." He rose, holding his arm out as he strode to her. "I am reminded of the times we went swimming in the lake." She closed her eyes as his hand touched her tresses, winding a long curl around his fingers. "Pae."

His voice was a breath sliding across her cheek.

"Richard, we cannot." Her tone was so soft she could barely hear the words.

His mouth brushed hers, and her lips burned with the caress.

"No?" His arms wrapped around her, heating her whole body.

"No." Although right now she could not think of even one reason not to do what they wished.

"Just let me kiss you." He slanted his head and pressed his lips to hers. She opened her mouth, allowing him in, meeting his warm tongue with hers.

The springy hairs covering his muscular chest called to her. She could have no more resisted touching them than she could have resisted one of Gunter's ices. Pressing her palms to his chest, she stroked, grazing his nipples with her nails. He felt hard, and warm, and wonderful.

Richard groaned as he pulled her flush against him. The blankets fell, and she slid her hands over his shoulders. His hard member pressed against her belly. His slightly callused hands roamed over her back, down to her derrière, lighting flames wherever they touched. Desire, long dead, rose, causing her to rock against his length.

Oh, God, she wanted him, wanted this.

"Richard." She panted as he ravaged her mouth.

"Hold on, my love."

She quickly wrapped her legs around him as he picked her up and opened the door behind them.

"A bedchamber?" Why had she not been paying attention when they'd arrived?

"Fortunate that we got the last one." He grabbed at the covers, pulling them back, and, somehow, managing to get them both onto the mattress without letting her go. He took her lips again in a ravenous kiss, then began pressing his mouth to her neck. "Tell me if I do anything you do not like."

She nodded, moaning as he pushed her breasts together, taking one nipple in his hot, wet mouth and sucking. "Good, so good."

"God, Pae, you taste like honey and lavender."

Frissons of lust shot from her breasts to her mons. She arched into him. "I want you."

He settled between her legs, and his shaft nudged against her. Once more she wrapped her legs around him, this time encouraging him to take her. Richard had nearly lost control when Pae emerged from behind the screen. He'd almost spent himself when Pae's blanket dropped. He had dreamed about making love to her for years, and now her beautiful pink-tipped breasts were his to enjoy, and he couldn't seem to get enough of them. Then she had spread her legs, allowing his member to feel her hot, wet mons, and his need to possess her, to make her his, surged.

He pressed slowly into her tight sheath, watching as her head dropped back giving him perfect access to her swanlike neck. He dragged his tongue along the soft line of her jaw and brought his mouth down on hers as he buried himself in her.

After almost twenty years, finally, he was home.

Moments later her breathing hitched, and she cried his name, convulsing around him bringing him with her. "Oh, God, Pae."

He wanted to tell her he loved her and always would. Instead, he held her close to him, tucking her next to his side and urging her to nestle her cheek on his chest.

Waiting for her to say something, anything, he listened to the fire crackle and pop, while the rain lashed the shutters. Instead, she wove his chest hairs around her slender fingers and sighed.

Finally, she turned her head, her sky-blue eyes gazing at him. "I did not expect this."

"To happen?" He gently pushed her hair off her face.

"That, of course." Her lips curled up into a warm smile. "Yet mostly how we were together." She glanced away, a small line forming between her brows. "The passion. I was prepared to say no."

He dropped a kiss on her head and grinned. "You did."

Turning, she gave him a quizzical look. "But then you kissed me, and it was so different from anything I had experienced."

"I don't understand." Or rather he did not want to believe that she had been denied a husband who cared about her.

"There was no madness before. It was as if he was performing a duty by seeing to my needs, as he called it. When *we* kissed"—she pressed her lips to his fingers—"I knew neither of us could stop."

He put his finger under her chin and tilted her head up. "I love you, Pae."

Her blue eyes shimmered with tears. Not what he wanted to see. "I love you as well, Richard, but I'm afraid it is too late for us to have a life together."

"Fate brought us together again." He gently kissed the corner of her mouth. "Perhaps it will show us a way forward."

"I hope so too." She lowered her head to his chest. "Though I do not see how it can work."

With the pad of his thumb, he brushed away the lone tear that had leaked from under her lashes. Somehow, he would find a way for them to be together.

They made love again slowly, sweetly, then she dropped off into a doze as he listened to the rain still beating a tattoo against the windows.

Slipping out from under the covers, he tucked them around her, making sure she remained warm before making his way into the parlor. He shook out and turned their clothing. Lifting the dome off the tray, he saw it was as he had expected. The tea was cold.

Richard tugged the bellpull and waited. Fifteen minutes

later, the summons had still not been answered. Unfortunately, his pantaloons were still not dry enough to don. He gave the bellpull a hard yank, and a few minutes later, the same lad as before knocked on the door.

"Sorry, me lord. We have a terrible lot of people here, what with the rain and the mail coach and all."

"I need more tea, the soup that was promised, and some bread." The boy nodded, but appeared a bit panicked. "Is there something wrong with my request?"

"No, me lord, it just may take a bit. We're not used to having the mail here, but the bridge washed out."

Richard dragged a hand over his face. "Going to London?"

"No, the other way."

That was something at least. Still, it occurred to him that Pae's family would become worried if she did not return soon. "I'll also need paper, pen, and ink, as well as someone who can hand-carry a message to Town. He'll be well rewarded."

The lad nodded, and to show he would be appropriately appreciative, Richard flipped him a crown. "Thank ye, yer lordship."

A few minutes later the writing instruments arrived. Fortunately, the inn had their name at the top of the paper. An unlooked-for extravagance, but fortunate as he couldn't remember the name of the place.

Dear Lord Worthington,

Lady Worthington and I have been held up due to the weather. I shall convey her safely home as soon as we are able to travel.

Please acknowledge that you have received this letter.

Yr servant,
Richard, Viscount Wolverton

He was affixing his seal when the food arrived. "Send this as soon as possible." He handed the boy another crown. "Wait for an answer. There is more when I know it's been delivered."

"Yes, me lord. My older brother's to take it."

Once the lad left, Richard carried the tray to the bedroom and climbed in next to Pae. Her long, golden hair curled around her shoulders. Moving it carefully, he drew her to him.

Turning in his arms, she opened her eyes. "Is everything all right?"

"Everything is perfect. I ordered hot food and sent a message to your stepson that we have been held up. Are you hungry?"

"A little. I would really like a cup of tea."

"You should have some soup as well. I would not want you to catch a chill."

"There is no need to worry about that." She took a sip of tea and sighed. "As you know, I am never ill."

"Nevertheless." He gave her a wicked grin. "I predict that you will need your strength."

An hour later, after they had once again made love, the rain stopped. She was his now. Unfortunately, he had no idea how he would keep her. Would she agree to continue seeing him once they returned to Town and her children?

Chapter Seven

The next morning Patience woke with a headache. That was strange. She had felt fine when she'd gone to bed. "I can't be ill."

"You can be, my lady." Reid's no-nonsense voice seemed to echo in the room. She came over and fluffed Patience's pillow. "Master Walter woke up with something this morning as well."

Walter, Grace's fourteen-year-old brother, was Patience's daughter Augusta's closest friend. "Augusta?"

"Pink of health, but her ladyship is taking no chances. They have been moved out of the schoolroom floor to separate chambers." Reid set Patience's tea down on the table. "Lady Augusta is insisting on nursing him."

"Naturally."

"Her ladyship said that if you didn't mind she may, but none of the other children is to be around them."

Patience did not feel up to the argument she would have

with her daughter if she attempted to keep Augusta from her friend. "Do we know what it is yet?"

"No, my lady. Master Walter is being made to breathe under some sort of tent to clear his nose."

Patience tried to sniff and found herself breathing through her mouth. "I think I may need a tent as well."

"I'll get it started right away."

She took another sip of tea. The steam coming off the cup seemed to help. Thank goodness Grace had it all in hand. From what Charlotte had said, her sister was ruthless whenever any of them became ill. As if the fever was an enemy to be vanquished.

Yet why did it have to happen right after the most glorious day of her life? The memory of Richard's hands on her made her nipples hard and desire for him speared through her body.

Then she sneezed.

How was it possible to feel so miserable and so lustful at the same time? It was probably Fate's way of punishing her for wanting too much, Richard and her children.

The tent turned out to be a large piece of cloth set up with a bowl of some herbal concoction. Nevertheless, it worked. As had the plaster on her chest that the cook sent up.

Her maid entered the room holding a small vase of bluebells. "These came for you. Lord Wolverton brought them himself."

How she wished she were well enough to see him, to be in his arms again, but she could not even rise to write him a note. "Thank you for bringing them to me."

"He asked after you, and was told you're not feeling well."

That was an understatement. "I am sure I'll be better tomorrow."

At least well enough to have a visitor.

The doctor had been called and pronounced that she and Walter had lung ailments that must be watched carefully. He prescribed saline draughts, rest, and beef tea. But by later that day, her head felt ready to split apart, and she was shivering.

Quiet voices spoke near the door, and a few moments later, her maid was pouring another draught down her throat. "I am not a child."

Her voice sounded more like a frog's than hers, and it was peevish. She detested peevishness.

"No, you are not, my lady," Reid said calmly. "But the way you're shaking, more would go on you than in you."

"My eyes hurt." She closed them against the faint light in the chamber.

"That's to be expected. You're running a fever."

Every bone in her body ached, and she turned, trying to find a comfortable position and not able to.

Richard.

The last time she had slept well she had been in Richard's arms. Patience wanted him now, but he wasn't there.

The day after Richard had been told Pae was ill, he was in the reading room at Brook's having coffee and waiting until he could try to see her again. All he'd been able to think about was her boast that she never took a chill, and now she was sick.

If she was not better today, he would send for some fruit from his succession houses. They would be much better quality than what one could procure in London.

Another gentleman entered the room, drawing a chair up next to his.

"What is my stepmother to you?"

He glanced at Lord Worthington's stern face and carefully folded the paper, placing it on the low table next to him. "Why do you wish to know?"

"Because she has been asking for you. She's running a fever."

Richard stared at the younger man for what seemed like eons before he finally understood. "I'll come straightaway."

As he started to rise Worthington's hand clamped down on Richard's arm. "I'll ask you again, what is she to you?"

He looked straight into the other man's eyes. "The only woman I have ever loved."

Worthington gave a terse nod. "I was afraid it was something like that." He released Richard's arm. "My carriage is outside."

In short order, they were in the curricle and the horses were trotting down the streets of Mayfair.

"How bad is she?"

"Bad enough to concern me. She is never sick."

"I know." If only he had gotten her to the inn more quickly or insisted she get straight under the covers after he had undressed her.

"I don't suppose you could be obliging enough to be a peer without an estate?" There was a hopeful tone in Worthington's voice that Richard didn't understand.

"No. I have a rather large estate in Kent."

"Well, this is a damnable muddle," Worthington grumbled. "We'll have to sort it out later."

They arrived at Stanwood House, and Richard jumped to the pavement, taking the stairs two at a time. The door opened and Lady Worthington came forward.

"Thank you for coming. I'll take you to her immediately." She began to climb the staircase. "It is the fever, of course, but she started asking for you and will not calm."

"Thank you for coming to get me."

She nodded, then pointed to a woman who looked to be in her fifties. "Please follow Reid."

The servant's lips were set in a grim line. "Come this way, my lord."

He was led to a large, airy room at the back of the house, then through a door to a bedroom. Pae's pale hair had been neatly braided, but she lay so still that for a moment he thought the worst.

"We just gave her a draught for the fever a while ago, but she's worn herself out." A chair with a footstool already stood next to the bed. "Make yourself comfortable. I'll be in the dressing room. Tea and barley water as well as some books and newspapers are on the table by the window. There's a bowl with cold water and a cloth next to the bed."

He almost grinned at the bow to propriety in having the maid close by. "Thank you. I hope I will be able to do some good."

"Anything is worth a try at this point." Reid left the room.

Richard ambled to the table and picked up a copy of the same paper he'd been reading at Brook's, then poured a glass of barley water for Pae when she woke, and a cup of tea for himself. Once everything was situated to his liking, he sat in the chair, put up his feet, and waited.

Unfortunately, he did not have to wait long. She began to toss and turn, crying out as if she was in pain. Without bothering to feel her head, he wet the cloth, and wiped her face and neck. It had been a very long time since he'd had to nurse anyone through a fever, but that type of knowledge was never lost.

When she settled a bit, he sat on the bed, lifting her so that she could drink some of the barley water. He made a note to ask for lemonade as well. "Come, my love. Have some of this and you'll feel better."

"Richard." His name was no more than a moan.

"I'm here, Pae. Drink some of this. It will make you feel better."

She opened her fever-glazed eyes and stared at him, but obediently drank the water. "You're really here?"

Her voice was so faint he could barely hear her.

"Of course I am." He put the glass down and held her head against his side. "You didn't think I'd desert you."

"You missed my come-out ball. I waited for you."

His heart squeezed painfully. He wanted nothing more than to whip his younger self. "I'm sorry. I tried to make it. I just got the date confused." By almost a year. He was supposed to have returned the previous autumn. How stupid he'd been. "I won't leave you again. You have my word."

She closed her eyes, but the respite was never for long, and her sleep was fretful. Day stretched into evening. He caught the occasional sounds of soft voices from the parlor, but the only person to enter the room was Reid.

Late that night she offered to shift him, but he refused to leave Pae's side. He had disappointed her once, with disastrous results. He would not do so again.

Finally, as the gray light of dawn filtered through the windows her fever broke. She had been so restless that he'd taken his boots off and climbed in bed with her, holding her, dosing her, and making her drink barley water and lemonade.

"Richard, what are you doing here?" A single candle was the only light other than the fire, and, even though he couldn't see her eyes, her voice, though weak, was lucid.

Thank God she is going to be well.

"I'm sorry, I must have fallen asleep."

When he started to move to the chair, she stayed him. "No, I mean here, in the house."

"Worthington brought me." Richard reached over for the lemonade. "You must be parched."

"I am a bit." A smile trembled on her lips.

Damn. She was so pale.

He poured her a glass of lemonade. "Drink some of this, and I'll give you the soup Cook made for you."

"I am not really hungry."

"Still, you must eat. Especially after I went to all the trouble to set up a warming plate in your fireplace."

"Maybe a few bites. I am so tired. How long have I been ill?"

"Since the day after we visited Richmond. About three days." He eased himself out of the bed, then fixed a bowl of soup for her. She didn't eat more than a few spoonfuls, but that was enough to convince him she was on the mend.

"Will you hold me?"

He had no doubt that all hell would break loose if Worthington found Richard in Pae's bed, but he didn't care. Taking care of her was all that was important. "Yes, my love, for as long as you wish."

Sometime later, while she was in a healing sleep, Bolton, his valet, appeared with a tray. Richard wasn't even surprised to see the man. "How long have you been here?"

"Only about an hour, my lord. Word was sent round that you would need a change of clothing. I have arranged everything in the chamber next to this one. Have you eaten at all?"

"Yes." Richard grinned for the first time in hours, possibly days. Tea had been sent up numerous times as well as breakfast, luncheon, dinner, and the lemonade he'd requested for Pae. "One will not go hungry in this house."

"Excellent. I shall be in the servants' hall if you need me."

Bolton set out the plates and silver before leaving. Richard moved to the table to break his fast, but his attention never left Pae.

Several minutes later, Reid entered, and he put his finger over his lips. "The fever broke and she is resting comfortably."

"I'll order a bath for you."

"There is no need. I shall remain here."

The maid placed her hands on her hips. "I think you should have a look in the mirror, my lord. There is no reason to frighten her ladyship."

He glanced over and the man staring back at him had several days' growth of heavy beard, his clothing was rumpled beyond repair, and his eyes were bloodshot. He looked as if he'd spent last night in a flash house and was tempted to take a sniff of himself, but didn't. "I see what you mean."

But bloody hell, he didn't want to leave Pae. They might not allow him back in her chamber.

Chapter Eight

"Richard?" Patience glanced around her chamber, but the only one present was her maid. Had she dreamed him? She'd had so many strange dreams. Most of which she couldn't remember. Yet he, his presence, had been so clear she could have sworn he was with her.

"Lord Wolverton has just gone to bathe and change, my lady. He'll be back soon."

"Bathe?" she repeated stupidly. If only she did not feel so weak.

"After spending the last two days and nights taking care of you, he looked like something the cat dragged in." Reid stopped what she was doing and looked at Patience. "No need to worry. He's in the next room over. Have some lemonade. His lordship had it made for you."

She had a memory of him pressing her to drink lemonade, and she took a sip. "I'm hungry."

"Now that's a good sign." Her maid fluffed up her pillows and helped her to sit up a bit. "I'll get you some soup, and as soon as you're done eating I'll comb your hair and re-braid it. That will make you feel better as well. As soon as you're able, I'll call for a bath."

She sniffed and caught a sour odor that must be coming from her. "If you can help me, I think I'd like one now."

Reid stood, her hands on her hips, seeming to evaluate Patience's request. Finally she gave a sharp nod. "I'll call one of the maids. We'll remake your bed while you're in the tub."

An hour later, she felt much more the thing. Although still fragile, at least she was clean.

Richard strolled into the room looking more handsome than ever, and she held out her hand to him. "I thought I had dreamed you, but Reid said you nursed me."

He lowered his large frame onto the chair next to her bed. "If I had my way, I would always be here to care for you."

She should be blushing or embarrassed, but the love they had shared at the inn had seemed so right. It still did. "If only you could." She turned away, not wanting him to see the tears filling her eyes. "I'm sorry."

"No." He moved to the bed, causing it to dip as he pulled her into his strong arms. "We'll find a way. I don't know how yet, but we will."

He pressed his warm lips to her cheek and she rolled into him, caressing his lean cheeks. "Kiss me."

His mouth brushed hers, before she drew his head down, and trailed her tongue along the seam of his lips. His tongue swept the cavern of her mouth, and she tilted her head to deepen the kiss. Desire swept through her.

She wanted him. Wanted to touch his naked body. Wanted him inside her. When her hand strayed down to the placket of his pantaloons, he covered it with his strong fingers, stopping her.

"You know as well as I that we cannot make love here. Not only is your maid in and out of this room, if Worthington found out he'd murder me. And I couldn't blame him."

She turned over onto her back, still cuddled in Richard's arms. "I'm sorry. That was foolish of me."

Patience couldn't believe she had so far forgotten herself. Not only would Matt murder her lover, but he could force her to leave the house and her children as well. If only she and Richard could marry.

"No, my love." He pressed his lips to her hair. "Wanting to express our love is not foolish. Merely ill-advised at the moment." He reached out, taking a book off the bedside table. "Shall I read to you? It is a book by that lady author."

Wishing they could stay like this for the rest of their lives, she replied, "Yes."

"It is a truth universally acknowledged, that a single man in possession of a good fortune, must be in want of a wife." Richard glanced at her. "I don't know about all men, but I certainly am, and I've already found her."

"You mustn't." She laid her palm on his chest. "No matter how we feel, I cannot leave my daughters."

"And I would not ask it of you, my love. Still, there must be a way."

Richard read until Pae had drifted to sleep again. He started to put the book down, but realized he was enjoying the story. What a wicked sense of humor the author had. He wasn't at all fond of Darcy, and that Bingley chit deserved to be taken down a notch or two. A toad-eater if he'd ever seen one. But the heroine, Elizabeth, was a woman to be cherished.

Pae's maid brought in a tray of food, glanced at the bed,

and whispered, "I thought you might be getting hungry again. How is she doing?"

"Better. At this point, I think she needs rest and nourishment." And me, he wanted to add.

After Reid had set the dishes out, she left the room again.

He cuddled Pae closer. Neither of them had mentioned it, but the fact she could be pregnant was a real possibility. She was only thirty-six, after all.

He must have drifted off to sleep himself, for the next thing he knew, she was stirring next to him. "I may be able to find something more solid than soup if you are up for it."

Her lips tipped into a weak smile. "That sounds delightful."

He helped her into a sitting position, then went to the table and surveyed the offerings. "There is an omelet, some sort of pudding, sliced meats, and bread. I believe the omelet and pudding are for you. Ah, and the grapes from my succession house have arrived."

Pae giggled, and Richard's heart soared. "When did you have time to send for them?"

"As soon as I discovered you were ill." He placed half of the omelet as well as some of the grapes on a plate. After maneuvering himself back onto the bed, he speared a small piece of the omelet and held it to her lips. "It will be my honor to feed you."

She grinned, but ate what was on the fork. After she had finished, he held out a grape. She bit into it, and for some reason it was the most erotic act he'd ever seen.

"Pae," he groaned.

The kiss was hot and sweet, and all he could have wanted.

A cough sounded from the other room.

Richard quickly moved into the chair next to Pae's bed just before Reid entered the chamber.

"The children wish to see you, my lady." She glanced at him. "Perhaps, my lord, you would . . ."

"Of course." He squeezed Pae's hand before standing. "I won't be far."

As he walked out the door to her parlor, he caught a glimpse of part of a skirt whisking around the corner of the corridor. Probably a maid in a hurry. *God knows they have enough to keep them busy in this house.*

"Did you see him?" Charlotte asked as Louisa dashed through the door, closing it behind her.

She leaned against the door, catching her breath. She hadn't run like that in a long time. "Only enough to verify that it *is* the gentleman who is visiting Lady Bellamny."

"Lord Wolverton?" Her friend lowered the letter she had just opened as Louisa nodded. "I am still amazed that Matt has allowed Wolverton to remain in your mother's chamber."

"As am I, but according to my maid, who had it from Reid, Mama was in a dreadful fever, calling for him, and they could not make her calm enough to get the fever down." Louisa moved to sit next to Charlotte. "My mother is in love with him."

"I know. Alice, Eleanor, and Madeline heard them declare their love, as they put it." Charlotte squeezed Louisa's hand. "The question is will she marry him?"

"I wish I knew." Louisa sighed. "I overheard them talking. She is concerned about my sisters and me."

"I see you've picked up the Carpenter habit of eavesdropping." Her friend grinned.

She returned the smile. "It does have its uses, and the children are correct. It is practically the only way to find out what is going on when Matt decides to start hiding information."

Since their families had been combined, she and her sisters had never been happier. Even Theodora had stopped getting into so much trouble. It was as if they had just been waiting to join Grace's family to make them complete. "I want her to be happy. If this Lord Wolverton can do it, then I think we should do everything possible to help achieve that end."

"I agree." Charlotte angled her head to the side. "Won't you miss her?"

"Of course, but I shall marry in the next few years, as will my sisters, and it would be selfish of us to demand that she remain here when we will soon be gone." Yet would her sisters feel the same? They were younger, especially Theo. They might not realize how much their mother was willing to sacrifice for them. "I need your help to think of a plan. Then we must present it to the others."

"You're right, of course. Whatever is decided will affect us all."

"And Matt must agree as well. I know he will not allow my sisters and me to permanently leave his house, and I do not think any of us wish to live elsewhere. However, there has to be a way to accommodate what Mama truly wants with what he believes is best for us."

"Let's give it some thought. Once we have developed a scheme, we can present it to him and Grace."

Louisa mused about how her sister-in-law had thought she could never wed because of her brothers and sisters. Then Grace had met Matt and they'd fallen in love. If anyone knew how important it was to be with the man she loved, she did.

A knock came on the door and May, Charlotte's maid, entered. "Her ladyship is well enough for visitors, my ladies."

"I wonder if Lord Wolverton is still here," Charlotte whispered.

"I suppose we will find out." Louisa rose. "Let's go see how Mama is faring."

The twins and Madeline were leaving the parlor as Charlotte and Louisa arrived. "How does she look?"

"She is tired and pale." Madeline's lower lip trembled as if she was about to cry. "She fell asleep while we were talking to her. I am afraid. I've never seen her like this before."

"Come here, sweetie." Louisa wrapped her arms around her sister. "Reid says she is on the mend and will soon be well. You would not have been allowed in if she was not recovering. Mama will soon be right as rain, just like Walter is." Madeline nodded, but tears glistened in her eyes. "Why don't you think of something to make her feel better?"

Alice, who with her twin, Eleanor, had been holding on to Charlotte, piped up, "We can give her the handkerchiefs we've been working on."

"The flowers will make her feel better," Eleanor added.

"There, just the thing." Louisa gave her sister a hug.

"What about Richard?" Madeline asked. "He seems to make Mama happy. Maybe we can keep him here."

Oh, dear. Well, they *had* been eavesdropping if they knew his first name was Richard. "Let me think on it. Perhaps there is a way to give him to Mama as well."

Reid ushered Charlotte and Louisa through the door. Lord Wolverton sat in a chair near the window reading a news sheet. She glanced at Charlotte, who grinned. "My lord."

Setting aside the paper, he rose. "My ladies?"

"We"—Louisa waved a hand at Charlotte—"would like to thank you for helping to take care of my mother."

"I was happy to have been of assistance." As he responded, his gaze strayed toward the door to Louisa's mother's bedchamber. A shadow clouded his eyes. "She is still weak."

"I think we are the last ones, and we shall not remain long."

"Thank you."

"He certainly looks like a man in love. We shall speak as soon as we return to our parlor," Charlotte whispered as she and Louisa strolled into her mother's bedroom. "We will find a way."

At least, Louisa hoped there was a scheme that would make everyone happy.

Chapter Nine

A week later, Richard stood in a small parlor in Bellamny House waiting for Pae and the rest of the Worthington party to arrive. The day her fever had broken he'd returned here to sleep, but little else. He had visited Pae almost every day, yet they were always in the morning room, where an amazing number of people seemed to require something that had been left there. A man could barely manage a kiss, much less anything else, before being interrupted.

Today, however, he fully planned to take advantage of the fact that most of the guests would be outside enjoying the events planned for the Venetian picnic or in the ballroom, which had been decorated with a profusion of flowers and potted plants to resemble the garden. Strains of music from the quartet Almeria had hired had already begun to drift on the air.

It would be a simple matter to spirit Pae up to his chambers without anyone noticing.

He glanced at his timepiece. *Will they never arrive? What if she's had a relapse? Although yesterday she had been much better.*

Finally, he heard Worthington's voice.

A few minutes later, Pae entered the drawing room, glanced around, and smiled. "Almeria whispered to me that you would be here."

A moment later his arms were around her. "I've missed you. Each hour is a day."

"Each day a year." Her hand cupped his cheek. "I cannot bear being away from you, my love."

Pressing his lips to hers, he coaxed them open. She sighed, sinking into him as she explored his mouth. "I want you in my life permanently."

"And I wish to be there, but how? I cannot think of anything that would allow us to—"

Not wanting to listen to her protests, he kissed her, taking ruthless possession of her mouth.

Naked lust lanced through him as his hands roamed her body. Cupping her lush bottom, pulling her against him.

He lifted his head, pleased to see desire swirling in the depths of her eyes as she fought for breath. "Come with me."

Pae nodded.

Taking her hand, he led her to the door, glanced around the empty hall, then led her up the stairs and down the corridor.

When they got to his door, he kissed her again. She deserved more than a quick shagging while a party was going on. She deserved a life with a man who would love her, and, God help him, some way he would discover how to accomplish just that.

He pulled the door latch up, stepping through as the door

swung open. By the time they reached the bed, her gown's tapes were almost unfastened. Next went the petticoats and her stays. Richard carefully pushed down her fine linen chemise. His groin tightened as the fabric uncovered all but Pae's nipples. "You are the most beautiful woman I have ever seen."

Eyes glazed, she watched as he reached out one finger and began tracing the line of her shift.

"Richard?" Her voice was as soft as a feather.

"Yes, my love." Bending, he lifted one smooth satin breast and licked.

She moaned as a light shudder ran through her. "Richard"—she swallowed—"how do we do this without anyone knowing?"

It took a few moments for him to realize that she was referring to crushed clothing, and not being caught together *in flagrante delicto*.

Devil take it, he would never be able to rearrange her hair if he mussed it as he'd wished, and her gown would have to be saved as well.

Bloody hell! He had to worry about his own kit too, and he damn sure wasn't going to take her against the wall or bent over the bed. He would make it work.

Glancing at the low dresser gave him an idea. "Trust me."

He made quick work of retrieving her gown from the floor, hanging it carefully over the wardrobe door. Once he had her back in his arms, Richard carried her to the dresser, all the while pressing kisses down her jaw and neck until he once again took a delectable pink nipple in his mouth and sucked.

Her breath hitched as she arched, pressing her other breast to his eager mouth. "I've never known a woman like you, sweetheart."

Her fingers speared through his hair, as she panted. "So good."

"I'll make it better still." Using one hand to steady her, he trailed his fingers up her stocking, over her frilly garter to the bare skin of her thigh. It amazed him how something this simple could make him harder than he'd ever been before.

When he stroked the soft curls of her mons, she buried her head into his neck and cried out, "Now. Please now."

Patience thought she would die waiting for Richard to claim her. She had never in her life been so ready, or wanted a man more. Finally, hard and hot, he filled her, and the tension and need that pounded through her broke on a cry.

A moment later, Richard groaned and shuddered in her arms. Their hearts beat a tattoo as they hung on to each other, not wanting to let go. What had she ever done to deserve a life that denied her either her children or the man she loved?

Several minutes later, he drew back and kissed her gently. "We should probably go down."

"Yes." She nodded, not wanting to leave his arms. "We shall be missed, and that would cause talk."

Silently, he tied her tapes. She glanced in the mirror and was surprised to find that other than her lips appearing slightly plumper, she did not look as if she'd been ravished within an inch of her life. That was for the best, of course. Yet strangely, it did not make her feel better. Now that she had made love with Richard, she would have been perfectly happy to return home.

This must be why people had honeymoons. So that they did not have to mingle with others. An image of them sitting together in some sort of study rose in her mind, and her throat closed painfully.

He turned her around. "Pae, we'll find a way."

Closing her eyes, she nodded, knowing it wasn't true, but that he felt better thinking he could wrest control of their future from fate.

She gave her skirts a shake. "We should leave."

"I'll go first and wait for you."

"That would be best." At least then she would have a chance to collect herself. She forced a smile. "I shall see you soon."

Patience waited five minutes before departing Richard's chamber and making her way down the corridor to the public areas. She had attained the first floor and was walking through the gallery leading to the ballroom when she heard the sharp click of boots on the polished wooden floor. She glanced up and saw the one person she wished to the devil.

"My lady." As Sir Grant ambled toward Patience she was put forcibly in mind of a slithering snake. "Surely you have some time to spend with another of your admirers."

Straining her ears, she listened for the sound of footsteps, low voices, anything that would indicate someone else was around. But there was nothing but the faint notes of the orchestra coming from the ballroom, which was too far away for her comfort. Raising her chin, she gave him her iciest stare. "I beg your pardon?"

"Come now. There is no use playing the chaste widow with me. I know what you're up to. I saw you in that inn near Hammersmith, and I have no doubt you have just come from another tryst."

The closer he came to her, the more she wanted to run. The only problem was that she would have to pass him to get to where the rest of the guests were. Why had she agreed to Richard going ahead of her? "Excuse me. I must get back."

Raising her chin, she began to make her way around him as rapidly as possible.

He grabbed her arm, jerking her to a halt. "I don't think anyone will miss you for the short time it will take me."

Her mind blanked for a moment. He could not think that she would . . . ? Anger and fear surged. *Oh God! Where is Richard?* She yanked her arm. "Let me pass."

Sir Grant's brandied breath assailed her nose. "I like my women buttered."

"Buttered?" Her voice was so faint she didn't think he'd heard her.

"They are easier to please, and if there is a brat, no one will know whose it is."

At first all she could do was stare at him, when what he had said finally hit her. He wanted to have relations after she and Richard had . . . "That is the most vile and disgusting thing I've ever heard. Release me now!"

His fingers dug into her skin above the edge of her glove. "But effective. Just do what I say, and your reputation will remain intact. I merely want a piece of what you're giving away so freely."

She whirled around, pushing him as hard as she could. He stumbled back, but caught himself in time to imprison her other arm. Patience's back hit the wall. Holding her wrists together, he pinned them above her head. His other hand went to his breeches, and she kicked out, and screamed.

Please, someone hear me!

"*Pae!*"

Suddenly, her attacker was gone, and the solid crack of a fist hitting bone was the last thing she heard as she sank to the floor.

"Pae, my love." Richard's arms came around her, enveloping her in safety.

She clung to him, shivering like one of Cook's blanc-mange.

Then her stomach twisted, and a vile gorge rose in her throat. "He was going to—going to . . ."

"I know, my love, but it's over now, and I'm here. No one will ever harm you again." He glanced over his shoulder. "Get the coach. We'll meet you in the hall."

"Give me one minute to clean up this rubbish, and I shall be happy to."

"Matt?"

Richard nodded, holding her closer. "When you didn't return, I went looking for you, and he came with me."

"Sir Grant"—she took a breath, but she was shaking so hard her teeth clicked together—"knows. Everyone will know. We cannot continue."

"I agree completely." He kissed the side of her head. "This state of affairs is not to be borne."

She heard a man moan in pain.

"There," Matt said. "He won't try to harm another woman for a while. I'll get the carriage."

By the time she and Richard were in the hall, the Worthington town coach was waiting. There was no sign of Sir Grant.

Richard bundled her into the carriage, then turned to Matt. The men spoke in low tones for a few minutes before Richard joined her. She was thankful it was him and not her stepson. There was no way she could have explained her behavior to Matt.

She was cold, so cold.

Wrapping his arm around her shoulders, Richard held her close to his warmth. "I should not have allowed you to go alone."

"You could not have known."

"I knew he was a lecher. I did not know he was a rapist. I

should have been there to protect you." Her body warmed as she cuddled against him. "But you are my main concern. Shall I stay with you?"

"I'll be fine once I am at home. Just hold me." Tomorrow she would have to tell him they could no longer be together. As much as she loved him, she could not leave her daughters. Nor could she risk a scandal that would harm their reputations. Yet how could she bear to live without him in her life?

Chapter Ten

Richard saw Pae safely into Stanwood House before returning to the Bellamnys' town house. As neither he nor Pae had actually made an appearance at the party, he decided to make use of the library. A brandy would not go amiss at the moment.

He opened the door. Almeria Bellamny was standing next to the desk. "How is Patience?"

"Well enough, I suppose. Who told you?"

"Worthington found me after you left. He will inform anyone who asks about her that she is still not feeling quite the thing." Almeria stared at Richard for a moment, her black eyes hard as stone. "I shall ensure Sir Grant is never invited to another *ton* party. However, that will not stop him from attempting to blacken Patience's name. At the very least, she will be subjected to the improper advances she has successfully avoided for years. What I wish to know from you is how could you have been so careless?"

Richard dragged a hand down his face. "I did not think—"

"Clearly." She bit the word off.

"No one seemed to be around." He finished lamely. He should have been more careful especially after seeing Sir Grant at the inn. "Almeria, I love her, and she loves me."

"In that case, I suggest you do something about it that does not include ruining her reputation." She swept out of the room, leaving Richard to stew in the juices of his own making.

He poured a glass of wine, but instead of drinking it he held the glass up and watched as the light played on the cut crystal and the red of the claret as they cast myriad colors on the walls. If only he had not been responsible for his estates, he could have made his home with Pae at Worthington's estate.

Richard shook his head. That would never work, and he did have duties he could not escape even if he wanted to. Worthington seemed sympathetic, but would he be helpful? And what about Patience? Could she bear to be parted from her daughters for even part of the year?

Richard tossed back the wine. Something was bound to come to him, and it had better happen soon.

The following morning, Richard knocked on the door of Worthington House and was admitted by the butler.

He handed the servant his card. "I would like to see Lord Worthington."

Several minutes later, he was ushered into a comfortable study, paneled in and painted a muted green. The chairs, sofa, and a large daybed were all of cognac-colored leather.

Worthington came forward. "I thought I might see you today." He held up a decanter of brandy, and Richard shook his head. "Tea then," Worthington said as he tugged the bellpull. "If you are concerned about what occurred last night getting around, I have already taken care of it. I also ensured that that blackguard will not be invited anywhere again."

"You and Lady Bellamny."

Worthington grinned. "That is who will do the deed. If only I could have put him on a ship to India, I would have. Unfortunately, he is the nephew of a friend of Prinny's."

Richard waited until the tea was brought and he had a cup in his hand. Although Worthington and Almeria had taken care of part of the problem, to Richard's mind it was not the more important part. "I need to marry Patience."

"Why?"

He jerked back. That was not at all the response he'd expected. "Because I'm in love with her, damn you."

"That is all very well and good." The man lounged in his chair, touching the tips of his fingers together, his stern features a mask Richard was unable to penetrate. "But why should I help you make her leave her family? What can *you* offer her that she does not already have?"

Richard felt a sudden kinship with any young man seeking to offer for one of Worthington's sisters. "I offer her a position in Polite Society."

"In case you hadn't noticed, she has one."

Blast the man. "She would be the mistress of several houses."

"Very well," Worthington replied, clearly unimpressed. "You do know she has not managed the skill of budgeting?"

"She told me. She may have her own secretary if she likes."

Still, his countenance remained impassive.

What the devil did the man want? Richard thought about what Pae had said concerning her dead husband, and he knew what he had to offer her. "I shall love her as she has never been loved before. I shall treat her with respect, and put her needs before my own. She will never want for any-thing. I will never leave her to go hunting or to Town."

Worthington's brow cleared and he rose. "Wait here. I'll see if there is anything I can do to help you."

Louisa was practicing a piece on the new piano Matt had bought when Theo and Mary ran into the room. "Mama still won't come out, and it sounds as if she's crying."

That wasn't good. According to the twins, Mama had re-turned yesterday from Lady Bellamny's town house and locked herself into her room.

Charlotte strolled in and stopped. "Walter just told me that Lord Wolverton is with Matt."

"It appears as if things have come to a head." Louisa rose from the piano bench. She and Charlotte had devised a plan and discussed it with Matt and Grace. Matt had decided that until Wolverton spoke to him about wanting to marry Mama, all should be kept from the children. Although Louisa and Charlotte agreed, they did not discourage the twins and Madeline from dreaming of a wedding. "It is time for a con-ference. Decisions must be made."

Several minutes later, Louisa stood with Charlotte at the front of the schoolroom parlor. They had gathered their brothers and sisters together so that they could present their scheme. The children had disposed themselves on the chairs and sofas scattered around the room. And though quiet, a restless current flowed through the room.

Louisa began, "It is clear my mother has fallen in love."

"That is what we thought as well!" her sister Madeline ex-claimed in chorus with Alice and Eleanor, the Carpenter twins. They were twelve and had become as close as could be.

Augusta, Louisa's fifteen-year-old sister, furrowed her brow. "What does that mean for us?"

Louisa gave her sister a grateful look. "That is what we must decide. I seriously doubt if Matt would allow us to live elsewhere."

"I don't understand." Theo frowned. "Why does anyone have to leave?"

"If Mama marries Lord Wolverton, she will wish to live with her husband, and he has his own estate. You know, like Cousin Jane moved to a house with her new husband, and Dotty is living with Merton."

"Oh." Theo drew out the word, then fell silent.

Mary held Theo's hand. "But we all want to stay together."

The tension in the room increased as the younger children exchanged nervous glances.

Charlotte cleared her throat. "Louisa and I have some ideas we would like to present to you. . . ."

In an amazingly short period of time, as far as Louisa was concerned, and with some changes to the original plan, a workable strategy had developed. "Theo, you are the youngest of the four of us; this will affect you the most."

The little girl nodded. "I want Mama to be happy."

Tears pricked Louisa's eyes as she regarded her sister. "We all do."

Just then, May, Charlotte's lady's maid, burst into the room. "Her ladyship's gone to see Lady Worthington."

"And that is the crux of the matter," Louisa said under her breath. "When I marry I shall make sure my settlements give me more autonomy when my husband dies."

"Thank you, May." Charlotte glanced at Louisa. "Everything seems to be settled."

"Yes." Turning, she addressed the other children. "I have a feeling we shall be summoned very soon."

* * *

Patience sat on one of two sofas flanking the fireplace in her daughter-in-law's study. After weeping until she had no more tears, she had finally decided to seek help. If Grace could not think of something, then Patience's love for Richard and his love for her was most likely a lost cause. "I simply do not know what to do. It is as if I am being torn asunder, and I cannot think of a way to make it all work."

"You love him a great deal," Grace said as she poured tea, and handed Patience a cup.

She took it gratefully. Some turned to spirits or laudanum when upset; she had always found tea to be of superior comfort when difficulties, or in this case, disasters, arose. "Yes, but I love my daughters as well, and Matt will never allow them to leave his control."

"No. He will not," Grace said in a matter-of-fact tone. "Although I am not technically a mother myself, I do understand, and I have been giving your situation some thought. I believe there is a solution. It is not perfect, but it might answer."

Patience stared down at her cup for a moment. At this point, she would consider anything. "Go ahead."

"The idea came to me when Charlie was home. We had never been separated before I sent him to school. It was difficult at first, but we soon became used to seeing him only on holidays. Before too long, the other boys will go to school as well." Grace paused, and Patience nodded. "If we put our heads together, I'm sure we could come up with a scheme where the girls will visit you and you will visit the girls, just as the boys will see us on their holidays."

Patience drained her teacup, then poured another cup. "That might work."

"Let us discover what the children have to say. After all, they are the ones who will be most affected by any change."

Part of her desperately hoped her girls would not want

her to leave at all, and the other part wanted them not to mind so very much. Yet, at the end of the day, all she wanted was for them to be happy. All of them, she and Richard included. "Very well. Let us do as you propose."

Grace glanced at the mantel before tugging the bellpull. A few moments later Benson, her butler, appeared. "Yes, my lady."

"Please have the children attend us."

"Right away, my lady. I believe they are all still in the schoolroom."

A few minutes after he left, footsteps echoed from the floors above. It never ceased to amaze Patience how well run this house was. She folded her hands in her lap and waited. A few moments later, a knock came on the door. Louisa and Charlotte entered.

Louisa glanced at Patience, then Grace. "Benson said you wished to see us."

Grace indicated the chairs next to the sofas. "We do, but we shall wait for the others before we explain."

Although Louisa and Charlotte must have noticed how close Patience and Richard had become, neither girl said a word. Instead, they exchanged a glance and took their places.

A moment later, what sounded like a stampede approached and the younger children surged into the room scattering into their usual places. Her next eldest daughter, Augusta, who was fifteen, sat in the chair next to Walter's, Grace's fourteen-year-old brother. They shared a passion for foreign languages and travel. Though not old enough to attend the Thornhills' drawing rooms, they had been invited to the couple's house numerous times to look at their foreign artifacts and discuss the Thornhills' journeys.

Twelve-year-old Madeline sat in between Grace's twin sisters of the same age, on the sofa Patience occupied.

Her youngest daughter, Theodora, eight, was as usual to

be found with five-year-old Mary Carpenter. Philip Carpenter, the youngest boy, also eight, sat with them next to Grace.

"Well, then," Grace began. "We would like your opinion on a certain situation which affects all of you."

The twelve-year-olds clasped their hands and sighed dramatically.

"Are you announcing your betrothal, Mama?" Madeline asked. "We have already discussed what we should wear."

And to think the three of them would all come out at the same time. Patience repressed a shudder. "What alarming children you are."

Her remark was greeted by a trio of self-satisfied smiles.

"I am not announcing my betrothal."

The smiles faded.

"Who is getting married?" Augusta stared owlishly at Louisa, then nodded. "I'd forgotten."

Theodora rolled her eyes. "The only thing you do not forget is anything to do with the globe."

"Theo," Louisa said sharply, "do not roll your eyes. It isn't polite."

"If you are not getting married, what is this about?" Madeline asked.

Chapter Eleven

Patience poured another cup of tea, drinking it quickly. Come to think of it, a glass of wine or sherry would not go amiss at the moment. Yet, now that the children were here, she had no idea how to approach the subject.

The door clicked shut as Matt entered the room. He focused on Madeline. "If your mother were to wed, where would she live?"

"With her husband, of course. All married ladies live with their husbands," she added earnestly.

The twins nodded their agreement with the answer.

"Very well," he continued. "Where would you live?"

Madeline frowned as if she did not understand the question.

Augusta looked at him as if he had suddenly become deranged. "Here and at Worthington."

"We have already discussed it," Theodora said.

Naturally, they had. They had done the same before he

and Grace had married. The only question Patience had was *what* had they decided.

Louisa cleared her throat. "It is clear Mama is in love, and it would be selfish of us to keep her and Lord Wolverton from being together."

An ache started in Patience's throat and now familiar tears pricked her eyes. "But I love you as well."

"We know that, Mama." Madeline reached over, took Patience's hand, and squeezed it. "We love you, too, but you won't be far, and during the Season, we will be across the street."

Her incipient tears halted. Really, she needed all her wits about her when dealing with her children. "I beg your pardon?"

"That is what I was about to explain." Louisa glanced at Grace. "Charlie said he wished to rent this house during the Season. Since Lord Wolverton does not have a townhome of his own, he can rent this one. Mama will not wish to miss the Seasons, after all."

"Hmm." Matt stroked his chin. "That settles four months of the year. What about the rest?"

"Mama always goes to Brighton during the summer," Louisa continued. "I am sure she will wish to spend the Christmas holidays with us, and perhaps if she would rather spend time at her new home, then we can all visit in the summer."

"Yes, of course." Patience said in a voice that was a bit faint. Did she truly spend so much time away from the girls? Of course she did not go straight to Brighton from Town. She always spent a few weeks at Worthington before traveling down. Yet this was the first time the girls had come to Town for the Season. With Louisa making her come out, Matt had decided it was better for everyone to be where he could watch them.

The idea of leasing this house during the Season was brilliant. She would only be across the Park from her daughters and the rest of the children she had come to love.

"I looked in Debrett's and found that Lord Wolverton's estate is in Kent. That is only three days from Worthington," Louisa continued. "There is no reason why she cannot visit us in autumn, or, perhaps, we can visit Kent." She glanced at Matt. "None of us has seen Kent or the sea."

Matt seemed to study all ten pairs of eyes carefully before glancing at Grace. "It could work. Do you think Charlie would have an objection to leasing the house to Wolverton?"

She grinned. "I think Charlie will do what he can to keep all the children together."

"In that case, I suggest we make ourselves scarce while Lord Wolverton and your mother have a talk." He fixed a stern look at the children. "And there will be no listening at keyholes."

Patience felt like giggling until what Matt had said finally struck her. "He is here?"

"I left him in the front parlor."

"Everything will be fine, Mama," Madeline assured her.

"Indeed it will," Walter said as Augusta bussed Patience's cheek.

"We will be right outside if you need us," Theodora said in a loud whisper.

"Not on your life." Matt took her small hand in one of his and Mary's hand in the other. "We are all going to the Park."

Patience swallowed as the last of the children left the study. "That was remarkable."

"I am going to make it a point not to be surprised by anything they do." Grace shook her head as the door closed. "I predict that Louisa is destined to be either a great political or diplomatic hostess."

"At the very least." Suddenly nervous, Patience smoothed her skirts. "How do I look?"

"Extremely presentable." Grace rose. "Would you like tea or wine?"

"Wine, if you will. I know it is early, but . . ."

"There is no need to explain." Grace kissed Patience's cheek. "It has already been a trying day. Shall I have it sent before Wolverton is allowed to come to you?"

"No. I do not think I could stand the wait." Nor did Patience think he could. He was more likely to attempt to try to find her on his own. She stood and shook out her skirts, wiping her hands down the silk. "I must admit, I am the slightest bit nervous. The last time a gentleman wished for private conversation, my parents had already approved of him."

Grace hugged Patience and she returned the embrace. "There is really nothing to be nervous about. He loves you quite a lot. The proof is that Matt was unable to scare him away."

"Yes." She wanted to laugh and cry at the same time. "And I am sure he tried."

"Well"—Grace grinned again—"he wanted to ensure Wolverton was the right gentleman for you."

Unlike Patience's first husband. She straightened her shoulders. "I am ready."

The door did not even close before Richard strode into the room. "Pae."

He stopped and for a moment appeared hesitant, and a little frightened. "Richard. I was told you wished to speak with me."

Coming forward, he stopped mere inches from her. "I should warn you right now, I will not take no for an answer."

It was all she could do to keep herself from throwing her arms around him. Instead, she gently prodded him. "You must ask me the question first."

Reaching out, he gently stroked the line of her jaw with one finger, then drew her to him. "Pae, please be my wife. I do not know how we'll work everything out with the children, but I'll do anything you want. Anything they want."

She raised up on her toes and touched her lips to his. "I would love to be your wife. All you have to do is agree to lease this house during the Seasons and spend Christmas with the children."

His breath tickled her ear as he trailed his tongue over the outer edge. "I agree."

"Then, yes, I will marry you."

"I have waited years for this. I wish we had not lost so much time." He pressed soft kisses over her cheek until he reached her mouth. "Pae, I love you. You won't be sorry. I'll make sure of it."

She had waited years as well. Yet if he had approached her when the girls were younger, and before Matt had wed, she would have had to continue to refuse him. "I know you will. Let us simply be happy we are together now."

Richard did not know what had happened after Worthington had left him in the parlor, but he would have agreed to almost anything to keep Pae with him. "How soon can we wed?"

Her eyes widened. "I had not thought of that. When would you like to marry?"

"Tomorrow." He grinned as she gasped. "But I realize that is too soon. What do you say to next week?"

She smiled, and he almost changed his mind. "Perfect. There are three young girls who would be terribly disappointed not to be able to plan a wedding."

"And we mustn't disappoint the children." He lowered his head, pressing his lips against hers. On a sigh, she allowed him in. If only they had somewhere they could go to be alone. "When shall we tell everyone?"

"Matt has taken them to the Park. We shall make our announcement when they return."

He pulled her down on his lap as he sat on the sofa. "Do you think we'll be left alone until then?"

"Richard! You cannot possibly be thinking—"

He kissed her again, cutting off her protest. "I have, but I realize this is neither the time nor the place. On the other hand, a little kissing would not be amiss."

"Not amiss at all."

The following week was filled with modeste appointments as well as the general mayhem that seemed to abound in Stanwood House.

Patience's second wedding would not be the grand affair her first one had been, but it would most likely be a more joyful one.

Richard was at the house so often he began taking the younger children to the Park with Matt. The twins and Madeline had insisted on not only helping design their dresses, but designing Patience's gown as well. Fortunately, Madam Lisette explained rather forcefully that their mother did not need to look like a wedding cake. However, the mention of cake reminded the girls that they needed to speak with Jacque, Grace's cook.

Shortly after the children had descended to the kitchens, Jacque had ascended to Grace's study. "Milady, I cannot have *les jeunes filles* in *ma cuisine. C'est dangereux.*"

Grace had listened patiently before responding, "I understand. Please tell them they are to return to the schoolroom."

The next day, the trio was gathered in the morning room with Patience and Grace.

"I don't understand why we are not allowed in the kitchen anymore," Alice said, pouting.

Nodding, Eleanor agreed, "All we wanted to do was give Jacque some ideas. How are we to be great hostesses when no one will let us help them?"

"Well"—Madeline crossed her arms over her chest—"I do not think it is fair." A moment later she smiled. "The flowers! We can help with them."

The three girls piled out of the morning room toward the garden, and Patience rubbed her brow. "How much damage can they do?"

"Oh, not much." Grace motioned toward the window. "I have already warned our head gardener, and anyone else who might be the victims of their largesse. I have decided they may assist with decorating the ballroom."

"I hope that will satisfy them."

"A few well-supervised trips up a ladder and having to follow Penny's instructions to the letter should quell their attempts to help."

Mrs. Pennymore had been the Carpenters' town housekeeper for years, and ran the house with a kind but firm hand. "That will definitely do it."

Patience found herself staring into the garden, yet not seeing anything.

"It will all be fine," Grace said. "I promise you. I will write you so often about the children you will feel as if you are here."

"I know you will. The girls are in good hands." Still, that wasn't it, at least not all of it. "I have never managed my own home before. I will be expected to know things that I do not."

Leaning over, Grace took Patience's hands in hers. "You will learn, and Wolverton does not seem to be the type of man who will become angry with you, and I am always a letter away. Make allies of your housekeeper and cook. The rest will fall into place. I promise you."

What Grace said was all true. She had witnessed Grace do exactly that before her marriage to Matt. Still, there was a fear she had not previously voiced, even to Richard. "What if I cannot give Richard an heir?"

Grace's brows came together as they rose, wrinkling her forehead. "My mother was several years older than you are when she gave birth to Mary. Had my father lived, there would have been more children. As to their sex, that, my friend, is for God to decide."

"You are right. I am worrying over nothing." Still, her qualms would not go away.

Squeezing Patience's hands, Grace said, "Your concerns are never nothing. These are things you had to give voice to in order to be able to work through them. I had my doubts before marrying Matt, yet our union has proved better than I could have hoped for. Speak to Richard."

The evening before the wedding, Richard still had a strong feeling that something was wrong with Pae. Her stepson had told him about her first marriage, and even though the man had been dead for several years now, he had the strong desire to plant the old earl a facer. It also made Richard want to punish himself for not absconding to Scotland with Pae before her marriage to the man.

After dinner he suggested a stroll in the garden. The moon was full, and small lanterns twinkled throughout.

When they reached the rose arbor in the back, he wrapped his arms around Pae. "Will you tell me what is bothering you? Whatever it is, I will do my best to make it better."

She took a shuddering breath and blinked as if she was holding back tears. "What if I cannot give you an heir? What if I only have girls?"

By not marrying her when they were young, he had

caused her to suffer. He had, in truth, been responsible for the pain of her first marriage. "I vow to you that I will love and cherish all of our children, no matter their sex. All I have ever wanted is you by my side. Can you forgive me for not returning in time?"

"It is just like you to take the blame for something that was not entirely your fault. If I had not been so angry and hurt when you did not come home, I might have been able to talk my parents into allowing me to wait for you—"

He placed one finger over her lips. "With me not present, there was no way your parents would have allowed you to turn down an earl. Your father viewed my voyage as a way of escaping my duties at home."

"I suppose you are right. It is time for me to stop blaming both of us and be thankful we found each other a second time."

He coaxed her lips apart as he kissed Patience. "I love you."

"And I love you."

The following morning Richard was more anxious than he had thought possible. Rubbing his hands down his black breeches for a second time, he asked his friend, "Do you have the ring?"

"Right here." Bellamny patted the pocket on his vest. "You look as nervous as a cat."

"Believe it or not, this is worse than being chased by headhunters. I'm terrified she will change her mind."

"I know what you mean," Worthington said with feeling. "But the children are here. She will not fail you."

Yes, the children were there. They seemed to fill up the church. "What are the twins and Madeline wearing on their heads?"

Worthington gave an imperceptible shake of his head. "After the girls were stymied in their attempts to take a hands-on approach with the wedding plans, Grace and Patience allowed them to design their own bonnets."

Richard had never seen anything like it. Not even his mother's hats were so—so full. "I shall make a point of complimenting them."

"I'd appreciate it if you did not encourage them. They were in the process of raiding the garden when Louisa and Charlotte suggested the girls use silk flowers and fruit instead of denuding the flower beds."

The noise level began to rise and Richard glanced to the entrance. Pae had finally arrived. She wore a blue gown the color of her cerulean eyes, trimmed in darker blue ribbon. "She is exquisite."

"I do not believe I have ever seen her happier," Worthington commented.

"Thank you."

"Well, Wolverton"—Bellamny grinned—"it's finally your day."

It was indeed. A day he had waited almost twenty years for. Richard greeted the young cleric who joined them. "I believe we are ready to begin."

Smiling, Pae joined Richard in front of the clergyman. Grace had taken a seat between the youngest girls, and Almeria Bellamny stood next to Pae.

"Who gives this woman away?"

"I do." Worthington took her hand and gave it to Richard. "I know you will take good care of her."

They spoke their vows clearly and firmly. When the vicar pronounced them man and wife, a sigh emanated from the pews.

"Is he our step-papa now?" Theodora asked in her straightforward fashion.

Richard turned to Pae. For some reason, he had not actually thought about his relationship to the children. After all, Worthington was their guardian.

Fortunately, Pae responded. "Yes, he is your step-papa."

Theo seemed to consider that for a few moments, then said, "I hope he is better than the last one."

"*Theodora Vivers!*" Patience cried, her hand covering her eyes.

Worthington barked a laugh. "You can hardly blame her. I'm not sure she ever met my father."

Fighting the sudden rush of tears clogging his throat, Richard bent down and put his arm around his stepdaughter. "I promise to be the best step-papa I can be."

Author's Note

I often say that one must look at the Regency as a different culture with different customs. That is especially true for this book.

In our modern age we expect widows to remarry. After all, what's the problem? However, during the Regency most widows did not remarry, and for some very good reasons. The most common was money. If a widow was left well off, and if her settlement agreements were done properly, as they should have been, then she was in charge, possibly for the first time, of her own funds. In the event of her marrying again, she might lose all or much of her money to her new husband. She also did not have a man telling her what to do. Unlike married women, widows could enter into contracts, buy property, and manage their own funds.

Another reason a widow might not want to wed is her children. It was not uncommon for a mother to either have to share guardianship with a man of her husband's choosing, or in the case of Patience, not have guardianship at all. Very few women were given sole guardianship of their own children, and almost never if one of the children happened to be a boy or an heir.

But wait, it gets worse. Once a mother remarried, she could not have guardianship of her children at all. Why? Because married women were not legally allowed to have guardianship. A fact you might remember from *Three Weeks to Wed*. Once she lost even partial guardianship, she could be barred from seeing her children. Fortunately, this is a romance, and as we all know, romances must have a Happily Ever After.

For those of you who wonder if Patience will have a child, I assure you that will be answered later in the series.